ELUDE

C.MILLER

Text Copyright © 2012 C. Miller

First Paperback Edition: July 2014
Second Paperback Edition: February 2023

Cover Art: C. Miller

ISBN: 9798371131225

THE
REAVE SERIES

REAVE
ELUDE
ASCEND
TO FALL

PROLOGUE

THE RULES

I'VE DISCOVERED THAT THE RULES in life change as you're living it. Your mind grows and adapts with time, which alters so many other things, potentially your entire perspective on the world. Somewhere along the way, you begin formulating the long and perpetually shifting list of what's acceptable or expected and what is not. Your own list would always be different—by varying degrees, depending on your person—from the accepted norm of everyone else. But some behavior and decisions seemed entirely unyielding where acceptability was concerned . . . so long as you were on the outside looking in.

Who was the mysterious person that decided what was wrong and what wasn't? Where are they when your back is against a wall and you're forced to make those decisions yourself? Who says a choice is the right or wrong one? Why should anyone do something strictly because it's the acceptable thing? Shouldn't we all have some sort of say in the matter? Was it wrong to follow through with decisions that went against the grain if it caused other people's lives to hang in the balance?

What about your own life?

I'd contemplated over those questions—and more—often during the past week, after I'd learned the truth.

I had learned that a person I'd grown to trust was in fact a brother I'd never known existed. I had learned that my father was not dead, as I was sure he had been for the last ten years of my life. I had learned that my father, by occupation, was a murderer. He was a Reaper—trained from birth to be an assassin—as was my secret brother and nearly everyone else I'd come to care for in this world.

As was my dead mother I'd hardly heard a word of in my life. It was quite clear to me now why my father had been unwilling to speak of her when I was a child.

Reapers. Learning everyone in your family either was or had been one was a rather substantial shock to the system.

Although it likely should've been, my father's occupation was not so much of a problem for me, and it wasn't a problem for me in the ways I was quite certain others would believe it *should* be. Despite how I felt about Reapers now, or the care I had for a few of them, it was unsettling to discover I'd been raised by one. It was more unsettling to wonder what he'd been doing all the years I had believed him dead. I was certain that would've been enough on its own, but it seemed so insignificant when compared to the undeniably personal blows he'd struck me with.

He had hidden the knowledge of what he was from me to be discovered more than half my life later by the brother he'd never mentioned me having. He had left me to rot in our small house in the wilderness. He had left me there to be given away by his friend and in the process sentenced me to a life of servitude.

He'd just left me to it all.

Even though all that would've been so much more than enough, life seemed to have a way of making things so much *more* than you could ever anticipate.

It was not any part of my past, or his place in it, that set my blood boiling at the mere thought of him. There was something that made me despise this . . . *man* with every fiber of my being, one particular thing that made even the significant issues pale in comparison.

He would not allow me to change the life he'd abandoned me to. My father would kill the boy I loved, simply because he did not want that boy to *have me.* As if I were in fact the object I'd been told I was all those years of his absence.

I could not stand for it. This man they'd told me of, this Reaper . . . he was *not* my father.

So I would leave.

I would leave New Bethel with someone I loved. I would escape from this hell I'd been stuck in for most my life, and I would hope with everything I had inside me that father would not find us.

It was the only thing I could do. *Hope*.

I would move forward and hope that the rules would no longer apply if I refused to abide by them.

CHAPTER ONE

A REAPER GUARD

MY BODY HAD BEEN IN PAIN for weeks on end, but it had developed into a new sort of torment. Focus and intent during my days spent inside the sixth room had shifted to something else entirely after the truth had come out about my family. I still did all the other things I'd been doing for weeks, but there was more than just the physical, stealth, and sensory training. I did not need to do so many movements any longer, as most my days were spent flailing around on the floor with Chandler. The flailing more than made up for the lack of time spent on designated movements.

The mental anguish did seem to worsen the exhaustion I'd been struggling through, as if internal torment could substantiate itself, but my body was not in pain from mere exhaustion. It was entirely covered in bruises, which were but one effect of the efforts expended on shifted focus and intent. Chandler would grab me by my clothing and toss me about the room as though I were made of nothing more than air. Shortly after, I would get dark red dots in those places where he'd been grabbing.

He told me the dots had something to do with blood under the surface of my skin, but I'd not been paying proper attention during the explanation. It was irrelevant to me. Knowing why did not change the fact that they were there or that I couldn't stop the events which caused their existence from happening. The only means of stopping were forfeit or endurance to some later point that seemed impossible to reach.

I would drink that unpleasant clear drink they always gave me—*Bryon tea*, they called it—and within a day, the bruises and markings would be gone. Then, as my training continued, more would appear beneath the surface, darkening my pale skin to vibrant hues of red, blue, and purple. It faded to pink, yellow, and green much faster than it should've done.

There seemed to be no end to the vicious cycle. There would always be more markings to display the extent of my incapability. It felt very much like wearing my failure on my skin.

I could not count all the Reaper training shirts I'd gone through in only a week. They would rip and Chandler would hastily retrieve another for me while I stood in my windowless room, covering with my hands and arms what the torn fabric no longer could.

He never looked at me while I was exposed and, in more than one sense, *shamed*.

After several of those instances, and the realization that he never looked, I was not so uncomfortable with his presence while in such a vulnerable state. It was strange.

On the second day of new training, he placed a stack of shirts by the door. That way he wouldn't have to leave the room to retrieve them, abandoning me to my vulnerability. Walking about the Valdour House for fabric was a waste of time we didn't have.

Ahren and Chase had both attempted to speak with me on several occasions. I would find Chandler every time they did, which wasn't difficult because he was always near. All I had to do was look at him and he would promptly ensure we resumed work without further distraction. He never told them not to speak to me of course, but we would both just pretend as though they weren't even there. It was easier for me to manage if Chandler was at my side, pushing me forward.

I was unsure whether I was more angry or hurt over their deception. If I hadn't overheard the beginning of the argument which led to my discovery and gathered that Chase truly had wanted to tell me, I likely would've been far angrier with him than I was. I could understand him believing it was Ahren's right to tell me that he was my . . . *brother*.

Still, Chase should've told me after realizing Ahren had no intention of divulging the information himself.

I did not know if Ahren would *ever* have told me any of it willingly. He didn't trust me enough.

I went back and forth with it all.

Would it have been wrong of Chase to tell me those things?

Not anywhere near as wrong as my blood standing next to me for months and not telling me as much, I thought.

It had taken me some time to get it sorted enough inside my head to discern the appropriate feelings and allocate them to where I believed they justly belonged.

I was furious with Ahren, but I was hurt by Chase.

Chandler never spoke a word of it to me; he kept my focus where it needed to be. He did not speak on behalf of the other two, as I at first expected him to. It eventually struck me that there was no intention of it, no matter any thoughts he had on any matters. And I knew he had those, as they could be seen in his eyes. He did not speak on anyone's behalf, nor did he ask me any questions at all unless they pertained directly to my training.

I preferred it that way. It was some of the only peace I'd been able to find in a world that seemed to be crashing down all around me.

I was not speaking to Agatha either. I'd gone to my quarters that first night after discovering my entire family was not dead and that I had more family than I'd ever realized. When I spoke the unbelievable words, I saw the knowledge of it already on her face. Ahren had told *her* the truth, but he had not told me, nor had she.

I felt so utterly betrayed by them all. I wondered if anyone would've ever told me. Perhaps after we'd gone.

Amber approached me once. She'd found me that next night as I was walking with Chandler to my quarters. I stared into her eyes, not hearing a word if she said any at all, seeing a girl I now knew had been a replacement daughter to my father.

He would not have needed a replacement, had he taken better care of the original.

I wondered how many of my words she'd sent back to him and how many of those difficult questions had been asked due to his curiosity and not her own. How many of my deepest feelings had she betrayed to a person who'd abandoned me and then wanted to prevent me from having a life of my choosing?

I was unsure what she saw behind my eyes when she looked into them or what she saw on my face, but she made a quick departure and did not approach me again. Whatever she saw must've been accurate enough in reading me, if it kept her away. I believed I understood what Chase had meant before about female Reapers, but I could've been wrong.

Chandler no longer haunted my dreams as he'd done after first meeting him.

It was always my father there. Every night, my entire sleeping vision would be taken up by a face I'd not allowed myself to picture in such a *very* long time. I had not forgotten that face, no matter how hard or long I'd pushed the memory of it down. His face tormented me.

Chase no longer did the killing in my dreams as he'd done after first meeting him, but he was still in them sometimes. When he was there, my father would kill him and then smile at me. I remembered that smile well. I would hear him say, 'It's for your own good,' in Camden's voice as his mouth moved.

I would wake up screaming or something close to it and, immediately after, find Chandler sitting rigid at the edge of my bed. He would stare at the wall and hold my hand until I fell back asleep.

He never asked me what I dreamt about. He never lied and told me it was all right. He never spoke to me at all in those times. He simply sat there, for some reason allowing me to hold his hand. I preferred that as well.

I sometimes would look at the outline of his face or his hand with mine in the darkness, and I would often contemplate kindness. Its variances.

I sometimes couldn't.

Before sleep would return to me, I'd spend some time staring at the backs of my eyelids, picturing my father accompanying Chase back to this House when he'd been a child. I would picture my father killing the leader whose face stood out so much more vividly to me than all the countless others, though I'd only seen him the one time through a haze.

He called it . . . a show of good faith.

My father had come here to murder a man and he'd not known I was stuck between the stone walls of this House. What would I have done if I'd happened across him that day with his bloody hands?

What would he have done if I'd seen it? Given I clearly knew nothing of the man who'd once been my father, I could only speculate. But if I had no idea what I'd have done . . . how could I get far in my speculation for him?

So at some point every night I held Chandler's hand in one of mine. With the other, I clutched the hilt of a knife that had been given to me. Since, it had been strapped onto my arm at all times, as instructed, hidden under the sleeve of my non-Reaper clothing.

It was the only way I could sleep somewhat peacefully. It was the only way my mind would slow enough for sleep to take me back into its clutches.

I never felt safe enough otherwise.

But safety was only a word, an illusion or delusion. Safety was a lie people told themselves in order to sleep, to make it through each day. It was only a word for a feeling, nothing more.

IT WAS ONE WEEK AFTER HEARING THE TRUTH that a new face was added to the harrowing dreams of my father. Ahren, standing behind my father as he murdered the person I loved. He—Ahren—looked at me before it happened and had tears running down his face. I watched his mouth silently form the words . . . *I'm sorry.*

I did not wake up screaming at the new, painful and unexpected appearance. I shot up in bed, taking gasping breaths of air, none of which seemed to reach deep enough into my chest. Chandler was still there, almost as if he'd been waiting for it. I wondered if he *had* been waiting. I wondered if he always did now.

I got out of my stiff bed quickly rather than reach for his hand, quiet as I grabbed my regular clothing. I did not want to wake Agatha and be bombarded with more of her persistent questions which I would not respond to.

I didn't hear the door open and then close, but before I began changing out of my nightclothes, I looked around the dark room and found that Chandler had gone. After I was acceptable and had opened the door leading to the corridor myself, I closed it and stared up at him to say, "I need to go somewhere alone."

"To see my brother?" He almost seemed hopeful for a moment that I'd finally decided to speak to Chase so he and I could sort everything out between us. Chandler did not act like it, but I knew he loved his brother.

Was a person required to love their blood? It was more than possible he was simply tired of dealing with the nonsense of our situation, whether we spoke on it or not.

"To see *my* brother," I told him firmly, realizing that had been the first time I'd directly referred to Ahren as such aloud, at least with a claim. "And I'm going alone."

"Aster." His voice was soft, such a stark contrast to its usual tone. He could be quiet, when not working. *Soft*, though . . .

"Time is winding down so quickly." I stared at the floor and slowly shook my head. I felt so *heavy*, everywhere. "If I cannot walk these halls alone . . ." I laughed once under my breath, though there was no humor in it. "You're not always going to be there to watch my back."

"If you wanted me to be—"

"You'd be killed if you went with us." There was nothing more to say to that, so I turned and began walking away.

"It's going to happen regardless," he said to my back.

I stopped moving, staring down at the stone floor but keeping my head up.

"Your father will kill me once he learns I assisted in your escape. Even if it was only preparing you for it and not attempting to stop you." He paused. "I knew better before I agreed to this. I'll likely be the first in line. Your father will still kill me for this."

I turned back to him, and the desperation and guilt that had been building in my torso as he spoke was so easily distinguishable when I said, "I *won't* allow that to happen."

The words mocked me in the almost painful silence that followed.

I could barely hear myself ask, "Do you believe me?"

I watched him open and then close his mouth. I didn't tell him to close it before he'd managed to do as much himself, as he always did with me. He looked to his right at the stone walls of the corridor enclosing us, and he nodded his head.

I nodded my own as I finally understood why Chase always asked me that particular question.

Do you believe me?

He did it only to have the reassurance I believed in him and his capabilities so that he may possibly find the belief somewhere in himself. It was nothing more than that.

I walked away with my new understanding and left Chandler standing alone outside the door to my quarters.

IT WAS NOT LONG AFTER that I found myself staring at the Reaper Guard standing in front of Ahren's office door, pretending in plain sight to be something so far away from what he truly was. A Reaper in Guards' clothing, leather armor and a standard-issue sword hanging at his side. We were all so easily fooled, so content to accept without looking.

Without seeing even when we *did* look.

The true Guard standing at the Reaper's left said, "He's not in there, Miss. He's actually sleeping for once."

I did not acknowledge the words that had been spoken as the Reaper Guard and I stared one another down in the dim hallway, both of us waiting for our own separate things. Points proven, dominance established? Who knew why he waited?

He eventually smiled. "You should leave."

At my right, his left, I heard, "She's allowed to do what she wants; you know that."

The Reaper did not look at him to clarify. "I was talking about you."

The Guard laughed the word, "*What?*"

The Reaper's eyes were still on mine. "Give me one minute with her and then return to your post."

A rather long moment passed before the Guard walked away.

When he was properly out of earshot, the Reaper's smile widened. "What can I help you with?"

"Take me to my brother," I ordered.

"He's sleeping." That smile transformed into a grin, and he narrowed his eyes a bit. "Didn't you just hear?"

I stepped up to him, shook my head, and very slowly said, "I don't care."

His head tilted as he stared down at me with that same expression still on his face. I worried for an instant that he was going to give me further grief simply because he could, but he relaxed his body significantly and said, "He stays on the other side of the House."

"Oh." I stepped away and frowned. "He never told me." I shouldn't have been surprised, because Ahren had not told me a lot of things. Where he slept seemed so small in comparison.

Or did it?

"Well, now you know," he said, still grinning.

I smiled tightly at the Reaper and began walking away, but I stopped when he spoke again.

"Would you like me to walk with you? You seem distracted. That's a bad thing for you to be."

"No thank you," I told him. Again, I had turned before . . .

"Are you sure?"

I took a deep breath to calm myself before responding. "I'm quite sure." I forced another small smile in his direction.

I was very confused as I looked at his face and watched it change slightly.

"I'll be here . . . if you change your mind."

After, I was very confused over his words when paired with the expression that had taken over his face.

I was baffled enough over it that I found myself really looking at him, for just a moment. He was quite tall, with slightly wavy hair which was cut relatively short like all the Guard, or Reapers pretending to be Guard; it was only a few shades darker than the blond of mine. There was something striking about his eyes, but I was unsure what exactly and it wasn't worth wasting time over.

He was just a man. He was just another Reaper pretending to be something he was not. He was just another person with a body, taking up space in the world. That was all.

I laughed, unable to keep my discomfort from sounding through. "I suppose you'll be here for a while, if you intend on waiting for that to happen."

He laughed, not uncomfortably at all, and by that point the other Guard was walking back.

I felt it necessary to say, "Thank you for your help."

He nodded, and I finally walked away without enduring further pestering or being forced to prolong the puzzling interaction.

I made my way to the other side of the Valdour House to speak with my brother.

CHAPTER TWO

SIBLINGS

TANLEY AND STEWART always stood guard at the one means to get from the active half of the Valdour House to the forbidden, where I'd spent nearly all my waking hours over the last few weeks. Once I arrived at their post on the way to speak to my brother, Stewart left it to accompany me. I needed him because I didn't have a clue where to find Ahren.

Stewart did not try conversing with me, which was somewhat unusual for him. On the few occasions he'd followed me away from his post before the door at the short hall, he'd spoken a great deal. I presumed my lack of desire to converse with anyone apart from my brother was apparent, but I was still a bit stunned that Stewart allowed me my peace.

He seemed to enjoy picking at me sometimes.

Ahren's room was very far away from that sixth door where my days were consumed. It was all the way at the end of the House and up a rather long flight of stone stairs, which eventually opened up to reveal a small area and one wooden door.

Once standing in front of it, Stewart left me to return to his post, offering me only the stiffest of smiles before his departure. I didn't like the way it made his mouth look, but it was one instance I wouldn't have returned the expression regardless. I doubted my ability to smile at all with the unpleasant churning in my stomach at the thought of interacting with my brother.

After waiting until Stewart's disheveled blond hair disappeared around a corner, I knocked on Ahren's door. The sound echoed strangely in the small, stone area enclosing me.

Not ten seconds passed before Ahren was there in front of me with a knife in his hand.

A frown pulled down at my mouth. "Surely, if I was someone to kill you . . . I wouldn't have knocked."

Ahren cleared his throat and concealed the knife somewhere on his person—I did not know where—and stepped aside. I stopped just inside the door and did not move any farther when he closed it behind us and gestured for me to sit down.

I did a quick assessment of his quarters—noting the heavy drapes which were in place rather than removed like I'd seen Chase have them in his before—and the lavish blankets and pillows on the bed. This room was one of only a handful in the entire House that had long strips of smooth wood for flooring opposed to the stone.

I stopped looking at his room and brought my full attention to him, our eyes meeting. My voice was near a whisper when I asked, "Why did you not tell me sooner?"

His gaze touched on something irrelevant—a wardrobe—for a moment, guilt clearly evident in his expression. I could see then just how tired he was, with the horrible dark circles under his eyes. The look of it did not suit him, as there was *something* about his face that wasn't quite . . . *right* when it didn't hold a smile.

Even if it at times wasn't a very *nice* smile.

"My objective . . ." he began, none of the guilt carrying into his tone, "was to infiltrate and earn your trust before telling you. Father wanted to be sure you would not be biased against us because of what we are."

"You still have not been honest with me about everything yet," I accused. "I've been thinking over it all constantly. You said your plans changed once I mentioned to you that I wanted this city destroyed, but you'd already begun instating Reapers long before then."

"I instated them for our safety." Though he said it so plainly, I did not believe that was the full story or that it could be so simple.

I was far too accustomed to Ahren and his partial-truths by now to take him immediately at his word, no matter how much I would've liked to. Reason and honesty did not necessarily make a statement the truth, nor did easiness.

"He wanted you to use Chase, didn't he?" I asked, trying a different approach. "He wanted you to use Chase to get to me, thinking it would sway my feelings toward Reapers in general."

"Yes." He clenched his jaw for an instant. "His story with you . . . Well, it's very *moving*." He paused. "Wouldn't you agree?"

I wasn't sure if the question had been rhetorical, but it seemed pointless and I wasn't going to answer it. "Is Chase aware of that?"

"Yes," he repeated.

"Was he in on it?" I wasn't entirely successful at keeping the wariness and hesitation I felt out of my tone. Was any of it even real?

Ahren looked away again and said, "To an extent." He sat down on the floor at that and looked up at me after getting himself settled.

That time, I sat when he gestured for me to. We faced one another, a few feet separating us as we'd done many times before. I felt incapable of removing the frown from my face as I waited for him to speak.

It took him a little while.

"Chase was being honest with you when he said he always wanted to take you away. But there was a bit of time, after learning you had family that could keep you far safer than he ever could, where he thought it may be the best thing for you to go with us. He thought you would *want* to go with us." He seemed to think on something for a moment before getting back on path. "But then he came to know you and fell in love with you." He chuckled a bit under his breath. "I'd already written our father a letter and informed him of the way you felt about each other. So when Chase arrived to speak with him on the matter, he was already aware of it. And as Chase told you, it didn't matter to him." He briefly pursed his lips. "What a sad thing, to realize you're in love and then be told you can't have it."

He would know, I thought.

Quietly, I said, "But surely he would let us be together, if we didn't run away."

"No. I can assure you he wouldn't." Ahren seemed to say the words carefully so I would fully understand them. He barely sighed. "It's so funny that they're both trying to save you from this life, in their own ways. Chase knows what it is you want, though, doesn't he? He knows you want to be free of this, so he's willing to take you anyway, even though . . ."

"My father will kill him for it." I finished the sentence for him, though it seemed somewhat unnecessary after doing so.

Ahren leaned back a little and nodded his head in response, which also seemed needless.

We both sat in silence for a short time, while one question plagued me. I eventually voiced it.

"Is he truly that awful?"

He shrugged. "It would depend on your definition of the word, or the way you want to look at it."

"I don't remember him being that way," I said quickly. I had been repressing all memories of my father for ten years, but I'd not forgotten any of it despite any attempts. He'd never been awful, at least not to me when I was a child. I'd never seen him be awful in any way, not to anyone or for any reason. But these two people were clearly separate, and I had to fully accept what that meant.

"I was taken from him when I was born, his wife was killed, and you were abducted," Ahren said. "Can you blame him for wanting to protect you from that?"

I sat there for a moment, staring at the floor and thinking over it before finding certainty. I looked into Ahren's eyes to answer his question. "Yes. I can." I almost stood, but I stopped myself and took in a deep breath.

I'd spent the week and a half before learning he was my brother repeatedly asking him one question that he would not answer: Who do you imagine while you're training?

Upon learning he was my brother, it had been replaced in my head with another that seemed indefinably more important, though perhaps not as telling.

"Ahren . . . do you love me?"

He blinked hard at me, like my query had caught him entirely off guard, and then he seemed to force a smile. His voice was quiet when he said, "Very much."

I looked away and nodded.

"That question you keep asking me . . .? I imagine our father."

"Why?" I asked, bringing my eyes back to his once I'd recovered from the shock he'd inflicted upon me by answering out of nowhere. *Finally*. "Has he done something to you?"

Ahren forced another smile at me, but I saw tears welling in his eyes when he reached out and took my hand. For a moment, he simply sat there and stared down at our hands joined together. "He sent me here with the intention of saving my sister. And then he expects me to destroy her heart. So yes." He appeared to be struggling to keep the smile on his face. "He has."

I squeezed his hand.

"I won't do it." The words spilled out of his mouth in a torrent. "He doesn't know, but . . . I won't do it."

"Would he kill you?" I whispered. "Like everyone says he's going to kill them? Would he do the same to you for helping me?" I truly didn't know this man we were speaking of, so how could I be sure? I didn't know that I could be sure of anything.

"No." Though it was not a firm answer, he sounded convinced. "But I will be punished for it."

"Punished how?"

He shook his head and looked away, which I knew meant he would not answer that particular question.

I had no idea what questions to ask in order to receive a truthful response. All I felt I could do was shake my own head and whisper, "I wish I could keep everyone safe." It was such an impossible thing to wish for, but the desire was still there and would not go away. It was a waste of time and energy to desire something that could never be.

"Would you like to see a picture of our mother?" he asked, the words coming out rapidly.

What?

My mouth fell open as he pulled his hand away and jumped up from the floor. He went over to a desk with papers strewn across it and pulled out another from inside a drawer. I remained firmly where I sat, still trying to process what he'd said, until he gestured me over. He couldn't have been serious.

I was hesitant as I walked toward him, sure this was some sort of trick. What a cruel one it would be.

A few seconds later, I was staring down at the drawing of a woman.

"Where did you get this?" It was in such great detail, though the colors were very basic—only skin color, hair, and eyes.

"I stole it," he replied.

When I glanced up at him, he was grinning at me.

"They have portraits of us all, to keep track of us. I took this when I was younger. You look just like her, see? The nose and cheekbones. You even have her mouth. See there?" Each thing he mentioned he pointed at, as though I needed his assistance in such a way to know what he was speaking about. "Father said we both inherited her hair color and his eyes."

My jaw quivered as I looked at the drawing. Though I had never seen a portrait of her before, there was absolutely no denying it. It was almost as if I were looking at a slightly distorted reflection of myself. My jaw was not the same as hers, nor were my eyebrows, but this woman was undeniably . . .

My mother.

Ahren stopped staring at the drawing when I brought my attention back to his face. I hardly felt the tears in my eyes, but I knew they were there.

He smiled hugely at me, as if showing me this had made him so very happy.

Perhaps it had. Perhaps he'd been waiting for this shared moment for a long time.

I threw myself forward, wrapped my arms around him and whispered, "Thank you."

"You're my sister." He said it as though it were all that needed to be said on the matter. I almost believed I heard a note of reverence in his tone, like having a sister was the most amazing thing in the world. I might've been mistaken.

"And you're my brother," I said against his chest.

It was the first time he'd ever heard me say it, and it must've made him happy because he leaned down and kissed the top of my head. I spent a moment working through it to the best of my ability.

After, I sighed and stepped back. "I should let you get some sleep. I'm sorry for waking you, I just . . ." I shook my head, staring off at a wall. "I keep having these horrible dreams."

"You can wake me whenever you want." He reached a hand out and mussed up my hair.

I frowned at him because I still could see no purpose to the action, apart from a desire to frustrate me. Perhaps that was reason enough to do it.

It was just as I began to walk away—trying to smooth my hair as I went—that he asked, "Are you going to stop by Chase's room on your way?"

Though his tone had been politely casual, he was pretending to be occupied with something on his desk when I looked back at him.

"I hadn't thought about it," I lied.

Only then did he look at me. He frowned at me as I had at him, which clearly said that he did not believe me.

It was clear that no verbal response had been needed from him when I said, "Well, I *had* thought about it. I just didn't think I should."

"I'm not necessarily saying you should or shouldn't." He cleared his throat.

I turned away.

"He was going to tell you."

I closed my eyes. I was determined not to be frustrated by everyone waiting to tell me things until I'd already begun to leave.

I turned back to him to say, "He *didn't* tell me."

"He started to that night you stayed with him."

"I would remember if he'd attempted to start a conversation on the matter." It came out a bit too harsh.

Ahren grinned a little and looked away. "He told me you interrupted him. That you told him *the past didn't matter.* He was going to tell you."

I replayed the night I'd stayed with Chase over in my head and when I hit that particular point in the conversation, I put my hand over my face. I *had* interrupted him when he'd been about to tell me something, but I'd thought he was going to say something else. And then I felt a jolt go through my body when I realized . . . "He didn't say what was going on when he was about to tell me, did he?"

"He told me the two of you were standing there talking."

I released a giant breath of relief.

He narrowed his eyes at me. "Why? Is that not true?"

"No, it's true." I spoke to a wall rather than his face. "We were standing there talking." I cleared my throat purposely, as if that might explain why my voice was sounding slightly more high-pitched than usual.

It would be extremely awkward to tell my brother that I'd been standing in front of Chase with my shirt off at the time in question. Everything had been covered of course, but my shirt had not been in an entirely acceptable position, given it hadn't been . . . *on.*

"Aster?"

I hastily tried to change the subject. "I believe the Reaper in front of your office door was flirting with me."

My attempt at a diversion was successful because Ahren blinked hard several times at me and shook his head. "*What?*" His voice was disbelieving, but then he laughed awkwardly and said, "I'm sure he wasn't."

I nodded shortly. "I'm quite certain he was."

"Well, you're not particularly exceptional at distinguishing that sort of thing." He sounded almost apologetic.

"You're right." I laughed a little and turned to leave.

That time, he allowed me to make it all the way to the door before he spoke again. "You can go ask Chase your question and then return to your quarters."

I gaped. "What is *that* supposed to mean?"

"I'm your brother." He shrugged. "I have to say it. I never said you have to listen to me." I laughed again and had put my hand on the doorknob when he added, "You *should* listen to me."

"Go to sleep," I said, still chuckling a bit under my breath. And then I paused on my way out to remind him of a very valid point. "He'll hear you if you're roaming the halls down there to see if I returned to my quarters."

A sheepish sort of grin appeared on Ahren's face. "And he can tell you all about it in the morning."

I shook my head at him and the situation as I stepped out of his room and into the small, stone area. I stood there for a moment outside his door, contemplating. Then I opened it again, just enough to see him standing where I'd left him.

"I love you too," I told him. "Just so you know."

He smiled hugely at me, and I finally walked away.

CHAPTER THREE

FRIENDSHIP AND FLUKES

HASE'S ROOM WAS ALONG THE WAY of getting back to my quarters. I glanced left in my walking and found I was quite pleased with myself for passing by the door. I continued about my way but then abruptly stopped moving when I rounded the next corner. I closed my eyes tightly, took in a deep breath, released it in a huff through my nose, and then turned around.

I stood there for a moment once I arrived at what I'd initially passed, thinking over all the numerous ways things had changed. It felt like so long ago when I would step in front of Chase's door and he would open it without me having to knock. Now he would stand just on the other side, waiting for me to open it myself.

When had life changed so drastically? When had I begun making decisions for myself? When had I been allowed to start making them?

When I opened the door, Chase was *not* just on the other side of it as I'd expected him to be. He was standing near one of the walls, speaking in a hushed tone to Chandler.

"I'm sorry," I said quickly. "I didn't know—"

Chandler grinned at me a little, which was the most he ever did if we weren't training.

I stopped speaking.

Chandler said, "I thought you weren't coming to see my brother?"

"Well, I hadn't planned on it." I sounded guilty, but I hadn't anticipated . . . "I can—"

"I was just going." Chandler began walking over toward both me and the door. "Will you be going back to your quarters?"

"I . . ." I started and then stopped, trying to formulate the correct response to the simple question. "Yes, of course I will."

Chandler nodded at that and left the room without another word.

Chase had been staring at the floor, but when I began walking over to him, he looked at me. The closer I came, the more I realized it almost appeared as though he were bracing himself for something horrible.

When I stopped moving, I took in a deep breath and sincerely said, "I'm very sorry."

"Chandler really was getting ready to leave," he said. "He'd just stopped by to discuss something with me."

"I wasn't apologizing again for intruding." I fought against a very small urge to laugh at him. "I'm apologizing for how I've acted towards you lately."

He narrowed his eyes at me. I was unsure if he did so due to confusion or because he thought I was being dishonest with him. He didn't say anything.

"Ahren just said you'd tried to tell me about everything."

He looked away and nodded.

"Why didn't you say as much this past week?" I asked. Wanting and trying were very different, in my opinion, and he'd *tried*.

"Because almost doing something still isn't doing something." His voice was quiet. "I didn't want to pressure you into forgiving me. It would defeat the purpose."

I smiled at him when he glanced at me, and he returned it, though he seemed hesitant. I stepped closer and wrapped my arms around him.

It was amazing how quickly you could forget what it felt like, being close to a person.

"How much time do we have left?" I whispered against his chest.

He leaned down, resting the side of his face on the top of my head. "Not much." We'd never had very much time.

22

I nodded and remained standing there for a moment, trying to enjoy the feeling of closeness to him, but I simply could not do it. His words were like a dark cloud hanging directly above my head.

"I should go," I said quickly as I stepped away. Rather than run from the room in an attempt to escape the unpleasant feeling as I was tempted to do, I forced a smile at him. "I've already missed enough sleep tonight. I don't want to be tired tomorrow."

He returned my forced smile, nodded, and looked away.

I lingered at the door when I made it there, watching him from where he stood across the room. His shoulders were slumped over, which was so unlike him, and his face appeared distant as he stared down at the floor.

It looked to me as though he were carrying too much weight on the tops of his shoulders, like there was an invisible heaviness pushing him down.

"I love you," I told him quietly.

He looked up at me and smiled again, only it appeared genuine then. "I love you too."

I WAS NOT ENTIRELY SURPRISED to find Chandler waiting for me when I rounded the corner into the next hallway after Chase's room.

I spared a forced smile for him as well before asking, "What did you need to speak with him about?"

"What did you need to speak with *your* brother about?" He shot that back at me, not unkindly but seeming to merely be making a point.

I glanced up at him and he grinned.

I said nothing.

"That's what I thought."

I would not have told him, if he hadn't taunted me over it. Was it wrong to divulge personal information simply because you were rising to some provocation that likely hadn't even been intended as such?

Perhaps it was not wrong at all to look at the floor, no matter the reason, and admit, "I needed to ask him if he loved me."

When I peeked up at Chandler again, he hastily looked away from me, bringing his eyes forward as we walked the hallways of the House together. He seemed stunned that I'd told him what I just had.

"I needed to discuss me going with the two of you." He cleared his throat and almost uncomfortably added, "We'd all be more likely to survive that way. At least for a bit longer."

I was brought back to sitting on the floor of my quarters with Ahren when I'd called him out on being a Reaper.

What are a few secrets between friends, Sir?

Perhaps that was what friendship was all about—divulging personal information to a person you believed you could trust.

I wondered at what point in time Chandler had become my friend.

A small, stunned laugh escaped from my mouth. "We're friends now, aren't we?"

"No." He answered immediately then frowned at me for just an instant, to make the meaning behind the word official.

"Well, you're *my* friend," I told him with a grin, "whether you'll admit to it on your end or not."

He continued to stare straight ahead as we walked, but I did see him smile a little for a brief moment. It had been so very brief.

Brevity didn't seem to matter so much on this occasion.

CHANDLER WAS MUCH ROUGHER ON ME the next day than he'd ever been before. I did not know if that was due to my declaration of friendship and he was secretly punishing me for saying it aloud. It might've simply been because we had such little time remaining. Either would've been understandable.

Reality seemed to slip away from me while inside the room past the sixth door now.

Initially, when the focus of my combative training had shifted a week before, I could pick up every minuscule detail of what happened to me as it was happening. Now it was all bangs and slams combining together, creating a fuzzy haze that distorted the picture in front of my eyes.

It was a sound that brought me out of the daze sometime around midday. It was a sound I'd never heard before, something between a choke and a gag. I blew out the blood pooling inside my mouth in a spray as I shook my head and tried to discern where I was and what had happened.

I was inside the sixth room.

My mouth was bleeding quite badly, which shouldn't have been happening.

I blinked hard when I found Chandler on the floor.

At first, I believed him to be playing a joke on me. He *had* to be joking.

One of his hands was on his throat and the other was . . . *down farther*. But it was his eyes closed tightly in something I realized was pain that brought the realization of his seriousness down on me.

"All the stars." I dropped down beside him and tugged gently on his arm. I only realized after a few seconds of tugging that I likely shouldn't have been touching him at all. I jerked my hands back to myself, wondering why my instinct had been to touch when I didn't have the vaguest clue as to what was actually wrong with him. *Strange.* "Are you all right?"

His face flinched and he removed the hand from his neck, putting it up in the air in front of my face, clearly telling me to give him some time. I spit more blood out onto the floor while I stared at his face, keeping my hands in tight fists near my chest. I looked up when I heard the door open.

For a very short time, Chase stood in the doorway, tilting his head as he took in the mad scene before him. By the time Chase was over to us—he had walked *remarkably* slowly—Chandler had removed both his hands from the parts of his body he'd been clutching with them and opened his eyes.

"Did he let you do that?" Chase asked when his gaze finally moved away from Chandler and fell onto me.

"I . . . I would imagine so," I answered quietly. I spit more blood onto the floor, noting there was not as much of it as there had been initially.

I caught movement in my peripherals—Chandler shaking his head.

"Did you punch him in the throat?" Chase asked me the question calmly and *very* slowly.

"I . . ." I shook my head. "I don't know." I didn't know how any of this had even happened. I couldn't believe it *had* happened.

I could remember when Chase had first been showing me options for physical defense and he'd explained about hitting a person in the nose with the palm of your hand.

Unless you've trained for an extremely long time, you won't get your hands anywhere near a Reaper's face to do it.

The throat was too near the face.

I knew for a fact that nothing was a lack of skill on Chandler's part.

I saw movement in my peripherals again which brought me back from the memory and my thoughts on it. Chandler shook his head once more and tapped at a spot on his arm, directly beneath his elbow.

"She *elbowed* you in the throat?" Chase was still speaking so deliberately.

Chandler nodded then and began to stand.

Chase did not try to assist him, but I did. It was an immense struggle to hold up a good portion of his weight.

He was so large.

Chandler steadied himself on my shoulders and he looked down at me. He patted me once and then again on my left shoulder and said, "Good girl." His voice sounded quite raspy and painful.

It was not a joke.

I had hurt him.

Chase attempted to help Chandler when he began walking away, but he was shrugged off. I turned my head while Chandler was walking, but I glanced at Chase for an instant when he spoke.

"What are you doing?"

"Letting him have his dignity." I said the words under my breath then spit the last remaining bits of blood from my mouth onto the floor. I used to bleed for much longer, I was sure. "He wouldn't want anyone watching him like he was a wounded animal." I knew that because I would not want it either. I also knew . . .

He would not want me to apologize.

Chase said, "You know he's going to come harder at you now."

"He already was," I stated blankly.

"No." Chase shook his head. "If you managed to injure him at all, he's going to increase the difficulty."

"To punish me?" It was more a statement than a question.

"Because he'll think you're ready for it," he responded, his voice also impassive.

When I finally looked straight at him again for more than a glance, his head was tilted at me.

"You might want to spend a few minutes mentally preparing yourself. He's going to hurt you when he gets back."

"He's already hit me in the face today," I said. "That's the first time he's done it. We weren't supposed to be touching faces."

"Getting hit in the face doesn't hurt."

I almost laughed and corrected him that it did in fact hurt quite badly, but he spoke again before I had the chance to do so.

"Not in comparison to other things." He paused for a moment and frowned. "For your sake . . . I hope that wasn't a fluke."

Chase walked away from me then, going and finding a place on the other side of the room. But when Chandler returned a few minutes later, I watched Chase take one look at him and hastily vacate the room. Only then did I truly look at Chandler's face and, when I did, I wanted to hastily vacate the room as well.

He was smiling as he strode over to me.

MY SCREAM DROWNED OUT most of a strange popping sound that occurred near my head. When Chandler released my left arm from his hands, it hung dead at my side.

"I have to put it back." Chandler's voice was so calm when he reached out for me again.

I took several quick steps away from him, holding onto my seemingly dead arm with my opposite hand.

I'd not realized that my eyes were closed tightly as my face contorted in pain until he said, "Aster."

I looked up at him.

"I know it hurts, but I have to put it back."

I gave him a stiff nod, which was all I could manage, and he stepped over to me again.

He hesitated before touching me. "This is going to hurt too. You shouldn't look."

ELUDE

Rather than following his instruction as I usually did, I watched as he popped my shoulder back into its proper place. I watched until I screamed again at least, and then black spots filled up most my vision. I wanted to collapse into a heap on the floor, but Chandler kept my weight on him and forced me to remain standing.

"You should take a little time off," he said. "Let it heal."

"I don't *have* time to take off!"

Firm, he said, "You need to let that arm rest."

"How many days do we have left?" I asked him, desperate despite the pain.

He pursed his lips together into a hard line and looked away. Then he took a deep breath and almost let it out as a sigh before his gaze fell back on me. "I can secure it to your body, but you're going to be useless with it messing up your balance. You don't have time to get used to it. And it would heal before you could get used to it anyway."

"Work around it," I told him flatly. Saying what I had was far better than screaming at him for doing something that would make me useless for a time when we had so little of it, I thought. I was already so unbelievably useless, and I'd not needed his assistance in worsening it.

He nodded and left the room.

Only when he'd closed the door behind him did I sit down on the floor and allow my head to fully realize how much pain my body was actually in; it made me remarkably dizzy. And I continued sitting there in my agony, thinking about pain, until I heard the door open again. I was unsure how much time had passed.

I stood and forced my face into blankness. It was not easy to do.

Chandler was not alone when entering the room. Ahren was with him, and my confusion over his presence did strange things to my head, which seemed to be sputtering as it attempted to function through the pain.

Chandler's face was impassive—businesslike—as he walked toward me, but Ahren was clearly struggling to keep his face under control. I almost thought he was angry, but I could've been mistaken. He had a glass of liquid in his hands, and it was not clear, like the Bryon tea. It was greenish brown and, upon closer inspection once I could see it properly . . . *thick.*

"What is that?" I imagined my tone would've sounded hesitant, had I not been sucking in air through my teeth to speak.

Ahren frowned. "It's disgusting is what it is." It was a bad attempt at a joke, I thought, and it did not answer my question. "But it will help."

I winced when I released my injured arm from my hand to take the glass from him. I began drinking it, but two swallows in, I gagged.

Ahren's hands darted out, one taking the glass from me and one covering my mouth.

I did not become ill as I had thought I would, and I glared at him once I could. "I could've choked on it, with you covering my mouth that way."

"Plug your nose while you're drinking it." Ahren made the suggestion without acknowledging my remark. "It's not so bad when you do that."

My eyes widened at the idiocy of what I'd just heard. "With what *hand*?"

Chandler snorted and reached his hand out, pinching my nose extremely hard between his fingers. I wasn't entirely certain the hardness was wholly on purpose; he was just so strong.

Ahren extended the glass back to me and I began drinking it again, Chandler's hand following on my nose as I moved.

It truly wasn't quite as bad when not smelling as well as tasting it, but it was still disgusting, as Ahren had said. I gagged twice more during the process. Each time, one hand from somewhere grabbed the glass and another covered my mouth to prevent me from losing any of it from either source.

By the time I was done getting that horrid substance down my throat, I discovered I felt very lightheaded, and not strictly from the pain.

I swayed on my feet. "What . . . what was that?" My voice was distorted in my ears, far too loud and deep-sounding.

I was very quiet.

I was not loud.

Hands grabbed and steadied me. The contact felt very strange on my skin.

"Fandir root," someone said.

I only realized I'd had my eyes closed tightly once I opened them and saw the world twisting and spinning in front of me. I swatted in front of my face with my good hand, and it seemed to leave a trail of blurry light where it passed.

"You've poisoned me." I heard the disbelief in my voice just before I slipped away into blackness.

CHAPTER FOUR

DODGING

ONSIDERING I HAD DIED, I was not expecting to wake up again. I did not believe it worked that way.

I looked down at myself in a daze, finding my left arm secured to my body with some strange sort of bandage wrapping around the entirety of my torso. I felt nothing when I attempted to move it. I felt nothing of my body in general. It existed, I could move it, but I couldn't quite *feel* it.

I blinked hard as I looked up, finding Chandler, Ahren, and Chase standing a good distance away. They were all stealing glances at me, for some reason. The simple colors in the room hurt my head horribly—they were much too vivid, somehow—so I closed my eyes. I rested my forehead against the tops of my knees and breathed. I was breathing and I was not dead.

What had they given me?

"Are you done rambling?" Ahren asked.

When I opened one eye to peek over at him, he was much closer to me than he'd been before.

"I was sleeping." My voice still did not sound quite right, almost like my ears were underwater. My entire body felt like it was underwater. Movement was much more difficult than it should've been, *sluggish*.

Numb. That was it. Numb, like sleeping on an arm wrong, only without the unpleasant tingling sensations.

"No, you just thought you were sleeping," Ahren said. "You've been talking nonstop for the last twenty minutes."

"I could never speak for twenty minutes straight," I shot at him as I closed my eye again. My voice was much quieter when I spoke next. "I could never think of so much to say."

"Which is why you could speak for twenty minutes," Ahren stated. "You weren't thinking at all, at least not really."

"What does that even *mean*?" I nearly begged. "You're hurting my head with all your talking."

I thought I heard Ahren snort once, but I might've been mistaken, both about the sound in general and its origin.

Chandler was closer as well when he said, "You can only have what we gave you if you've got permission to have it. People use it for surgeries, sewing up knife wounds and the like. It makes it to where your body can't feel anything, which nearly paralyzes you for a short while. It also makes a person believe they've lost consciousness when they really haven't. It's very useful."

"Why are you wasting something like that on me?" I asked the question harshly, but I still kept my face on my knees. I could've handled the pain, I was sure. I had dealt with enough of it in my life, so I was sure I could have. It just might have taken me some time to acclimate to a new sort of it.

"Because we know where to find it," Chandler replied.

"Then why are people not allowed to have it?" I asked, curious.

"Some people use it for reasons we don't allow," Ahren answered. "It's harmless, yes, and though there's enough of it, we don't need people wasting it for . . . *recreational* purposes."

"Why would anyone *want* to drink that?" I demanded. Only then did I remove my face from my knees. What he was saying was simply absurd.

"To escape from life, even if just for a few moments?" Ahren shrugged. "Who knows why people do what they do?"

"People are stupid," I grumbled as I replaced my face where I'd had it.

I heard several snorts and I was unsure who they all came from, but I felt inclined to continue on because of them.

"You're given such a short time in life, and it will only be what you make of it. Why try to escape from something when you could simply try to fix it instead?" *Right* did not necessarily equate to easier; I imagined it rarely ever did. That still didn't mean it was not the better thing to do.

"Why indeed?" Ahren said, I imagined rhetorically.

I sighed. "Were you all conversing with me while I was incoherent?"

"Why do you think we were on the other side of the room?" Ahren asked. "You were making us uncomfortable."

"*What*?" I snorted and looked up again. "What could I possibly say that would make *anyone* uncomfortable?"

Chandler said, "Words you wouldn't say in front of people, as long as you had your mind to tell your tongue to keep hold of them."

I almost thought he was about to laugh for some reason, but he did not do it. He grabbed me by my right arm and pulled me to my feet instead. I hardly felt it.

I glanced at Chase, who was still standing quite a good distance from me, and he distinctly looked away. It was strange, but I could do nothing for that.

"What are we doing?" I asked. It was far better than further pressing the subject of things I'd said when I'd had no control over my tongue. I wasn't entirely certain I wanted to know any of those things anyhow, and their behavior told me some. "I feel indescribably more useless than normal. You shouldn't have given me that."

"We're going to work on dodges," Chandler said, which made me frown. We'd never worked on dodges before. Then he grinned. "A few good bangs to the head might get you back to normal more quickly anyway."

A FEW GOOD BANGS TO THE HEAD did not get me back to normal more quickly.

Well, it was possible they might have, but after quite a few of them, I was dizzy from that instead. Every time I had a brief moment of immense satisfaction, over successfully dodging one thing, Chandler would immediately come at me with his other hand—or elbow, or fist—and hit me someplace else.

I knew the purpose of this activity. It was not being successful with the dodging, as I would've assumed. It was anticipating, not the first move of your opponent, but the next.

It was not, 'If you move this way, you will not get hit.'

It was, 'If you move this way and then immediately *this* way, you will not get hit twice.'

I'd been participating in combative training with Chandler for some time now and believed I had a decently good general idea of his fighting tactics. He always seemed twenty steps ahead of me despite that, if not more. He could not only anticipate two of my dodges in advance, but more. It almost seemed as though he were strolling casually along inside my head, knowing every move I would make before I thought to make it, while also knowing his own intentions at the same time.

I couldn't have kept up, even if both my head and body had been more responsive.

There was so much to it. Trickery, I realized, worked wonders. Feinting one way, only minutely, would make him believe it was the way I was going. But when he realized I'd discovered as much after several successes, he anticipated those as well.

He laughed for a moment, once, when I moved the upper half of my body one way and then kicked his legs out from under him from the other. He took me down with him of course, quickly setting my body away from him once he hit the floor. That stopped me from landing more on him than the floor itself.

He shook his head after that small laugh and said, "You're not attacking."

"*You're* attacking," I pointed out.

"Sometimes the best way to learn something useful is to not attack when it seems the sensible thing to do." He tapped on my head a few times with one of his fingers. "It's in *here*, more than anywhere else. It's not anticipating. It's *knowing*. You get inside another person's head, and then . . . all the attacking will fall into place." He paused for a moment to smile tightly at me. "If you're capable of getting far enough ahead, you can stand back and watch a person fall on their own blade."

I took in a deep breath. When I released it, it sounded like a sigh.

He stood, pulling me up with him by my good arm as easily as he'd taken me down with him. He then straightened a looping of the bandage around me before looking me in the eye in a certain way he had that I knew was checking to ensure I was prepared to carry on.

He saw whatever he was looking for, and we did carry on.

TRY AS I MIGHT, I could not get inside Chandler's head. The remainder of the day only proved as much.

Still, at the end of it he said, "You did well today."

"When are you going to stop lying about that?" I asked him as I plopped myself down onto the floor.

It had been such a nice lie to hear initially, but I did not want to hear nice things any longer. Nice would not get me anywhere. Nice was irrelevant.

Despite knowing as much, part of me secretly enjoyed hearing it. I would never admit such a thing aloud though, especially not to Chandler.

"I'm not lying." He sat down beside me, leaning his back against the wall as though he were somehow exhausted from beating me throughout the entirety of the day. "You were better than I could've expected. Much better at that than attacking."

"Saying I'm better at *anything* than attacking truly isn't saying very much."

Chandler did not laugh at my words, but he smiled.

I looked away and asked, "Why doesn't Chase help with this sort of thing? He's hardly in here with us at all anymore."

"He doesn't want to hurt you," Chandler said. "And he leaves while we're doing this because he doesn't like seeing me hurt you, either."

"But he knows what we're doing is necessary," I stated.

Chandler nodded thoughtfully. "Sometimes getting hurt is the only way to truly learn anything in the world." Then he smiled a little. "That doesn't mean people who care about you want to watch it happening."

"Have you been hurt very much?" I asked him curiously. I could not imagine he had been.

He breathed in deeply and stretched his arms out wide. "It's why I'm so ridiculously intelligent."

I snorted and shook my head at him.

"You're going to need to take that bandage off before you go back to your quarters." He gestured at me. "It should be partially healed by now, but it will still be incredibly weak for a while."

I sighed. "Good thing it wasn't my dominant arm."

He grinned a little and looked away.

"You did that on purpose, didn't you?" My eyes widened a bit. "Pulled my weaker arm out?"

"Everything I do is on purpose," he said unapologetically. "We're all that way, as long as we have our heads."

"What do you mean, *have your heads*?"

"Getting emotionally involved in anything takes your head from you," he stated. "It makes you think with your heart and not your brain."

"That's why you won't admit we're friends." My voice was quiet, almost as though I were telling him a secret. "Isn't it?"

"We're not friends." He said it firmly, but he smiled a little which I believed cancelled out both his tone and the words he'd said.

I told him, "I learned today that thinking with your brain doesn't always get you very far."

He narrowed his eyes, which made me smile.

"When your opponent is smarter and better-trained than you . . . all you've got is your heart."

He chuckled a little and smiled wider than he usually did, which accentuated the few characteristics his face shared with Chase's. "And what did that get you?"

"A dislocated shoulder and likely a concussion." I grinned. "But am I improving?"

"Yeah." He patted me a few times on my knee. "You're improving." He sighed and pulled me up by my good arm. I was surprised he'd allowed me to sit for as long as he had because I knew Chandler did not like to see me sitting. "Let's get that bandage off you."

I let him unwrap me from the contraption and, as he was doing so, I said, "Chandler." I waited until he stopped to look at me before I warily asked the question. "What was I speaking about earlier, while I was incoherent?"

He immediately got back to work, but I saw him smile a little in that usual closed way he had before he responded with, "Several things."

The smile was a relief, but I pressed, "Such as?"

"Well, you spoke about your father, for one," he said. "And you talked about being afraid."

"Afraid of what?"

He did not answer me and gave no indication that he would.

I quietly added, "I don't see how either of those things could make anyone uncomfortable."

He laughed a bit under his breath. "What are you afraid of that would make everyone uncomfortable to hear you speaking of it?"

I began going through a list inside my head of things I was afraid of, or things I'd always *believed* I was afraid of.

I'd barely realized that I needed to make a different list when Chandler stepped in front of me and asked, "What are you afraid of that would make your *brother* uncomfortable?"

I felt my eyes widen in absolute horror when I quietly answered with, "*Your* brother." His brother and where things would inevitably go. I shook my head. "All the stars. *Please* tell me I wasn't really."

"Would you like to go talk to him about it?" When he looked at my questioning face he clarified with, "Chase."

"Oh no." I shook my head again, quicker then. "No, if I was speaking about such things freely, I don't believe I want to see him right now."

He shrugged. "Go ahead and change your clothes. I'll walk you."

I nodded and proceeded toward the room that held my normal clothing in a horrified daze. I could only imagine what things had come out of my mouth, and thinking they'd all heard them . . .

I glanced at Chandler before entering the room, feeling . . .

I was unsure.

Embarrassed? It wasn't quite right.

I did not know the word.

I could not find it.

I carried on.

Changing into my normal clothing was an unpleasant task. Though my body still felt somewhat numbed, my arm was not quite functioning properly. Every time I moved it to either remove or replace clothing, it sent strange jolts of pain down my entire left side.

It must've been apparent when I stepped back into the hallway because Chandler said, "You wouldn't believe how much more painful this would be for you if we hadn't been giving you Bryon tea for weeks now."

"What?" I asked, bemused.

"It builds up in your body when you drink it consistently. Makes it heal more quickly than it normally would, along with increasing your pain tolerance."

I knew I'd been healing faster than I should have, but . . . "How could it possibly do that?"

He shrugged again. "It just does."

"Is it not allowed either?" I asked. "Like that farfawhatsit thing?"

"The Fandir root?" He laughed. "You could say that, but it's not something you find by itself in the wild. Reapers make it."

"That clear drink?" I asked. "You all *make* it?" I'd never thought to ask questions about it because they rarely told me anything when I did, and I supposed getting thrown about was a reasonable distraction.

"You'd be surprised what can happen when you put certain things together."

It was just then that we were passing by Chase's door. I attempted to hide the fact that I was glancing at it, but Chandler snorted at me anyway. He thankfully said nothing on the matter. I was grateful, as I sincerely doubted my ability to form proper thoughts beyond the few that kept repeating. There was no telling what would've come out of my mouth.

Right before we were about to pass through the door that would take us to the normal side of the Valdour House, I quietly asked, "What did I say about that, while I was out of my head?"

Chandler stopped with his hand on the doorknob and grinned at me. "That you weren't afraid anymore."

That made no sense at all.

Still quiet, I admitted, "But I *am* afraid."

He shrugged. "That's what you said." He began to turn the knob, but . . .

"Did—"

He halted, focusing in on me with his hand still where it was.

"Did I say anything horrendous? About . . . *intimacy*. Or such."

He almost laughed. "Do you imagine you even out of your right mind would say something *horrendous* about it?"

Shortly, I nodded.

He did laugh then, beneath his breath. "You said a few things. None of them *horrendous*. Mostly that you're not afraid."

I didn't want to tell him again that I was.

He began looking away, but . . .

"Chandler?"

He focused in on me again.

"Did I say anything about you?"

"Not a word."

Relief flooded through me.

"Don't worry. My feelings wouldn't have been hurt if you spent all twenty of those minutes talking about despising me for all I've done to you." Then he opened the door.

I followed him through it, but it took me a moment to say, "I don't."

He glanced down at me. And I looked up at him.

He didn't say it, but I saw it—that he was glad I didn't.

I told him again, "You're my friend."

He smiled a little, in a small and stiff way, and then looked forward. We passed by Stanley and Stewart. I was able to offer them each a small smile.

Chandler and I had only walked one hallway before . . . "Are you not going to say anything?"

I glanced up at him. "Hmm?"

"On me potentially . . . *accompanying*." He glanced down.

I shook my head.

"How do you feel about it?"

I kept my gaze forward to nod.

In my peripherals, I saw him nod.

I tried to force some lightness into my tone to ask, "Would it make a difference to you?" I looked up.

I watched the corners of his mouth tug upward, but he said, "Nah."

Mine began pulling up.

We walked.

CHAPTER FIVE

PRACTICE MAKES PREPARED

COULD NOT FALL ASLEEP, despite how exhausted my body was and my best efforts to do so. If Chandler would've asked—which I knew full well that he wouldn't, but if he *would* have—I'd have blamed my restlessness on my shoulder. In truth, I laid there staring through the darkness at the stone wall directly in front of my face, contemplating fear.

It was such a funny thing, I thought. Fear was like rules, I could see that now. As you went through life, it adapted and changed. You could find yourself horrendously afraid of something one day and then realize there's actually nothing to fear after being exposed to it. Or realize possibly that there *was* something to fear, though perhaps not as much as you'd always believed. I wondered if preparedness of any sort, or possibly acceptance, made a difference in perspective. And perhaps fear had everything to do with perspective, or perspective had everything to do with fear.

I had been afraid of Reapers, until I'd been around them. Still, I was afraid of most of them, though I would not admit as much to anyone apart from myself. Did being afraid of a portion of a whole, no matter the size, make you entirely afraid of it? I was not certain it did, but nor was I certain it didn't.

I had been afraid of my feelings for Chase until I'd realized there was nothing *too* horribly frightening about them. Well, it was not the feelings that were frightening to me still, though they had been before. Now it was what those feelings would allow me to do or to look over.

It was terrifying, thinking of all I'd done on account of those feelings.

Why, then, was I still so afraid? The feelings themselves had not directly harmed me, but was it a certain potential I feared?

I had been afraid of men, so very afraid. But Chase touched me and didn't hurt me when he did. Chandler hurt me, yes, but not in the way I feared. Was it all right to be touched by a person if you knew, with certainty, they would not hurt you? Was it all right to be hurt if you knew it was beneficial? Was that actually something worth expending your energy being afraid of? Given what was coming, and all the truly frightening things that would likely happen . . .

I did not believe it *was* worth it.

I didn't realize that I'd stood from my bed until I was already standing. And I remained standing for only a few short seconds before I caught the silhouette of Chandler, sitting with his back against the door, tilting his head at me. Then I crawled back into my bed, willing my mind to be quiet and give me some peace.

Still, no matter what I attempted willing my mind to do, it kept getting stuck somewhere—on *hurting*.

There were all different sorts of pain in the world. Every day it seemed I discovered a new sort of it, and they all felt so disparate from the next while being so undeniably similar. But there was one question that kept popping in my head.

How could you *ever* know with any amount of certainty that a person would not hurt you?

Hope. You could only hope they wouldn't.

CHANDLER NO LONGER NEEDED TO SHOUT in my face to wake me at an odd time, nor did I believe he enjoyed it now as I was sure he had before. Sleep was different now from what it used to be.

ELUDE

I felt my normal clothing being dropped on top of my blanket and I jolted upright, ignoring the pain in my shoulder because of the sudden movement. I found it still dark outside when checking the single tiny window near the ceiling, but I did not have the vaguest clue as to the hour.

I could hardly see Chandler move as he pointed over his shoulder at Agatha's lightly snoring form. He brought one finger to his lips, telling me to be quiet.

Rather than leave the room as he always did while I was changing my clothing, he simply walked over to a wall and faced it. I got out of bed slowly, listening for slight changes in Agatha's breathing. When I realized the soundness of her sleep, I hurriedly began the process of stripping down and then replacing my nightclothes with my normal ones. The faster I finished, the less likely a confrontation with her would be. There was a fine line, though. I had to be efficient more than fast.

Agatha must've felt safe with Chandler in the room, because she no longer insisted that one candle be lit as we slept. He was better than a tiny bit of light, in terms of security. I enjoyed sleeping in pure darkness while I could, so I wouldn't have complained about the change even if I had been speaking to her.

I'd only taken one step in Chandler's direction when he turned and began walking toward the door, not making the slightest sound as he went. I frowned, thinking about how strange it was for him to have been listening to me changing my clothes. I said nothing on the matter as I followed him.

It was only when we'd made it a good distance away from the door to my quarters that I whispered, "What are we doing?"

He shook his head and said nothing on that subject or any other. After we'd climbed the stairs that brought us out of the servants' quarters, I walked as though I were taking a casual stroll through the House as he followed a good distance behind me. I was permitted to do that now if I wanted—walk after hours without question. I hoped Chandler intended for me to go to the other side, because it was where I headed. After we got past Stanley and Stewart, Chandler walked beside rather than behind me.

Though he did gesture again with his finger for me to be quiet before we passed by Chase's door, Chandler still didn't speak at all until we went into the room where I always switched clothing. When

I reached for it, he shook his head and grabbed a different, new pile. It was quite a bit more fabric than the other.

He looked at me significantly and said, "We only have one chance to practice this."

"Practice what?"

Everything suddenly became very real when he answered with, "Our escape. We're leaving in two nights."

"Oh." I said the word on a breath, my eyes going wide at the information. "Why are we practicing? Aren't you afraid we'll get caught?"

"I'm more afraid that when the time comes you won't be able to scale the wall."

I gaped. "I won't be able to *what?*"

He frowned. "Did you think we were going to walk out the front door?"

"I . . ." I didn't know.

His frown deepened when he put a few fingers beneath my chin, pushing my mouth closed. It had taken me that long to realize what he'd said.

Our escape. Chandler *was* coming with us.

In that moment I was somewhat glad for the shock of being told I would be required to scale a wall. I did not want him to see the relief I felt at knowing he would be there, not thinking he might or could but knowing he would. There was relief and . . . something else.

What was it?

I didn't know that either.

He said, "We have a rope for you to climb out the window."

I was hardly listening to him as I attempted to discern the other feeling.

Pleased. I was *pleased* he was coming with us. *Happy.*

He was my friend.

And my friend was saying something very important.

"Ahren will make sure there's a rope on the wall surrounding the House on the night of."

"I'm confused," I said apologetically. I was entirely unsure as to whether, in that moment, I knew which way was up and which was down. That was what I got for focusing on feelings, but I doubted closer attention paid would've mattered as much on this occasion as I would've liked to believe.

He sighed loudly and replaced the clothes where he'd found them. Then he nearly dragged me over to a window by my right arm.

Something was definitely wrong with me.

Slowly, he said, "You're going to climb down the side of the House." He pointed off in the distance. "You see that wall over there? The same one you've seen a million times through the windows?" He paused for a moment. "It surrounds the House."

"Yes, I know that." I didn't bother to conceal my unhappiness over his clear implication that I was an imbecile. I *felt* like one, but that was irrelevant.

He pretended as if I hadn't spoken at all. "One side of the House lies against the city. The other side?" He shook his head. "There's nothing there apart from trees and open space. You can't see it from inside the House, but that's what it is."

"Really?" I asked in disbelief.

He nodded in response.

I simply could not believe that past the allowance of my viewing, there was . . . *nothing*. I should not have been surprised, and I needed to get back to the important matter at hand. "So I'm to go down the side of the House and then . . . climb a rope up that giant wall. . . ."

Again, he nodded.

"How do you propose I do that with my shoulder being out of sorts?" That was also an important matter at hand, I thought.

"Deal with it and do it," he answered impassively. "Now change into those clothes and I'll come back inside."

"Isn't Chase going with us right now?" I asked as he began walking away.

He halted and shook his head. "If we happen to get caught, I might be able to play it off. There's no way I can play it off if Chase is with us. Most the Reapers in the House don't know he's here."

"But . . ." Panic rose in my gut. "I thought you all said they knew?"

"You're the one who assumed as much," Chandler stated. "Just because nobody contradicted you doesn't mean you were correct. I don't want you to think about that right now. I want you to change into those clothes. Just—" He closed his eyes for a few seconds that felt longer than they likely were before opening them again and looking at me. "Just do what I tell you to do."

I looked away and nodded.

Once Chandler had gone from the room, I spared a very small amount of time studying the new clothing. It was not like my normal clothing, nor like my Reaper training clothing, nor like the all-black clothing Chandler wore while he was following me around outside the sixth room. It seemed relatively close-fitting but was not stiff.

I shook my head and put it on.

When I had finished, I put on a very strange pair of gloves that had no fingers attached to them. I didn't know what purpose they could serve or who in the world had thought to make them that way. What point was there to wearing gloves with no fingers? Had the person making them simply become bored with the task? I had no idea why they might want me to wear defective gloves.

I nearly wanted to scream when Chandler walked back into the room not even five seconds after all my clothing was properly in place. Could they hear *that* well, or had his timing been a fluke?

He grabbed a rope that was lying on the other side of the room then tied it to a bedpost. "Now," he began, "you're going to watch me *very closely*. When we really do this, we have to do it quickly."

"How can we all climb down the same rope quickly?" I asked. "Will there be more ropes?"

"Chase and I don't need ropes."

"You can climb up and down walls without ropes. . . ." I attempted to wrap my head around his words. I remembered that Chase had climbed up the outside wall of the House once before, but I'd always assumed there had been a rope involved *somewhere*.

"Depends on the wall. But these walls?" He nodded. "Yes."

"How is that possible?" I almost whispered.

"Practice," he said nonchalantly. "But after you watch enough people fall off walls and break their bodies on the ground . . . you learn to hold on in any way you can."

I hadn't realized that my mouth had fallen open again until he stuck his hand forward onto the bottom of my chin and pushed it upward once more. Then, he opened the window.

Attempting to be casual, I peeked over the edge. My casualness was instantaneously destroyed as I stepped back and closed my eyes. I'd never known I had an aversion to heights, but then again . . . I'd never been faced with the prospect of what I was currently faced with.

"What happens?" I tried to force my voice into indifference as I looked up at him. "If a person were to fall from this height?"

He smiled a little and shrugged. "Depends on how they hit the ground." He narrowed his eyes. "If you don't want to find out, keep hold of the rope."

I paid absolute attention to Chandler as he was showing me the appropriate way to hold the rope, though in the back of my mind all I could think of was my injured arm. Surely it would make something that was implausible absolutely impossible. I shouldn't have been thinking of it at all if I wanted to survive the endeavor. I needed to focus on his instruction completely.

So I did.

I pushed all concerns over the low functionality of my arm from my head.

Along with that, I also pushed away the new knowledge that most the Reapers in the House were unaware of Chase's presence, what that might possibly mean, and how much more dangerous this situation was than I'd initially realized.

It being more dangerous than I'd realized was absurd, because I'd thought of a *great* deal.

Though, try as I might to keep my attention strictly on Chandler in front of me as he demonstrated proper rope handling . . . I couldn't stop a few thoughts of bodies hitting the ground from coming through.

Once Chandler had shown me the correct way to hold the rope several times to ensure there was no mistake, he said, "I was going to climb halfway down and then back up so you could see it."

I nodded my head in understanding. "So you could come back in here and ensure I actually go out the window."

He almost grinned but didn't. "I'm going to trust you to do it yourself. Don't let me down."

I blinked hard at his words, looked away, and then nodded again.

Before heading out the window, he said, "Watch me very carefully."

I would not remind him it was dark and that I couldn't watch much of anything very carefully. But it was when he was already out the window and I was looking into his face that I said, "We're going to get caught."

Then, he did grin. "No, we're not." And then he was gone.

I leaned out the window, trying to watch the way his body worked as it was doing this seemingly impossible task, but before I knew it . . . he was already at the bottom. It was sort of like the instructions—done and over so fast.

I could just see the outline of him in the moonlight—a hand, waving me down.

I would not have trusted myself to go out the window without him standing there to push me forward in whatever way he deemed fit, but it was the prospect of disappointing him that sent me crawling out on my own with the rope in my hands.

My body dangled where I held on, and the injury in my left shoulder protested so hard against what I was doing. I was glad for all the body strengthening I'd been enduring the past month and also for that clear drink. If not for those things, I was certain I would've shaken myself right off the wall.

Though I wanted to close my eyes, I did not. I put my feet on the wall, took one step down, and then another.

I didn't look at the ground as I made my slow descent, and though I wanted to cry in terror, I somehow managed not to do so. I focused on my breathing and on putting one foot below the other, on keeping everything the way it needed to be and imitating as closely as I could. *Survival*. I focused on my hands in those gloves, holding tightly to the rope, and I believed I somewhat understood their purpose after putting them to use.

I jumped when I felt a hand on my back, but before I could scream, my body was away from the wall and a hand was over my mouth.

"See?" Chandler whispered in my ear.

I breathed out and felt my body relax against his. Although I was quite accustomed to touching him—more so than I was with any other man, I realized—the contact was strange and somewhat uncomfortable. I tried not to jolt at any of the revelations so as not to make anything needlessly awkward.

I barely heard him speak, but I could clearly hear the pride when he said, "You did it."

He released me, and I could not explain why, but I turned and hugged him. I only realized after my arms were there that there was no reason for it. I certainly expected him to at the very least perhaps pick me up and move me away from him.

He didn't.

His arms wrapped around me, and I believed he laughed without a sound possibly twice.

I paid attention to his hands—where they were and how they were.

Not long passed before he patted me twice at the back and whispered, "All right."

He released me again. That time, I stepped away. I expected to see a smile on his face, as I'd heard one in his voice, but there was not one to be found when I looked.

It was nothing. He held my hand every night. We were quite physical with one another during my training.

Being bodily close should not have been strange at all. People touched one another sometimes. It was normal. It was all right. Varying levels of intimacy should not have thrown me in such a way. It was just so . . . peculiar.

Chandler seemed both unfazed by the recent proximity and my absurd reaction to it when he pointed to each of his eyes then up at the window. I nodded my head as he began to climb, and I watched him as he'd silently instructed me to do.

You'll get accustomed to friendship eventually, I told myself.

I hoped I would.

Halfway up, I was certain he'd released the rope, as his body had flattened against the side of the House. He was faster that way, and I suspected he'd initially gone slowly only to show me the proper way to do it when I could actually see him clearly enough in the moonlight. I heard no sounds at all. No scraping of hands or clothing on wall, no breathing or straining, and absolutely nothing as he slipped back in through the window.

I did not allow myself to wonder how many people's windows he had silently snuck through, or what he'd done once inside.

How could anyone stand a chance against that when we all lumbered about?

I grabbed hold of the rope and slowly began pulling myself up the wall, away from the temporary and false freedom of being outside the Valdour House. I ignored the screaming protest from my shoulder, and I did as Chandler had told me to do.

I dealt with it, and I did it.

CHAPTER SIX

AFRAID

HANDLER PULLED ME IN through the window, somehow managing not to yank on my left shoulder at all during the process. He hauled the rope I'd climbed back in and closed the window without making a sound. I wanted to ask him if my attempt had been dreadful, but instead I said what I thought he might say in response to the unvoiced question.

"I didn't die."

"No, you didn't." He laughed, and his amusement carried into his tone when he spoke again. "You should get some sleep. There are only a few more hours until dawn."

I was struck with confusion and a sense of panic that I tried to quell. "Aren't you coming with me?"

Chandler was always with me now.

He sounded nonchalant when saying, "No, I'm thinking I'd like to sleep on a bed for the rest of the night." He moved the rope over to inside a wardrobe. "Who knows when we'll be able to do that again after we leave?"

"Oh." That sounded perfectly reasonable to me, though I had to admit the prospect of Chandler not being there was strange.

What would I do if I woke from another of my nightmares?

Did I have enough time left in the night for bad dreams to be a legitimate concern?

I didn't want him to see how frightened I was at the thought of waking and not finding him right there, so I forced my voice into calmness to say, "All right, but I don't suggest you tell Ahren that you didn't accompany me back."

"He won't ask." He barely shook his head. "Goodnight."

"Goodnight," I told him, then watched him make his way to the door.

He'd never said that to me before.

I kept waiting for him to stop on his way. Perhaps tell me to do one thing or another.

Don't hug me again for no reason.

You crossed a line.

Why did you do that?

I've changed my mind.

He did not say another word.

Chandler was not anywhere to be seen in the hallway when I peeked out after changing back into my normal clothing, so I began making the return journey to my quarters alone. I glanced at Chase's door as I passed it, but I didn't make it all the way to the next corner like I had the previous night before I stopped.

I turned around and walked. When I got there, I did not barge in. I gently tapped on the door a few times.

It took Chase a good while to answer, and it was clear I'd woken him when he did.

Rather than apologize for that, I said, "I climbed up the wall of the House."

He narrowed his eyes and then rubbed at them as he laughed quietly. "Did you?"

"With a rope, but yes." A bit of pride swirled in my torso. "And I'm still alive."

"I can see that." He chuckled. "Do you want to come in, or no?"

I nodded my head stiffly and he stepped aside.

"I didn't figure you would want me to," I told him once I was properly inside and he'd closed the door behind us. "After . . . the things I said earlier."

"You didn't have any control over what you were saying."

I wasn't entirely certain that made a difference.

I glanced over at his bed, finding the blankets askew as they always were after he'd slept in them. "Do you always have trouble sleeping?" I asked him distractedly.

He nodded in response when I looked back at him.

"Why is that?"

He rubbed at the back of his neck in an uncomfortable manner. "There aren't very many things in life you can truly escape from."

"You're haunted by your life and the things you've been forced to do," I said quietly. "It's why you're always staring off, isn't it? Remembering things?"

He looked away. "Yeah."

"It's sad," I said. "That you aren't even allowed peace in your sleep."

"If you knew what we're actually talking about . . ." He brought his eyes back to mine. "You would say I deserve no peace."

I thought on that for a moment, wondering what that sort of torment must be like. "Aren't you glad, then, that your life of being forced to do horrible things is over? At least now, if you do something, it will be your choice."

"It doesn't change anything. It doesn't *erase* anything."

I took a deep breath and walked over to his bed, grabbing the edge of his blanket and holding part of it in my hands. He'd followed me, though I'd not heard him do so.

"You remember when I stayed in your room with you a few weeks ago?" I asked. "I told you Stanley had offered to escort me back to my quarters and then that I'd decided to stay because I was afraid to stay."

"Yes, I remember."

"I had a conversation with him about fear." I looked at the floor and felt a sad smile pulling at face. "He told me he prayed I always had reason to be afraid in my life, that I would always have something I would be afraid of losing." I looked back into Chase's eyes to say, "I pray you never forget the things you've done. If you forgot . . . you would lose every bit of the humanity inside you. Those things, being *haunted* by them?" I shrugged stiffly with my right shoulder. "It makes you human. And it's all right."

He said nothing for a long time, and he would not look at me. I stood there, patient as he either thought over my words or dealt with some unknown thing. Those words and what they meant, perhaps, or possibly something else entirely. One could never be certain of the thoughts that plagued another.

Eventually he asked, "Do you want to stay again?" He still hadn't looked at me.

"Yes."

He nodded his head and muttered, "I slept better with you here."

I followed him as he began walking away toward a dresser, I assumed to find some nightclothes for me. When his hand was extended to open a drawer, I grabbed hold of it.

He was clearly very confused when our gazes finally met. "I thought—"

I told him, "I don't want to sleep."

He pulled his hand back to himself and stared around the room for a moment like he'd forgotten where he was. It took him a bit of time to bring his attention back to me. "Are you afraid?"

"Yes," I admitted, "but I don't care."

"You've thought about it?"

I nodded in response.

"And you're *sure*?"

I was smiling a little when I nodded again.

I waited for him to move, but he did not.

Quietly, I asked him, "Do you not want to?"

He inhaled a deep breath and took the step separating us. It felt like it had been such a long time since we'd kissed when he pressed his lips against mine.

For a long time, I stood there enjoying the feeling of kissing him, but then he backed away a little and rested his forehead against mine.

"Are you going to slap me?" he asked.

"I'm not sure." I replied honestly, though I did not believe I would do what he'd inquired about.

He laughed quietly once and, when he kissed me again, he was still smiling. I fought against a small feeling of panic when his hand grabbed the back of my left leg and pulled my feet up from the floor. There was the panic, but there was also a feeling of safety as he stood there effortlessly holding my body. It was so easy to tell myself in that moment that Chase would never let anything bad happen to me, that he was strong enough to keep me safe and keep us alive.

That feeling of safety squashed the panic like a disgusting bug on the floor.

He started walking when I wrapped my arms and legs around him. Then, before I knew it, we were on the bed. It took me an extended amount of time to realize that absolutely nothing whatsoever was happening.

I opened my eyes—which had been shut tightly—and found him staring down at me. When looking at his face, I discovered . . . he was afraid, too. Somehow, that made me less afraid.

Agatha's explanatory talk several weeks ago had prepared me for this. I knew, generally, what to expect and how it would work. I knew it would hurt, but at some point along the way, the hurt would stop and be replaced by something else. She didn't clarify with *what*, only saying it was pleasant. And that was all right—the hurting.

I took a deep breath to strengthen my resolve and then I sat up slightly to remove my shirt.

I looked up at his face again when my back was replaced on the bed. He was staring at the wall above my head and in front of him. I wondered why it was that, when I knew Chase was afraid, it always took my own fear away. Or . . . enough of it, at least.

I reached my hand up to his face and said, "It's all right."

His eyes lingered on mine before they were cast downward, like he was ensuring I'd given him permission.

I was *not* expecting for him to smile as though he were amused. I'd not been expecting that at all.

I blinked hard in confusion for a moment until he began unstrapping the knife that was attached to my arm. Once it was detached, he tossed it onto the floor beside the bed. I almost wanted to tell him that, though I may slap him, I would certainly never stab him. I then wanted to tell him that I wanted the knife back where it had been. Then I realized it would likely be potentially dangerous—having knives attached to your body with what we were intending to do.

"You should probab—" I stopped speaking immediately when his hand went flat against my abdomen. I was unsure how much time I'd wasted thinking about knives, but I knew I hadn't been paying attention to his face. How had I not been paying attention to things in such a moment?

I hadn't realized I'd closed my eyes tightly again until he kissed me once and then asked, "Should probably what?"

He kissed me again and I struggled to force my brain into thinking.

What *had* I been thinking about?

I felt his fingers prying one of my eyes open, so I opened them both.

He was smiling when he asked the question again. "Should probably what?"

The smile did not help matters any, so it took me several excruciatingly long seconds to respond with, "Remove your knives."

He appeared to be extremely confused for an instant as he looked down at me and then over his shoulder toward the door. And when he looked back at me again, I wondered if he *ever* took all his knives off himself.

I smiled and said, "We'll be all right."

I heard him breathe out once before he moved and began pulling something out from the top of his trousers. It was my turn to be confused again as I tried to fathom how I'd not been able to notice it before, especially given that I'd stayed with him.

It was a strap that looped around his hips. On the left side was a rather large knife in a sheath that ran alongside his leg, and then on the other, four small ones. He watched the strap as he tossed it onto the floor. Then he sat down beside me and began undoing straps that were attached to each ankle. Each one, he watched as he tossed. He put one on the floor on the side of the bed where my knife was, and one on the floor near the end of it. Easy access, I supposed. Multiple options.

He remained sitting there, staring at the door and tilting his head to the side as he listened for some sound that simply was not there. Only when I rolled over and wrapped my arms around his waist did he seem to remember I was in the room with him and why he'd been required to remove his weaponry in the first place. He jolted a bit at the contact, but then one of his hands began running along the length of my back.

His fingers did not seem as if they were counting the scars on my back from my numerous beatings throughout the years or analyzing them in any way now. When he touched me, it felt as though they weren't there at all.

But they were there.

When he laid down, I pulled myself up close beside him. One of his hands continued to run along my back and the other touched my face.

And there was something about the way he was looking at me, something spectacular.

So it took me a while to respond when he asked, "Are you afraid?"

I contemplated it again. I contemplated it for what felt like an eternity before the unplanned word came out of my mouth. "No."

He watched me for several seconds, and when he decided I was being truthful . . . he smiled.

MY BODY FELT VERY STRANGE when I woke. It was a pleasant sort of strange, like breathing in too deeply. I was sore, yes, and though I'd grown quite accustomed to soreness over the past month, it was a different sort. Even that was not entirely unpleasant—not in comparison to other things, at least.

I only had an instant to somewhat enjoy the feeling of it before Chase kissed me on my forehead and jumped out of bed.

I smiled a little as I watched him by the light filtering in through the window. He had a knife attached to his arm. He must've put it there sometime after I'd fallen asleep, somehow. It was only when he'd put his trousers back on and was walking toward the door that I heard shouting coming from the hallway.

I hunkered down beneath the blankets just before the door opened. I was easily able to make out Ahren's voice loudly asking, "*Is my sister in there?*" before it closed and I was left alone.

I jumped out of bed then as well and was nearly done putting on my clothing when a fist punched straight through the door. I blinked hard at it for a moment and then completed the process.

Once I was properly clothed, including both my knife and my shoes, I threw the door open. Ahren's hand was bleeding everywhere, though he did not seem to notice the blood dripping down his fingers as he stared at me.

"Don't be an imbecile," I told him unhappily.

He glared at me and asked, "Do you want to *talk* about being an *imbecile*? What if he gets you *pregnant*, Aster? What *then*?"

"What if the sky falls down and the world decides to end?" I asked.

In my peripherals, I saw Chandler purse his lips together.

I kept my focus on Ahren. "If everyone lived their lives on what-ifs, no one would ever have a life to live."

"Was that *really* your decision?" Ahren asked in disbelief.

"No, he broke the door and prevented me from leaving."

Though my response had been full of sarcasm, Ahren puffed himself up the instant the words came out of my mouth.

Quickly, I said, "I'm not serious! Do you honestly believe he would *ever* force me to do something I didn't want to?" I shook my head. "Don't be ridiculous."

"*Ridiculous*." Ahren said the word on a breath, looking down at the floor. He brought his eyes to mine again and went on more firmly. "*Ridiculous* is the mental image of my sister trying to escape from Reapers while she's pregnant. I don't want you to end up like our mother." Then he stormed away.

I watched his back while he went.

We all stood there in a strained silence long after Ahren rounded the corner out of our sight. Chandler spoke first and was clearly apologetic when he did.

"He shouldn't have said that."

"What he shouldn't have done was punch through the door." I finally looked away from the emptiness of the hallway. I tried to look up at Chandler and could only manage it for what felt an instant. Then I quietly added, "He was well within his rights to say what he did, though." Or at least . . . I *thought* he was.

"Do you regret it?" Chase asked from behind me.

"No." I turned to him. "I don't believe what we did was wrong, but I can understand his concerns."

He nodded his head in understanding then said, "You may want to go fix things with your brother."

"You're right." I immediately began walking away in the direction Ahren had gone.

"Aster," Chandler said to my back.

I stopped moving then looked over my shoulder.

He cleared his throat before informing me, "Your shirt is on backwards."

I brought my gaze down and felt my face burning. "So it is."

"You should *probably* fix that."

I looked to Chase and shared a small smile with him before going back inside his room and fixing my shirt like Chandler had told me to.

CHAPTER SEVEN

PLANS

RESOLVED MYSELF TO BE ENTIRELY CALM as I made my way toward Ahren's office. Truly, I did not think too much on what I would say to him once I arrived. I was more concerned over how strange walking there felt.

It felt *very* strange.

My mind was still inside Chase's bedroom—processing what had happened inside it, at least—when I found myself standing in front of the same Reaper who had flirted with me and the same Guard who had been with him that night. The Reaper's eyes were narrowed at me and he had his head cocked to one side.

I cleared my throat. "Is he in there?"

The Guard said, "Yes, he is. I'll inform him you're here, Miss."

Once the Guard had stepped inside and closed the door behind him, the Reaper grinned and said, "That's interesting."

Confused, I asked, "What's interesting?"

"The way love is able to twist and distort little girls' minds." He shrugged. "It's interesting."

"*Excuse* me?"

"No time." He nodded his head slightly toward the door.

An instant later, it opened and the Guard reemerged. "He's ready for you, Miss."

Rather than go inside, I stood there gaping at the Reaper. I was too afraid to let him out of my sight, knowing he'd *somehow* discerned Chase's presence here by the way I was behaving. I couldn't just leave him, knowing he would likely go find and attempt to kill Chase for my father.

Would we have to leave sooner? Did this Reaper have to die to be kept quiet? If so . . .

Who would kill him?

The Reaper looked at the doorway—though I did not—when Ahren said, "Leave the door."

"But Sir?" the Guard said.

"Three minutes," Ahren said. "Leave the door and return in three minutes. The two of you, step inside." I saw him gesturing in my peripherals as the Guard made his leave.

The Reaper grinned at me again before doing as he'd been told. Only when he was all the way inside the room did I follow after him.

Ahren turned to us and was clearly unhappy when he asked, "*What* is going *on* with the two of you?"

"She's worried I'm going to kill Chase." The Reaper said it nonchalantly then turned to me and smiled. "Aren't you?" I was unable to tell whether his tone was taunting or playful, but either of those options were wildly inappropriate and damn near infuriating.

I gaped at him, then at my brother.

Ahren sighed. "I can assure you he won't."

"How can you assure that?" I demanded.

"Because *this*," Ahren held his hand out toward the Reaper, "is my other best friend. He's one of very few people in this world that I trust."

And *that* was apparently why Ahren had not believed me when I'd told him about my interaction with this particular Reaper. With the understanding that he was no imminent threat despite what he knew, I turned to him and asked, "Why would you call me a little girl after you flirted with me?"

Ahren sighed. "Are you on this again?" His tone was full of exasperation.

I ignored him as I looked at the Reaper, who was still smiling as if he were thoroughly amused. But there was *something* else on his face. What *was* it?

I didn't have the vaguest clue.

"It's what your father and brother would think, isn't it?" The Reaper laughed quietly, and his gaze went down my body then back up to my eyes. "Clearly you're not."

I struggled against the strange and intense heat rising on my face.

"*Did* you flirt with her?" Ahren asked in disbelief, his voice much louder than normal.

I felt a surge of pride in myself for knowing as much when the Reaper shamelessly admitted, "I did."

I pursed my lips together tightly in an effort to refrain from laughing when Ahren balled his hands into fists. The one he'd punched through the door was cleaned now, at least. I did worry he was going to get it bleeding again, though.

"I don't know why you're angry with me," the Reaper said. "At least I didn't sleep with her. Should I take you to another door so you can punch through it, too? Would that make you feel better?"

I disguised a laugh as a cough and turned away.

Ahren said, "Get out."

The Reaper shrugged and turned, but Ahren spoke again before he could walk away.

"And for *god's sake*, don't ever let my father figure out you were stupid enough to do that."

The Reaper smiled at me once more before he left the room. I was unsure if my brother saw it, as I was somewhat distracted by another—*tamer*—wave of heat on my face.

After the door had closed, leaving the two of us alone, I watched Ahren sort of slump over where he stood and put his face in his hands. From between them he mumbled, "Having a sister is exhausting."

"Only because you make it so," I told him with a little chuckle as I walked over and placed my hand on his arm.

"I'm not sure if I'm behaving correctly." He almost sounded distracted, which was unlike him. "After the fact, I feel as if I've been somewhat unreasonable, but at the time . . . I'm not able to think clearly."

"I'm sure it's a bit of both," I told him apologetically. "But there's no cause to be upset over a person flirting with me. I'm sure if he's your friend he wouldn't try to hurt me, as Camden did. You must know he likely did it solely to get a rise out of you." It made so much more sense after knowing, as did all things.

Or most all things.

"And what of . . ." Ahren stopped speaking and his face contorted strangely, which made me laugh.

"Chase?" I offered.

He nodded.

"You were right about what you said. It was hurtful, yes, but . . ." I sighed. "I'll admit in all my thinking of it, that was one aspect I hadn't even contemplated. I've been too concerned with my other fears on the matter."

"Would you have still . . ." Ahren paused to clear his throat before going on. "Done it if you *had* thought of that?"

"I would have," I told him honestly. "I needed to prove to myself I could do something I was afraid of, given what's coming." I did not believe it had helped matters any that I'd been riding on some strange sort of euphoric feeling induced by climbing up and down the wall without getting caught and surviving the entire endeavor. I would not tell Ahren that part though, as I didn't believe it would be very beneficial in sorting things out with him. I also certainly would never try to explain to anyone the weighing of separate fears that I'd done beforehand.

"You need to be careful, Aster." Though his voice was quiet, it was also firm.

I pursed my lips. I didn't believe telling him that he needn't be hypocritical—as I knew he'd done the same thing with Evelyn—would benefit the situation either.

"I won't always be there to look out for you."

My brow furrowed hard. "Aren't you coming with us?"

"*What*?" he asked in a stunned tone. "No. Of course not."

"But . . ." It was all I could say for what felt like an eternity.

I hardly registered the expression on his face as I continued shaking my head.

"But I just found you." Quietly I admitted, "I don't want to lose you."

He opened his mouth, then closed it again. He blinked several times before looking away at a wall. "I don't want to lose you, either."

"Then come with us," I whispered.

"I can't kill our father," he stated. "It would be better for you if I didn't go, if you expect that of me."

"Would you stand by and let him kill Chase?" My jaw started quivering as I thought of my dream where he'd done as much.

"I don't know," he said. "But I *do* know that I've stood by and let people who meant far less to me do more than that. The fact is . . . I don't know. It's not a good thing to go into a situation without knowing how you would handle it. I worry my presence would do more harm for you than good."

"I don't believe that," I told him firmly. "I understand you've had more time with our father than you have with me, but I don't believe you would stand by and—"

"I don't *know*, Aster."

I blinked hard at the wall that he'd looked away from and cleared my throat. My voice sounded very small when I spoke again. "Will you think about it, at least?"

As quietly as I'd spoken, he said, "I'll think about it."

I sniffed a little and suggested, "You should come and watch me today."

"Why?" He'd not been inside the sixth room while I was training for quite some time. Chandler would not allow it.

I forced a smile at him. "To see how useless I still am. It might sway your decision on the matter."

He frowned. "Chandler said you've gotten much better."

I laughed and informed him, "Chandler lies, just like the rest of you." I for a moment wondered if Chandler considered it lying at all, if he might in some way actually believe it. Then I got myself back on path. "And, if you still decide against going with us . . . at least if you come watch me, you'll know what you're leaving me to."

He narrowed his eyes. "You're trying to manipulate me."

I shrugged. "If being honest is manipulative."

"You've never been as weak as you've played yourself off to be." He shook his head and sighed. "But I will go with you."

I smiled.

He clarified, "To *watch*."

"I knew what you meant." I took his arm. "Come along, brother. Let us go see how horrible your sister is at fighting."

SURPRISINGLY, THE FIRST THING AHREN DID upon our arrival in the sixth room was apologize to Chase, both for his reaction and also for attempting to punch him and bashing his hand through the door in the process. I believed he apologized, not necessarily because he was truly sorry, but because he felt foolish.

He might've only felt foolish for missing. I suspected Chase was glad he had, with as much force as had been in the swing.

I hadn't known my brother was so strong.

The two of them stood by one wall talking quietly with one another as Chandler and I fought in the middle of the room. I didn't downplay my abilities because Ahren was there watching; my shoulder and general lack of skill did enough of that for me. I didn't believe that was manipulative of me, but I would not deny the possibility that I could've been mistaken on the matter.

At the end of the first activity, I was stunned to find Chase still inside the room, watching me as he talked with my brother. They were both still there as I practiced dodges. They were both still there as Chandler and I practiced stealth and sensory training, though they participated in none of it. But I believed I was the most stunned when, after lunchtime and having waited for food to settle, all four of us began running around the perimeter of the room together.

As all eight feet hit the floor, I wondered when Chandler had shouted at me last. I thought back on it and discovered I could not remember when exactly. The past month was one giant blur of time and I found myself wondering if the rest of my life would pass in much the same way.

I didn't struggle as immensely as I had initially when we ran fast, but at the end of it, I was still gasping for air.

Ahren said, "You *have* improved." He was not even slightly out of breath.

"Not in the ways that matter," I informed him.

Chandler said, "Everything matters."

I sighed. "It's this damned arm. I know I was doing better in the fighting before my arm. Perhaps not very much, but every little bit must count for something."

"It'll heal completely soon." Chandler smiled a little. "But you need to keep drinking the Bryon tea."

I asked, "Will we have any of it while we're gone?"

He nodded shortly.

"That's good." I nodded as well. "We'll still have a lot of training to do after we leave here."

Chase said, "After we're done traveling and finally get where we're going."

"You know . . ." I began thoughtfully. "I'm afraid of what we're preparing to do, but I believe I'm excited as well. I've never really felt free, and having the prospect of it in front of me is . . ." I almost laughed. "Well, it's kind of amazing. Do you know what I mean, or is it insanely ridiculous to be excited given the circumstances?"

Chase smiled warmly. "I know what you mean."

"That's good, because I'm not entirely certain I fully understand it myself." A small laugh did escape from my mouth then. "Where is it we'll be going, by the way? I've never asked." I'd never thought to ask, but would I have received an answer if I had?

"Well, I had to change my initial plans, given that I informed your father of them," Chase said. "Good thing he didn't know I found multiple suitable locations. The place where we're going is by the sea."

I stopped moving then, as the four of us had been strolling casually around the room, and I turned to face him. Everyone else stopped with me.

"By the sea?" I asked.

He nodded in response, almost hesitantly.

I heard myself breathe out loudly as I looked down at the floor. "I've seen drawings of it in the books of the library. I never thought I would ever get to see it for myself." I looked back up to him. "Is it beautiful?"

He smiled nodded again, but it was not hesitant. "You'll love the sea." He sounded convinced.

I did not doubt I would. "Will you tell me about it?" Excitement began building inside me.

"Well, it's—" Chase stopped speaking immediately.

The smile dropped off his face as he stared at the door the instant Ahren grabbed hold of my good arm.

I glared at Ahren, but he also was staring at the door behind me and did not notice the look I'd shot him. His hand began shaking where it held my arm, and I knew with certainty.

I somehow knew it the instant before I heard it behind me.

"Flower."

I did not close my eyes, like I wanted to do. I would know that voice anywhere, and though my stomach felt like it had sunk to the floor . . . I knew what I had to do. *Necessity.*

I turned around and said, "Hello, Father."

CHAPTER EIGHT

FATHER

"AREN'T YOU GOING TO HUG ME?" My father asked the question with a smile that seemed too easy, too . . . *pleased*. He looked precisely the same as I remembered—older, yes, but he still had the same face. I hardly registered his dark hair that held only the slightest hint of grey now or his green eyes that used to seem so warm to me. Like sun shining on grass.

I was entirely focused on his hands. I watched those hands intently.

He had come alone into the room at least, though I did not doubt more of his Reapers stood just outside the door. The Valdour House was filled to the brim with his Reapers, after all.

My voice was blank when I said the word, "No." It was almost difficult—when looking at him standing there—to for an instant forget everything I'd learned recently and remember being a child, safe in his arms instead. But I was not a child, and he was the biggest danger to me now. "Can we please drop the pretenses?"

He did not drop the smile from his face, but it did change somewhat and he did narrow his eyes at me—only for an instant—before they settled in behind me on Chase. "So glad to see you're still alive and that the information I had received was false." He'd almost sounded convincing in his delivery of the words.

"*Are* you?" I asked him harshly before Chase could respond in any way.

The smile finally left his face when he admitted, "No."

My hands clenched into fists at my side.

"How can I be when he's trying to take my daughter away from me right when I've found her again?"

"What are you *talking* about?" I demanded as I quickly worked everything out inside my head. This was so far past bad, but keeping them all safe was much more important than anything else. It was more important than our plans.

Our plans.

The thought of it brought an ache to my chest, which I pushed so far down it had no hope of reaching me again now. "All three of them have been trying to convince me to go with you this entire time."

"Have they?" Both his eyebrows rose, and he grinned. "I'm quite certain you're lying to me, Flower."

"*Am* I?" I nearly shouted.

The grin wavered on his face.

"Why would I want to go *anywhere* with a man who abandoned me?"

He blinked hard where he stood nearly halfway across the room.

When he took a step closer, I said, "You're close enough."

I was surprised he stopped moving, but I pushed that down as well.

"Is that what you think?" His voice was quiet enough then that I could only just hear it. "That I abandoned you?"

"What I think is irrelevant, isn't it?" I asked him. "What I *know* is that you're not going to allow me to live my life. You're not going to allow me to leave here, unless it's with you. Are you?"

"No," he said. "I am not going to allow you to leave here unless it is with me. But you need to understand—"

"*You* need to understand," I said firmly as I began walking toward him. I hoped upon all hope that the other three stayed where I'd left them because I could do nothing if they moved closer to him. Not now. Perhaps not ever.

I shook my head as I stared up into my father's face when I was only a few short feet away from him.

How long had I secretly dreamt of seeing that face again?

How long had I secretly dreamt he would come and save me from this life?

As long as it had taken me to realize that I did not need saving.

"I am going to tell you what will happen now." I could not remember a single time in my life where I'd told my father how anything was going to be, but nothing was the same as it had been then. Too much time had passed.

His grin returned. "What will happen now, Flower?"

"I *will* come with you. Willingly," I said, which made the grin on his face morph into a genuine—if not stunned—smile. "But I have conditions."

He seemed amused by that, but I went on.

"The first of those is that you will allow me to continue my training."

"That's not—"

I held up a hand and went on. "The second of those is that Agatha will come with me. She will not be a servant wherever we go. The third is that Chase and Chandler will also come with me. The fourth is that no one, and I mean absolutely *no* one will harm them. Not in any way, to any extent, by any means."

"Why would I agree to that?" Curiosity was evident in his tone.

"I'm more than aware of the fact that you do not care about my feelings," I told him. "But I understand that you want me to come with you to keep me alive. You wouldn't have gone through all the trouble you have if there weren't some things you *do* care about. So you will agree, not because I want it, but because of what will happen if you do not."

His eyes narrowed. "And what would happen?"

I stepped closer and, through my teeth, said, "I will hate you. Until I draw my very last breath . . . I will *hate* you."

He shook his head slowly. "You clearly do already."

"No," I informed him. "But I am very close."

For the briefest instant, I saw that he'd not expected things to be this way, but then he straightened his face out and that particular opportunity for further insight was gone. His expectations and wants were as irrelevant to me as mine were to him.

He seemed to ponder over my words for a moment as he looked down at me. "How am I supposed to ensure their safety? If they were sent—"

"They will *not* go on missions for you," I told him firmly. "Do not misunderstand the words I am saying to you. They belong to me. *Not* you. And you *will* ensure their safety."

"If they belong to you, shouldn't that be your responsibility?"

"If you're forcing me to go with you, it will be yours," I said. "My last condition is that you need to understand something. I am not that child you left in the house in the wilderness ten years ago. You will not treat me as such. You will not tell me what to do, nor will you dictate my life, my time, or whom I love. Are we clear, Father?"

It took him a very long time to say, "As glass, Flower."

I nodded and told myself I could take my breath of relief later, when he could not see or hear it.

His tone was different—businesslike—when he spoke next. "You should prepare yourselves. We have a death to fake, and I need to retrieve some cargo to take back with us. Then, we're leaving." He began walking away.

"Cargo?"

He stopped and turned back toward me with a smile on his face. "Yes. Just a little something that needs taking care of."

My stomach dropped as understanding struck me. "You're going to allow me to accompany you while you retrieve it."

"I will not." His tone did not have to be as that of most people in order for you to understand . . . you could not get past his word. "And I *believe* you're out of things to bargain with." He immediately began walking away again.

"I have one more thing," I said quickly to his back.

He halted, and when he looked at me this time, one of his eyebrows was raised slightly.

I closed my eyes for a moment and took a deep breath before saying it. "If you allow me to go with you now, I will allow you an attempt to make amends with me."

"Will you?" His head did not tilt to the side like most other Reapers, nor were his reactions so easy to read on his face or detect in his voice, even when surprised as I knew he must be. And even the easiest Reapers I'd come in contact with were difficult to read.

I pursed my lips then nodded my head in response.

"No matter where we're going and what I'm retrieving there?"

"I already know where it is you're going," I almost whispered, then looked away. "And what you're retrieving to bring back to your home with you."

"And you'll agree to that, just to accompany me?"

I nodded again as I stared at the wall.

"With that, you've eliminated your only remaining bargaining piece." I glanced at his green eyes, watching them stare at me when he said, "I thought I taught you better."

Then, he turned away.

I HAD NEVER BEEN to the place where prisoners were held in the Valdour House, though I'd heard stories about it.

It was on the side we were already located. It mirrored where the servants' quarters were on the normal side but was deeper underground, past the point for tiny windows near the ceiling. There was no chance to discern the time of day, by natural means or any other. I'd heard that alone could drive a person to madness. The only sources of light were lanterns.

I could hear my heart pounding in my ears as I followed behind my father. I could not hear Chase, Chandler, or Ahren's footsteps behind me, but I knew they were there. I also knew they were being followed by four of my father's Reapers who'd not bothered pretending to be Guards. I supposed they'd accompanied him here.

No one spoke at all.

When we'd stopped outside the bars separating us from Camden, I touched my father's arm and urged, "Let me speak to him alone."

"That wasn't part of our bargain," he stated.

"I deserve that much for what he tried to do to me."

My father studied me.

I stared into his eyes to add, "Please."

He nodded and Ahren stepped in front of us to unlock the cell door. I did not look at anyone behind me as I stepped forward, taking a lantern one of the Reapers had extended. I most certainly could not look at Chase. My eyes were locked on Camden's, who was sitting against a wall with his hands in shackles.

I placed the lantern on the floor at his left and my right, kneeling in front of him.

I stared intently at his face, which had always flushed when he'd first spoken to me, analyzing and contemplating. I wondered now if he'd always done it on purpose, as he did not hold that innocent quality any longer.

Then again, being horrible enough to try to rape a girl meant he'd lost his innocence long ago. Perhaps he was quite good at pretending and had spent a very long time practicing.

I barely asked, "Do you know what's going to happen?"

He blinked at me and then took in the scene of Reapers on the other side of the door. He said nothing when our gazes met again.

"Ahren?" I said to Camden. "He is my brother."

Camden's mouth parted slightly in stunned understanding, as he'd received the answer to the question he'd asked me that horrible night on why Ahren cared about me.

"That man right there?" I said, knowing he would be watching closest. "That's my father."

"Reapers." Camden's voice broke on the word.

I nodded.

"Why are you here?" I did not know whether he meant them inside this House or me here in his cell with him. Either way, it was irrelevant.

I asked him the question again. "Do you know what's going to happen?" I noticed my voice sounded like a strange mixture of pleading and nothing at all.

"They're going to kill me." He clenched his jaw after answering.

I analyzed his face again, seeing a terrified resignation there. But I also noticed that, though his face had healed somewhat strangely due to Chase beating him that night, he was otherwise unharmed. Chase had not returned to punish him further, as he surely would be more damaged. I'd always thought he would. I'd been so sure of it. Was I disappointed or relieved with that knowledge?

I did not know.

I pursed my lips for a moment in an attempt to keep my jaw from quivering. "We're leaving." My voice was quiet. "My father is going to take you with us, to teach you a lesson."

"I'm sorry," Camden said quickly toward the direction of the cell door.

I could see on his face that the prospect of what my father was planning was far more terrifying than simple death, as I had assumed it would be. I'd thought over the same thing for myself many times in the past month.

Firm, I said, "Don't apologize to him."

Camden brought his eyes to mine. "I'm so sorry." I could not tell whether it was sincere or if he was simply saying it to reason with me and my father. That, too, was irrelevant.

"Don't apologize to me," I told him, my voice quieter.

"Please." He whispered so quietly that it was hardly more than his mouth moving. I could see desperation so clearly on his face when he said, "Don't let them take me."

I forced a smile at Camden as I heard Chase's voice in my head.

One day . . . One day you wake up and really think about it. You think about the mission from the night before and wonder why. And you wonder how you could've done what you did. So, before every mission, you start asking more questions. You don't want to go anymore when you hear the answers, but what else can you do? You know they'll just kill you and send someone else if you refuse. So you go. You go so they don't send someone worse instead. At least you know you'd kill them quickly where the one they'd send in your place may not. And you pretend. . . . You pretend they've done something horrible.

I had to act quickly in case anyone had been listening hard enough to hear Camden's whispering. I'd done enough practicing with Chandler to know how to grab the knife strapped to my arm in an instant. And I knew precisely where to put it. The knife was not long enough to hit the heart in the easiest place from below the ribs, so he'd shown me the tiny spot to get to it appropriately from above.

I acted quickly and I did what I'd been trained to do.

Death is not as fast as a person would like to believe, if you've not trained your entire life to make it so.

I hadn't.

I did not know how to break a person's neck, nor did I feel confident in my strength to do as much, so sticking a blade in Camden's heart was the best way I knew.

I did not want to do it, but I pulled the knife back after it hit its mark so he could bleed out faster and have less time suffering.

I heard a commotion by the door, but I did not look away from Camden's face. Light caught on it strangely from the lantern. He'd just gone into shock by the time my father yanked me up from the ground by my bad arm. I hardly felt it.

"What did you *do*?"

What had I done?

Don't feel it, I told myself.

"What you wouldn't," I answered blankly. Then, I walked through the cell doors.

I ignored the stunned expressions on the faces of my father's Reapers. I glanced at Chase, Chandler, and Ahren for a moment. Ahren was stunned like the rest. Chandler's face was almost but not entirely impassive, but I could see it on Chase's through the shock there. Some sort of understanding.

I heard his voice in my head again.

Until I've seen you kill and seen how you react to it . . . I'd still be worried about you in that scenario.

Chase had just seen me kill a person.

I forced my face into blankness as I stepped past him and walked back up the stairs. I wanted him to know he could depend on me to do what was necessary, no matter how horrible it was.

Once I was away from those particular stone walls, I felt my hand shaking where it held on tightly to the hilt of the knife. I would not look down at it. I kept my eyes straight ahead.

Everything seemed so strangely normal as I stepped through the door that would return me to the other half of the Valdour House. Everything seemed so normal apart from Ahren's friend standing there impatiently with Stanley and Stewart.

He rushed over to me. "They said your father was here." Then, his eyes went down. "Did you kill him?"

I looked up at him, finding that I could not speak.

"Aster, did you kill your father?" His eyes had widened, and by that point Stanley and Stewart had joined us.

I shook my head.

"Who did you kill?"

"Cam . . ." was all I could manage to get out of my mouth. I was certain I said it several times, attempting to get his name out. I could not get it out.

"Camden," Stanley said on a breath. "*Why*?"

"So my father . . ." I started and then stopped because my head did not seem to be working. "He's taking me. I have to . . ."

"Come on." Ahren's friend began ushering me away.

"He's taking me," I said again. "I have to go."

He stopped moving and leaned down close to my face. I hardly noticed that he forced a smile at me. I saw it, but . . .

Why couldn't I *see* it?

He said, "You have to get that blood off you is what you have to do right now. Everything else can wait."

I tried to look down at myself on reflex though I did not want to, but his hand went under my chin, preventing it.

"Don't look. It won't help anything."

"Don't tell them," I said quickly.

"Don't tell who what?" His brow furrowed as he looked at me, and I noticed then that he had very peculiarly colored brown eyes, which might have been why I'd found them so striking before. They were warm eyes, like my father's used to be, though very different. "Did nobody see you do it?"

"Don't tell them I'm not all right." *Desperate.* I was desperate because . . . they could *never* know.

He looked behind me at something for just a moment, then leaned close to say, "Your secret is safe with me."

I nodded and let him put his arm around me. I walked when he began leading me away, but I was not able to pay any attention to where we were going. I heard people speak to him several times, but I did not know what any of them said or what he replied to them with. I felt like I did not know anything. I felt like I did not know myself.

Who was I? I had always known what I was, hadn't I?

I'd been wrong.

Had I been wrong?

A little voice whispered a word in my head. Though so quiet in comparison to the indistinguishable waves of speaking around me and the unrelenting screaming that felt as if it would rip my head apart . . . it was the only thing I heard.

Murderer.

CHAPTER NINE

BLOOD

'D NOT REALIZED that Ahren's friend and I had stopped moving. I'd not noticed him cleaning the blood off me with a wet towel. I hadn't registered anything he'd said or done—though I distantly knew he'd been speaking—until, "The first kill is always the hardest."

Then it all rushed to me.

I looked up at his face as he was busy cleaning me off. Why was he doing what he was?

"It sticks with you forever."

"Don't they all?" I heard myself ask.

He blinked hard as he stopped what he was doing and looked into my eyes, appearing to be stunned that I'd responded to him. What had I missed? Had he been speaking all the while?

"Yes." He answered me with a sad smile. "But not like the first. When you get over the shock of it, you'll start asking yourself the questions."

"What questions?" I always had so many questions and discovered so few answers. All answers seemed to lead to more questions.

"Are you a monster?" He wiped at one of my hands that he was holding in his.

I did not look at it.

"You'll go over everything, trying to rationalize it. I hope you had damn good reason to do what you did because, if you didn't?" He paused to shake his head. "You're not going to like the answer you come up with."

"I didn't want my father to torture him," I said quietly, feeling wetness in my eyes though I heard no crying sounds. Only when the wetness spread did I realize that my eyes had been too dry, like I'd never blinked at all in my entire life.

"And now you'll ask the next set of questions," he said. "Could you have done things differently? Was there anything else you could have done? Do the reasons for doing bad things actually matter?"

"I'm certain there will never be an end to it." I whispered my words to the wall. How did I feel when realizing my list of questions that required answers was transforming into an enormous pit I hadn't the slightest hope to climb out of? Would I ever manage it?

Endless. Impossible.

Were there actually answers for questions like the ones he'd voiced?

I felt his hand briefly touch on my chin which made me look at him again.

"There won't be," he said apologetically. Then he made to wipe my chin off with the towel where his finger had been.

"That's—" I said quickly when I saw the fabric. I stopped speaking and stepped away. "There's so much blood." Only then did I look down at myself, hearing a choked sound escape from my mouth.

It was as if my mind had blocked the sight of it from reaching its appropriate place inside my brain as it had happened, or perhaps it had been the lighting. I did not know. But now, looking down and seeing the sprays of it on my clothing, it was all too real.

I heard myself heaving, though my ears were ringing loudly and I was so lightheaded I could hardly register the fact that I was getting ill all over the floor.

The heaving stopped, though my stomach persisted in its churning. My eyes were closed so tightly that it almost hurt in a strange way, and the coolness of the stone floor on the palms of my hands felt both familiar and foreign at once. My thoughts were such a jumble— horrible words and images dashing to the front, only to be overtaken before the point of coherency by the next.

What had I done?

Killed a man. I had killed a man and his blood still covered me—an inescapable truth.

I didn't fully realize that I'd stood from the floor at some point and had begun attempting to remove my clothing until arms went around me.

Ahren's friend said nothing, but he held me close to him despite my flailing and hysterics about needing to get the bloody clothes off. He did not move at all until my flailing and hysterics turned into sobs, and then all he did was partially slacken his hold.

There aren't very many things in life you can truly escape from.

I felt outside myself as I cried against his chest. It seemed as though nothing was real. I was not being held by my brother's friend who had flirted with me once in the middle of the night a few days previously. I was not covered in blood. I had not killed a person. I had not made a deal with my father to go with him. My father was not here. I was leaving with Chase and Chandler—and hopefully Ahren—in one night.

But it *was* real. All those things had happened, they were all true, and I was not escaping as planned. The only similarity between departure and escape was going from one location to another. The journey and destination were so very different.

There was no escaping any of this.

And my brother's friend belonged to my father.

I pushed hard against his chest.

He mustn't have been expecting anything at all like that from me because he fell backward. He braced his fall with the backs of his arms so he didn't hit his head, but in the time it took him to do that, I was on him.

"Who informed my father I was leaving?"

"*What?*" Shock, or something similar in appearance, was clear in his expression. It took him several seconds to answer. "I don't know."

"Someone *has* to know." I nearly shouted at him, but somehow contained it on the chance I'd been followed. *Likelihood.* "My brother did not do it. The shock on his face was apparent when he saw my father standing there. So it had to have been someone who knew Chase was still here. I do not believe it was Stanley or Stewart, so who does that *leave*?"

His eyes grew wider. "You think *I* did?"

"Who else *knew*?" I did shout at him then. I couldn't stop it from happening, despite some sort of reason breaking through the madness, warning me.

And I'd been worried he would try to kill Chase. He didn't need to.

I hadn't even realized that I'd attempted to punch him until he grabbed hold of my arm and frowned at me.

"Don't do that." His eyes narrowed. "You think I told your father? Why would I? What reason would I have to betray my best friend and his sister?"

"You—"

"Flirted with you once?" he asked with a short, humorless laugh. "Do you think it's *Chase* your father doesn't want you involved with? It's what we *are* in general. I'm not stupid enough to waste my time trying to get involved. And if you believe I would do something like that for such a ridiculous reason . . . you're as unintelligent as Ahren said you pretended to be when you first spoke."

"I was *going* to say . . ." I began slowly through gritted teeth, "that you belong to my father. Perhaps you *are* stupid, to assume I would say such a petty thing."

"Understand something, *Flower*." His voice was quiet. "I belong to *no one*."

"You all belong to someone, the same as I've belonged to this House for the last ten years," I informed him. "At least I could see that. Please release my arm."

"A word of advice," he said without heeding my order. "Don't attack a Reaper unless you're certain you can kill them. And don't *ever* attack me again. I was just trying to help you."

"Help me," I said on a breath.

"Who do you think was going to put the rope up tomorrow night for you to scale the outside wall? Your brother couldn't do it because he's watched everywhere he goes. You know your father wouldn't kill him for assisting in your escape, but I can assure you he would kill *me* for it if he found out. So yes. All I've been doing is trying to help you, and looking at it now . . .? You're right. Apparently I *am* very stupid." He released my arm. "Get off me."

"I'm sorry." The words were hardly more than a whisper when they came out.

"Get *off* me." He repeated it so slowly that every word sounded like a complete sentence.

I moved fast then, sitting my rear down on the floor. He stood before I was entirely done with the process and began storming toward the door.

I told him, "I would never have wanted you to endanger your life on account of me."

I wouldn't have thought he could've heard me, as I'd said it so quietly, but it was apparent he had.

He stopped moving, and I watched as it seemed like several muscles on his back twitched before he faced me again. He smiled. "It won't happen again."

I nodded my head and looked down because that was what I always did. I managed not to repeat the choked sound as I was faced once again with the blood covering me. But I felt my face contorting for a brief moment before I heard Ahren's friend say several of the angry words Chandler liked to use with me during our training. I still did not know what any of them meant, as Chandler never informed me when I asked him, but the point of them was always clear.

I looked up at him in only enough time to see his head shaking before he stepped over and pulled me up from the floor by my uninjured arm.

"You're going to get me killed." He started dragging me away.

"I . . . I don't know what you mean," I said apologetically as I stumbled along beside him. "I wouldn't want you to be killed."

"Please be quiet."

I said nothing else as he hurriedly dragged me through the House.

WHEN WE ARRIVED AT MY QUARTERS, I expected Ahren's friend to place me there and leave immediately, but he did not. He stepped inside and grabbed some clothing for me. I did not take it, as it seemed all I could do was stand there staring at him while I tried to process something. *Anything.*

"If you don't want them to know how you feel about what you did, you need to get your head straight before they see you," he said. "I'd imagine someone will be here for you shortly."

I took the clothes from him then and looked away, knowing he was right. I thought about necessities, wondering why they couldn't offer a respite from their difficulty.

I heard the door open and then close again, so I assumed he would be gone when I looked. He was not.

He stood facing the door for a moment before turning to me, his hand lingering on the knob. "How did you manage to hold it together until you were away?"

"Because I had to," I replied. *Necessity.*

I watched him almost turn away again then seem to think twice. "Why did you let me see you break down?" He clenched his jaw.

I opened my mouth to speak, but I could not locate the appropriate answer inside my head. It took me a while to find it. "I don't need to prove anything to you." Before he could leave, I quickly asked, "Where's my knife?"

"I'll make sure you get it back before you leave."

"I . . . I need it now."

He reached his hand somewhere, and I caught a flash of silver and nearly black dark red before it was hidden by his shirt. It took several seconds, but I saw no red on it when he walked forward, though I did not look particularly closely. I extended my hand, but he replaced the knife inside the strap on my arm.

I looked down at the floor and said, "Thank you."

"Change your clothes," was all he said before he was gone.

I did not look at the dirty clothes as I took them off and put on the others. I did not look at the blood that had soaked through them onto my skin. I would worry about that when I was able. I could handle it being there now, so long as it was concealed from me. I would deal with it once things had settled and I was allowed a moment's peace to come to terms with what had happened and what I'd done.

It was not thirty seconds after I'd changed that my father stepped through the door.

He did not knock.

He seemed to be alone, but I did not doubt that he had several of his Reapers nearby.

He attempted to come over to me, but I held my hand up and shook my head. I assumed he would ask me if I was all right, but he did not.

"I'm sorry." The words sounded so believable.

I asked, "For which thing in particular?"

"I didn't know your arm was injured," was what he chose to say.

I heard myself laughing that, out of all the things in the world he had to apologize to me for, he had chosen to mention yanking on my injured arm.

"If I had known . . ." He trailed off and cleared his throat. "Did you plan on doing that when you realized where I was going? You did, didn't you?"

"Yes." I did not believe telling him as much would do any further harm. "And you cannot say that, if you'd known, you wouldn't have agreed to me accompanying you. Could you? Not with what I offered. You could possibly say that, had you known, you wouldn't have agreed to allow me inside his cell. But even still . . . I had the right to it, didn't I?" Very deliberately I asked, "Who are you to deny me what is rightfully mine?"

"I'm your father."

"I had a father when I was a child," I said. "You have his face and his voice, but you are not my father. I can see now that the man I loved was not real. And if he ever truly existed at all . . . it does not change the fact that he is gone now."

All the amusement that had been held on his face before he'd watched me murder a person was gone. There was only sadness and desperation when he took a step closer and asked, "What can I do to make amends? *Please* tell me."

"Nothing you are willing to," I replied. "Perhaps I will come up with something at a later date."

He and I stared at one another for a long time before he looked away and nodded. "Things will be much different for you where we're going." His tone was somewhat soft then, like I'd always re-membered it being. "You can have anything you could possibly want there. My city isn't like this one."

"I cannot have what I want there, no matter how different your city is from New Bethel," I informed him. "I want *freedom*. You're unwilling to allow it."

He cleared his throat again and continued on as if I hadn't spoken. "Things will be different in other ways as well. Most people don't know Ahren is my son, you see. We've always kept it quiet to protect him. Everyone will know you're my daughter. That, coupled with your lack of training, will put you in great danger by Reapers from other cities. So I require you have several Reapers who will accompany you everywhere."

"You're not serious," I said in disbelief. "I tell you I want freedom and—" I looked away and heard myself laugh. I took in a deep breath and struggled to rearrange my thoughts. "It's bad enough, what you're preventing me from having in life. You wish to take away my privacy as well?"

"I wish to keep you *alive*," he said significantly. "That's all I'm trying to do."

"*Keep me alive*." The words fell out under a breath. "It's funny then, Father—the things you're doing. You're going to parade me around your city and wait for Reaper attacks until the day I die." I paused to smile at him. "If you had simply allowed me to go, I'm quite certain I could've kept myself alive. Now, if I die . . . my blood will be on *your* hands. I very much hope you're satisfied."

He looked away again for a moment. "I'll allow you to choose the Reapers who will stay with you, if that offers you any comfort."

"And you won't demand that I have more than just Chase and Chandler?"

"You will *need* more than Chase and Chandler," he said, "but I won't insist on who the others are." He paused. "You should gather all your things. We're leaving as soon as you're done. We must be out of the city before nightfall."

The corners of my mouth tugged upward. "Would you like to see the only thing I own in this world?" Apart from what was on my person.

He blinked at me as I stepped over to my bed and reached beneath my pillow.

I pulled out a small piece of paper with a heart drawn on it and showed it to him. "This is all. I'm prepared to leave now, Father."

He looked away from the paper and cleared his throat. "Any of my Reapers who are here that you want to accompany you . . . you should find them now."

"Why?" I asked curiously.

"Because the rest are staying behind." He took a deep breath and said, "I cannot express to you how happy I am to finally see you again. I thought I'd lost you forever." He quickly walked to the door.

Before he'd opened it, I asked, "What happens at nightfall?"

He hesitated, and I watched him take another deep breath and wipe near his eyes with one of his hands. My right hand twitched at my side.

When he turned to fully face me, his voice was entirely even when he said, "I'm sure you already know the answer to that question, Flower."

I should've asked him who had told him I was intending to leave, but I did not ask him the important question. Instead, I heard myself say, "You didn't seem as stunned as everyone else by what I'd done."

He stared down at the floor between us. "It's in your blood."

I let him leave then, as I could not think of anything to say in response to such a statement.

CHAPTER
TEN

DEBT

I DID NOT ALLOW MYSELF ANY TIME to contemplate over my father's words about blood. As soon as I was sure enough time had passed for me to not catch up with him, I bolted from the room.

I ran quickly, taking the familiar path to where Stanley and Stewart were always posted to prevent anyone from slipping into the other side of the House. I was relieved to find them standing there, precisely where they were supposed to be. I hadn't known whether they would bother now that my father had arrived.

They seemed to jolt a little when they saw me but otherwise appeared as unfazed by my presence as they usually were.

"I need to ask the two of you a question."

I was not surprised when I received no form of response from either of them. I rarely ever did when they were standing at their post. It was only when they would leave it that they would say much of anything.

"My father insists I have Reapers who stay with me all the time when we get to his city. I don't—" I took in a deep, frustrated breath. "I don't trust anyone."

A confused frown appeared on Stewart's face. "What do you expect us to do about that?"

"Will you . . ." I paused again before spitting out, "I know it's a horrible thing to ask, but will you do that for me?"

"You trust us?" Stewart seemed baffled by the thought of it, which was not entirely surprising.

I nodded in response.

"How do you know we weren't the ones who told your father about your plans to leave?"

"Because Ahren wouldn't have trusted you with the information if he had any inclination that you would do so."

"Of course I will do that for you," Stanley said. He seemed to be ignoring Stewart.

I was relatively certain he was quite accustomed to doing that very thing—ignoring Stewart—when no one else was nearby. Or perhaps he simply didn't wish to dwell on subjects none of us had the time for.

"I'd do anything to be done with standing in this damn hallway," Stewart said. "I'm in."

I heard myself finally release a somewhat relieved breath. I hoped I would get a complete one soon.

"Prepare yourselves to leave," I told them. "My father said we must be gone before nightfall."

They seemed to be puzzled for a moment over what they should do as they stared down the hallway.

"I don't care about that stupid door," I said. "It doesn't seem as though it matters anymore, does it?"

I walked away at that. Just before I rounded the corner, I turned to look at them, finding that they'd already vacated the premises. When I'd seen that they were gone, I took off running again.

I stopped when I reached Ahren's office door. I shouldn't have expected his friend to be there, as he'd helped me earlier and had clearly not been working at the time, but . . .

I *had* expected it.

I stood there for far too long in disorientation, as I'd not even contemplated this possibility through all the madness. I did not know what to do or how to find him.

A normal Guard member asked, "Can I help you?"

"I need you to leave the door," I told him.

"*What*?"

"You heard her," the replacement Reaper said.

The Guard shook his head in obvious frustration, but he did as I'd instructed. I wondered now when people had started listening to me, but I knew it had absolutely nothing to do with my person and *everything* to do with my family. Did the *why* matter with such a thing? It did not change the fact that people were listening.

Didn't why people listened matter, though?

"Your brother isn't in there," the Reaper said. "He's playing dead. There are too many questions when loose ends aren't properly tied. Too many questions is much too dangerous in this situation."

"I'm not looking for my brother." I struggled to keep down the growing impatience. "I'm looking for the other Reaper."

His brow furrowed. "Who?"

"I don't know his name." This was so frustrating. "He was here this morning."

"What do you want with Jas?"

"I just need to speak with him!" I tried so hard to get a handle on my panic. "*Urgently.*"

A short laugh came out of his mouth. "I'll take you to him."

I followed him as he began walking away. When we came upon the Guard, who was standing one hallway over and looking quite put out, the Reaper told him to return to his post. I had no idea why he was being so helpful, but I supposed it didn't matter. He was helping me and there were so many other things.

After walking for a moment, I blurted out, "Aren't you worried the Guard will cause problems with your plans for this evening?"

"A lot of them are in on it." He grinned. "The answer would still be no, even if they weren't."

"Why would they be *in* on it?" I asked in disbelief.

"Because they were treated better while your brother was here than they ever have been before." He shrugged. "We've spent enough time planning this. We've weeded through all of them properly."

Instead of thinking on that—what *weeded through them* actually meant and what they'd been doing beyond guarding and patrolling—I asked, "Aren't you worried you'll all be killed by the Reapers of this city?"

He stopped moving then, and he laughed a little. I did not think it was funny in the slightest. "Do you know how many of them we've already got to?" I assumed his question was rhetorical. "You'd be surprised what people will do when they're unhappy with their situation in life."

"You've convinced some of the Reapers in this city to kill their own people?" I asked on a breath.

"It wasn't difficult." A bit of a smirk played at the edges of his mouth as he shook his head a few times. "It's a shame you weren't able to see the way Reapers in other cities operate before being exposed to your father's and ones with . . . *their own reasons.*" A few seconds of silence passed. "I'm sure you already have a distorted view on what we are, given you're in love with one of us and that your brother plays nice with you. When you go to your new city and you see us . . . keep in mind they're not all like we are. Your father is very good to us and it shows in the way we behave. When the other Reapers come for you, perhaps you'll understand."

"What do you mean?" I asked quietly.

"You thought of us as monsters, didn't you?"

I nodded in response, though I had no idea how he knew as much.

"That would be accurate," he said. "But your father has given us a purpose. It does not change what we do, but it changes what we are. Or perhaps you could look at that the other way around. Either would be true enough."

My brow furrowed. "And what is that purpose?" What could make that happen?

"We're trying to fix this world," he said significantly.

I shook my head in confusion, though he did not explain.

"When you meet another Reaper, someone who has no ties to you . . . you'll understand."

"So your purpose is to take out other Reapers?" Was *that* what he'd meant?

"No." He shook his head, then his eyes narrowed. "I thought you had urgency?"

I pursed my lips and nodded. I said nothing else as he began walking again. Different sort of Reaper or not, I'd been around enough of them by now to know when a conversation with one was over.

I WAS AWARE THAT I WAS IN THE GUARD QUARTERS, despite never having been there before, when the Reaper stopped moving and pointed to a door. I'd heard a few of the server girls speaking about it.

Before he could leave, I said, "I hope you're able to wake up in the morning." I thought it was better than telling him I hoped he did not die in his endeavors tonight. I did not want to speak directly of death.

"As do I," he said with a surprisingly warm smile. "Good luck to you."

He'd not completely made it down the hallway before the door I was standing in front of opened.

"What are you *doing* here?" Ahren's friend demanded. He seemed more stunned than angry.

"I . . ." I despised not knowing what to do, and past locating him . . . I had no idea. "May I come inside?"

He frowned, but he stepped aside and allowed me to enter.

"I need to speak with you about something," I said before I'd even stopped moving.

"I gathered that." His voice was humorless as he closed the door behind us.

"Firstly, I need to apologize," I said. "For attacking you, of course, and also for assuming you were the one who told my father."

"It was understandable." He sounded somewhat uncomfortable. "You don't know me. I would've assumed the same thing. I suppose I need to apologize for being an ass."

"Why would you call yourself that?"

It took a moment, but he laughed a little and clarified with, "The way I acted. What else is it you need?"

"You said earlier that you were going to get killed because of me."

He narrowed his eyes at me and said nothing in response to the statement.

Though I waited for something, I didn't know what he possibly could've said. It was ignorant for me to hope I'd receive any bit of assistance with this.

I took a deep breath. "I want you to return to your city with me now. My father insists I have Reapers around me all the time because other ones will come to kill me or some nonsense."

"What does that have to do with what I said?"

"It's clear you're already preparing yourself for tonight." I gestured at his all-black clothing and the knives strapped to him. He had several knives on his arms alone. "I believe you will have a higher chance at survival if you come with me instead."

He narrowed his eyes even more and, again, said nothing.

"You see . . . it's my fault this is happening here," I went on uncomfortably. "It's my fault the Reapers of your city are going to kill the ones here, because of something I told my brother. If you stay and die, then what you said earlier would be true."

"And you believe me going with you is the best thing to do?" he asked slowly.

"It's entirely logical," I told him. "I have hardly anyone in this world that I trust. If you're my brother's best friend and you were willing to risk your life for me when you didn't know me at all . . . I should trust you, shouldn't I?"

"There's a difference between trusting a person with a task and trusting a person." Very slowly he added, "It would be a good idea for you to learn how to discern which of those would be the most intelligent thing to do in any given situation."

"Will you come with me?" I asked, my voice impassive.

"If you insist I do."

Quickly, I told him, "I'll insist nothing of you."

He smiled a little. "Only that I keep your secrets for you?"

"Asking and insisting are two entirely different things," I informed him. "I won't even ask you to follow me around all the time when we arrive there. I'm only asking that you leave with me."

His head tilted a bit to one side. "Why should it matter to you if I live or die?"

I stared at the floor for a moment and took another deep breath. "My brother has had many things taken from him that shouldn't have been. I don't want the death of his friend on my hands. And . . ."

"And?" he pressed when I did not continue.

"It was very kind of you," I said. "To help me. Even after I attacked you, you still helped me despite your anger toward me. I don't wish to be in your debt. I feel as though ensuring you live past the night will make us even."

"You're very strange." He grinned. "Most people hold others to a higher standard than they do themselves. You want to call us even for me being kind to you only after you feel you've saved my life, is that correct?"

"Why should a person expect more of someone else than they do of themselves?" I asked curiously. "One should always strive to be better than what is expected of them, wouldn't you agree?" I smiled a little. "Besides, if you died, I could not repay you at all."

"Most people don't help another with the expectation that the other will be in their debt." A small, uncomfortable chuckle came out of his mouth. "You don't owe me anything."

"Do you know how many times I've been shown kindness in the last ten years?" I asked. "Apart from the past several months, of course."

"Not many, I would expect."

I smiled again. "If you knew how few, you would understand why I feel indebted to people for showing it." I took a deep breath and asked him once more. "Will you go with me?"

He seemed to be pondering over it as he looked away from me and stared intently at one of the blank, stone walls. I remained silent while he thought. I would not ask him another time. His eyes met mine briefly before he closed them and shook his head.

I took that to be his answer, so I turned and headed toward the door. It opened before I made it halfway there. My father stepped inside, followed by nine of his Reapers, Chase, Chandler, Agatha, Stanley, Stewart, and Amber.

"What are you doing in here?" my father asked me. He did not seem angry, only curious.

"I was—"

"Just helping me gather my things," Ahren's friend said from behind me. When I looked, he had a bag in his hands and was slipping it onto his back.

My father seemed to take that as a satisfactory answer because he nodded his head. "We're leaving now. The correct people are in the appropriate places."

"Where's Ahren?" I asked quickly. Surely whatever loose ends were already tied.

"Waiting to slip away," my father replied. "He's to meet up with us shortly."

"You're leaving him to his own defenses?" I demanded. "Knowing what is to happen here tonight?"

"Your brother can take care of himself."

"If he's injured or worse, Father, you and I are going to have many more problems than we currently do," I informed him. "I don't believe it would be beneficial to your cause."

He frowned, but he said nothing more on the matter. He removed a bag from his back, opened it, and handed me a set of all-black clothing; it was not exactly like theirs.

"You can change in here," he instructed. "We'll all be waiting for you just outside the door."

Everyone took that as their cue to leave, apart from Agatha. Once they had, I began doing as I'd been instructed. I didn't think about how strange it was to be changing my clothing inside a man's room, nor did I think about the blood that had been concealed by fabric until Agatha gasped at the sight of it.

"*My flower*!" she exclaimed as she ran over to me. "What *happened*?"

I began slipping the clean shirt over my head. "It doesn't matter." It was the first thing I'd said to her in what felt like such a long time. I looked at the floor and shook my head once the shirt was properly in place. My voice was nearly a whisper when I added, "Nothing seems to matter very much currently."

"Aren't you happy?" The words barely slipped out of her mouth.

"*Happy*?" I asked, baffled. "What reason for happiness is there?"

"Your father will keep you alive, my flower. *That* is reason for happiness."

I blinked hard at her as I heard a strange sound escape from my mouth—some short mixture of a laugh and an exhale of breath.

"Perhaps," I managed to say through my stunned disbelief.

I did not know how she'd managed it, but I knew now that it had been Agatha who'd gotten word to my father. It was written so clearly just below the surface of her face. She could not hide it from me while I was looking.

I should have looked at her sooner.

CHAPTER ELEVEN

LAST LOOK

AS I WALKED THROUGH THE HALLS of the Valdour House for what would be the very last time, I wondered if this day could get any worse than it already had. I knew it was possible, as I could imagine a multitude of horrendous scenarios that would in fact make it so. The day as it stood would've seemed unfeasible on the previous, but I simply could not imagine anything graver as a tangible possibility.

I had to admit, at least to myself, that my father's presence might've been the one thing that would stop those other options from becoming plausible.

Still, I could not even enjoy the smell of the air as I'd expected to once we walked into it. I was far too concerned about my brother to think of much else.

I never could've imagined leaving and feeling the way I did. Addled to the point I could hardly function, afraid of things I hadn't thought to fear, and plagued by an unyielding sense of hope-lessness in realizing . . . my escape from the prison I'd occupied most my life would grant me no true freedom. All those unanticipated thoughts and feelings were because I'd never considered leaving New Bethel at the mercy of my father, even after discovering he was still alive.

It had been so *ignorant* of me.

I did not look behind me as I made my way, nor did I allow anyone to carry the bag my father had given me when they offered. I did not speak to anyone. I did not look at anyone. I looked only at my father's back as I followed behind him.

We did not go far, stopping in some stables that were very close to the House. I'd never been to them, of course. I'd never even known they existed, as they could not be seen from the allowance of my viewing for the past ten years.

There were horses already prepared and waiting for us, along with a covered carriage. Agatha climbed inside it without a word, followed immediately by Amber. I stood there staring at my father.

"Get inside," he urged.

I smiled. "No thank you."

"Aster." He frowned. "You don't know how to ride. You need to get in the carriage."

"I'm quite sure I can manage."

"We don't currently have time to give you riding lessons." Impatience was only just seeping through his tone. "Please get inside the carriage."

I stood there staring at him, unwavering. I would not ride in the carriage with two people who had betrayed me, and I did not care what he said to me on the matter. He'd come here for me and was on limited time, which temporarily gave me an advantage.

Chase said, "Bring an extra horse and she can ride with me for now."

"Forgive me for saying so . . ." my father started slowly, "but I don't particularly trust you with my daughter right now."

"Forgive *me* for saying so," Chase began, "but you don't know your daughter anymore. She won't get inside there. We can stand here arguing about it all night, but I can guarantee you she won't do it."

"She can ride with me," Ahren's friend said evenly from behind me.

My father nodded his head in what appeared to be satisfaction. "Let's go."

Once he'd turned his back to me, I offered an apologetic look to Chase. He sighed but said nothing at all as he walked over to a waiting horse.

I followed Ahren's friend to another horse. It was huge and massively frightening, but I would not admit that aloud.

After a moment of assessing the creature in front of me, I whispered, "I don't know what I'm doing."

"Put this foot here." He gestured to both a specific foot and a specific place on the saddle. Then he pointed to another place and said, "Grab there and pull yourself up."

The entire process had always seemed like it would be much simpler from books.

Only then did I realize how utterly small the saddle was, as I'd been far too focused on the horse.

Still at a whisper, I asked in disbelief, "How are we both supposed to fit on there?"

He grinned then patted on the saddle. "We'll fit."

I did as he'd instructed without giving him further grief. It didn't work very well and he had to push me a little, but after some struggling . . . I made it.

I fidgeted a bit, realizing how uncomfortable the strange sitting was after what I'd done with Chase the previous night. I was almost entirely certain Ahren's friend snorted quietly, so I struggled to keep my discomfort to myself in the hope he would not see it.

I sat there feeling indescribably awkward until he pulled my foot out of the contraption and easily made his way up behind me. Somehow. The awkwardness intensified significantly when he moved my body and I was struck by the realization that I was very nearly sitting in his lap.

"This is extremely uncomfortable," I muttered under my breath.

He chuckled. "You'll get used to it."

I found myself startlingly glad that he'd misinterpreted the meaning of my words.

I glanced at Chase and my face felt as if it were going to melt away, though he only returned my glance for just an instant.

Desperately wanting to change the subject, I said, "I'm going to fall off." I felt very unstable on the animal and I did not like it at all.

Ahren's friend said, "No you won't."

At that point, the horses began filing away.

My stomach plummeted when ours moved forward.

"This will help you get a good feel for riding anyway. Just pay attention to what I do and how it feels."

If my face had felt like it was going to melt away a few moments previously, I did not know what it was feeling after his words, only that it was a good deal worse.

I cleared my throat and managed to say, "All right."

He snorted. That time I was sure of it, as it was much louder and *much* closer to my ear. "*Relax.*"

It was a very difficult thing to even contemplate doing, given his words paired with the proximity, and his arms which were around me and holding onto the reins. I did not know if what I'd done with Chase lessened or worsened this aspect of the situation for me, but I knew I was much more aware of the body behind me than I likely would've been before. I wouldn't have thought that possible, before, had I ever thought to think of such a mad thing. But I had a far more thorough understanding of bodies now.

Relaxing was even more difficult to contemplate doing when we were free of the stable, out in the open air, and I realized . . . "We're going to be seen."

"Yes." His voice was completely void of amusement now. It was completely void of anything.

"Why are we leaving this way?" I demanded.

I watched one of his hands pointing briefly toward the sun, which was very nearly setting in the sky now. "Because it's time. You can close your eyes if you've seen enough death to suit you for one day."

"Won't we get *attacked*?" This was so unbelievably dangerous and ignorant.

He chuckled. "You can keep your eyes open and see."

It was not two full minutes into riding when I saw the first Reaper of New Bethel. He was talking—what seemed to be—happily with some random person from the city as we were approaching. He looked at us as we passed, seemingly without thought, smiling in clear amusement at something his companion had said. He saw Chandler first, and I watched him tilt his head, confusion taking over his face. The smile faded. But I watched realization dawn as Ahren's friend and I passed directly by him.

So close. We had passed so unbelievably close to him.

I was still alive. *How* was I still alive?

I turned around and peeked past Ahren's friend's arm to see what would happen.

The Reaper would throw knives at our backs, I knew. We were going to die after two minutes of being gone. I wouldn't even make it past the outer wall. I was going to die in this city as I'd always feared I would.

He'd only taken one step forward when his head quickly twisted to one side. I caught the briefest image of a person in normal clothing behind him. They'd faded back into the crowd before his body hit the ground.

I said, "All the stars," under my breath only a few short seconds before a lady noticed the body and screamed.

I looked up to the face of Ahren's friend with wide eyes and saw that he was smiling as he stared straight ahead.

His strange eyes met mine as he said, "Open it is, then."

WE DID NOT GET ATTACKED and I saw no blood, but I heard screams from the people of New Bethel following behind us in our wake, like we were leading some morbid procession through the city. The people were not getting killed—I knew that because I'd asked—only seeing the killing of their Reapers as it happened in front of them. I did not look directly at Chase or Chandler to see how they felt about their brethren being slaughtered like animals by my father's Reapers and their own, but I did catch a muscle in Chandler's shoulder twitch once in a glance.

The horses became somewhat unruly when the citizens began running around aimlessly in the streets, attempting to get to their houses or perhaps out of the city entirely. I doubted they could manage the latter. All the while our pace was so much slower than it should've been, and none of my companions once turned to see what was behind them. I was unsure why they kept their gazes forward, but I'd not wanted to look back after witnessing the death of the first Reaper.

He had died so easily. . . .

We were all naturally weak, in our ways.

I looked at the houses we passed and at the people filling this dilapidated, broken city. I had never seen any of it before, and now . . . I found I was glad I hadn't.

Inside the House was so clean. At our hands or not, it was clean and kept. The city was not.

Perhaps nothing was clean and kept without someone to do as much for those who wouldn't.

I realized I wanted to close my eyes, not necessarily to miss any possible deaths, but because I did not want any more memories of this city. I did not want to remember the shabby buildings. I did not want to remember the frightened people. I wanted to cover my ears so I wouldn't hear the questions, shouted and whispered.

What's happening?
Have you seen them?
Where are they?
What's happening?
Are they going to kill us all?

I didn't want to hear the screams. I didn't want to hear the questions or the responses.

I did not want any more memories of this horrible place taking up residency inside my head.

I already had far too many bad memories of it to suit me, but I felt overloaded by them now. Old and new swirled together in my head, all the bad being brought to the surface by the horrible things transpiring around me.

A man shouting instructions. A man dead on the floor with blue lips. A Reaper's head twisting so far at the neck, his face disappearing from view. The face of a man before it went into shock before disappearing from view.

A little girl screaming for her mother. A little girl being tied up, beaten, and crying for her father.

No, I did not want more memories of this place. I did not want the new to latch onto the old, making them impossible to forget.

It was inevitable, though. Inescapable. It was as if life was determined to prove a point, or many of them.

I had asked for this.

So I did not close my eyes or cover my ears like I wanted to. I kept them forward and open, watching the horse's ears twitch at the nearby noises. Once, when a lady screamed right next to us, I patted the horse's shoulder. I could not comfort the lady, but I could comfort the horse. It seemed in that moment as though it were just as frightened as the lady.

Still, the horse walked on despite its fears, unable to voice them. Unable to express them in a way anyone would see or notice. But would they care at all even if they did?

The horse walked on and carried me along with it.

My stomach dropped again when the houses disappeared. Looking forward in the fading light, I saw a large wooden gate slowly coming nearer. It opened before we reached it, and a Reaper smiled at my father as we passed through. Once we were clear of it and my gaze settled in, I realized . . .

There was nothing there. No buildings, no people.

I looked around myself in something that felt like desperation, and I found absolutely nothing more than a wide expanse of open space.

Knowing and witnessing were not the same.

In that moment it was so easy to forget that I was not free. The feeling of it welled deep inside me as I heard the gate of New Bethel closing behind us. For such a short instant there was nothing else inside me. No houses in my mind, filled to the brim with unwanted things and memories. No people or phantoms to haunt my dreams. It all disappeared in the open expanse before me, apart from the word.

Freedom.

But then I looked at my father and felt the awestruck smile fall away from my face. I resigned myself again to watching the horse's ears as I came to terms with the loss of something that had never truly been mine to have and all the things that flooded forward as reality truly set in for what seemed like the first time. At least the first time since a little girl stopped crying for her father.

Several minutes after we'd passed through the gate of New Bethel, Ahren's friend drew me from my thoughts with, "Are you uncomfortable?"

"No."

"Comfortable?"

"No," I repeated.

He chuckled. "Well, which is it, then?"

"Neither."

He chuckled again then said beneath his breath, "Your fidgeting is making *me* uncomfortable."

It took a moment for what he likely meant to strike me.

"All the stars, I'm *so* sorry!" I wanted to put my hand over my face in embarrassment, but I didn't want to draw attention to myself.

My body went rigid when I felt him leaning closer to me.

His mouth was right next to my ear when he whispered, "I'm sure it doesn't feel very good, but you need to stop moving around like that. It would be unfortunate for your father to realize what the two of you did last night, don't you think? Just relax."

I could not relax, but I could be still.

I was not surprised that my father came up beside us only a few seconds later. "Why are you whispering in my daughter's ear?" He did not necessarily sound angry, but he certainly did not sound happy. If he had issue with my ear being whispered in . . .

"Because she's concerned about her brother and I didn't believe she would want everyone to hear me reassuring her of his safety," he lied easily. Had it been a lie? "Full of pride, if you didn't know."

"Are you happy now, Father?" I snapped at my father rather than point out that Ahren's friend knew nothing at all of my pride. He'd lied for me.

My father said, "Aster, Ahren will be fine."

"He'd better be."

My father pursed his lips and stepped up his horse's pace to get in front of us, almost as though speaking to me were a taxing thing he couldn't bear to deal with any longer. The thought of that prospect nearly put a smile back on my face.

After twenty or so more minutes of riding, I was pulled out of my distraction over just *how far* past uncomfortable I actually was by a pounding sound. Our horses were turned, and we saw someone riding up fast.

When they got close, I realized it was Ahren and released a giant breath of relief. I did not care if my father saw or heard it that time. But when I discovered my brother was covered in blood, my next breath caught in my throat as I tried to jump off the horse toward him.

Arms wrapped around my stomach and, next to my ear, I heard, "He's fine. It's not a good idea to flop off a horse."

"Are you all right?" I asked urgently, ignoring the voice and focusing on my brother, which was infinitely more important.

"Of course," Ahren said. "Got into a bit of a scuffle on my way out, obviously, but I'm fine."

"Obviously," I heard myself say under my breath.

My father seemed entirely unfazed. "Were you followed?"

Ahren looked to him. "No."

"Good." My father nodded. "We'll ride for several more hours then make camp. I want to put a good deal of distance between us and that city, just in case a few of them manage to escape."

That seemed to be the end of the conversation as he trotted his horse toward the front of our procession. Had he always been so short with words?

Ahren brought his horse up beside us and quietly asked, "Why is my sister in your lap?"

I frowned at him, but behind me I heard, "Because she refused to get in the carriage and your father refused to let her ride with Chase."

I tried not to gape at my brother. "That's *really* what you're concerned with right now?"

Ahren shrugged. "I was just curious."

"Go away." I said that to him mostly because the sight of him covered in blood in the moonlight was horrible to see.

He frowned, but he complied. As soon as he was gone, I heard and felt his friend laughing behind me.

"Stop laughing. You're making me uncomfortable," I snapped.

"Or comfortable," he said quietly.

"Please be quiet." I repeated his words from earlier in the day with haughtiness in my tone.

He laughed. "If you insist."

I could not explain why I did it, but I attempted to pinch his leg where it rested behind mine. I was unsuccessful, as he grabbed hold of my hand before I could get anywhere near achieving my goal.

"What did I tell you earlier?" He laughed again, and I could tell he was trying to be quiet when he did it.

"That wasn't attacking." For some reason, I was glad he could not see the tight grin on my face.

"It was close enough." He released my hand quickly.

When he did, I glanced several horses over and found Chase looking at us with a curious expression and his head slightly tilted.

I focused on the horse's ears again, attempting to discover why I felt somewhat guilty over the exchange. It had been completely innocent.

Suddenly, the horse turned around and stopped.

"What are we doing?" I asked in confusion.

"Taking your last look at New Bethel," Ahren's friend said behind me.

I looked down onto the city from our position at the top of a large hill, watching the distant lights from candles and lanterns flickering below. I wondered how many of my father's Reapers were wandering the streets and if they had already completed their massacre.

"You'll never see it again."

I barely said, "I've heard that before."

I glanced out of the corner of my eye at my father, who distinctly looked away from me before turning his horse back around the appropriate way and proceeding forward.

Chapter Twelve

THE FEELING

FTER SEVERAL HOURS OF RIDING on the horse with Ahren's friend in the darkness, the lower half of my body went painfully numb. I could hardly see the horse's dark ears in the moonlight, but every so often I would lean forward and pat it a little in front of the saddle. It was strange and I had no idea why I thought that was a suitable thing to do, but it kept me somewhat occupied.

When I was not patting the horse, my mind wouldn't slow down. I kept picturing Camden's face—the look he'd had on it when pleading with me not to let them take him. Had he known I would kill him or had he believed I could somehow convince them to leave him in his cell? I would not have been able to have done the latter, I knew. And I doubted anyone had known I was capable of killing until they'd seen me do it.

I'd known I was capable of it, hadn't I? Hadn't I known I would be required to do it at some point? I'd made my decision after searching myself. If I'd known that I was choosing *this* . . .

Would it have made any sort of difference at all?

No.

I'd wanted to teach Camden a lesson after what he'd attempted to do to me. I'd wanted to punch him repeatedly in the face, as Chase had done. But I had not wanted to kill him.

Had I been wrong to do what I'd done? Was torture truly a worse fate than death? Had it been mercy for me to kill him or had it simply been evil? Or had it been some horrible combination of both those things?

Was such a combination even possible?

Every time I found myself thinking on that subject—or any subject similar in nature—for more than a minute or so, I would receive some sort of nudge from behind me. Occasionally, Ahren's friend would just bump his leg slightly into mine. I didn't know if he was fidgeting or if he somehow knew what I was thinking about while I was thinking about it. I imagined he was reminding me that I didn't want anyone else to know how I felt about what I'd done.

I did not know how he could be inside my head, especially when he was so unfamiliar with it, but he didn't move at all when I was thinking of other things. The timing made me almost entirely certain of the purpose in his movement. So every instance I received a nudge, I patted the horse to tell him I'd heard his silent message and that I would fight to rearrange my thoughts, even if I could only successfully manage it for a brief moment until the next.

Eventually, that became increasingly less effective at distracting me.

"Your name is Jas?" I asked him, hoping that conversing with someone would help me get my mind away from the feeling of dried blood on my skin.

He said, "Jastin."

"Which do you prefer to be called by?" I was curious. No one ever asked me if I preferred to be called by Aster or Flower. They simply called me whichever they wanted with no thought at all on how I felt about it.

"Depends on the person," he replied. "And you prefer your name, don't you?"

"Yes, I do, actually," I admitted. I did not like to be called Flower because it was what my father had always called me. I had always believed he'd done it to feel closer to my mother, though I could've easily been wrong. I didn't mind so much when Agatha called me it because she'd always been like a mother to me. I wondered, though . . . "But why did you call me Flower earlier, if you assumed I don't like it?"

"To make you angry."

I contemplated turning around to see if he was smiling because it sounded to me as if he were, but I did not. I frowned at the horse's ears instead. "Why would you believe that would make me angry?" It was a silly thing for a person to get angry over, I thought.

"What is a flower?"

Before I could answer him, he went on.

"It's nothing more than a pretty thing, is it? Something for people to look at and enjoy? I don't believe you want to be thought of in that way."

I heard myself very quietly ask, "You enjoy looking at me?" I could not explain why the words had come out of my mouth. They simply . . . *had*.

"No." His voice went to the blank tone Reapers so often spoke in.

"That's a very good thing," I told him. "I don't, by the way—want to be thought of like that."

"It's not as bad as you'd think."

"How do you mean?" It had sounded quite bad, given what he'd just said about it.

"We make some of our poisons out of flowers." He replied quietly with a small chuckle. "They're useless if you look at or touch them, but *some*? Well . . . it's not always so bad to be seen as less than what you are. Sometimes people looking over the potential you have inside is the best advantage you could ever possibly have." He paused for just an instant before adding, "You should keep that in mind."

I realized I was smiling a little. "That *doesn't* sound so bad."

"Do you want to take the reins?" He asked that at a normal volume and in a normal tone.

"What?" I shook my head. "I wouldn't know what to do."

"Just keep him moving forward. He'll naturally follow the others," he said. "Here, take them. My arms are tired anyway."

He rattled them around a bit in front of me, and I took them from him so the movement wouldn't startle the horse. I didn't know if such a thing *would* startle a horse, but I did *not* want to take the risk, especially while on its back.

The horse kept moving along with the others, just as he'd told me it would. After about five minutes of holding onto the reins with no incident whatsoever, I said, "You were lying—about your arms being tired." I had seen Reapers do much more strenuous things for much longer periods of time without their bodies becoming tired.

He chuckled. "You should know by now that we're all liars."

"What are you doing with your arms now?" I turned around to see.

They were lazily tucked behind him on the back of the saddle. I only glanced at his face for an instant and saw that he was smiling at me before he lurched forward and grabbed the reins. Only *then* did I realize I'd somehow gotten the horse turned around sideways.

Once Jastin had tugged a little and righted it, he rattled the reins for me to take them again.

My face burned horrendously as I ignored the curious glances from our companions. I kept my eyes forward after that, and every so often I patted the horse to apologize for being incompetent. The horse didn't seem to mind.

I did not speak to Jastin anymore, and he did not speak to me.

I WOULD NEVER HAVE ADMITTED to the feeling of relief that verged on excitement I felt when my father declared it time to make camp. I was determined not to feel it.

"Pull back a little," Jastin said from behind me. "It'll get him to stop."

I pulled back a little, but the horse did not stop.

He chuckled. "A little more than that."

I did as he said and the horse stopped moving. It snorted once, and I had an errant thought that the horse might possibly be relieved at the thought of this day ending as well.

"Ahren, go wash the blood off you in that stream over there," I heard my father say from a good distance away. I'd not forgotten the way his voice always carried when he spoke, even when his tone was soft. I'd been able to hear him from so far away through the trees as a child.

Where's my Flower?

I shook my head of the unwelcome memory.

"How do I get down?" I whispered after I checked to ensure my father was not paying enough attention to potentially hear me.

Jastin slid off the horse easily and stuck my foot back in the place he'd shown me to put it when getting on. Why couldn't I remember what it was called? I had read the word before.

"Throw the other one over," he instructed.

I did as he said and had a very awkward moment of one foot being on the ground while the other was in the air still attached to the saddle. It was made even more awkward by the fact that the lower half of my body was numb. My standing leg gave a little and in the time that it took me to realize, Jastin had already freed my foot, righted me, and walked away with the horse in tow.

I pursed my lips tightly and took in what I could see of my surroundings in the darkness and moonlight.

We were in a rather open area with a stream nearby. Upstream led into trees to my left and downstream led into more open, empty space.

I found myself walking—uncomfortably—over to my father, who was fiddling around with something or other in the back of the carriage. He turned around to look at me before I'd reached him, and he didn't look away.

"Father, I . . ." I stopped to clear my throat so I could ensure my voice would be strong. "I require that you allow me to go alone into the trees."

"Why?"

I cleared my throat once more and very quietly said, "I've not been able to get myself properly cleaned from . . . *before*. I won't try to run away. I simply need to get this off me."

"Oh." He almost sounded distracted. "Yes, of course. Just don't go far." I nodded and had turned when he asked, "Do you still have your knife?"

"I do."

"Good," he said. "Keep it on you always."

I nodded again at that and walked away, not telling him I'd been told as much when given it.

I for an instant when walking met gazes with Chandler near where the horses had been taken, but only just.

I'd made it halfway to the trees when I heard my father say, "Chase."

I turned and found that Chase had begun to follow me. He changed direction and walked to my father when beckoned.

I frowned and continued on my way.

I went much farther than I was sure my father intended for me to. I kept walking far past the point where I could no longer see the ending of the trees when glancing over my shoulder. Only then did I remove all my clothing and step into the shallow water.

It was quite cold in comparison to the warm air surrounding me, but the temperature hardly fazed me. The contrast of it seemed to wake me up and yet numb me to the world at once. I found I was somewhat glad for the cold water and the numbing effect of it as I stared down at my torso in the dim moonlight that was filtering through the branches above.

I should not have done it, but I touched the dried blood before attempting to wash it away. I watched a few small pieces of Camden's life flake off my body to get carried away in the peaceful current.

And then I cried.

I cried silently where I sat in the water, scrubbing with ferocity at my chest and abdomen with my wet hands. I saw that they were shaking when I stopped after a moment and stared at them. The red was not dry and stuck to me anymore like some horrible second skin. It was wet, but it still was not gone from me. It covered the palms of my hands and smeared up my arm, appearing to paint my body with darkness that was too *thin* to be what it truly was.

Then, I found I could do nothing more than put my forehead on my knees and keep crying.

It was a sound that brought me out of it, though I was not certain how much time had passed in my inert state. I jolted and looked up from my knees, finding both Agatha and Amber standing a good distance away.

I stopped crying as I stared at them. I would not let them see it.

I was sure my father had sent them to check on me, and I was so angry. I was angry at all of them. I was so angry that I was not even allowed my time to come to terms with everything. I did not know if it was possible, but I needed time to try.

Agatha stared at me as she tugged backward on Amber's arm, and I heard myself laugh under my breath once as they both frowned at me. Agatha could return my father's replacement daughter to him. And Amber could be the new replacement daughter for my replacement mother.

They had all taken absolutely everything from me. I'd had so very little in this world and they had all destroyed it. They had destroyed everything, along with the possibility and prospect for me to have something—*anything*—more.

I finished what I'd set out to do once they'd gone, and I did not cry anymore.

WHEN I WAS FINISHED removing the physical remnants of Camden from my body, I found something suitable enough to dry off with inside the bag my father had given me. I did not pay any attention to what it was, as it all seemed so irrelevant. I replaced my clothing after shaking it for what felt like an entire lifetime, then I trudged back to the camp they'd made in my absence.

All the horses were tied up to trees with their saddles removed and lying near them on the ground. There were makeshift bedding areas strewn about in a rather large circle. They'd made a fire relatively close by and were cooking something or other. I was not hungry, so I went and sat down on the grass very far away from them all.

I sat there, running my hands over the top of the grass and trying desperately to enjoy the feeling of it. It was only the second time I'd touched it with my hands in ten years. I found no pleasure in the exercise now, but I persisted in my attempt, hoping I would stumble upon it eventually.

Once, I heard my father say, "Chase," again, though it was much quieter than it had been before.

I looked over in enough time to see Chase sit back down. I was surprised to find I was happy for my father to be keeping him from me, at least for the time being. I was not yet ready to be alone with him after what I'd done. I did not believe I was anywhere near ready to face him.

At some point, I heard a footstep behind me.

I turned to look, finding Chandler there.

"Are you hungry?"

I looked back down at the grass. "No."

"Aster—"

"I'm fine." I forced a smile at him.

Still, he received the message and left me alone.

Once he'd gone, I gave up in my attempt at enjoying the grass and began plucking it from the earth and ripping it into tiny pieces. The blades of it made me think of knives, for some reason that had nothing to do with the word. It was sharp, but not sharp enough. I still could not enjoy the grass, but there was a strange and sad satisfaction in destroying it.

It took me some time to realize that the forced smile I'd offered Chandler had not felt right on my face. That gave me a great deal to think on.

It was not five minutes after Chandler's departure that I heard someone else approach.

Jastin stepped over and then sat down beside me, extending a bowl in the space between us. "You need to eat." His volume was quiet, but his tone said it was a subject that was *not* up for debate.

"I'm not hungry." I plucked another blade of grass from the ground.

"You don't want me to tell them you're not okay?" he whispered. "Don't *show* them you're not. How do you expect me to keep a secret you won't keep for yourself?"

I took the bowl when he extended it toward me again. He put his hands beside his legs to push himself up and I heard myself begin to blurt out, "Will you—"

He stopped what he was doing and looked at me in a confused sort of way, but I did not finish what I'd almost asked. Still, he did not stand up. He sat there with me as I stared down at my bowl of food and forced myself to eat it, and he did not speak to me. It was exactly what I'd not wanted to ask but had wanted him to do.

When I was finished eating, he took the bowl from me and left without a single word.

Ahren came over then, like he'd been waiting. There was a frown on his face. "Father wants you to sleep in the carriage."

"I refuse," I said, my voice even.

"I told him you would." The corners of his mouth began tugging the opposite direction. "Let me show you where you'll be sleeping. I'm sure you're exhausted."

I did not tell him that I wouldn't be able to sleep. Instead, I stood and followed him. He led me to a few blankets on the ground, precisely in the middle of the circle of other bedding areas.

I frowned deeply and said, "I'm not sleeping there."

"You're the least trained," he said apologetically.

"*Agatha* is the least trained," I informed him. "I don't want to be circled like I'm some useless . . ." I struggled to think of the appropriate word, but it struck me after a moment. "*Flower.*" It was the only word that made any sense to use.

"It's this." He pointed to the same one he'd shown me. "Or that." He pointed to the carriage.

I heard myself huff out a breath as I bent over and removed every piece of my designated bedding from the ground. I gathered it all into my arms and stomped away.

Nobody asked me what I was doing and nobody told me not to do it, but as soon as I'd settled myself in, I saw everyone else filing over with their own blankets and pillows in hand. I clenched my jaw as I stared up at the sky. I ignored them as they circled around me, silently making their beds into the exact formation I'd attempted to escape from.

I was angry.

For a long time, I was so angry as I laid there, staring up at stars I could not appreciate and watching the two Reapers who hadn't lain down periodically circle around us all, listening for sounds and watching for sights. But eventually the anger faded and all I was left with was some horrible, empty feeling.

It felt as though it were snaking its way slowly throughout my body, latching onto every fiber of my being and spreading like a disease, destroying every part of me it touched.

So this is what it feels like, a little voice said inside my head.

Killing a person did not kill a part of you, as I would've always assumed. It simply destroyed it, not eliminating but irreparably breaking. It destroyed it enough so that the only thing the broken part could do is watch your body keep moving without its function. It destroyed you on the inside.

I wondered how it was possible that the Reapers could go on living with the knowledge of this inside them. I wondered how they could be alive at all.

Did I have a heart? I put my hand over my chest, feeling nothing.

It's in there somewhere, I told myself. It had to be there.

It had to be.

I was certain hours passed, as the stars were not in the same places in the sky that they had been when I'd first lain down. I heard varying volumes of snoring around me distantly, but it felt as if the only real thing in the world were the tears making their way from the corners of my eyes and falling down my temples.

I felt frozen in the torture, not moving or making a sound apart from breathing. It seemed so silent around me, but there was so much screaming inside my head. The screams and cries of others blurred and twisted with my own voice shouting at me. All the words jumbled together, creating a horrible, unrelenting noise inside me. The comparative silence outside my person was painful.

I wanted to scream—at those voices, at the silence. I wanted to scream until my lungs burst and my throat ripped itself apart. I just wanted it to *stop*.

A hand reached out and wiped one of the tears away from my face as it fell.

I looked over and found Stanley frowning at me, and I watched his hand intently as he brought it back to himself.

I could remember the first time I'd been close to Chase, watching his hands and not allowing myself to think about all the people he'd killed with them. Stanley had killed with his hands, too. And now . . . I had killed with mine.

We weren't so very different.

I rolled over onto my side and took the hand that Stanley had placed on the ground between us in mine. My jaw quivered, so I forced a smile at him, feeling another tear falling. It made its way over my nose and dropped down onto my thin pillow.

Stanley did not force a smile back at me, but he covered our joined hands with the sides of each of our blankets so that no one would see how weak I was.

We weren't so very different.

I shoved my face into the pillow to hide that weakness along with everything else, and I called myself a murderer inside my head until the word blurred away with the world into nothingness.

CHAPTER THIRTEEN

RETURNING FAVORS

I WAS SMILING as I stared into Camden's face. He was far too weak to break free of my grip where I had him pinned against a wall. It made me feel so unbelievably strong to watch him struggling against that wall like a wounded animal, trying so hard to free himself from my grasp.

I let him struggle, finding such pleasure in his weakness. But eventually, the point had been made and it was time for the lesson to be learned.

I told him, "I'm going to remind you of what you are."

I heard myself laugh quietly, sheer amusement bubbling up in my chest as I watched his eyes blinking so hard in his confusion. Didn't he know what he was? If he didn't . . . he soon would.

I leaned forward to whisper. "It's for your own good."

I moved again, plunging my knife into his face, pushing through the hardness of bones that were determined to stop my progress. They could not stop it. They could not stop *me*.

Redness poured, and the smile stretched farther on my face.

I jolted upright with a horrible choked, gasping noise. I was up and moving before I realized that I'd ever even been asleep. I did not know where I was going, or even that I was going somewhere, until someone jerked me by the arm.

"Aster, I've said your name ten times." My father sounded concerned. *My father.* "Are you all right?"

A dream.

It had only been a dream.

Reality crashed down on me, reminding me that Camden was already dead. I'd already killed him and there was something more imminent staring directly at my face.

My father.

"Please get away from me." Though I had tried so very hard to keep it from my voice, even I could hear the pleading in it. I put my hands behind my back to conceal their shaking from him. I could not let him see it.

"Do you want me to send your brother to you?"

"No." I turned away from him and began walking again. I had to get away.

"Don't go far," he said to my back.

I did not respond to him. I put my hands over my face and rubbed at it roughly, vaguely knowing I was walking along the line of trees, away from the camp. Despite having removed my hands from my face at some point, I eventually tripped and fell in my distracted state. A part of me wanted to stay on the ground, stay on the ground where I belonged and *never* move again, but my body would not allow me to do that. I stood back up and resumed walking. I was certain I fell many times, though how many . . .

I did not know.

If I'd never taken a step, would this still have happened? Was there an inevitability to it? Was there any point in anything?

So many questions. Why couldn't they stop?

It felt as though I walked forever before my body finally halted itself. I did not sit on the ground when the moment was reached. I stood and stared into the darkness surrounding me. It was strange that my body had forced me forward and then would not allow me to move at all. I didn't even think I could blink.

Stars dotted themselves across the sky, so still. But they moved, didn't they?

Did they *really*?

Did stars truly move at all? Was being caught in the same cycle actual movement? There they were still, so small but so untouchable and safe despite their visibility.

As if to mock all my previous thoughts, a streak of brightness shot across the sky, a tail of vibrant green disappearing behind it. It reminded me of the bruises on my body, only beautiful. The strangeness of the sight caused me to blink several times in rapid succession, which was almost painful due to the dryness of my eyes. Each time they closed, I saw the briefest image of that brightness on the backs of my eyelids.

Until it also faded.

When the shock of what I'd seen was over, I kept my eyes opened, determined not to become distracted by something so pointless again.

THE SUN WAS ALMOST PEEKING OVER THE HORIZON by the time a body stepped in front of me. My gaze went upward and I found myself staring at Jastin, who was tilting his head at me in an analytical sort of way.

I barely said, "This is what it feels like."

"Yes," he said blankly, though I'd not intended it as a question.

"Does—"

"It doesn't get better," he said. "But you get used to it eventually."

"*How*?" I asked him, desperation feeling in that moment like the only real thing in the world. How could any person *possibly* get used to feeling this way?

Monster, that little voice said.

"Because it's the only thing you can do," he said. "And what you're going to do *now* is go back to camp and eat some breakfast. We'll pack everything up and then you're going to ride with me."

"I thought I would get my own horse." My voice nearly sounded dead when I heard it in my ears. How could I ever get past any of this?

"You know how you woke up back there?"

I said nothing and did not respond in any way.

"Do you want to do that while on a horse?"

"I won't fall asleep." I did not think I would ever allow myself to fall asleep again. This could not be escaped from, not ever.

"Oh, you *will* fall asleep," he said assuredly. "You only slept for forty-five minutes or so. You're going to nod off and then jerk awake who knows how many times today. If you want to fall off a horse and break something in the middle of nowhere . . . you're more than welcome to. Or you can ride with me and not have to deal with the consequences of that. It's your decision."

"Why can't I ride with Chase?"

"Because you don't want to."

I opened my mouth to speak, but no words came out of it.

"Do you?" He paused, waiting for an answer he likely knew I would not give him. "Have fun convincing your father if you do. Let's go."

I followed him when he began walking away, but it took me a few minutes to ask, "Why did you come after me?"

He kept looking forward. "Your father told me to when you left."

"Why would he do that?" Had he been standing there the entire time?

"Because he saw that I got you to eat last night."

"Why do you keep taking care of me?" I could not understand why he did. Was it loyalty to my brother or my father? Or was it something else entirely?

He stopped moving. "Why do *you* keep asking me so many questions?"

I said nothing as I stared up at his face, watching him close his eyes and take a deep breath.

He sounded exhausted when he spoke again. "Because you're letting me. Can we go back now, please?"

I began walking again and, under my breath, said, "You're the one who stopped."

I glanced over at him when he didn't respond and saw that he was smiling a little as he stared straight ahead.

He looked down at me, without the smile, and I looked away.

I was glad he did not speak to me anymore, and I was quite certain he was glad that I did not ask him any more questions.

I DID NOT GO TO SIT FAR AWAY FROM EVERYONE once we'd made it back to the camp and I had food in my hands. I sat down between Stanley and Stewart, who made the room for me without having to voice my desire to be there, and they did not complain about it in any way.

I'd only taken two bites of my unknown and unwanted breakfast when the discreet staring from everyone became unbearable. I looked up and met gazes with the Reaper directly across from me. He seemed to be around the same age as my father, though perhaps a little older. His nose sat a bit crooked on his face.

"May I help you?" I asked him firmly.

"Bad dreams?" He grinned. "I wonder—"

"Do *not* taunt my daughter." My father's interruption seemed to bounce off the loose circle of bodies.

I disregarded what he'd said, because I did not need his assistance.

"Yes, actually," I admitted to the man with the crooked nose. "I had a dream that some horrible men came to abduct me. And then, when I woke, I realized reality was so much worse than my mind had portrayed it to be." I smiled.

He laughed loudly.

I stretched my smile farther. "It *is* quite funny, isn't it?"

"My god," the Reaper said through his laughter. "She is *just* like Elena."

I shook my head. "Who?" Was I supposed to know who he was speaking of? I did not know anyone.

The Reaper stopped his laughing instantaneously and looked at my father in a confused sort of way. When he brought his gaze back to me, he said, "Your mother."

Quickly, I asked, "You knew my mother?"

He nodded, and I was momentarily distracted by my father standing and walking away.

I did not care why he left or where he went as some strange feeling built inside my chest, pushing at all the unpleasantness surrounding it. It almost felt like light pushing at darkness. "Will you tell me about her?"

The Reaper watched my father's back as he went and replied with, "One day perhaps, though your father could tell you so much more than I ever could." He frowned when he brought his full attention back to me. "You didn't even know her name?"

I shook my head slowly.

"Excuse me." He stood and walked away as well.

It was not three minutes later when I heard restrained shouting from a good distance away.

I ignored that as I stared down at my food and shoveled it into my mouth at a pace so slow that I wondered if I would ever manage to put the slightest dent in it.

"Your mother was the same way," I heard from the opposite end of the circle.

I looked over and found another Reaper tilting his head at me.

"I don't know what you mean." I did not know anything about my mother. I'd learned only a few days ago that I looked very much like her, and now, I had learned her name.

"Every time she opened her mouth to speak, it wiped all sensible thought from a man's brain." There was an almost mischievous grin on his face. "Only women like that can make one of us stupid enough to go against our better judgment."

"Why would anyone go against their better judgment on account of another person's words?" I asked him, curious. "Shouldn't people hold their own minds to such a value that they wouldn't allow another to make them . . . *stupid*, you called it?"

"Because they make you want to be better."

"It's sad, isn't it, that a person should wish to be better only if someone makes them feel inferior first?" I asked rhetorically. "It's sadder, I think, that striving to be better would make a person considered *stupid* by others or themselves." I smiled at him.

I kept smiling at him until he deliberately said, "*That* is *exactly* what I mean."

Then, I looked down and took another bite of my food, hoping he would find himself satisfied enough that he would stop speaking.

He seemed unable to stop himself from adding, "It's a useful skill to have in our line of work."

I forced another smile in his direction. "Clearly, it's not useful enough."

If my mother had been skilled with words, it hadn't been a useful enough skill to keep her alive. I'd never considered myself overly skilled with them, so I wondered what that said of my own fate.

With that thought in mind, I stood and began walking.

When I'd made it far enough away that I doubted anyone would see, I slipped into the trees and dropped the remainder of the food from the plate onto the dirt.

I STOPPED BY THE STREAM to clean off my eating utensils, and it was while I was in the process of doing that when Chase found me. I peeked over my shoulder at him and then proceeded about my business, watching tiny bits of food get carried away over the smooth grey rocks in the current. "Is my father distracted enough in his arguing that he wasn't able to call you back?"

Chase ignored my question. "You're avoiding me."

I closed my eyes and took in a deep breath. I'd finished cleaning the utensils by that point, so I stood, holding them in my hands and staring at him.

He waited for a response, but I gave him none as each of us waited for something.

"If this is about—"

I had to ask, "Do you remember when you taught me about pretending?"

"Yes, of course I do," he replied. "What does—"

"We had a very interesting conversation about lies," I said. "Didn't we?"

He blinked at me and shook his head in confusion. When he did not answer me verbally, I went on.

"We made a deal that you would never lie to me directly—that, if I asked you something and you couldn't answer it, you would simply remain silent."

"I remember." I could hear the wariness in his tone.

"The thing I didn't fully understand at the time . . ." A small laugh escaped from my mouth. I tried again. "The thing I didn't understand at the time was that there was no answer you *couldn't* tell me; there were only answers you wished not to." I took several steps closer and looked up into his eyes. Very quietly, I continued. "How many times did I ask you questions I should've had the answers to and all you did was remain silent?" I shook my head. "You would smile at me like you were playing a game, wouldn't you? Playing a game with my life?"

His mouth parted, but I knew he wouldn't say anything.

"You want to know what this is about?" I asked. "If this is about what happened yesterday or even possibly if this is about what happened between us." I smiled and very slowly said, "Consider this me returning the favor."

And then I walked away.

CHAPTER FOURTEEN

WASTE OF TIME

SHORTLY AFTER HAVING MY FIRST verbal exchange with Chase since leaving New Bethel, I was searching in the back of the carriage for the appropriate place to store my eating utensils. A war was being waged inside me as I moved things in an attempt to discover the rightful place for those utensils.

One side told me to toss the contents of the carriage about to make as large a mess as possible. It would inconvenience someone else and perhaps release a minuscule amount of my boundless frustration. I'd never purposely made a mess before and nothing seemed to matter any longer regardless.

The other side pointed out that the person I might inconvenience may not have done a single thing to me directly. And how dare I do such a thing for such petty reasons?

It was the thought made by the destructive side that shot to the surface and intermediated.

Nothing seemed to matter any longer.

I didn't realize I'd stopped moving altogether, staring unseeingly into the back of the carriage, until I heard a footstep behind me. The box for the utensils was just lying there next to my hand, staring me directly in the face. It was as I was putting mine where they belonged, with all the others, that the person who'd come up behind me spoke.

"*So*," was all I heard at my back. The word was dragged out for far longer than necessary.

I turned and found Stewart staring at me.

He smiled a little and bounced a bit on the balls of his feet. "How are you?"

I blinked hard at him for a moment—assessing him and the odd tone—before responding. "I'm fine. What is it you really want?"

"Is there something going on between you and Jas?" he blurted out with a grin.

"*What*?" Shock and disbelief battled momentarily to become the preponderant reaction. After those two fought a short but intense battle, confusion decided to interject and show its unwelcome face.

I didn't even know what Stewart was going on about, but then I thought on it and discovered he meant it in a *completely* ridiculous way.

Then I *really* thought on it. There was absolutely no possible way that Stewart cared whether or not there was something . . . *going on*.

I narrowed my eyes at him. "Who are you asking for?"

"Why *ever* would you come to that conclusion?" His innocent tone was clearly faked. "Don't you think I care about your life? Can't *I* be concerned?"

"Leave her alone, Stewart," Stanley said from beside me. I'd not heard him come up, which could've been attributed to how much mental effort I'd just expended. Similar to how a sprint could use all your energy.

I peeked around Stewart and saw that everyone was behaving normally, though Chandler—who was putting a saddle on a horse—was the only one who had his back distinctly turned to us.

"You tell Chandler . . ." I started speaking faster than my head could keep up with, so I tried to catch myself. "You tell him that, if I'm not allowed to have friends, he and I need to reestablish the boundaries of our own relationship."

Stewart laughed and sounded more like his usual pert self when he said, "I'll be sure to relay the message."

He'd begun to walk away, but my mouth was not finished despite my head telling it to be now that it had caught back up.

"You *also* tell him," I went on, realizing my voice was significantly more high-pitched than it normally was. "Tell him I have enough people wanting to run my life at the current point in time. And if he's intending to add himself onto that list, then he and I won't need to reestablish *anything*."

I could still see Stewart laughing when he was halfway between Chandler and where I stood.

My breath huffed out of my nose and my lips were pursed tightly together—which I felt incredibly foolish about—when Stanley said, "What Roger failed to mention to you earlier is that boys are generally stupid where *any* girl they care for is concerned. It's less about the girl herself and more about dynamics." He was smiling when I looked at him. "I'm sad to say it's something we rarely grow out of."

"That's unfortunate," I heard myself say as I glanced once more at Stewart's back.

"That it is." Stanley chuckled a little. "You'll have to forgive him."

"It's simply preposterous for him to have asked me that question," I said. "Even more so that he wouldn't ask me it himself."

Stanley tilted his head at me. "*Is* it?"

"Of *course* it is!" I exclaimed. I could in no way understand why Chandler would've sent Stewart to do it.

Stanley grinned and nodded his head as though he were satisfied about something.

He had made it only two steps away—in Chandler and Stewart's direction—when I heard myself say, "*Stanley!*" in an indignant and disbelieving tone.

He turned around and shrugged. "I told you. We rarely grow out of it."

And then I watched, openmouthed, as he went over to the two of them. I wanted so desperately in that instant to have someone to talk to, so I could go to them and shout about the stupidity of men until I felt better.

But I had no one I wanted to speak to, especially after what had just occurred. I also didn't believe it would've done any more good for the way I felt than tossing random things about without purpose.

Still, I contemplated for a *very* brief moment about going to tell my father, but I sincerely doubted that doing so would be beneficial in *any* way. All I did was simply stand there and stare at the three of them as they spoke to one another. And then, when my brother joined them, I seriously contemplated shouting about it to all four of them instead of someone else. *That* would've done some good, I thought.

I heard a clinking noise beside me which drew me from my open-mouthed gaping and contemplation.

I looked over and found Jastin putting some things away inside the carriage.

He smiled at me. "Something interesting happen?"

"Men are ignorant," was all my mouth seemed able to say in response.

He laughed. "Are we?"

"Yes," I answered firmly. "And I had no idea just how much until this very moment."

"What happened that struck you with the realization?"

"The four of them . . ." I pointed toward where they all stood by Chandler's horse, shaking my head. "Chandler and my brother sent them over here to ask me if something was going on between us."

"Between me and you?"

"*Yes!*" I exclaimed. "Isn't that simply preposterous?"

He chuckled. "Of course it is."

"That's *precisely* what I said!"

He kept chuckling.

I continued shaking my head as I stared in their direction. "Look at them. Over there *gossiping*. They look like the women in the kitchen who would speak about the servers as soon as they'd left the room. Stanley's much too old to take part in such ridiculousness. In fact, they *all* are. Don't they have better things to concern themselves with? At least Chase has the sense not to take part in it." I would've thought they *all* did, Stewart included no matter how he at times behaved.

Jastin's laughter grew louder, and it took me several long seconds to realize he was not laughing at the situation.

"Why are you laughing at me?" I demanded.

He wiped at one of his eyes. "Why do you care about what they're doing?"

"Because it's ridiculous for them to think such things," I replied. "Even more so for them to speak about me the way they so clearly are. There are *so many* other things."

"I repeat: Why do you care?"

Firm, I said, "Because they're *wrong*."

"If you know they're *wrong* . . ." he started, seeming to be taking great care in choosing his words. "Why should it bother you?"

"I . . ." I closed my mouth, as Chandler would've wanted me to do, and then I thought back to a very similar conversation I'd had with my brother before I'd known he was my brother. I looked shamefully at the ground to admit, "I suppose it shouldn't."

"Now, don't you feel better?"

When I looked up at him, he was smiling warmly at me and I *finally* discovered why I found his face to be comforting. It was as though a candle had been lit in the dark recesses of my mind, the place where I kept all my secret memories hidden from both myself and the world. I supposed it was the light.

Before I could stop myself from speaking, I said, "When I was a child and my father would be gone on his . . ." I heard myself laugh, "*hunting* trips . . . occasionally he would bring me something back. When he discovered I had a favorite gift, he always saved it for when he returned from being away for a very long time."

Jastin narrowed his eyes at me and was smiling in a very confused sort of way. "What was your favorite gift?"

"Honey." I felt an awkward smile trying to stretch itself farther on my face.

He chuckled beneath his breath. "Why did you tell me that?"

My cheeks burned, and I hoped it was not apparent on my face. Rather than telling him that his eyes were nearly the *precise* color of the favored gift from my father, I said, "I *do* feel better now. Thank you."

He narrowed those eyes at me as the laughing abruptly stopped, and a different smile slowly spread across his face. Then all at once, it dropped away and blankness took over as he focused in on something at my back.

My father said, "And do you remember why I only brought you back a little of it every time?"

The awkward smile instantaneously dropped away from my face as well. I heard myself exhale quietly, but I did not turn to face him.

I looked at the ground and repeated what he had always told me when I'd wanted more. "Because, sometimes, too much of a good thing is bad for you." I finally turned to him. "And do you remember what I always said in response when you told me as much?"

A sad smile overtook his face. "Good is good."

"You always told me wrong, Father," I informed him. "Good *is* good. You simply should have told me that, whenever you find good in your life . . . bad always comes to take it away." I forced a smile at him as I tried to ignore the wetness spreading in my eyes. "It's such a shame you never told me the truth to properly prepare me for life before you abandoned me to it. Wouldn't you agree?"

I did not give him any chance to respond. I simply walked away, crossing my arms in a feeble attempt to comfort myself. I'd not wanted to hear any answer my father possibly could've given, but mostly . . . I just did not want him to see me cry.

If I got away from him and my memories, I would not cry at all.

I WALKED TOWARD THE GENERAL VICINITY of the horses for something to do. All the traitorous boys had gone, so it seemed the best option to occupy myself until we left camp. At least I could be alone, if not occupied.

I could not recognize the horse Jastin and I had ridden before, so I simply stood there for a while looking at them all. Most seemed restless, as though they were all waiting to be ridden again so long as they did not have to stand still any longer. I wondered if they felt those were their only two purposes in life—carry loads and stand around, waiting during each until it would be time for the next. But one of them was chewing on some grass, almost lazily, as if it hadn't a single care in the world and wasn't waiting for anything. Stuck in a cycle.

I walked over to that one. I could use the companionship of something living that didn't have a care in the world. I seemed to have so many of them. I wondered what it felt like and if I could somehow discover that by exposure.

I decided it was a bad idea once I'd gotten closer and remembered just how big the creatures were. They were significantly more frightening without any sort of humanly gear on them. It popped its head up from the ground and made some strange sort of sound at me. I jumped a little because of it, and then when it didn't come charging . . . I smiled.

"I never liked riding," I heard a quiet voice say at my back.

I closed my eyes and tried to refrain from screaming at the top of my lungs when I turned to face Amber.

"Your father always told me I would get used to it, but . . ." She shrugged. "I didn't."

"Is there a point to this?" I attempted with everything inside me to keep my voice calm, though I could not stop my hands from balling into fists at my sides.

"I just—"

She was interrupted by Jastin loudly plopping a saddle onto a horse behind me and saying, "Time to go."

She looked from him back to me. "I just—"

"Big man says it's time to go, so it's time to go."

She looked at the ground for a moment before turning and walking away without any further objection.

I breathed out a giant breath of relief and whispered, "Thank you."

How many times had he helped me now?

"For what?" He grinned. "Did you not want to talk with her?"

I would've nearly believed the timing had been serendipitous—*innocent*—if not for that grin.

I said, "You know I didn't."

"Do I?" he asked. "How could I possibly know what you do and don't want?"

"Why do you lie?" I asked him curiously.

"Pray tell, what did I—"

He was interrupted by my father making a declaration that it was time to go.

Jastin held his hand into the air as if he were illuminating the entire world for me before finishing his question. "What did I lie about?"

"You saved me from having to speak with her."

"I don't know what you're talking about." He chuckled as he worked on getting the saddle properly strapped to the horse, the same horse that had made the silly sound at me. "And I'm failing to see how that means I lied, even if I *did* know."

"Why *do* you lie?" I asked him again.

He stopped messing with the horse and looked at me. He was smiling so hugely at me when he turned, but then he pursed his lips together and narrowed his eyes. He took a step closer and leaned down a bit.

His voice was very quiet when he spoke. "First you tell me some random story about when you were a child out of nowhere and you stand there blushing the entire time you're doing it. It wasn't an embarrassing story to tell me, was it? How could it be? And *then* you accuse me of lying when there was nothing said that could possibly be a lie." He paused to tilt his head at me. "I'm quite worried about your mental state."

He returned his attention to preparing the horse and I stood there staring at the back of his head thoughtfully.

For some reason that I could not explain, I stepped next to where he stood beside the horse.

Quietly, I urged, "Tell me a lie."

He glanced over at me for an instant and grinned. I stood there waiting while he finished what he was doing. As soon as he had, he faced me.

His face and voice were both entirely impassive when he said, "I believe it's intelligent for people to waste their time looking at pretty things." When he was finished speaking, he tilted his head and smiled as though he were pleased with himself.

"Tell me something true," I urged.

This, it seemed, was much more difficult for him to do. He frowned while he stared at me, and he seemed to be contemplating very hard on what to say.

I could almost see it click inside his head, as he grinned before he—just as blankly as the previous statement—said, "You have very pretty hair." Then, he laughed. "If you've found what you were looking for . . . can we go?"

I'd wanted to see the difference between when he told the truth and when he did not, but in fact, I had gained no useful knowledge from the exercise. He'd said both sentences in precisely the same way with the exact same expression on his face. There had been no nuances there to be found.

I assumed most people would be giving a person a compliment when they told them something about them was pretty, but it was clear he'd not meant his words as such. So all I had learned was that he thought it would be unintelligent for people to waste time looking at my hair. It was not helpful in any way whatsoever, but I was inclined to agree with him regardless.

It *would* be a waste of time.

I forced a smile. "Yes, we can go."

127

He patted on the saddle, and I pulled myself up. I did not need his assistance with the action then—his hands pushing me up—though he still gave it.

CHAPTER FIFTEEN

HATE AND SAFETY

FOR THE LONGEST TIME after we set out, all I could think about was that Jastin did not want to look at my hair and it was stuck directly in front of his face. It was absolutely ridiculous of me to dwell on something so utterly trivial, but I couldn't help it. After some time spent pondering over my preoccupation, I decided that ridiculousness taking up space inside my head was preferable to thinking about being a murderer.

It was also preferable to thinking more on what had happened before departure.

Holding the reins again would've helped to distract me from everything, but I did not have them. Every few minutes I would realize I'd been messing with my hair—moving and touching it unwittingly. I would feel ignorant about my behavior and thoughts then pat the horse for a while to keep my hands occupied.

When I was not doing that, I attempted to discover some distinguishing feature between our horse and the only other solid black one in the group, which was being ridden by the Reaper who'd told me my mother's name. After I found it—one quite small, stray white spot near the rear end of the other—I had absolutely nothing else to do.

When we stopped to eat lunch and the sun was in the middle of the sky, I went a good distance away from everyone else and put my back to them all. Then I began digging frantically inside the bag my father had given me in the hopes that I would find something to tie my hair up with.

The entire contents of the bag were strewn about on the ground, and I was sat there staring down at it all when Chandler came up and asked, "What are you doing?"

"Oh, am I allowed to speak with you?" I shot at him. "Pardon me, but I'm slightly confused about what I am and am not permitted to do."

"Aster, he's the only person you're talking to without being hostile." Chandler sighed. "What do you expect everyone to think?"

"That perhaps the reason for my behavior has something to do with most people instead of the one," I said. "That would be the most logical explanation, wouldn't it?"

"Look." He held up a hand. "I'm sorry for assuming—"

"*I* am sorry that you would not come to me yourself with your concerns. And you *wonder* why—" I stopped speaking before I said something to him I would be sure to regret, at least eventually.

"What were you going to say?"

I shook my head and then began tossing all the things from the bag around on the ground. I wanted to scream at them for not being more useful to me. Why was I even *carrying* this bag of useless things?

"What are you *doing*?"

"Trying to find *something* . . ." I picked up another thing and examined it for likely the fifth time. *Useless.* I threw it back onto the ground. "To tie back my *damned* hair."

Careful, he said, "Why do you seem so angry about it?"

"Because apparently my mental state is questionable." I pursed my lips. And then I had an idea that sent a jolt through me. "Would you cut off my hair? With one of your knives?"

"I don't think so." His voice still sounded unnaturally careful for speaking to me.

"That's unfortunate," I said to the ground. "I would ask Agatha, but I'm not speaking to her. She likely wouldn't do it anyway, as it's something I want done. Perhaps I will simply do it myself."

"Time to go," my father said loudly from a ways off.

Several of Chandler's angry words fell out under my breath as I began shoving the useless things back into the useless bag. I looked up halfway through the process and saw that Chandler was no longer standing next to me. I frowned deeply and finished what I was doing in near silence. I couldn't stop the words from coming out, but I *could* control the volume at which they came.

I had only stood and taken a few steps when I stopped moving and shoved every bit of my hair down the back of my shirt. It tickled and was quite unpleasant in general, but at least it would not be stuck in someone's face for the next several hours.

Jastin pursed his lips together when he saw me—in amusement, I was sure—but he did not say anything.

I pulled myself up onto the horse without being told to do so, and then he pulled himself up behind me.

JASTIN AND I HAD RIDDEN IN SILENCE for nearly half an hour, and I occupied the time mostly by waiting for random conversations from the people who were with us. If they were far away or speaking in hushed tones, I attempted to make out what they were saying. It was usually heard as incomprehensible nonsense when it reached my ears.

Butter gopher little longhair toothache.

I felt as though the wind were trying to steal the one thing from me that I could use to occupy myself, at least the only somewhat productive one.

Or perhaps I'd simply gone mad.

And then, he finally asked, "Why is your hair down your shirt?"

"So you don't have to look at it," I replied.

"And you want to cut it off so I don't have to look at it?" he asked. I did not need to contemplate turning around to see if he was smiling. I already knew he was.

"No, I want to cut it off because it's useless," I informed him. "I wish you boys didn't tell one another everything." They told one another everything and told me absolutely *nothing*.

"Well, Chandler came to ask me if I had any idea why you would be raving like a lunatic about your hair."

I turned around slightly then to frown at him. "He said I was behaving like a *lunatic*?"

He chuckled. "Not in so many words."

It did not matter that I *felt* as though I were behaving like a lunatic.

Had he thought I was?

I turned back around.

"How about this. . . ." Jastin began. "You give it a few days and think about it rationally. If you decide you still want your hair gone, I'll cut it off for you. I'm sure it wouldn't be pretty, but I'll do it if you want me to."

I peeked over my shoulder at him. "Would you really?"

"Sure." He smiled.

Pleased at that, I faced the front and found myself smiling as well. It was not ten seconds later that he removed one of his hands from the reins and pulled all my hair back out of my shirt. Then, he replaced his hand in front of me. I quickly grabbed hold of it all and brought it over one of my shoulders.

He laughed, which made me say, "You're making me uncomfortable."

He did not stop laughing. "I never told you I didn't like your hair."

"I don't care whether you do or don't," I informed him.

He seemed to think that was funny as well for some incomprehensible reason.

"You simply made me see there's no point in having it."

"Would it make you feel better if I told you I do?" And still, he would not stop with his chuckling. *Why* did he have to be so infuriating?

"No. Your opinion is irrelevant to me," I said. "What would make me feel better is for you to stop laughing at me."

"If you insist." Indeed, he did stop laughing, but I could still hear the smile in his voice.

"Would you *stop* doing that?" I demanded as I turned partially around again.

"Doing what?" he asked innocently.

I frowned as I realized *precisely* what he *was* doing. "Why are you messing with my head?" I whispered. I wondered now if he had made the comment about my hair just to make me feel insane, like pushing me over a ledge I'd been standing too close to. Had standing there been as good as asking for it?

He grinned lopsidedly and answered with, "Because you're letting me."

I glared at him over my shoulder for what felt like an eternity before I said, "I'm quite certain I hate you."

His grin slowly transformed into a rather large smile and all he said was, "Okay." I was unable to discern whether or not it sounded as if he believed my declaration.

I crossed my arms in front of me and resigned myself to staring at the horse's ears. I attempted to scoot as far away from him as I possibly could, but the curvature of the saddle only put me right back where I initially had been. I didn't know how, or why, but that only seemed to make the contact worse. So I huffed multiple times until I decided it was futile and gave up in all my attempts. Huffing did even less good than moving.

Given that hair was no longer an issue, all I could think about was my dislike for Jastin. But truly, I only disliked him half the time. And it was the other half of the time that made me come to the conclusion that thinking on it would not help matters any.

The lack of beneficial things to think over, coupled with the fact that I'd expended absolutely all my energy on being angry at the world, caused me to find myself dozing off for the first time. I'd not even fallen asleep but had nodded off enough to jolt.

I did not want to fall asleep. I did not want to see any of what I would see when I closed my eyes. So I forced my eyes to stay open, and the effort of that was what kept me occupied for a very long time. But the sun was so hot on my skin, and it made me so tired.

When the sun began setting in the sky and the light began to fade from the world, it became increasingly more difficult to manage. My skin burned, and my eyes felt strained by all the light of the day and by being open for so long. Everything felt so . . . *heavy.*

I felt my head lolling forward several different times and had jolted, but after multiple occurrences of it, I jolted when I realized I'd accidentally relaxed my body against Jastin. The embarrassment of that particular ordeal kept me awake for some time, fighting through a fatigue the likes of which I'd never experienced before.

Some time was not anywhere near long enough.

THERE WAS SO MUCH BLOOD EVERYWHERE. It covered the stone walls in sprays and spread slowly out across the floor like a glass of spilled milk on an uneven surface. I looked down at myself, finding my body covered in it. It was *everywhere* and I had no hope to get away from it because . . . I could not escape from myself.

I was just about to scream when I heard, "Aster."

I jerked forward with a rattling, choked noise that felt for an instant it would break my body apart. When I realized I was still sitting on the horse, I wondered how I'd not fallen off it. I looked down desperately to see the blood covering me, but all I saw was one of Jastin's hands holding the reins and his other arm wrapped around my stomach.

Dreaming. I'd only been dreaming.

I put my face in my hands and tried to breathe normally. I was certain I'd caused a scene and that all the Reapers were likely staring at me, but I would *not* let them see me cry. I focused on my breathing, and I told myself that I was not allowed to cry. I had been told as much for ten years by other people, and it would not hurt to tell it to myself now when it was actually necessary.

Push it down, I told myself. *It can't touch you if it's far enough away. It can't touch you.*

When I was certain I could hold myself together, I partially turned around and looked at Jastin over my shoulder. I clutched my shirt in my left hand so tightly that my fingers felt as if they were threatening to break. I hid it all with the back of my right arm.

"I'm so sorry," I whispered.

He shook his head and whispered back his response. "It's okay." I only realized his left arm was still around my stomach when his hand nudged the one of mine that was latched onto my shirt.

I quickly unclasped it and cradled my ribs. I switched back and forth between the two, not knowing what to do or how to possibly comfort myself from something I deserved no comfort from.

His hand did not touch mine again. I attributed that particular bit of contact to either some strange, possibly subconscious urge for one person to assuage another in distress when in close physical proximity or a conveniently timed accident. Or perhaps it had simply been a reminder that others were near and nothing more or less than that.

He forced a smile. "I can tell you something that might help?"

I nodded because I wanted to know *anything* that might possibly help.

"You have to think about something happy."

I shook my head then because I could not think of anything happy. Where was there *anything* good in the world to be happy about?

"You loved your father, didn't you?" he asked. "At some point?"

"Yes," I whispered. I had loved my father *very* much at some point. I was not happy that person was gone. The man with me now was a mockery to the memory of the one I'd loved, like life was putting him in front of me and laughing for taking away the only good I'd ever truly had. How could I be happy about that?

"Here's what I want you to do. . . ." he started. "I want you to turn around and close your eyes. You're going to think back to when you were little and your father had just come home from being away. I want you to think about how happy you were to see him."

"I'm afraid to close my eyes," I admitted on a breath.

"You don't have to be afraid," he whispered. "I'll hold onto you so you don't fall, and I'll wake you up if anything bad slips into your head. Okay?"

"How would you know?"

"By paying attention," he replied. "I'm taking care of you, remember? So there's nothing to be afraid of."

I nodded my head, which made him smile a little. Then I turned around, but I did not close my eyes.

It was a long time that I spent staring through the darkness at my father leading our procession. I thought of him the way he used to be, and I cried silent tears as I remembered what my life had been like as a child, when I was too innocent to know about the evil in the world. All those things I'd not once allowed myself to think of in such a long time, pushing so hard every single instance they tried to get near the surface . . .

There had been nothing in the world but me and my father, together, playing games where we would hide in the trees and then find the other. I pictured his face smiling at me as he taught me how to read; he'd always been so patient and proud no matter how awful I was at it. I thought about him crying at the dried grass in the field because it had reminded him of my dead mother's hair. I thought about him tucking me inside his jacket well after I'd become too big to fit properly.

Him standing at the door, taking up the entire space of the doorway, just watching.

Me sitting near his feet, watching the light fading, painting his face in oranges and reds.

Hiding, so he wouldn't stop humming.

Small fingers touching much larger knuckles. *How did you get these funny markings, Father?*

You remember when you fell and that branch cut your leg? Such a sad smile. *Just like that, Flower.*

You fell and hurt yourself, Father?

The saddest smile, but so genuine in every way. I thought about the stubble on his chin and how it felt beneath my fingers. Tears. Bedtime stories. A back, then a hand in the air.

I hadn't realized my body had slackened until Jastin pulled me closer to him with the arm that was still wrapped around me. My eyelids felt so heavy when they opened and blinked. My eyes couldn't focus. Everything blurred.

"It's okay to go to sleep," he whispered in my ear. *So heavy.* "I've got your back."

Another tear fell from my eye when I closed it. Then, I was no longer sitting on a horse with Jastin. I was curled up in bed with my father holding me close to him and protecting me from the world. And I was utterly and undeniably . . .

Safe.

CHAPTER SIXTEEN

WORDS AND MEMORIES

THAT WONDERFUL, SAFE FEELING was still coursing inside me when I woke. It pulled so hard on me, reminding me there *were* good things in the world and that I was just so far away I'd forgotten as much. I woke up feeling like a child. It was something I hadn't felt for a single moment since my father disappeared and I'd had my childhood stolen from me. But then I jolted when I realized I felt that way because I smelled the distinct scent of *my father*.

I jumped up immediately once it registered. Once I remembered that *good* was a temporary, fleeting thing which could be stolen or vanish in an instant then mourned forever. *Good* could be taken by force at the will of another. It could be broken, murdered. It could show its face then torment you in knowing . . .

You could never have it.

I looked down at the ground, finding my father sitting with his back propped against a tree.

He'd been holding me in his arms.

He wiped at one of his eyes sleepily and looked up at me with a sad expression on his face.

In order to prevent myself from attacking him—this man who could die and destroy my entire world, then return from the dead determined to repeat the process—I stormed off into the trees in the darkness.

I did not realize that I was saying Chandler's angry words aloud rather than inside my head until Jastin ran up beside me several minutes later and asked, "Where did you learn to talk that way?" He did not seem pleased about it.

I stopped moving and rounded on him. "Where were you?"

"What?" he asked in confusion.

"Where *were* you?" I repeated it louder then because he *clearly* could not hear me speaking. "You told me you had my back and then you gave my back to my *father*?" I'd trusted him with this and out of all the things in the world he could've done . . .

For the first time, I found Jastin lost for snarky words. He opened and closed his mouth several times, but no sound came out of it as I stood there shaking my head at him in both anger and disbelief.

But then he ran his hand through his hair and asked, "Are you saying you wanted to . . . *sleep* with me?"

"*No!*" I exclaimed. "Of course I'm not!"

My reaction or response seemed to put a little more of *himself* back into him.

"Then are you saying you wanted me to stay awake all night holding your hand?" he asked. "It wouldn't be helpful if *both* of us were falling asleep on a horse. The *same* horse." One of his eyebrows rose. "I can function all right on *one* night of hardly any sleep, but even *I* will start having issues if you insist on piling them on."

"I never asked you to hold my hand." Where had that even come from?

"Well apparently me holding your back wasn't good enough for you." He laughed. "Because you were definitely holding my hand the entire time you were asleep on that horse."

"I would *never*," I said indignantly.

"Oh, I guarantee you that you would." He nodded. "And that you *did*."

"You're lying," I accused. What a *ridiculous* thing to lie about. Did he just wish to make me appear foolish?

"*Am* I?" The lopsided grin I'd seen earlier returned to his face, then he shook his head. "You clearly don't know when I'm telling the full truth and when I'm not. I wonder why that is." He tilted his head thoughtfully for a moment before continuing on. "You can hear when people are telling you partial truths, can't you? Maybe you can't do that with me because you don't want to. So every time you hear something you think you don't want to hear, you tell yourself I'm lying. It's easier, isn't it?"

"I don't know what you're talking about."

"No?"

I crossed my arms and shook my head at him. I wouldn't repeat myself for his amusement, nor would I further dignify this preposterousness with verbal responses. But I honestly had no idea what I could've said.

"If you can tell when I'm lying, how is this one?" His grin stretched farther. "Tell me which of these happened when we stopped for the night."

My brow furrowed.

All at once, his face straightened out, and his voice was entirely blank when he said, "I handed you down to your father and argued with him about how I'd told you I was going to take care of you. He wouldn't let me stay with you of course, so I went and sat nearby to pay attention to your sleeping despite knowing I needed to sleep myself. Or did I hand you down to your father without a word and go to sleep with everyone else? You'd wonder how I could've known you'd woken up if I wasn't close, am I right?" His expression and tone did not change in even the most minuscule of ways. "Your father woke me and told me to come get you because I'm the only person you'll let yourself be around right now."

He finally paused in his speaking to grin at me, which I took to mean he'd finished laying the foundation and it was now time for the next part of the process.

As validation to my suspicion, he asked, "Which happened?"

"You're not stupid enough to argue with my father over me," I said quietly. "You made that point very clear after he came to retrieve me."

I'm not stupid enough to waste my time trying to get involved, I heard his voice say in my head. He'd answered his question for me.

"I'm not?" he asked.

I shook my head. If logical thought told me anything at all it was that, if the two scenarios were entirely separate as he'd laid them out to be, one had to be eliminated completely. It was easy to discover which when one part was so obvious.

"See, that's the thing, Flower." He pursed his lips together for an instant. "You don't know me at all. I told you I'd have your back, didn't I? You don't know me well enough to say for sure whether I'd do something stupid because I gave someone my word. And you don't know if I'm smart enough to hand you over to the *one* person you want to be away from more than the rest just to save my own ass." He was not amused at all when he asked, "Do you?"

I found I could think of absolutely nothing to say in response and no satisfactory action to offer, so I simply stood there frowning at him.

"Think about it," he pressed. "Would your father have sent me if I'd argued with him about you? Would he have let me come out here if I had?" He shrugged. "Maybe he would. Maybe I made a convincing enough argument that he would. You don't know that either, do you?"

I put my hands over my face and, for an instant, wished I could rip my own skin off it. There were too many words being said that didn't make enough sense, and my brain was not functioning properly. And he was just so damn . . . *infuriating.*

I did after a moment remove my hands from my face and drop them down into fists at my sides. "Stop messing with my head."

Was that all this was? Was anything even remotely true?

"Would you insist it of me?" he asked in mock-innocence. Then he tilted his head and smiled. "Who's the liar?"

"Time to return to camp," I heard in the trees. It was not my father's voice, as I would've expected.

When I walked closer to the sound, I saw the Reaper with the somewhat-crooked nose who'd argued with him the day before.

He pointed. "Keep walking that way."

I asked, "Aren't you coming?"

He looked toward Jastin. "We'll catch up with you shortly."

I did not want to look at him, so I walked in the direction that had been shown to me. It was not two minutes later when the two of them caught up with me. Jastin jogged past, but the Reaper slowed his pace to walk with me.

When I could no longer see Jastin at all, I asked, "What did you need to speak with him about?"

"Intelligence," he replied.

"I suppose it's unintelligent for *anyone* to speak with me at all." The words slipped out under my breath as I shook my head in frustration. Or perhaps I was wrong. Perhaps it was unintelligent for *me* to speak with anyone.

"I wouldn't say that."

"Well, what *would* you say?" I asked.

"Only that people should take mind to the things they choose to do in life," he answered cryptically.

"That sounds like the same thing to me." It sounded like the *exact* same thing.

"It's not."

I glanced up and caught a small smile on his face.

"It's something your mother told me once a very long time ago."

"Why would she say that to you?" I asked curiously. I wondered what he'd done to warrant such a statement, and despite just thinking that speaking might not be the best thing for me to do . . . I seemed unable to stop myself from asking the question. I supposed it had everything to do with the person who'd initially said the words to him.

"Because when you're young, you don't have a mind to take with things." He chuckled. "It's a sad day when you wake up and realize you finally have one."

"You were . . . *fond* of my mother," I said carefully. "Weren't you?"

He nodded. "Very much."

"That's why you argued with my father yesterday," I said. "Not because a girl had grown up without knowing her mother's name, but because you felt it an injustice to her memory. Am I correct?"

He looked over at me and forced a seemingly sad smile in my direction before looking ahead again. "It's a sad thing that you did not have the chance to know her. But if you had, you would understand why your father could not bear to speak of her after losing her."

I could see it then, that this man had been in love with my mother too. Perhaps it was simply the tone of his voice when speaking of her. I almost accused him of it aloud, but I would not do that. Perhaps I was wrong in my assessment. Ahren had been right before; I wasn't particularly exceptional at distinguishing that sort of thing.

I felt the initial flirting from Jastin had been too obvious for *anyone* to have missed, and I was sure it was just to poke at my brother whether he knew about it or not.

Rather than make a fool of myself with wild and potentially misplaced accusations, I asked, "What's your name?"

"Anders."

"You told me yesterday that you may one day tell me some things about her." I spoke slowly, being deliberate with the way I went about this. "Also that my father could tell me more than you were able." I paused before very quietly adding, "I'm quite certain you could tell me some things he may not be able to."

He stopped moving then which made me stop as well. When I looked at him, he was tilting his head at me.

"Perhaps," he said with a small smile. "But perhaps not. If you're curious about your mother's life, you will have to find all the available pieces and see how they fit together yourself." He paused. "I should warn you that some pieces are more difficult than others, both to find and bear. I should also warn you that when digging into another person's life . . . you will never like all you manage to uncover."

I thought on that for a moment before speaking. "May I ask . . ." I cleared my throat a bit. "What you were to her?"

The smile slowly spread farther on his face. "Her friend."

"May I ask what you were to my father?" I clarified with, "While she was still alive."

"I must admit he and I were not particularly fond of one another." He chuckled again. "Not for a very long time."

I nodded my head in partial understanding, which seemed to be all I could find.

"We should be getting back," he said. "I don't wish to have two go's with your father in two days."

"Then we shall have to continue this tomorrow," I told him jokingly. "To give you a small break in between."

He laughed a little and shook his head, but he did not say anything more.

I followed him and, once we were out of the trees, I said, "I'm glad to have met you, Anders."

I was glad to have met anyone that knew the woman who had given birth to me—had given her *life* for me—and would allow themselves to speak to me of her, even if only briefly. Given my new information, I realized she was becoming more mysterious and less clear than I ever could've anticipated.

Information was supposed to sharpen, not blur. But I'd never anticipated learning anything about her.

At least I knew she'd existed.

"Same," he said quietly. He walked away then, leaving me standing there alone.

The sun was mostly up by that point somehow, and nearly everyone was sitting around a fire eating breakfast. Had I slept the entire night?

I stood there staring at them all, and watching Anders rejoin the group made me realize just how far out of place I was with them.

I could go shove myself between Stanley and Stewart, as I'd done the previous day, but I did not fit there naturally.

I was not speaking to Agatha, nor did I want to be anywhere near Amber.

I did not want to be near my father and his Reapers.

I feared my brother, Chase, and Chandler would all ask me questions I didn't want to answer. Or that they would look at me in some disgusting, pitying way, as though I were feeling precisely what I truly was feeling on the inside.

Broken.

Chandler was one of the only ones not at the fire. He was at his horse, seeming to be brushing it. I thought about the night after the incident with Camden, being inside the sixth room. And I thought, perhaps if I just . . .

But then I thought about being given my knife.

Concealment at times is the only means to safety. Some people might look at your arm and see that knife there; most won't. You keep it hidden? You keep yourself safe.

I looked back at the fire and the grouping of most everyone, finding nearly all of them glancing my direction.

The ones I knew.

The ones I didn't.

I met gazes with Jastin when he looked up from the fire, toward me, and he quickly looked away. His face was entirely blank, but I saw no pity for me in his eyes. I thought, possibly, that the only thing held in them was a slight tinge of shame.

I slowly walked over and placed myself between him and my brother. And then I turned my back distinctly to Ahren so I couldn't see any looks he gave me or to present him with space to ask me questions I did not want to answer.

Jastin did not speak to me. He did not even look at me. I didn't want him to. But sitting there next to him seemed the only place I could be.

It was . . . *unfortunate.*

CHAPTER SEVENTEEN

A LACK OF PEACE

I WAS TO GET MY OWN HORSE because I'd slept through most the night. Adequate rest coupled with the fact that I technically had two days of riding experience was enough to suffice.

I did not mention that both my body and mind still felt worn down or that I only had *riding* experience and not any sort of knowledge as to handling the creature if it refused to follow the others or was in any way uncooperative.

I wanted to keep the same horse I'd ridden since leaving New Bethel. I had grown quite fond of him, and though I didn't know why, I thought it might be due in part to some level of trust found when sitting on his back unharmed. Or perhaps I felt some sort of attachment to the creature which had carried me from a place I despised, or some other emotional reason I wasn't quite certain of.

Or perhaps I was simply fond of it.

A minor argument had ensued due to the size of the horse in comparison to the size of me. I did not care that he was one of the largest and that I was the smallest in our party, apart from Amber and one almost startlingly short male Reaper.

I was adamant and persistent.

It felt like a small battle won when I got him, in a sense.

In another sense, it felt quite massive. Perhaps as massive as the horse himself.

My father declared that Jastin was to stay close to me on his own horse on the off chance I lost control of mine.

When I informed my father that it was completely unnecessary, he told me I had that option or the carriage.

I grudgingly agreed to being chaperoned.

My father *clarified for me* that he was being entirely reasonable, but I failed to see it. If it had been another horse, I likely wouldn't have argued.

One battle won and another lost.

There was some confusion about how riding was supposed to work when doing it alone, as I had to keep my feet stuck in the place where I put them to get on the horse.

Jastin only tried a little to hide the smile on his face when explaining it to me, but he left me alone as soon as he had, which I appreciated.

I spent a moment before setting out standing in front of the massive horse, watching its dark eyes as it looked from me, to the others around us, then back to me. I wondered what it was thinking as it shook its head, its mane flying around almost wildly, and made another of those funny sounds.

I smiled a little and reached my hand out, stroking down its face. It moved and I hadn't the faintest idea if it was trying to buck my hand off, or if it was trying to show me it approved of the contact. I almost thought it was the latter, but I pulled my hand back in case it was the former.

I wished in that moment that I could speak and it understand me, for some reason, but what would I even say? *Please don't kill me?*

I would probably say a lot of things to something living, if not for all the reasons one shouldn't.

I walked to its side, patted it a few times on its shoulder, and pulled myself up. Then we were off.

I felt strangely exposed sitting there alone, but it was nice not to be so cramped. I reminded myself several times that it was also nice not to be sitting on a boy's lap for hours on end. Very nice, indeed.

It was also nice to pretend I had some semblance of control in my life and which direction it went.

I SPENT THE FIRST HOUR OF RIDING ALONE sitting rigid as a board while I waited for the horse to take off running with me, if only to mock the faith I'd had in it or to prove me incapable.

It did not.

When I realized it likely was not going to do so—despite perhaps knowing it could get away with such a thing while I was alone on its back—I found myself glancing next to me every so often at Jastin.

I wanted to see how it looked to ride, as I'd not thought to do so before that point, and he was the closest person to me. Everyone else was spread out decently far from one another in a jagged line.

"Why do you keep staring at me?" he asked eventually. He'd not turned to look at me once until that point, but I should've remembered that being discreet did not matter much if at all when dealing with Reapers.

"I'm not," I said indignantly. I was not looking at *him*. I was looking at him riding a horse.

"You *are*."

I supposed it was close enough. I sighed before admitting, "I'm simply trying to see what it looks like."

"What . . . *what* looks like?"

"Riding."

"Don't you already have a good feel for it?" He looked forward and pursed his lips together.

"Clearly not good enough."

He snorted.

That made me ask, "What's funny?"

"Nothing." Slowly he stated, "So you want to watch me to see how it's supposed to be done."

"That's what I just said, isn't it?" I didn't mind the unhappiness I felt seeping into my tone.

He snorted again. His reactions truly made no sense whatsoever, given the subject at hand. "Do you want me to go fast? That way you can see how *that's* supposed to be done? I'm pretty good at it, or so I've heard."

I said, "No, I don't believe I would like that very much."

"Oh, I think you might." He laughed, then shrugged. "You'll never know until you try it."

"I'm quite certain I wouldn't," I told him firmly. "And I have no desire whatsoever to try it."

"My god, you're so much fun." He shook his head and smiled, exhaling a very satisfied-sounding breath.

My forehead scrunched in confusion. "How is speaking about riding horses fun?"

"Oh, is *that* what we were talking about?" he asked in a stunned tone.

"Yes, of course it is." Hadn't I made that clear?

He laughed loudly at that, for some reason.

"What did you—" My blood suddenly felt too thick in my veins, and I found myself wanting to lunge off my horse so that I could attack him. Rather than do as much, which would be pointless and more than likely result in me injuring myself, I said, "I'm telling my brother."

"Telling him *what*?" he asked, adopting that fakely innocent tone that he so often enjoyed using.

"That you're being inappropriate with me."

"*Am* I?" He sounded appalled and I wondered how one person could possibly manage to be so exasperating. "Then by all means . . . tell your brother. I can get him for you, if you'd like."

"You can't," I said. "You're not supposed to leave me."

"Do you want your brother?" His mouth was parted, on the verge of smirking.

My blood still did not feel as if it had returned to normal. "Yes, I do."

He smiled at me then whistled—once high, and once low. It was not a full minute before my brother made it to us.

"What's going on?" Ahren asked.

The very same smile was still on Jastin's face when he said, "Your sister wanted to speak with you."

Ahren turned his attention to me. "Are you all right?"

I simply sat there staring at him. I'd not anticipated actually having to speak with him. My threat had been an empty one.

Ahren's right eyebrow rose. "What do you need to say to me?"

I opened my mouth, and I expected to tell him what I'd threatened to tell him. Instead, all that came out was, "Hello."

In my peripherals, I saw Jastin turn his face away. I watched his shoulders heaving as he laughed in silence.

"That's all you wanted to say to me?" Ahren asked.

I opened my mouth and then felt it close again. Then I smiled at him a little too widely.

He turned his attention to Jastin, who had somehow managed to get himself to stop laughing. I noticed then that my brother had one hand forcefully relaxed holding the reins of his horse, while the other was clutching the front of his saddle so tightly that his knuckles had gone as white as bone. "That's all she wanted?"

Jastin shrugged. "I guess so."

Ahren sounded completely exhausted when he asked, "What did you do to my sister?"

Jastin shook his head and had a look on his face as though he were both entirely stunned and immensely offended. "What are you talking about?" And then he turned to me. "Aster . . . did I *do* something to you?"

I opened my mouth and then closed it once again, contemplating. Truly, Jastin had not *done* anything to me; he had *said* something to me. Words were not actions, though they *were* just as capable of eliciting responses and reactions. I was still juggling with technicalities when I responded with, "No."

I smiled then as I was struck with a realization.

"That's all you wanted?" Ahren asked me.

I told him, "I'm quite fine, really. I just wanted to say hello."

He shook his head and sped up his horse to return to the spot in the procession he'd initially been.

I kept smiling.

Jastin asked, "Who was the liar just then?"

"I was," I admitted. *Technicalities.*

"So why are you smiling?"

"Because I've just realized that you don't so much lie as distort your words into what you want a person to believe."

He grinned. "Is that so?"

I nodded. "Yes, I'm quite certain it is."

I remained remarkably pleased with myself for about a minute, which was all the time he gave me to enjoy the feeling of it.

Then he asked, "Why were you blushing when you told me that story yesterday?"

"Was I?" I asked nonchalantly. "Perhaps you weren't really looking at my face to see."

"I was looking, and you were blushing."

I narrowed my eyes at him.

"You were standing right in front of me and we were having a conversation. Why wouldn't I be looking at your face? *And*," he dragged the word out for much longer than necessary, "you're blushing again right now."

"I most certainly am *not*." My face burned.

He laughed. "I'm looking, and I promise you are."

"Perhaps I simply have a sunburn," I suggested.

"That developed in the last thirty seconds?" he asked. "Is that *really* what you're going with?"

I looked down at my arms, which were more than slightly pink, and I held one of them extended in the air between us. "I've been indoors for the last ten years. Clearly I'm sunburned."

"*Clearly*," he said dramatically.

After about a minute or so of angry silence on my part, I decided to inform him, "I don't believe I'll sit with you again when we stop to eat."

"You're breaking my heart." He put his hand over his chest. I was unsure what sort of look I was giving him in response to his statement, but whatever it was caused him to chuckle and ask, "What?"

I heard myself sniff before I said, "I stabbed Camden in the heart."

Breaking and stabbing were not the same, but it didn't seem to matter in that moment.

Technicalities.

I looked forward but had seen Jastin close his eyes tightly before I'd managed to look away from him.

He said several of Chandler's angry words before riding up closer to me.

"Don't talk to me," I told him before he could try.

He didn't, and I assumed he must've understood that technicalities didn't always make so much of a difference.

TRUE TO MY WORD, I did not sit with Jastin when we stopped to eat. I couldn't force or allow myself to sit with anyone else though, so I made a place of my own in the grass far away from them all. It was peaceful, in a way, but lonely. Occasionally I would glance over at the group of them, talking amongst themselves. I realized, sitting there, that I'd not felt so alone since the time my father had gone and never returned. I'd always had Agatha, and now . . . I did not even have her.

When my father approached me, I believed I finally understood what Chase had meant when we'd talked about never having peace. It seemed that every time I had a moment to breathe, or at least attempt it, someone would come to steal all the air from me. I wondered if I would ever catch a full breath again.

Did I deserve no peace?

Did I deserve to breathe?

I'd finished eating by the point my father arrived, so I sat there pulling up grass and ripping it into pieces. I didn't look at him, not even when he sat down beside me.

I asked him, "Where did you always go, Father?"

"What?"

"When you would leave me alone," I said. "Where did you go?" Then I thought of something else that seemed more important, in its way. "No. I have a better question to ask you." I did look at him then.

His brow furrowed. "What is it?"

"Evelyn," I said. "The girl Ahren was in love with. Did *you* send him to kill her family? Did you send someone else to do it when he would not? Or did you do it yourself?"

I could tell he hadn't expected me to ask him that question. He almost seemed startled that I knew of her at all. His eyes appeared to be slightly wet when he said, "That happened before I was in control."

"Did it?" I asked, somewhat rhetorically, only because there was . . . "It's so funny, Father, because you seem stunned that I would presume you capable of killing a girl your son was in love with. Why shouldn't I? You would've killed Chase if he'd gone away with me, wouldn't you have? That would make you *just* like the Reapers who murdered my mother. Wouldn't it?" I smiled at him. "Are we done with our conversation now?"

He blinked at me momentarily before standing and walking away. As soon as he'd gone, I could not keep the smile on my face any longer. I heard him declare it time to go, so I got on my horse and went.

CHAPTER EIGHTEEN

SPEAKING

DAYS PASSED. Endless days of riding on horses in the sun. They seemed so long, which I assumed was due in great part to an inactivity I was not accustomed to. There was so much space, so many uninterrupted minutes to do nothing but *think*.

It was torture. Every second, of every minute, of every hour.

My face and arms hurt from sunburn. It was a new sort of pain, more bothersome than truly hurtful, but like any pain it was worse when touched or thought on.

Every day that passed, I found the air growing hotter, and the sun somehow felt as though it were getting closer to the ground at the horse's feet.

My eyes were strained from all the light. The bright colors surrounding me appeared distorted by it, but if I would stare off for long enough at a time, the grey of stone would seem to overtake it. Grey would turn to red. Every time I closed my eyes . . . I saw red.

They were days of silence. I did not speak a single word to anyone. I ate alone. Jastin was still required to ride close, but he gave up in trying to speak with me after several failed attempts.

All I could do was *think*.

Hours upon hours of endless thinking—about where I was, where I was going, and all the things leading up to it.

They were days of silence, apart from the screaming inside my head.

I heard someone say the heat caused vivid dreams. I did not know that it was the cause of the torture I endured at the end of every day, but I couldn't deny that I'd never had such dreams before in all my life.

No matter how much death my mind had subjected me to in my sleep before . . . it had never felt like this. It was all so vivid—the colors more vibrant, the sensations more lifelike, and it was all so . . . *lucid*.

Every time I woke, I had to struggle to convince myself that what I'd seen—or experienced or *done*—hadn't been real. It was all in my mind. So I knew precisely what the heat was.

Punishment.

I could not follow Jastin's advice on how to keep the bad dreams at bay, though I didn't know if it would help or if I deserved the help. I would look at my father as he was now, leading our procession to his city. I could not imagine him as the father I'd known and loved as a child when my mind was clear, nor could I locate any other happy thoughts to dwell on.

I woke many times in the night due to my own sort of failed attempts. All the Reapers knew, I was sure, but none of them mentioned it to me or mocked me again for my bad dreams.

Sometimes I would walk at night in an attempt to clear my head of the madness inside it. Sometimes I would simply lie there staring blankly at nothing because nothing ever seemed to bring true relief. Sometimes my body would force me back into sleep because it was so exhausted and required the rest that my mind would not give it. I did not always have bad dreams when it reached that point of fatigue.

But every time I woke in the night, my eyes would find Jastin. I'd at first had to force them not to go where they naturally went then and otherwise. I kept hoping it would get easier, though I doubted it. I kept hoping it was like a muscle to be strengthened. That, too, felt like torture and punishment as did the thoughts I had on it. Some things were far more difficult to manage than others.

Every time my eyes found Jastin in the night, he was awake, and every time, he would look away from me. When I walked aimlessly, he would always come to retrieve me at some point, though he did not say anything.

It was so strange, but he started disappearing every evening when we stopped to make camp. He would be gone for hours at a time and had usually not returned by the point most of us fell asleep, but he was always there when I woke in the night. I did not ask him where he was going and he didn't attempt to tell me. I did not ask him how he managed to function on such little sleep, either. I hoped I would eventually discover the secret to it.

Chase didn't try speaking to me at all, but I would catch him watching me sometimes. When I would meet gazes with him, I would receive the look I expected to find on his face and would turn away.

I was sure that Amber had intent to speak to me on more than one occasion. Every time I saw her walking toward me, someone would intercept and turn her around before she could get close enough to actually speak to me. Sometimes it was Ahren, sometimes it was Chase, and sometimes it was Jastin. I even saw Stewart do it once when Jastin was gone and Chase and my brother were preoccupied speaking with one another.

Amber very well might've been as quiet as she believed herself to be, but she could not slip past so many Reapers who were paying proper attention.

More often as the days passed, Anders came to sit with me while I ate, but he did not bother speaking to me. I didn't mind him being near; I assumed he knew as much and that was the reason he did so. I had to admit, at least to myself, that I enjoyed his silent company very much. I found it comforting somehow. I'd had more than enough time to contemplate over the potential reasoning for the inexplicable feeling his proximity induced inside me, but I'd discovered nothing definitive enough to account for it. He was the first person I spoke to in more than a week.

"Does it bother you?" My words came out sounding very strange from the lack of use. I cleared my throat quietly.

"Does what bother me?" He did not seem stunned that I'd finally spoken again, which had perhaps been the reason for him sitting with me. It was possible he knew it was likely I'd speak to him eventually. It was also possible he'd been sent by my father. I did not know, but I'd contemplated that as well.

"That I look so much like her," I said. I'd noticed him frowning at me sometimes when he believed me to be paying no attention. They always believed I paid no attention to anything, and I knew as much because it was so blatantly obvious.

Anders looked at the ground for a moment before saying, "No." Then he stood and walked away.

Once he'd gone, I thought on what Stanley had said about boys rarely growing out of being stupid over girls. It was apparent to me now that lying was something Reapers rarely grew out of either, when they believed a situation called for lies.

I watched Anders as he slipped away into the trees rather than going back to join everyone else. He did not return until it was time for us to move on.

I felt a horrendous need to apologize to him, but I suspected that would only make matters worse. Only when seeing how badly my question had affected him was I struck with the realization that it had been horribly unkind of me to ask. I'd simply been curious.

Was I horrible to everyone now? Was this what people had meant when they'd spoken of Chase ruining me? If it had been, their concerns had been misplaced. He'd not ruined me.

I simply was.

IT WAS LATE IN THE EVENING on the same day when Jastin attempted to speak to me again. I wondered if he somehow knew I'd spoken to Anders earlier and had taken it as invitation or if the timing truly was serendipitous. There was no way to know. Asking him and taking anything he said as fact . . .

There was no way to know.

The sun was low in the sky by that point, draining the world of all color and brightness. It always seemed appropriate, somehow. Life was what and as it was.

"Can I ask you a question?"

I could easily see him in my peripherals, riding beside me. He'd asked me many questions in those first few days of not speaking, trying to pull me out of whatever was going on inside my head. I assumed he did it because he felt guilty.

Or perhaps he simply felt bad for me. There was no way to know that either.

I didn't look at him in acknowledgment, nor did I respond, knowing he would ask me whatever he wanted regardless as he always did.

"What did Chase say to make you feel like you couldn't go to him with how you're feeling?"

I finally looked at Jastin then, blinking hard in his direction.

He seemed satisfied that he'd provoked some sort of reaction from me, as I never looked at him anymore apart from when I woke in the night.

It was because he'd asked me such a strange question that I found myself answering it for him.

"Scenarios." I said nothing else.

After several minutes of silence, he stepped his horse closer. "Will you tell me what you mean?"

And it was the genuine caring I heard in his voice that caused me to explain.

"We had a conversation about what he would do in a scenario where three Reapers were sent. He said that, when I was thrown into the equation, he couldn't know for certain what he would do, or what he *should* do. I asked if he could manage them alone if I was not in the picture. He speculated then asked me for a solution and I gave him one."

"Which was?" he pressed.

"For him to teach me how to take care of myself so that, if a situation such as the one he'd mentioned were to occur . . . he would not have to worry about me."

"That still doesn't answer my question."

I hadn't technically answered it, no, but all this was down to scenarios.

I took a deep breath and clenched my jaw for a moment before releasing it to say, "He said that until he'd seen me kill and seen how I'd react to it, he would always worry about me in that scenario."

"And you think avoiding him is the best way to show him you can handle it."

I pulled my horse to a halt.

Jastin passed and then turned his horse around to face me.

"You think that's why I'm not speaking to him?" I asked evenly.

"You truly believe me to be that ignorant? That I would think the way I'm behaving would show him what I want to show him?"

"Then *why*?" His mouth was slightly parted where he sat there staring at me.

Very quietly I asked, "Do you know what it's like to have *so* much faith in everyone, and then . . . when there comes a point in time where everything is stripped away and you look at those people . . . and you see that no matter *how* much faith you have in them, they have *none* in you? Do you know what that's like?"

He did not say anything as he waited for the Reaper who'd been riding behind us to pass.

When he was properly out of earshot, Jastin said, "I don't know what happened for you to feel that way."

I heard myself laugh on a breath, and I wiped at my eyes with my sunburnt forearm. It didn't hurt so badly.

"I spent so much time training with them." I shook my head. "Not as much as you all have, clearly. But I spent the time hoping to prove to them that I could do what I *had* to do. And then, when the time came that I had to do it . . ." I paused in an attempt to regain my composure on the inside. "I looked at their faces and saw that *none* of them truly thought I could, even if they might've understood why I did. I saw it there." I shook my head again. "What was the point of it?"

He said nothing.

"Do you remember the question you asked me when you saw me after I'd done it?"

He nodded.

"You didn't ask me who had been killed. You asked me who *I* had killed," I said. "They all would've assumed someone else had done it with me close by, wouldn't they have? If they hadn't seen it with their own eyes, it's *precisely* what they would've thought."

He still said nothing.

"You asked me that day why I let you see me break down." I paused. "Does that give you proper explanation for the answer I gave in response?"

"You . . ." He stopped speaking, waiting for the next Reaper to pass, and then no one else was behind us. Very carefully, he asked, "You were letting me around you all that time because I asked you who you'd killed?"

"No." I wiped again at my eyes. "I wanted you around me because you were the only one who could see I already had that evil inside me. I wanted you around me because you didn't look at me like I'd lost a part of myself. It's sad, isn't it, that you could see it when you don't know me at all?"

It almost appeared as if I had slapped him.

He nodded his head a little after a moment spent in clear unhappiness and said, "The biggest part of you killed him so your father couldn't touch him. Have you asked yourself the other questions, or are you not there yet?"

"What do you mean?" I'd asked myself so many questions.

"Do you know how often we kill outside of missions?"

I shook my head.

"*Rarely*," he said. "And there's never a simple explanation for why. There are so many variables." He paused for an instant. "I'd assumed your biggest reason was what you'd said. It's in your nature to want to protect people. I thought your second reason was for what he'd tried to do to you, but I can see now that I've been wrong. I don't think that played a part in it at all."

I slowly shook my head in confusion. "There was no second reason."

"There is *always* a second reason, whether you know it at the time or not," he said firmly. He moved his horse very close to me then leaned over to whisper. "I don't know *what* you said to your father to convince him to bring the brothers along, but I know whatever it was wasn't true. And all that time, feeling weak and helpless . . . You needed to show them you would do whatever it took to keep them safe. Didn't you?"

As my breathing became heavier, I could hear it more than I could feel it while as I stared into Jastin's eyes through the growing darkness.

His voice was almost loud when he repeated the question. "*Didn't* you?"

"I don't know." I barely heard myself say the words. And for a time after that, the only thing I could hear was my own quiet sobbing at the thought of his words, mine, and what it all meant.

"You can't accept it if you don't understand it," Jastin said. "You weren't ready for this conversation before. Now you can move forward."

I laughed through my tears. "Move forward in accepting myself as a monster."

"Do you know how many people I've killed?"

I looked away and shook my head in frustration and exasperation. I *hated* that question.

"Before your father took control of our city, we started going on missions at a younger age than we do now. I was *fourteen* when they first sent me out." He almost whispered, "How many bodies do you think can pile up in nine years?"

I brought my eyes to his, and his voice was at a normal volume when he spoke next.

"Do you want to have a nice conversation about being a monster?"

I shook my head again.

"No?" He smiled. "Are you sure? I'd be more than happy to oblige. I'm sure the things I could tell you would make you feel so much *better* about yourself. I can, if it would make you feel better to know you're not the most horrible person alive. I promise by the time we finished you'd never have another doubt about it."

"Everything all right here?" my father asked as he trotted up to us.

I said, "Yes, everything is quite all right."

"Are you crying?"

"Yes, unfortunately," I admitted as I wiped away the last tears that I would let him see tonight. "I was just feeling sorry for myself due to my unfortunate situation. Would you like to see the tears I've wiped onto my arm? You've missed a great deal of them while I was locked away in that House. You could make up for lost time."

I watched my father's shoulders hunch slightly before he said, "We've made camp just over there."

"I'm quite certain I can manage to get there," I informed him. "I've done a lot of things on my own in my life. Or did you not wish for me to be alone with someone? Am I not allowed to have private conversations, Father?"

I heard him breathe out loudly before turning his horse and trotting away.

"The next time I make you angry . . ." Jastin began, watching my father's back. "Just don't speak to me."

I did not speak to him as we rode together to the newest camp.

CHAPTER NINETEEN

ILLUSIONS AND EQUALITY

I WAS NOT EVEN A LITTLE SURPRISED when Jastin made his way into the trees almost immediately upon our arrival at the newest camp. He'd only watched for long enough to ensure I properly tied my horse to a tree without getting trampled by it before he slipped away. I could only assume that was his reason for watching me during the process every time I did it, despite my horse never giving the slightest inclination that it wished to do me harm.

On the contrary, the horse had been the only pleasant thing in my life lately.

I couldn't understand the attachment I felt toward it, though I'd done a decent amount of contemplation on the matter. Like the feelings I felt around Anders, I could come up with nothing conclusive enough to make sense of the attachment to an animal.

But it almost seemed as though it were . . . *waiting for me* in the mornings now.

Not for someone or anyone else but me.

That brought about some small but inexplicable feeling of joy inside me. I was quite certain I only imagined the waiting and acknowledgement of my person, but when I really thought on it, I explained it away with logic.

If the horse was waiting, that was because it understood its place in the world, or at least the routine of it. It had nothing at all to do with me specifically and any bonds formed were all in my head due to some sort of loneliness.

Still, it did recognize me, at the very least.

That horse had been the only reason I'd smiled in over a week.

I often found myself wondering if I *had* gone mad.

As soon as Jastin had gone—doing who knew what in the trees—I did the same thing I did every evening.

I looked at Chase and waited for him to return my gaze. When I received the same expression that I always got from him now, I exhaled a breath and turned around to pat my horse, just like I did every night after receiving that expected look. Then I sat down and waited until I could eat, which would be followed relatively shortly after by most everyone going to sleep.

To pass the time, I pulled at grass and waited to hear something useful. This was the only time of day when I learned anything of relevance.

I knew, from previous nights, that we were still several weeks away from our destination. I knew that approximately two weeks before we arrived at my father's city was when we would pass the closest to another, given the speed of our travel. I knew both the name of that city—Maldir—and the Reaper in control of it, Bren. I listened to them talk for brief moments about particular threats in any given area. And they never, not once, realized I was overhearing them.

Enduring the torture that I rightfully deserved alone had its benefits.

I closed my eyes and thought of what Jastin had told me—that sometimes it was better for people to think less of you than what you were.

People had always thought less of me than what I was, but it had never been beneficial for me. Perhaps one day it possibly would be. For now, all I could do was keep listening and remain invisible.

Or perhaps that wasn't the only thing. . . .

It was after dinner that I went to my father and asked, "May I speak with you alone?"

Everyone sitting nearby looked over at me as though they'd forgotten I was even here with them, despite my existence being the reason behind their traveling. I knew they'd not forgotten, but I'd imagine it would've been an easy thing to do when a person was very quiet and very insignificant.

It wasn't difficult to be both.

"Of course," he said as he stood.

I followed him a good distance away and, when I was sure we were far enough that no one would hear us, he stopped moving. He seemed stunned I would willingly speak to him, or perhaps he was simply worried I would attempt to stab him while no one was near. Would he be able to stop me if I did?

Highly likely.

He waited for me to speak.

"I see that everyone takes shifts at night. . . ." I began. "Every few hours two people wake and the two who had been awake go to sleep."

"Yes." I didn't believe the wariness in his voice was intentional, but I could've been mistaken.

Slowly, I said, "I want to take part in that."

He blinked at me as if I were speaking a language to him that he could not understand. Still, it didn't take long for him to find some part of my statement to latch hold of regardless of not understanding. "You're not trained."

"I *am* trained," I contradicted him. "Not so well as any of you, of course, but clearly the task is more listening and watching than anything else. You can ask. I'm quite good at that, and I'm awake for a good portion of time during the night anyhow."

"And what would you do when one night it's *not* simply listening and watching?"

I tilted my head at him in confusion.

"Killing a person who asks you for it is not the same as trying to kill one of us."

"Is that so?" I asked. "And you believe me incapable of protecting myself or anyone else." I heard myself laugh once quietly. "I wonder how much faith you had in my mother's capabilities when you abandoned her to fight for our lives."

For the first time in my entire life, I saw my father angry. He puffed himself up and I worried for an instant that he was going to attack me. But I knew he would not, even if a part of him might want to.

I almost walked away, but I stopped myself and turned back to him. "Don't worry, Father." I shook my head. "I won't ever waste my breath asking you to have faith in me again. I can see now how pointless it was to try."

I briefly watched in satisfaction as the anger seemed to whoosh out of him at once. It appeared as though he'd deflated when I turned and left him standing there alone.

IT WAS NEARLY AN HOUR AFTER speaking to my father when Chandler and Ahren came over to where I was sitting alone. Chandler nodded with his head for me to stand and follow them, and I did as instructed.

When we'd walked far enough to be out of everyone's earshot, Chandler stopped and turned to me. "We just had a chat with your father."

"Oh?" I asked. "What about?"

Chandler frowned, but Ahren shook his head, almost as though he were amused with me.

"About you pulling a guard shift," Chandler replied.

I said, "My father made it quite clear he believed me incapable of performing the task properly."

"Why would you *want* to?"

I smiled, which felt so strange on my face, and I did not answer him.

Chandler sighed loudly. I suspected Chase had informed him of our last interaction and that he was clearly aware of what I was doing, which was not answering him when he wanted an answer. "He asked about your capabilities."

"And you told him I'm hopeless at combatives," I stated.

"I told him about what you did to me for me to pull your shoulder out," he said. "I left that particular part out, of course. We hadn't informed him about what happened to your shoulder, only that it was injured. But I told him you were quite exceptional with your sensory training, which you were."

I chuckled. "I suppose his reaction was wondering how much I've overheard of the things they've said."

"Well, yes," Chandler said, almost apologetically. He leaned in somewhat close then and almost whispered. "Why would you want to let him know about your skills? Just to pull *guard* duty? That doesn't make any sense, especially not in the long run. And if there's *one* thing I know about you, Aster . . . it's that you're full of sense."

I had to look away from his face, down to the ground. "It makes perfect sense."

"*How?*"

I forced myself to look back at him, far up at his face, and I could not keep the sadness I felt inside from coming out in my response. "I wish you knew."

"Does *Jas* know?"

I heard my brother sigh loudly behind him.

"I wouldn't know," I said. "You can ask him what he thinks when he returns and see what answer he gives you. Then, the next time you speak to me, I'll tell you whether he was correct or not. But I won't tell you the answer unless you figure it out for yourself. It's so much more gratifying to discover things on your own, or so I've heard."

In the end, you still learned from something, no matter the means or source. It was all technicalities.

"Is this some crazy, drawn-out plan you've been concocting in your head this past week?" Chandler demanded quietly.

"It's not so complicated as that," I informed him, my voice calm. "It's really very simple. And all of you are too blind to see it." I looked from his eyes to my brother's, then back again. "Are we done here?"

Chandler took a step back and huffed out a breath through his nose.

"Father has agreed to let you do it," Ahren said. "You'll be pulling the first shift."

"While everyone is still awake to give me the illusion I'm doing something productive and worthwhile." A tight smile pulled at my face. "Just like everything I did inside that sixth room. If you'll excuse me . . . I've had quite enough talking to suit me for one night."

I left them standing there, and I ignored them as they called after me.

I WOULD STILL DO A PROPER JOB with the task I'd been given, even if no one was going to take me seriously. I did not allow myself to think, pushing down all the thoughts that had been plaguing me. Armed with a different task, it was not so difficult to suppress those torturous thoughts that came in cycles and only seemed to grow larger in each passing. I cleared my head the way I'd learned how in sensory training, and I paid great mind to my breathing as I very slowly paced around my designated half of the bodies on the ground.

I'd been doing as much for nearly an hour when Jastin stepped through the trees.

I hadn't heard him at all until I'd seen him.

I was angry with myself—and also extremely embarrassed—when I looked at Anders as he was making the other half of the circle.

He was distinctly pretending as though he'd missed my indiscretion, and for some reason I doubted he would mention it to my father. I did not know if that made it better or worse. Was it possible it could be both at once?

Why was everything so complicated?

Jastin had stopped where he'd come out of the trees and stood there staring at me with his head tilted. After more than a minute which was likely spent trying to figure out what was going on, he walked over to me and whispered, "What are you doing?"

I pointed at the bodies that were all feigning sleep.

"Did you ask to?"

I nodded.

"Why?"

I whispered my first verbal response in the exchange back to him. "Apparently it's all part of some crazy plan I've concocted inside my head in my silence."

Crazy.

Lunatic.

"Is it?" he whispered.

I smiled sadly at him and shook my head.

It felt like he stared at me for a very long time before he said, "You just want someone to treat you like an equal, to have faith in you. Don't you?"

I hurriedly wiped at my eyes. "Go on and pretend to sleep like the rest of them."

"I'm going to sleep." The smile on his face was startlingly warm.

Then he narrowed his eyes. "I trust you won't let anything happen to me?"

I heard myself sniffle a little, and I wiped at my eyes again before whispering, "I've got your back."

He nodded and walked away silently toward his empty bedding area.

After that, I mostly watched the trees and listened rather than moving constantly. I would walk back and forth at intervals, but I knew that if there was a threat, it would likely come at us from the trees; it was what I would do. And I knew that if there *was* a threat, they would take me out first because, being female and less trained aside, I was the smallest one awake. I was the easiest target by far.

Every so often I would watch the bodies on the ground for a few seconds at a time. I knew most of them were awake because they were far too still. Reapers moved so much more in their sleep than what they were doing. But Stanley and Jastin had both fallen asleep. It was the twitching that gave them away—the random jerk of a muscle here or there beneath their blankets.

And it was a sound that had me looking over and finding Jastin sitting straight up. Even from a distance I could see him breathing heavily as he looked around himself. When his face turned to me, I watched him wipe at his forehead with one of his arms and then lie back down.

I felt a tear fall from my eye as I realized . . . no one could *ever* have any peace in this world.

IT WAS SUCH A MINUSCULE SOUND by Anders that sent my father and another Reaper to their feet. I walked as quietly as I could to where my bedding was laid out on the ground, and I frowned as I stared around the circle of bodies. I did not trust hardly any of these people, and I did not know half of them at all.

I'd made it halfway to my destination with my bedding tightly in hand when my father grabbed hold of my arm and whispered. "What are you doing?"

"Putting my back to someone I trust to protect it," I whispered in response. "And then sleeping peacefully." I hoped.

"I don't—"

"I'll not spend one more night the way I have been, and you're absolutely ridiculous if you're concerned about where I sleep in a grouping of people all sleeping near one another. What in all the world *are* you concerned about?" My response had almost been too loud.

The nearest Reaper flopped himself onto his opposite side and sighed.

My father said nothing, staring down at me in the darkness.

I said, "Let me go."

My father shook his head, but he released me.

Once he had, I walked the rest of the way and laid out my bedding near enough to Jastin to feel comfortable but far enough away to feel comfortable. I did not look at him once, despite the fact that he was sleeping and would not see me do it. I laid down and put my back to him.

It was not long after I'd been there when I heard a sound behind me—a rather loud, broken intake of breath. I peeked over my shoulder and found Jastin sitting up again.

He blinked very hard at me, and I watched his forehead crinkle in confusion. I could see the sweat covering it gleaming in the moonlight. He smiled—I could not tell what sort it was—then rolled over, putting his back to me.

I had slept with Chase before, and he'd latched onto my back. I'd felt safe then, like nothing in the world could touch me so long as he had hold of me. But the feeling of Jastin putting his back to me, as if he truly did trust me to protect it while he was protecting mine . . . it was entirely different.

I closed my eyes and when I fell asleep dreamt only of broken memories from my childhood that had been trying desperately to resurface. I did not wake from disturbing images fabricated by my mind and possibly exacerbated by the heat, only from minuscule sounds made by the people around me. I would dart up, my hand instantaneously shooting toward the knife on my arm, only to find the Reapers switching their positions for the guard shifts. But when I slept, it was peaceful.

For the first time in all my life, I felt . . . *equal.*

It was such a shame that equality between any two people always seemed to be found on the ground.

CHAPTER TWENTY

A SECRET

SLEPT FOR MUCH LONGER than I usually did, as the sun was mostly up in the sky by the time that I opened my eyes.

Everyone else was already awake, apart from Stewart, who I'd noticed had a tendency to oversleep quite often if not roused by someone.

When I looked around, I found Jastin walking toward the fire, away from my general direction.

Had he slept longer than usual as well?

Perhaps his direction had nothing at all to do with me and everything to do with timing.

It was irrelevant.

My body was stiff from multiple days spent sleeping on the ground, but I hadn't felt so well-rested in a while. After a moment spent thinking how funny it was that I'd taken a stiff bed for granted when I'd never believed I had anything to *take* for granted, I stood and went about my morning business as usual.

It was while I was eating, away from everyone else, that I noticed Chase and Jastin slipping off into the trees together. I tilted my head, staring at the spot they'd disappeared from.

How peculiar.

I was frowning as I placed my food on the ground and made my own way into the trees, not taking the path they'd gone but taking my own.

I focused on the days of stealth training as I carefully maneuvered my way through the branches and undergrowth. It was much different than walking quietly on a floor, as I kept making some sort of noise no matter how hard I attempted not to. I was not accustomed to there being so many things capable of making noise beneath my feet and all around me. I'd not been trained for this, which only reinforced what I already knew.

I decided I would have to come into the trees to practice stealth on this sort of terrain at some point every day. I could not ask Chandler to help me. I was quite certain I could manage it on my own. It would assuredly be a way to occupy my free time at the very least, and much more productive than ripping up grass by far.

Free time.

I had free time. I'd never thought I would, and I had almost no idea what to do with it, but that was not pertinent.

I would've worried about getting lost as I walked through the trees, if not for the fact that I began hearing voices after a short while. The closer I came to them further brought the realization that they were not speaking. They were . . . *shouting*.

I still wasn't near enough to hear what they were saying to one another, and the shouting set me on edge. It was peculiar enough that they were speaking in general, as I'd never once seen them communicate with one another directly unless required or hardly do more than acknowledge the existence of the other. But nearly screaming?

I began paying less and less attention to my breathing and footsteps as I made my way toward them.

I'd only just barely heard Jastin yell, "*Open your eyes!*" before a hand touched my arm.

I almost screamed, but I turned quickly and saw that it was only Anders. I breathed out a breath of relief, and I did not mind if he saw or heard it.

He took the hand he'd used to touch my arm and gestured for me to follow him.

I wanted to shake my head at him, but all I did was turn my attention back to the voices and pretend he wasn't there. Before I could make out anything else said, Anders grabbed my arm—only hard enough to both make a point and get the job done—and began pulling me away.

When he'd taken me far enough from where I wanted to be to suit him, he stopped moving and tilted his head at me. "You *are* a sneaky little thing, aren't you?"

I opened my mouth but could not think of anything appropriate to say in response, so I remained silent.

He chuckled a tiny bit. "If you'd had more training, you would've known not to leave your plate on the ground."

"I just wanted to know what they could be speaking to one another about," I admitted guiltily. I hadn't thought about my plate at all, past knowing I'd not wanted it in my hands any longer.

"Yes, and if you'd gone about doing things in the way you always did them, you could've slipped away without my noticing. For a little longer than what you did, at least. Then you would be hearing what they were saying instead of standing here with me. But I'm sure you already know what they're speaking about."

"I'm certain I don't." That was why I'd *followed* them.

He raised an eyebrow at me. "No?"

I shook my head, and then, he shook his. It had been an entirely different action, despite being the same thing.

He then said, "Did you know that Reapers operate in pairs?"

"No, I didn't," I told him, feeling my forehead scrunching. It was not something that anyone had ever told me, but I couldn't see how it was even remotely relevant to the current situation.

"They always do in our cities," he said. "Do you know why we put that into effect?"

I shook my head again.

"Before we began operating in such a way, we lost men as often as we had successful missions." His lips pursed for a moment. "It's difficult, what we do in particular, as we don't take out innocent families who cannot defend themselves. I should say . . . *innocent in comparison*. And Reapers?" He widened his eyes at me. "We don't grow on trees. It takes an entire lifetime to train us properly, and then, it can all be over in an instant. All that time and energy, all the life and potential . . . *wasted*."

"But while I was in that House, no Reapers ever visited together." I was so confused. "Chase told me Reapers are required to take one another out quite often. I got the impression they were around one another as little as possible."

"*Our* cities operate that way. I did not say the others do, though they will all send out pairs or teams when particular missions call for them," he clarified. "I must admit that, a long time ago, things were not the way they are now. We're taught to be competitive with one another; it makes the killing feel less real and more like a game. So, in truth, you could say it's instilled into us from birth to naturally despise one another."

"Then how do you function properly in pairs?" Being sent on missions to kill one another was completely different from spending your entire life despising something, I thought. One was internal, the other external. It changed everything but the action.

"We changed the curriculum for our Reapers when we took over our first city."

"*We?*"

He smiled. "Your father and I. He could never have done it alone. How could he have gotten close to other Reapers to create a revolt when he was outnumbered and had no one watching his back? It would have been . . . *impossible.* I'll not answer the question you likely want to ask me next. It is your father's right to explain it to you."

"Then what *will* you tell me?" I asked him that instead of the questions I wanted to ask.

Was it your fault my father was always gone? Was it your fault he never came home?

"Your father and I shared a common hatred of our broken system, as it took the same thing from the both of us." He smiled again. "It gave us reason not to continue wasting our time hating one another, so we focused all our energy into the system instead. It still should've been impossible. I cannot tell you how many times we discussed our imminent deaths." He paused to chuckle quietly under his breath and shake his head, like he was recalling such discussions. "But we're both still alive, as you can so clearly see."

I tried as hard as I could not to think on my father having such a conversation. I could not imagine anything he might say on it, certainly not anything he would.

I did not know this man.

A thoughtful expression appeared on Anders' face. "It was such a simple concept—trusting another person. So simple, and yet so difficult to do when trust is removed from us. We began testing it, sending pairs out together for simple missions. It was a horrendous effort at first, I can tell you. But then we realized that you cannot force one person to trust another, so we began allowing our Reapers to choose their own partners. When possible, at least."

"You allow them to make such choices in their lives?" I had never heard of such a thing, especially not to such an extent.

"Unbelievable, isn't it?" He chuckled. "And now, with our younger ones, when two people seem particularly taken with one another, we allow them to remain close rather than ripping them apart. They're not required to keep their closeness hidden from the adults in order to prevent it from being stolen from them. The pairings break occasionally of course, which is only natural as people go through their lives. Breaking of some sort is inevitable when one person gets close to another."

My brow furrowed minutely.

He tilted his head. "Do you know how often we lose our Reapers now?"

I shook mine.

He smiled before saying, "*Rarely.*" I heard him take and then release a satisfied breath. "Do you want to know why that is?"

"I do," I admitted.

"Because while one Reaper is infiltrating—playing a specific part that needs to be played—another is disguised as a normal person, always watching their back," he said. "We don't simply train our Reapers to pretend to be certain people now. We train them to be insignificant as well. *Insignificant* is a word we'd always found . . ." His nose crinkled a bit. "*Unacceptable.*"

I nodded in understanding. "Like the man who snapped that Reaper's neck in New Bethel while we were leaving."

"*Exactly.*" A pleased sort of smile appeared on his face. "And the number one can play their part effectively because they don't need to check over their shoulders constantly as we were always trained to do." He paused. "If you ever see a Reaper of ours alone, you should know that they are not. Any seemingly lone Reaper has been designated a specific task and another is directly beside or behind them. You may not see them, you may not notice them, but they're there. It's a good thing for you to always keep in mind."

"And . . . is the number one always the number one?" I asked that rather than inquiring as to why he was telling me something my father likely did not want me to be made aware of.

"They switch back and forth as they see fit," he said. "Some of us prefer to be invisible."

"Wait," I said quickly as something struck. "Were your tactics different when you were infiltrating New Bethel?"

He shook his head at that.

"But the Guard. I never saw more than one of your—" I stopped speaking immediately when he smiled.

Had almost all the Guard members been replaced by Reapers?

Had I looked past them all that time when I thought I was seeing them?

How could I have missed such a thing?

I pursed my lips then forced myself to ask, "Why are you telling me this?"

There had to be some sort of reason for it.

His openness made no sense.

There was *always* some sort of motivation behind things.

He was silent for a moment as he listened, then he smiled hugely. "Would you like to hear a secret?"

"About my mother?" I whispered.

He nodded his head and two words spilled out of my mouth before he'd even finished the action.

"*Yes, please.*"

"Reapers never used to put much stock in their women, as they are naturally built physically weaker than men. It's a dire mistake people make." He scrunched his nose again in what was unmistakably distaste. I watched him rid himself of it then move on. "Your mother was sixteen when she was sent on her first mission. I was four years older and had been going on them for quite some time already. Her first task was to seduce a leader from a neighboring city." He ignored my stunned gasp and my contorted face. "One of our Reapers was giving him inside information, and it was her mission to gain his trust and find the name."

I couldn't . . .

He paused to frown before saying, "She messed up because she was so afraid. She wasn't supposed to kill him, but he discovered what she was after a short time. She was able to get the name, but as

I said . . . she wasn't supposed to kill him. Too many possible repercussions. Infiltration is *much* more dangerous than kill orders. Typically."

Quiet, I asked, "How did she get the name if she killed him?"

He smiled. "I should suspect you wouldn't enjoy hearing the answer to that particular question." Then he breathed out deeply. "I can still remember the look on her face when she returned. It was so much like the look that has been on yours when you believe no one is paying attention to you."

He shook his head as though he were trying to rid himself of the memory. His voice was normal when he went on. "It was quite a while before they agreed to send her out again, and the next time they did, I was between assignments. So I accompanied her without them knowing, and I watched her back. She was . . ." He shook his head again, but he was smiling now. "*Exceptional.*"

"*Really*?" I asked, an inexplicable excitement rising in my chest.

"Oh yes." He chuckled, nodding. "She blamed her success on my presence, which I thought was ridiculous at the time, but I can see now that she was correct. She could perform properly because she wasn't so afraid when she knew she wasn't alone. So every time she was sent on a mission after that point, and I wasn't away on one myself . . . I went with her."

"Why would you go, if you thought it was ridiculous?"

"Don't you know?" The curiosity was apparent on his face. He waited a while as he stared at me before continuing on. "At first it was because I wanted to ensure her safety, but then she began accompanying me on mine when she did not have one either. And then, when we began taking more active roles in one another's missions, we realized that . . ."

"Realized what?" I pressed when he did not say anything more.

"We were quite the pair, she and I." He laughed once humorlessly. "Even after she began seeing your father in the way she eventually did, we still worked with one another for a time. He knew, of course. He even threatened to expose us on more than one occasion, but he never did. I suspect he was too afraid of losing her if he forced her to choose. But then she became pregnant with Ahren, and after she had him, I woke up one day and . . . they were both gone."

"Were you one of the Reapers who hunted them?"

His right eyebrow rose. "Why do you think it was Reapers from another city who caught them?"

What was he saying? "You killed the Reapers they sent from your own city?"

"I would have killed *any*one for her," he said firmly. He looked away and wiped at one of his eyes.

"Why are you telling me this?" I whispered. Looking at his face in that moment, as he stared at a nearby tree and seemed unable to look at me, made me feel as though he were torturing himself.

Did we all deserve the torture we endured in some way?

"To give you a very important piece of advice," he replied. "Trust is the most valuable yet most difficult thing to find in the world. You can break it, you can destroy it, but the catch is . . . it's the *one* thing that cannot be destroyed by outside forces, only by the people it belongs to. It's like . . . *magic*. Do you know the word?"

I nodded.

I'd seen the word before, in books. It was a nonsense word, a word used to describe anything outside the short limits of human understanding.

Thoughtful, I asked, "Wouldn't you say that love is like magic?"

"No," he said assuredly as he shook his head. "Love can be destroyed by a great many things. It is still special in its way of course, but inarguably less magical. There is *nothing* in all the world even remotely comparable to trust—no word, no action, no feeling. Trust exists in a tiny space between two living creatures, but in that space . . . it's *boundless*. Its importance is one thing, but its *potential*?" He was staring into my eyes as he shook his head again. "Nothing can even begin to compare."

"So you pulled me away from something I wanted to hear to tell me this advice." I nodded my head slowly and was ashamed to admit to myself that I was extremely confused over the intended purpose behind all this. I knew there *was* a purpose, but it was beyond my grasp.

"You said you didn't know what they could possibly be speaking of," he stated. "Until you find yourself aware of it, you don't deserve to hear what they say."

"And you believe *you* know what they're speaking of?" I found I was feeling both defensive and remarkably unhappy because of what he'd said.

Deserve.

Was that all the purpose to it? Was it only him making an assessment of what was *deserved* and what wasn't?

He smiled. "Oh yes, I'm quite certain I do." Then he sighed. "Now come along so I can show you the proper way to sneak."

"What?" I asked quickly.

He pulled a bow off his back, which I was apparently too dense to have noticed before. "In order to be believed, you must have a believable story. In most instances, the safest way to travel is not in an obviously straight line. When dealing with Reapers, you must *always* have the stops along your journey plotted precisely before you ever set off, no matter the direction. If you fail to do so, it's highly likely you'll never reach your desired destination."

He paused and stared at me for a moment. I waited during that time for him to ask me if I understood what he was truly saying to me, but he did not.

Instead, he informed me, "You and I are going hunting to explain our absence together."

I blinked hard at him in confusion. I had never been . . . *hunting*.

Before he could walk away, I asked, "What was the secret about my mother? You said my father knew about the two of you working together. Where was the secret?"

"I never told anyone about how her first kill broke her," he answered.

"Why would anyone have asked?" I'd been told that Reapers did not care so much about anything, so long as what they wanted done was done. This seemed to be another of those instances where technicalities did not matter so much.

"They wouldn't have." He said that then smiled sadly. "But she asked me never to tell anyone anyhow. I believe she wouldn't mind me making an exception for her daughter while that daughter is going through the same thing. So I'll break a promise I made to your mother to let you know . . . You're not alone." The smile stretched a bit farther, but his expression remained the same. "I thought it might help you."

CHAPTER TWENTY-ONE

LIKE

NDERS CARRIED TWO LIFELESS RABBITS in one of his hands as we walked through the lush trees in what I assumed was the direction of the camp. I didn't have the vaguest clue how he knew which way was the correct one. It all looked the same to me past a few things that I thought I'd seen before but very well might not have. As we made our way, he said, "Your mother was so funny about hunting."

I glanced up at his face. "How do you mean?"

"She had no qualms after a time about killing people, but no matter what I did . . . I could *not* get her to hunt with me." He laughed under his breath at that, and though admittedly *funny*, I found no humor in it. "She said she couldn't force herself to take the life of a creature that never harmed anything in the world. Humans are the only creature that harm things for no good reason. Once you realize that? Well . . . It's not so difficult."

Choosing the tolerable path to take, I asked, "So, did she not eat meat then?"

"Oh no, she most certainly did." He laughed again, louder then. "She simply couldn't kill an animal. She would cook them when I'd return with them, but she would never even accompany me. She'd always rather sit alone, waiting, than see it happen."

"It sounds as though the two of you spent a good deal of time alone with one another." I said that to the ground, then I cleared my throat uncomfortably.

I looked up at him when he made no reply and found him staring straight ahead with a smile on his face.

I frowned as I returned my gaze to the ground as we walked. I did not know precisely how I felt about the ideas I had toward the relationship my mother had shared with Anders, perhaps because I didn't fully know about it. I was unsure that discovering all the facets of it would help.

I decided to feel that, no matter what had happened between the two of them, I should not have any sort of problem with a person loving my mother. I should not have a problem with someone having cared for her in her life, because that would be ridiculous. She was lucky to have had a single person care for her, and there was nothing else to it.

"That other Reaper . . ." I began slowly. "Roger, I believe his name is. He said every time my mother opened her mouth to speak, it wiped all sensible thought from a man's brain."

Anders thought that statement was extremely funny, as his raucous laughter so clearly proved. "You could say as much."

When he did not elaborate further, I asked, "Was she kind?" I'd wondered that many times, especially since the conversation we were speaking of.

"Only when she felt particularly inclined to be so," he said with another laugh. Then out of seemingly nowhere, the sound stopped, his face evened out, and he whispered. "Prepare yourself for a scene from your father."

It was not thirty seconds later that we stepped through the trees and were swarmed by the hulking mass of my father. He was physically very large, but he appeared even more so when in such a state. Though I'd seen him angry when inquiring about guard duty . . .

I'd never seen him like this.

"Where have you *been*?" He did not shout the words at me. His attention was entirely focused to my left, but I still struggled not to flinch.

"I took Aster hunting." Anders held up the two rabbits, unfazed.

"Why would you take my daughter hunting?" my father asked in disbelief.

"If you haven't noticed, we're running low on food and your *daughter* is *bored*," Anders said nonchalantly. "I figured I would kill two birds with one stone."

Or rabbits, on this particular occasion.

"Am I not allowed to enjoy myself at all, Father?" I asked the question in an innocent tone when his attention had turned to me.

His anger had abated, enough that I could ignore what remained of it, at least.

"You enjoyed going hunting?" He seemed to be having a very difficult time processing the situation, struggling with the appropriate way to handle it.

His indecision was an opportunity.

"Very much." I smiled. "Anders even allowed me to shoot his bow once."

That was something my father had *never* let me do when I was a child. I was allowed to *touch* his bow only after asking permission to do so, and I was watched extremely carefully by him all the while.

My father frowned, though he did not seem to be angry at all any longer. "Just tell me the next time you decide to wander off."

"Should we have designated times for me to relieve myself?" I asked him. "Or am I not allowed to do that without your permission either?"

I watched my father close his eyes and shake his head before turning and walking away. When I looked at Anders, he was rubbing above his top lip with one of his fingers to conceal a small smile with his hand.

I asked, "What?"

"Ahren is very much like your father in disposition, at least in some ways," he said. "But you are *exactly* like your mother."

"I'm not," I said quietly. There was simply no way I could be. I'd not ever known her to inherit her personality traits through exposure to them.

"I can assure you wholeheartedly that you are," Anders said, then his nose scrunched a bit like he was sharing a joke with me. "That's the only reason your father tolerates your tongue. Watch what happens if someone else attempts to speak to him the way you do as many times as you have. I bet it would surprise you." He paused and his grin grew wider. "We all have our limits. You should keep that in mind."

He still seemed amused when he began walking away, but he stopped moving when several words came out of my mouth.

"May I accompany you?"

He turned back to face me.

I clarified with, "Some other time when you go to hunt?"

He tilted his head as if he were confused, or perhaps as if he'd truly thought I'd not enjoyed myself with him and had lied to my father about it. He must've seen the truth on my face because he smiled warmly at me. "You may accompany me anytime you'd like."

I felt foolish when I realized how hugely I was smiling so I pursed my lips together and nodded my head.

I could not explain the feeling I had when Anders walked away, but it was a good feeling welling inside me for a change. Though it was not *good* the likes of which I knew was somehow capable in the world, it almost felt that way. When surrounded by so much of the opposite, drowning in it, the smallest thing in the midst of it all almost felt like a full breath. I only wondered how long it would take before this got pulled under and disappeared with all the rest.

Still, it was there for now, and it was a good enough thing that I'd forgotten about Chase and Jastin entirely until I looked around and found them sitting very far away from one another. They did not appear to have gotten into a physical altercation at least, which was another good thing.

I realized, standing there, that I did not feel like being alone at the current point in time. It was selfish, and I had no problem with that, but I couldn't help wishing to prolong what I was feeling for as long as I was able. I was sure I could keep it from being pulled under, at least for a little while.

I went and found my brother where he was sitting. I sat down beside him, took his hand in mine, and then turned away from him so I wouldn't have to see any looks he gave me. His hand only twitched a little.

It was not five minutes later when my father declared it time to set out. I looked at Ahren then, preparing myself for a deflating feeling that would come when I saw the usual sad look in his eyes. But he was smiling at me when he pulled me up from the ground by my hand. And I smiled all the way to my horse because of it.

I WAITED ALL MORNING for Jastin to mention his argument with Chase to me, but he did not. I was unsure why, but I'd expected for him to, and I found it . . . *bothered* me that he didn't. I wasn't agitated, just a bit confused and . . . unsettled.

He did not mention the argument or the fact that I'd slept next to him the previous night. He did not ask me why I'd done it. He did not look at me, or speak to me, once. I was unhappy when I discovered . . .

I wanted him to.

When we stopped for lunch, he disappeared into the trees and almost didn't make it back in time to eat before we set off again.

It was after another hour or so of riding in silence that I maneuvered my horse closer to his, which I could do properly now. "Are you attempting to stay away from me?" When he looked at me in clear confusion, I said, "Is that why you always leave when we stop?"

He shook his head.

"May I ask you why you go, then, if that's not why?" It was the only reason for his behavior that made sense to me.

"Thinking and looking." Then he quickly asked, "So how much of our conversation did you overhear?"

I sat there and found I could do nothing more than blink at him.

"Your father said you left the camp shortly after we did." He stared straight ahead. "He saw us leave, but he didn't see that you had until after you were gone. It's why he was so concerned when we came back and you weren't with us. Isn't that funny?"

"I was hunting with Anders," I said quietly.

"*After* you followed us to eavesdrop." He made his accusation with a grin. The grin faded slightly—I saw him struggling to keep hold of it—when he repeated the question. "How much did you overhear?" It sounded much different the second time. *Weaker.*

"Not much," I admitted, nerves playing around in my stomach. "Only one thing, actually, before Anders pulled me away."

"He pulled you away?" He seemed quite baffled at the prospect.

I frowned. "He told me that, until I knew what the two of you were speaking to one another about, I didn't deserve to know what was being said."

Jastin laughed. "That's funny."

I shook my head at him in confusion, because I could not find any humor in it.

He clarified with, "That you don't know what we were talking about."

Careful, I said, "Well, I assumed it had something to do with me."

He snorted and nodded his head, not in response but what somehow seemed to be amusement. "*Did* you?"

"Yes," I admitted, being overtaken by a wave of extreme embarrassment. Had that been horribly presumptuous of me? I supposed . . . I supposed it had. "That's why I wanted to listen. And, truthfully, I was worried Chase was going to get the wrong impression about . . ."

"You sleeping next to me?" He finished my sentence for me with a grin.

"Well, yes," I said quietly. I'd worried several people would. . . .

I sat there for a long time watching him looking forward as he said nothing.

"Is that what happened?" I pressed.

"What?" He asked the question as if I'd just woken him or that he'd somehow forgotten we were in the middle of a conversation. Or perhaps like he'd forgotten my existence in the world entirely. "What were we talking about?"

I frowned at him due to his behavior.

He laughed again. "Don't worry. Everything got straightened out."

"That's good." I almost whispered the words as I tried to figure out why I felt so strange.

"*Is* it?" he asked, leaving no room to mistake the taunting he'd intended to be there.

"Why is it . . ." I started then clenched my jaw because I did not want to continue on. When I decided that possibly having an answer to the question would be a better alternative than the embarrassment of asking it, I did. "Why is it that you treat me one way when it's light outside and then the opposite of that when it's dark?"

He raised an eyebrow. "It's easier, isn't it?"

I shook my head in confusion. "I don't know what you mean." Truly, his answer made no sense to me whatsoever.

"Don't you?" The way he was staring at me—with his eyebrow once again raised and his mouth slightly parted—made me see that he clearly expected me to know.

I shook my head.

He laughed again before saying, "Maybe I'll explain it to you one day, then."

"One day when?"

"One day when I feel like it."

My voice was almost entirely blank—apart from a bit of astonishment I couldn't keep out of it—when I said, "I really don't like you."

He grinned. "During the day."

"More like *never*," I clarified for him. "Trusting a person and liking them are two completely different things."

"No." His tone was thoughtful. "You like me at the *exact* times I want you to like me." He looked over at me, I suspected to give me the full effect of his grin.

I couldn't discern what I heard in his tone when he spoke next, but I did not like the way it made me feel.

"You can't help yourself, can you?" He laughed and asked, "Are we done conversing for now?"

"Yes," I told him unhappily. "I'm quite certain we are."

"That's good."

When I glanced at him ten minutes or so later, he almost appeared miserable, for some reason.

FOR A BRIEF TIME later in the day after the sun had set, I contemplated attempting to converse with Jastin, simply to see if he would act differently toward me. But I did not, and then my opportunity to do so passed.

Chase didn't look at me at all once we stopped, and I sat alone for a long time before Anders walked over. He did not bother speaking to me and, again, I found myself simply glad for his company. I wondered if I would ever discover why.

Anders didn't have the first guard shift with me again that night. It was a different one of my father's Reapers who had never attempted to speak to me.

I could feel his eyes on me as much as the empty space as I paced quietly. I knew he was watching me for weaknesses so he could report them back to my father. I tried my hardest not to show him any, though I was sure he saw some regardless.

Jastin did not return while I was on my shift but an hour and a half or so after the first switch. My bedding was already next to his, as far away as I'd had it the night before, and I had my back turned to where he would lay. I'd actually laid both ours out, to ensure they were where I wanted them. I kept his in his usual spot of the circle, but I felt me doing both was staking some sort of claim to my right to be where I wanted.

I doubted anyone cared at all, but it made me feel better.

My eyes were closed as I fought to hear a sound while he was slipping himself under his blanket. But my eyes shot open when I felt a hand touch my hair. It was brief enough that I was almost certain I'd imagined it, or that it had been accidental, but then I heard him exhale a seemingly frustrated breath through his nose and roll over.

My gaze shot to the nearest person who was awake, which was Anders. When our eyes met, he distinctly turned away and walked his designated half of the perimeter.

I could not fathom why Jastin would've touched me at all, let alone a part of me he'd declared useless.

I did not get much sleep that night as I pondered over it.

CHAPTER TWENTY-TWO

SURPRISES

AS WE WERE RIDING TOGETHER late the next evening, Jastin said, "You're still angry with me, aren't you?"

The sun was just barely beginning to set, pink and orange lighting up the sky before all brightness would once again fade from the world. No matter how pleasing it was to the eye, I found it so sad. It almost seemed like a futile last-ditch effort, the world clinging to something good that could only exist for such a brief time.

All its beauty would disappear before its next coming, and it was *never* the same; it was only similar enough to have the same name.

Always so appropriate.

It took me a moment to come out of my distraction from the sunset. They looked so much different when you weren't watching them through a window, and they felt so different after you realized.

"*What*?" When I thought back and realized what it was that he'd asked me, I said, "No. I'm not angry with you. Are you disappointed?"

His forehead scrunched for an instant until he presumably understood what I'd meant. His voice was quiet when he said, "I don't like making you angry."

"I'm inclined to believe you do." I glanced over at him to add, "Sometimes."

"Is that what you think?"

"I think you enjoy it while you're doing it and then feel guilty afterward."

He seemed to think on that for a moment. "Why do you keep forgiving me for it?" He shook his head a bit. "You don't forgive people easily."

"Because it doesn't bother me." My answer was truthful enough to pass. "I know you mean no real harm by your taunting. You've not done me some great injustice with your words. I'll admit you make me feel insane occasionally, but I believe it's easier when I know you do it on purpose without true maliciousness."

"How would that be easier?" Indeed, he was looking at me as if he thought I *was* insane. "Shouldn't it be the other way around? You should forgive people for things they do to you accidentally, shouldn't you?"

"Perhaps," I said. "But for now, I'm simply finding myself glad a person understands me enough to know what would bother me and what would not. How can I stay angry at you for that?" I glanced over at him again. "Besides, on occasion you've kept my mind from dwelling on things I'd rather not think of. I should be thanking you, shouldn't I?"

"I'd rather you didn't."

I shrugged. "Then I won't."

I looked over at him for a bit longer than a glance and contemplated tormenting him about his reasons for touching my hair when he believed me to be asleep, but all I did was smile at him.

He did not return it, but that didn't bother me either.

WE DID NOT LEAVE AS USUAL after eating breakfast the next morning. Jastin and my brother had slipped away into the trees with bows attached to their backs before the sun had even risen. They didn't give me the opportunity to ask if I could accompany them, though I very much doubted they would've allowed me to if I had.

I would've liked to have gone.

At the very least, I would've liked to have not been woken by Jastin getting up. That left me with nothing to do but sit around watching the Reapers as they slept and eventually woke. I took turns between that and observing the sky as it lightened once more, the clouds illuminated by light bluish greys and purples as the stars faded and ultimately disappeared.

Thinking over the similarities and differences between the sun rising and setting kept my mind somewhat occupied.

After a good deal of time spent in absolute boredom once I'd formulated an opinion on the process, I found myself sprawled out on my stomach across the grass, watching Anders draw pictures for me in a blank book.

He told me stories as he did it. I sincerely doubted any of them held even the smallest bit of truth, but I found myself laughing at his words and pictures regardless.

"Those sound a great deal like the stories my father used to tell me when I was a child," I said then chuckled. "Only he did not replace the characters with different, ridiculous variations of himself."

"Who says they're not true?" Anders sounded both aghast and curious at once.

"Only logical thought," I told him through my laughter. "But I'm enjoying them immensely anyhow."

"Your mother used to tell me I was the most ridiculous liar in all the world." He grinned. "When we would return from our excursions together, she would get so angry with me for the things I would tell people. She would say, 'Andy, I was right there and that *never* happened.'" He adopted a very unhappy female-like tone to his voice to repeat my mother's words to me. "But she never contradicted me in front of anyone and she never told me to stop doing it."

I realized that I was not laughing but giggling when I said, "That's very funny." I supposed my mother had enjoyed his stories as well, and it somehow made me feel closer to her, as though we were sharing an experience we weren't actually sharing.

It was strange.

Anders looked at something in the distance and sighed. "I should leave you alone. Your father is getting increasingly unhappier with me as time passes."

"But—" It was remarkable how fast I was struck by the sadness his words induced.

Was it ridiculous for me to wish he'd continue wasting his time on me, at least for a little while longer?

"Perhaps if you attempted to speak with him without being hostile, he would not feel as though I'm stealing you from him." He sounded quite apologetic.

I didn't want to come off as childish, as I would've done if I said I did not wish to speak with my father at all. Instead, I informed Anders, "I'm no longer a piece of property that can be stolen from a person."

He smiled and shook his head before standing and walking away.

I could not stop myself from doing what I did next. I looked at my father, and I glared at him. Why did even the smallest bits of happiness keep getting stolen from me? I was just contemplating stomping over so I could scream at him when I heard laughter.

I looked toward the trees and saw Jastin and my brother stepping out of them. Jastin had a giant mass of brown something thrown over his shoulder and Ahren's hands were covered in blood.

I ran over to the two of them and realized it was a giant animal on Jastin's shoulder, which should've been obvious, but all the red had overridden logical thought. I caught one look at its big, beautiful eyes before I felt my jaw begin to quiver.

"Are you *crying*?" Jastin asked as he was placing the animal on the ground.

Its dead weight hit with a muted thud on the grass.

I pursed my lips and wanted so badly to look away, but found I couldn't force myself to tear my gaze from the animal despite the desire to do so.

"It's very beautiful," I heard myself say quietly.

Then I heard Jastin chuckle and my brother sigh.

"That's a nicely sized deer," my father said in clear appreciation from relatively close behind me. "Aster, are you crying?"

I felt even more foolish about it when asked by my father. Perhaps it had something to do with the amusement and lack thereof in their differing tones.

"Is this why you always cut them up before you'd bring them home?" I asked him, my gaze still being held by brown eyes near the ground. "So I wouldn't have to see it?"

"Well, yes," he said apologetically, which brought my attention to him. The smile that appeared on his face was undeniably forced. "Do you remember how much you loved that stew I used to make from it?"

"Would you make it now?" I asked because I *did* remember.

He narrowed his eyes at me, either as if he were confused or wary. "It takes a very long time."

"We've already been gone a very long time," I pointed out. I did not see how making it now would cause any harm. I decided then that it was futile to ask him for something, but I still thought of what Anders had just told me. I forced a smile at my father and politely said, "Don't worry about it. Forget I asked."

I was momentarily distracted by a bit of movement in my peripherals. I looked over and unfortunately found Jastin removing his bloody shirt and bending over to dig around in his bag for a new one. I averted my gaze as fast as I could manage, though I felt as if my eyes would not blink properly after what they'd just seen.

"*Jastin,*" my father said in exasperation.

"What?" he asked nonchalantly as he stepped closer.

I just barely—and accidentally—caught a partial view of his abdomen as he slipped another shirt on.

Why did muscles look different outdoors? Was it the light?

Stop it, I told myself. It was just a body, not anything I hadn't seen before. He was just a person and I should've been used to this. Still, my brain seemed to be sputtering.

"Come on," Jastin said, not paying me the slightest attention. He looked only at my father, for which I was indefinably grateful. "What's a little bit of time to make your daughter happy? My ass could use a break from sitting on that horse anyway. Tell me yours couldn't."

"A bit of a break truly wouldn't hurt anything. . . ." My father seemed to be taking great care in thinking over it, and that surprised me. "We're in relatively safe territory where we currently are anyhow."

And I smiled the first genuine smile at my father in ten years.

I did not think he saw it.

It only remained on my face until he looked at Jastin and said, "I would appreciate you not speaking that way in front of my daughter."

"You should hear her when she's angry." Jastin laughed. "I don't even think she realizes what she's saying. Trust me when I say it makes *ass* look tame in comparison."

"Did you—" My father began to speak in Jastin's direction, but then he stopped himself and closed his eyes. He took a deep breath and smiled at me once they opened again. "Go on. You should find a way to occupy yourself for a while. As I said, this takes quite a long time to make."

For some reason I couldn't quite explain, I was very pleased with my father for not pressing my bad language when I was angry or accusing Jastin of being responsible for it.

Any bad language I'd picked up and actually used was Chandler's fault.

If my choices after exposure to him could be considered his fault.

I smiled at my father again, and I was sure he saw that one because of the expression on his face that followed it. It was the most he'd looked like him, and it hurt.

It hurt so badly.

Before I could do more than get started in walking away, he said, "Your mother used to cry."

I stopped and looked back at him.

"When I'd bring animals home," he clarified. "That's why I never brought them for you to see. You were so much like her, even then. I didn't ever want to see you sad."

I felt a prickling behind my eyes as I realized that had been the first time that I'd ever heard my father speak a word about my mother, apart from the reasoning behind my name.

She took one look at you and said you were the most beautiful thing she'd ever seen. She said it was only appropriate.

Will you tell me more, Father? Please.

So sad.

I forced a tight smile at him as I wiped at my eyes and turned away.

I WENT AND SAT ALONE on the grass, distinctly putting my back to where my father and Anders were cutting up the deer. I could not stop myself from glancing at them over my shoulders occasionally, and every time I did, I had to wipe at my eyes.

That poor, beautiful creature . . . it had never stood a chance. It was different to me than the rabbits had been. I thought, perhaps, that the difference in reactions might've had something to do with the deer reminding me of my horse.

It was not fifteen minutes later when I heard a very quiet whistling in the trees behind me—once low, and once high. I turned at the sound and found Jastin smiling at me, his body hidden from the rest of our party by a very large tree. He motioned with his hand for me to come with him.

Strange.

I briefly glanced at everyone as they were sitting around chatting with one another, but mostly I wanted to ensure that Chase did not see me, after them having argued.

When I was certain he wouldn't catch me doing it, I stood and slipped into the trees.

I didn't ask Jastin where we were going or why he'd pulled me away from the camp. In all honesty, I was simply glad to not have to remain sitting there alone, stealing glances at a dead creature while it was being cut into pieces. But eventually, when we kept walking and did not stop, I asked, "Where are we going?"

I received nothing more than a smile in response, but it was not long after that when we came upon a relatively large body of water. He stopped moving then, so I supposed this was it. It was pretty, but I had seen a great many pretty things since I'd gone from my confinement and could not understand why he'd pulled me away to see it. I gave him a puzzled look, but he was still smiling.

I gestured toward the water. "Is this what you wanted to show me?"

He said, "Sit down and close your eyes."

"Why?" Wariness from the abnormality of it all began to take over me.

"Because I said so." He laughed. "Just do it."

I frowned as I sat down on the ground and closed my eyes as instructed.

"Promise me you'll keep them closed."

"I promise." I pursed my lips for a moment. "You're not going to do something awful to me, are you?"

He didn't say anything, but I could hear his laughter trailing away.

I sat there for what felt like quite a long time, periodically sighing in both frustration at the situation and confusion at his strangeness. But at some point, I heard his footsteps coming closer. I was more than a little tempted to lunge at him. I was also tempted to turn around, but I did not because I'd promised.

"Keep them closed," he warned as he came closer. When he was directly in front of me, I heard him sit down. "Hold out your hand."

"My *hand*?" What in the *world* was he going to do to me?

"Yes, I have something for you," he said. "Hold out your hand."

He was going to stick some horrible sort of creature in my hand, I knew, so I could not explain why I huffed out a breath of air and extended it in front of me, palm up. Whatever it was that he placed on my hand stuck there.

I opened my eyes and stared down at a massive chunk of honey-comb.

CHAPTER TWENTY-THREE

STRIKING DEALS

Y BRAIN SPUTTERED. It tried so hard to form a complete thought—moving a little, stopping, and then repeating the process. I had doubts as to whether it would ever return to full functionality.

I did the only thing I felt I could, which was analyze the very basics of this.

I could feel that my mouth had dropped open as I stared down at the sticky contents of my hand, *larger than* my hand. I closed my mouth and pursed my lips together when I gained the mind to do so, because I did not want to look ridiculous. I heard myself sniffle before my jaw began quivering.

I looked up from my hand to Jastin's face.

There was a sheepish sort of grin on it, almost as though he were embarrassed or wary. I had no idea which it was, and I doubted my chance for success if I attempted to figure it out in my current—utterly *baffled*—mental state.

"You found this for me," I said quietly as I attempted to wrap my mind around what was happening.

Why did my head not seem to be working?

It was just a . . . *thing*. It should not have stopped my head.

It was just a thing.

Jastin bit down on the corner of his bottom lip and narrowed his eyes. I was quite certain his head was telling him to lie to me in that moment, but he said, "I did." Perhaps he only told the truth because it would've been ridiculous not to.

"How many times were you stung?" Did that matter? It seemed a reasonable question before it came out. *I* was *being* ridiculous.

"A few," he replied.

I looked down at my hand again and took in a deep breath. "Is this what you've been doing in the woods? Looking for this? For me?"

"I happened to stumble across it last night." He shrugged. "It's not a big deal."

I sighed before shaking my head and looking at him again. I slowly said, "It was simply coincidence you decided to go hunting the morning after you'd found it, so we wouldn't leave."

Was that all it was? Were things nothing more than things and timing nothing more than timing? Was that all?

"How could I possibly know you would ask your father to make something that takes hours to make?" he asked. "You don't like to speak to him, let alone ask him for things. It's just the way things played out."

I'd contemplated his timing so thoroughly, breaking down every questionable scenario. The conclusion I'd reached was that there was *always* something more to it. I'd been fuzzy on the *what* and the *why*, attributing it to some form of caring, or loyalty, or responsibility.

This was an opportunity.

I took another deep breath, holding it in my lungs. It felt as though I needed to choose my words *extremely* carefully and put a great deal of thought into them before they came out of my mouth.

"I understand that the sun is currently shining . . . but will you please put that aside and be honest with me?" I paused for just a moment. "Is this what you've been looking for when you're gone?"

It was a very long time that he spent staring at me before saying, "It's possible."

All the stars.

I sniffed again and wiped at my eyes with my free, non-sticky hand. "Why would you do that?" I asked the question quietly, though I believed I was finally beginning to understand.

His face turned a bit red before he looked away from me. "To make you happy."

"Are you *blushing*?" I asked in disbelief.

He frowned at me and spoke in a snooty tone. "Certainly not."

When he saw me smiling at him for mocking me, he looked away again.

"It's not a big deal," he repeated. "I was actually hoping to bribe you with it."

"*Bribe* me?" My brow furrowed. "For what?" I could not think of anything I had that he could possibly want.

"To not cut your hair."

"Because you like my hair." I fought so hard to keep the grin off my face, but I could feel it tugging up on the corners of my mouth.

He wrapped his arms around the front of his legs and laughed. It sounded very uncomfortable. "What makes you think that?"

A smile completely took over my face—I could do *nothing* to stop it—and he then brought his gaze to a nearby tree before speaking again.

"I just thought it would be ridiculous for you to cut it all off because of something I said to you."

"So why didn't you propose the deal before you gave me this?"

"I just wanted to give it to you." He glanced up at me for an instant before pursing his lips and looking back at the same tree.

"It seems a reasonable request." I nodded. "I'll agree to it."

"Will you answer a question for me instead?" He looked at me and tilted his head. "*Truthfully*."

I nodded again.

"Why did you tell me the story about it?"

"Because of your eyes," I admitted, my face burning. "But you already knew that, didn't you? I'm sure you know what color your eyes are." I took a deep breath and spent a long time releasing it before speaking again. "Chase accused you of falling in love with me. Didn't he?"

"No." Jastin grinned. "He accused me of manipulating *you* into falling in love with *me*."

Slowly, I asked, "And what did you tell him?"

"That I'm not stupid enough to try and you wouldn't be stupid enough to fall for it if that was what I was doing." He narrowed his eyes. "Are you?"

I cleared my throat. "I should hope not." It took me a few long seconds to ask, "What reason would you have for doing such a thing?"

"Something about some master scheme by your father to tear the two of you apart," he said dismissively. "But you and I both know your father would never ask me to do that, don't we?"

I narrowed my eyes and stared at him for a long time, and all he did was sit there with a grin on his face.

"Either that statement was true and you wish for me to believe it's not . . ." I started carefully, "or it's untrue and you wish for me to believe it is."

"Why would I tell you that if I was trying to manipulate you into falling in love with me?" His tone was sarcastically innocent. He only stared at me for a moment before continuing on. "Either way, you don't know me to find the answer."

"Perhaps you're right about that." I smiled. "But perhaps you're not. Perhaps I know you better than you believe I do."

He said nothing initially. Instead, he sat and looked at my face. Then, he said, "Did you ever think maybe Chase is right? Has it crossed your mind at all?" He chuckled quietly. "Did you ever think that maybe every interaction Anders has with you has been because your father wanted it to happen? Did you ever think that maybe every word I've ever said to you, everything I've ever done, has been on his orders? Has it crossed your mind?"

The grin faded away and he tilted his head. "You would think he wouldn't just allow you to be with me if you decided you loved me instead, right? A Reaper is a Reaper is a Reaper, isn't it? But what if he could depend on a person to not fall in love with you? Get you to send Chase away and then have them leave you once he was gone? What about that?

"Maybe I *did* know you would ask your father to make that food." He shrugged. "Maybe that's why your father mentioned it, so I could bring you out here alone. Maybe it was all planned. Maybe I touched your hair the other night because I knew you were awake and would know I'd done it. It's all possible, isn't it? I can assure you that if all of what I just said is true . . . I've done worse." He shook his head. "You shouldn't put it past me. You shouldn't put it past Anders. And you *certainly* shouldn't put it past your father."

"Or *perhaps* . . ." I said to the ground, then paused. "Perhaps my father saw that you were falling in love with me and sent you out here to put an end to it."

I leaned forward closer to him, watching in satisfaction as his body clenched up from the proximity.

I put my mouth quite close to his and whispered. "Congratulations. What a job well done." I forced myself to smile and laugh when I sat back down all the way. Then I said, "You can go ahead and send Anders for me."

As soon as Jastin stood and was behind me, I could not force the smile to remain on my face any longer. And as soon as I was certain he was gone, I stared down at the damned honeycomb in my hand and contemplated throwing it out into the water.

I did not throw it. I simply sat there and cried.

THAT WAS HOW ANDERS FOUND ME—with my face resting on my knees and the hand that wasn't sticky wrapped around the front of my legs. He sat down beside me.

I looked over at him with a quivering jaw to ask, "Do you only spend time with me because my father wishes you to?"

He frowned. "Is that what Jastin told you?"

"You didn't answer me."

"I can assure you, every conversation your father and I have had on the matter is the exact opposite."

"And how am I to know you're not lying?" I demanded.

"Logical thought." Through my blurry vision, I watched one of his eyebrows rise.

"Logical thought is telling me *everything* that happens is all part of some plan." I almost shouted, though logical thought begged me to find some composure.

Anders looked out at the water and breathed in deeply through his nose. I saw him wipe at one of his eyes. "I know you've gathered I was in love with your mother. Have you found yourself wondering if she felt the same way toward me?"

"I have," I admitted. I did not ask him what any of this had to do with what we were speaking of, as I trusted there was some sort of connection. There was always something.

"She most certainly *did*," he said firmly. "And now the next question along that path is why she was with your father if she loved me. Am I correct?"

He looked at me with wetness in his eyes and I nodded.

"She knew how I felt, though I never told her as much. No matter how I tried to convince her otherwise . . . she knew. She was with your father because I would never admit to it."

"Were you afraid?" My voice was quiet, cautious.

"Of course I was." He said it as though I should've known. "I was afraid that if I gave her what she wanted—" He paused to regain his composure by taking several deep breaths. "She would end up *exactly* how she ended up."

"Do you regret it?" I whispered.

"Do I regret not having her blood on my hands?" He shook his head forcefully for a brief moment. "But I regret not giving her what she wanted while I could. I regret that more than anything in the world, more than anything I've ever done in my life. If you knew the things I've done . . . you would know what it means when I say that to you." He paused before continuing on. "You may ask yourself if your father has any involvement over my wanting to spend time with you. You may ask yourself whether I only want to because you remind me of her. You may ask yourself if it's out of loyalty to anyone, or if perhaps it's nothing more than that I feel badly for you. None of those assumptions would be correct."

"Then why?" I asked. It made no sense at all, if not for those reasons. I'd thought of them all and come up with nothing to explain it.

He put a hand over his mouth and rubbed at it absentmindedly. I heard him sniff loudly as a tear fell down his cheek. "Because you should have been mine," he answered into his hand before removing it. "But then it would be me you can't stand looking at, wouldn't it?"

"You would be dead right now," I said which made him bring his attention back to me. "You would've never left my mother to fight for us alone. Would you have?"

His jaw quivered slightly before he said, "I don't know. If I was staring down into the face of a child I'd made with her . . . I don't know. I willingly gave up my opportunity to find out the answer to a question I've been asking myself for a *very* long time. And now I'm going to have to have a serious discussion with Jastin for bringing more lies into our lives. We have more than enough of them already."

"So I was right," I said under my breath. "My father saw that he was falling in love with me and made him put an end to it."

"Oh, I'm certain your father did nothing of the sort." He sounded so certain. "This has nothing to do with your father and everything to do with the discussion Jastin and Chase had a few days ago."

"What do you mean?" Why did I feel so leery?

And then I realized . . .

I *wanted* to blame this madness on my father.

"It's in Jastin's nature to play with people rather than allow them close." Anders wiped the last remaining tears from his eyes. "So it's natural for Chase, and everyone else, to assume him to be playing with you. I don't know what Chase said to him exactly, but I'm quite sure the two of them struck some sort of deal for him to back off."

"How could you know that?"

He smiled sadly at me. "Because I'd imagine it would be somewhat similar to the deal I made with your father when your mother became pregnant with Ahren."

Chapter Twenty-Four

Girls

I HELD HANDS WITH ANDERS as we walked through the trees together. I was unsure why I'd reached for his, why he'd taken mine, and why we continued to walk in such a way. I told myself it was natural.

I did not think about the honeycomb he'd wrapped tightly between several large waxy leaves, put in my bag, and instructed me to save for a time I could appreciate it. Instead, I thought about how easily this man could've been my father. I glanced at his face once and saw that he was crying silently as he stared straight ahead. I did not look at him again, but I kept hearing his words repeating loudly in my head.

You should have been mine.

Could that torment a person? Was it even an attachment to or fondness for me at all, or was it nothing more than regret? Would he have felt it at all—at least the likes of which he did—if not for the way everything had come about?

It was so strange to think that one person's mere existence in the world could affect another, let alone to such a degree.

Did my existence torture him?

I spent some time speculating as to how my mother might potentially feel about all this, were she alive to feel.

I couldn't help thinking that, if my mother *were* still alive, she would want me to have some sort of relationship with him. I did not know if she would've admitted as much, nor did I know why I was so certain she would want it. Perhaps she would want it because she was dead. No matter the confusion, that was the conclusion I came to. As I had no way of knowing, it was all I had to go with.

So I did not care if Anders was lying about my father's involvement in our interactions or any of his reasons for spending time with me.

I did not care because it was what my mother would've wanted, I felt sure, and it was what I wanted.

I wondered . . .

Did she wish I *had* been his?

Why had she done the things she'd done?

I couldn't stand all the endless questions.

I believed I began to understand more and less at once about the complications of love as I walked through the trees with the other man my mother had loved in her life. Had it been her anger towards Anders' denial of his feelings for her that had pushed her to my father? I had to believe she'd loved my father as well. She would not have risked her life running away with him twice if she hadn't, would she have?

It was possible.

How could one person love two different people at once?

I could see that Anders had not wanted to force her into a life where she could never have the things she wanted. He simply hadn't realized that not giving those things to her didn't change the fact that she could not have them. I wondered . . .

If she had her life to do over, would she have done things differently?

There was absolutely no point in thinking on it. Her decisions had cost her life, and she would never have the chance to do things differently or to give me answers for the reasons she'd had for doing them. I could never know any of it with certainty, only waste time speculating over things that were impossible to discover.

I decided to think about my own life instead because it was possible, though highly unlikely, that I may actually get somewhere with it. It was more achievable than having a conversation with someone who was no longer living.

If Anders was correct and Jastin and Chase had struck some sort of deal over me . . . what reason could Jastin have had to agree to it? And why was I *so* damn angry he had?

No.

I knew *precisely* why I was angry.

I was not a piece of property to be bargained over by anyone, and Chase did not *own* me.

I FOUND MY BROTHER when Anders and I stepped through the trees, back at the temporary camp. I walked over to where he was sitting with Chase and Chandler, and I looked only at him. He seemed to be quite distracted over something, as he was staring off at nothing in the distance with a thoughtful expression on his face. He took one look at my face when I got close and jumped a bit before jumping up.

"May I speak with you alone?" I asked.

"Of course," he said as he shot a confused glance at Chase.

Chase narrowed his eyes at me, which I caught, but he said nothing to either of us.

My brother led me back into the trees and walked a good distance away before he stopped and turned. "What's wrong?"

"Do you know of the deal that Chase and Jastin made with one another?" I asked as I struggled to force my jaw not to quiver. I simply needed to know whether he'd taken some part in it as well.

"Deal?" He shook his head, but only for a moment. He then was entirely still, apart from his narrowing eyes, when he asked, "What . . . *deal*?"

"I can see you have no idea what I'm talking about." I nodded my head and took a deep breath.

"Aster," Ahren said firmly. "What *deal*?"

I heard myself laugh once. "Apparently I'm far too ignorant to be trusted to form proper opinions of people." I forced a smile at him. "It's nothing to be concerned over. It's nothing more than I should've expected from the lot of you."

"*What*?" His mouth was hanging open a bit, which was both humorous and infuriating at once.

"It's the way you've all been treating me since we set out, isn't it?" I asked him, my voice impassive. Then I realized what I'd said and corrected myself accordingly. "It's what you've all done to me the entire time I've known you—pretending to trust and have faith in me then going behind my back with everything of importance."

My brother's mouth dropped open farther. "*That's* what this is?"

"Of course it is," I told him with a painful laugh. I shook my head and wiped at my eyes. "And now I've had the one person who doesn't treat me like that . . . *bargained* away from me. For *what*? Petty, improperly placed jealousy?" It was either that or something *far* worse—love being twisted into a need to have power. I refused to believe it was that. I refused to believe that of him. "I'd like to thank all of you for being ignorant and continuing to treat me like I'm worth nothing more than the dirt beneath your feet. I am so sick of you all pretending to love me when none of you truly have any idea what the word is supposed to mean. I very much hope you're all satisfied, because I have no desire to speak with any of you again."

I walked away at that, and I ignored my brother calling out for me.

I stepped back through the trees shortly after and found that I didn't care so much if absolutely everyone saw me crying hysterically. I spent a brief moment looking for Anders, but I could not find him so I went and found my father next to the fire instead.

"*Aster*!" he said as he shot up from the ground. "What's happened?"

I shook my head and sat down. When he sat back down next to me, I was shocked that I took his hand in mine. I stared at the food cooking over the fire, and I cried while holding my father's hand, finding it didn't feel the same as it had when I was little. I supposed that happened when you grew.

I'd not been doing that for a full minute before I heard shouting. I ignored it and looked to my father through my blurry vision.

He was staring off toward the direction of the sound, appearing as though he were on the verge of jumping up. When he looked at me again, I shook my head once more. Even in my current state I could tell . . . he was torn.

The shouting suddenly grew louder as more voices joined into it. And then, all at once, that sound went away and was replaced by another.

"Sonofa*bitch*." My father said it under his breath, which made my eyes widen in his direction. "Aster, I have to go stop them before they all kill each other."

He was gone the instant I dropped his hand.

I watched him run over to a rather large group of people who all appeared to be rolling around on the ground with one another.

There was a snort beside me, and I looked over to find Roger watching the scene as if it were one of those plays Chase and I had spoken about what seemed like such a long time ago. He nodded in the direction of it and said, "All sensible thought."

"What the hell *is* this?" My father's voice carried over to me at an almost normal volume once the struggling sounds stopped, which meant it had been *very* loud at the source.

"I've never seen Reapers fight that way," I heard Amber say from relatively close by. She sounded stunned.

I decided I was going to ignore everything said by everyone. I did not want to hear any of it.

"Boys get stupid over girls," Roger said nonchalantly. "She likely said whatever she did to her brother with the sole intent of creating the scene you just witnessed."

I heard myself release a very loud breath as I stared blankly at the fire.

Ignore them, I told myself.

"She *wouldn't*!" Amber exclaimed.

"Girls like her always do that sort of thing on purpose." Roger chuckled. "If we took bets on it, how many do you think would say it was intentional? Maybe half and half? Splitting is the point."

"Shut up, Roger," one of my father's Reapers warned.

"You don't know her at all!" Amber said indignantly—and loudly.

"Look at her sitting there," Roger said, "pretending as if none of it is even happening. Look at her eyes, little girl. What do you see there behind the tears? Do you see it there?" He chuckled again. "Believe me when I say I don't have to know her. Her mother was the exact—"

Roger stopped speaking immediately when there was the sound of a fist hitting flesh.

I stood on reflex and found both Roger and another Reaper being restrained by two younger ones.

Roger's nose was bleeding everywhere, pouring red down the front of him. It ran down his chin, his neck, then disappeared somewhere on his black, short-sleeved shirt.

I walked away once Amber began screaming obscenities at them all. I decided the best thing for me to do was get as far away as I possibly could from absolutely everyone.

An errant thought popped in my head as I left the scene. With all the shouting at my back, I realized Amber seemed to have a much firmer grasp than I had, where bad language was concerned. No matter what had just come from my father's mouth . . .

I knew she had not gotten it from him.

IT WAS NOT LONG THAT I SPENT WALKING when I heard a misplaced footstep behind me. I turned and sighed when I saw one of my father's Reapers.

"May I help you?" I wiped at my eyes, not looking at his face.

No peace.

"I'm just ensuring you don't decide to run away and get lost in the woods," he said. I could see his grin in my peripherals.

"I'm not in the mood for company," I informed him. "If you haven't noticed, everyone who gets within a ten-foot radius of me today seems to be getting into fights with one another."

"I don't care." He shrugged. "I still have the sense to do my job."

"And what job is that, exactly?"

"Keeping you safe," he replied. "It's what we're all supposed to be doing. Didn't you know?"

I assumed his question had been rhetorical.

"If I promise to sit here and not wander, will you leave me alone?" I could not stop myself from being somewhat hopeful he'd allow it when I sat down.

He grinned wider and sat down where he stood.

"That's not what I meant," I informed him. I'd intended for him to return to camp.

"I don't care what you meant," he said. "Or what you want."

I wondered, briefly, if that was the most honest thing a Reaper had ever said to me. I respected the statement, or at least his willingness to make it without seeming to have some ulterior motive. It was nice to have a bit of straightforwardness and truth.

It was a very long time that I spent taking turns between crying and huffing in frustration at the ground. I expected the random Reaper not to say another word to me, and I hoped he wouldn't past a small tickling of curiosity as to whether such honesty would carry over from one statement to the next. But eventually he did speak again, and I suspected it was because he was sick of hearing my noises.

"You're in love with Jas."

"*Excuse* me?" I demanded through my tears, my gaze darting to his face where I found another grin. "I most *certainly* am *not*."

"Don't worry," he said slowly, in obvious amusement. "I won't tell your father." He paused to chuckle. "Though it *is* quite likely he's figured it out in your absence, if he hasn't already. Roger might be an asshole, but you know he's right. It's *all* in the eyes. It just depends on how hard you have to make people look. Just remember, Aster . . . we'll always be looking."

And I was so angry.

So much so that I removed my knife from the strap on my arm. I hardly noticed the Reaper standing and rushing over toward me, and I didn't care at all about what he thought I was doing. I grabbed my hair tightly and began sawing it off above my hand.

The Reaper stopped moving, and I ignored his presence entirely.

I expected to feel better when I stood, holding all my detached hair in my hand, but . . . I did not. I couldn't feel better because what I'd done did not change anything.

I almost threw the contents of my hand onto the ground, but then I discovered a *much* better use for it.

I stomped back through the trees the way I'd come, and when I found my father speaking with the lot of bloodied people, I ignored them all.

I found Jastin and threw every bit of my hair at his face.

And then . . . I walked away.

CHAPTER TWENTY-FIVE

BLINDNESS

"HAS EVERYONE LOST their goddamned *minds*?" My father's voice rang out, both disbelieving and appalled, once I'd turned my back on them all. He then shouted my name several times before he grabbed hold of my arm and jerked me to a halt.

I pulled my arm away from him and stared up into his face.

"What happened to your hair?" he asked.

"I cut it off," I told him with a smile I realized was not a smile; it was a *smirk*. I was almost entirely certain I had never made such an expression before in all my life, at least not to such a degree. "Clearly, as it was in my own hand when I returned."

His eyes were wide as he stared down at me. "*Why*?"

I shrugged. "It seemed like a good idea at the time."

He put his hands over his face, and it appeared as though he wanted to rip his own skin off.

I understood the feeling.

Though it was likely forced, his voice sounded calm when he said, "And do you want to explain to me why you just stormed up and threw your hair at someone?"

"It seemed like a good idea at the time." I repeated myself, that time without the expression.

He took a deep breath and it came out as a giant huff. "I'll tell you what. . . ." He nodded. "I'm going to walk away and let you all work whatever the *hell* is going on out for yourselves."

I smiled and began walking away in the initial direction I'd intended, which was away from them.

"Ahren, grab your sister," I heard at my back.

I turned for an instant and smirked at Ahren's bloodied face. Then, I kept walking away. It was not twenty seconds before my brother had me thrown over his shoulder like that poor, dead deer had been on Jastin.

"Let me *down*!" I shouted as I pounded my fists against his back.

I flailed, but he did not release his hold on me until he'd dropped me in front of everyone else. And I felt so utterly humiliated by it that, as soon as he put me down, I punched him in the face without a single thought as to what I was actually doing until after it was already done.

He said several angry words before wiping his mouth across his arm, which left a satisfyingly red streak. "Do you feel *better*?"

I smiled at him, and he spit red out onto the bright, green grass.

"Would it make you feel better to hit us all?" he asked in the same, harsh tone.

I would not tell him that it appeared as though they all felt better from punching one another. I simply stood there smiling at him.

"Why is it that she always hits *me*?"

I did not care to look and see who he'd asked the question to.

Jastin said, "Because you're her brother."

The sound of his voice made my blood feel like it was boiling in my veins, and for the briefest instant it felt as though I'd lost all control of myself.

I focused on Jastin. "*You* shut your mouth. I don't want to hear *you* speak *at all*."

He looked away when my eyes met his. I ignored the split in his lip, and I did not wonder which of the boys had done it to him. He began plucking my hair off his slightly torn shirt and dropping it onto the ground.

"Aster—" Chase started which made me round on him.

"*Oh*." I interrupted him with a laugh. "Do you deem me *worthy* of conversation now? Only *after* you've behaved like an imbecile?" I gestured to his face, where he had a split above his eye. "Does that mean you and I are finally equal? Should we strike a deal with one another to pretend this never happened?"

"What is this *deal* everyone keeps going on about?" Jastin asked in exasperation.

"Aster believes you and I made a deal for you to leave her alone," Chase said, then looked at me. "Isn't that right?"

"Ah," Jastin said behind me. "So glad to finally understand now why I got punched in the face. Too bad it *doesn't* explain why I have ten pounds of hair stuck to me."

"You know *damn well* why you do!" I shouted at him.

He leisurely continued plucking it off him and dropping it onto the ground near his feet. The only acknowledgement I saw that he'd even heard me speak was a small, seemingly satisfied smile on his face.

Chase said, "This is *exactly* why I told him to leave you alone."

I turned around and glared at him again.

"There was no deal." Chase shook his head. "I told him to leave you alone because he's incapable of caring about any living person besides himself and your brother. I told him to leave you alone before he hurt you." He looked behind me and asked, "And what was it you said to me, Jas?"

"I said . . ." Though Jastin was not laughing, the amusement was undeniably clear in his voice. "*No.*"

I forced a smile at Chase. "Clearly he changed his mind."

It wasn't until Jastin stepped past me and went to stand in front of Chase that I realized something very . . . *strange.*

Jastin never faced me with his right side. Every time we'd ridden next to one another, I'd always been on his left. He did everything with his left hand. I had never looked at his right arm when I'd not been torturing myself inside my own head, but he distinctly turned that side of his body toward me now and I saw it.

Countless scars, no more than an inch long, running the entire length of his arm. They were too perfect, too neat and organized not to have been placed there purposely.

"I'm curious . . ." Jastin began quietly while my breath caught in my throat. "Now that all you have to do is find a way to get her father's permission to be with her . . . what happens next? Will you get married and have little babies together?" He was clearly taunting. "Maybe he'll even let you *keep* them. What would it be like not to have little Reaper children, I wonder. What would it be like to have a family?" He tilted his head and continued on with it. "Or will you still try to run with her? Get her pregnant and then get yourself killed? Leave *her* to fight with a child? It's what would happen, isn't it?"

Jastin laughed on a breath as he stared down at Chase. I'd never noticed that he was slightly taller.

So irrelevant.

Perspective.

"I'm just curious what it feels like to get what you want," Jastin said with a smile. His speaking was so slow when he continued. "And to be too *blind* to see what's in front of your face."

I wondered, for an instant, if Chase was going to attack him. It appeared as though he were seriously contemplating it.

But then he glanced at me and clenched his jaw, and I knew that he would not.

Jastin turned to me when Chase did and saw where my eyes were. I couldn't help going back to it.

"Oh, are you finally looking at my arm?" Jastin's question brought my gaze to his face, and I found him grinning widely at me. "Would you like to see the rest?"

He did not give me a chance to respond. He pulled his shirt over his head, holding it in his left hand. He held his right arm out in a dramatic sort of way, twisting it around and then lifting it.

The scars did not stop on his arm, because he'd run out of space on it.

They ran down his entire right side.

It was . . . a *tally*.

A tally of all the people he'd killed so he could not ever forget.

Jastin pointed a finger at me and—still with the grin—said, "*Blind*."

I didn't . . .

"She's never even looked at me, you idiot," Jastin said as he turned back to Chase, now without the grin. "Can you see that now? Look at her face." Chase did not look at my face, which made Jastin shake his head. "Stop being an asshole to her. She deserves better and *every bit* of this could've been avoided."

"And you think *you* would know what she deserves?" Chase laughed. "You don't know her at all."

"*No?*" Jastin leaned down in Chase's face and spoke through his teeth. "Why do you *think* I changed my mind?" He smiled hugely before whispering a question I almost didn't hear. "How does it feel to be wrong?"

Jastin laughed and stepped back. He did not replace his shirt, instead walking into the trees with it still balled up in his hand.

I did not know if he'd changed his mind simply to prove Chase wrong, because his words just now had been true . . . or if he had only done it because he was a coward. I didn't know, but I was certain it was one of those reasons. Were they all accurate, or was I completely wrong?

"Who's going to watch my back?" I heard myself say on a breath as I stared at the space he'd disappeared from. I'd not meant for it to be acknowledged. I'd not even meant to say it aloud.

"What?" Chase asked. All the hostility seemed to be gone from him now. I was also unsure why that was, but I found . . . I didn't care.

When I looked at his face, I saw that his brow was furrowed in confusion.

Chase said, "We all have your back. You know that."

"None of you trust me with yours," I said quietly. I attempted to force a smile onto my face, but it was far too painful and I gave up in trying after a few seconds. "And now I've lost the one person who did."

I walked away, but for a small amount of time I could hear the conversation I was leaving behind me.

"That's what this is about?" Chase asked.

"That's what this has been about the entire time," my brother told him.

I WENT AND SAT DOWN BY THE FIRE between Anders and my father. It felt both right and wrong at once, for a number of reasons. I wiped away the silent tears fighting to make their way down my face as they were falling.

"Everything sorted?" my father asked.

"Yes, everything is quite all right," I lied.

"Aster," I heard quietly behind me.

I closed my eyes tightly.

No peace.

"Amber," my father said. "I don't believe now is—"

Perhaps I could find no peace because I refused to make any.

"It's fine," I said as I stood up. Truly, this day could not get any worse than it already had, not with everything as it was. Perhaps if I spoke to Amber and allowed her to say whatever it was that she needed to say, she would leave me alone and a small bit of peace could be found.

I ignored her stunned face as I walked away to a suitable distance and waited for her to catch up.

"I suppose I should thank you, shouldn't I?" I asked her quickly once she had. "For standing up for me earlier."

She pursed her lips together and said nothing.

I released a frustrated breath that sounded somewhat similar to a sigh while I waited for her to speak. It took her far too long.

"For a long time, I couldn't figure out why you hated me," she carefully began. "Even after they told me you knew your father was alive . . . I couldn't figure it out. Not until I tried to speak to you before and saw how angry you got when I mentioned him." She frowned. "You feel like I stole your life, don't you?"

"I will admit that's likely part of it," I told her. "But no."

"So it was about our talks, then? Because you wouldn't speak to me again after you found out."

I said nothing to that.

She looked away, nodding her head. "I wrote him a letter after the first time you and I spoke. I told him you were thoughtful, and kind, and caring." She finally brought her eyes back to mine. "I never told him *anything* you said to me."

"No?" I asked, only believing parts of it.

"I *didn't*," she said firmly. "All the things I asked you . . . I asked because *I* wanted to know." She shook her head, appearing distracted, and it took her a while to continue on. "I won't apologize for loving your father, but I *am* sorry it upsets you. Do you know how often he spoke of you?"

I did not respond in any way. I just stood there staring blankly at her.

"*All the time*," she said. "Most my life I heard about you, and then I finally met you and you were so much more than I could've anticipated. Because your father didn't know you anymore to tell me what sort of person you'd turned into in his absence." She sniffled a little and wiped at her eyes. Then she looked over her shoulder, I presumed to make sure no one had seen. "I understand that you hate everyone right now. In a lot of ways I can't blame you for that, but . . . I don't want you to hate me."

"Was it through you how Agatha got message to my father?" I asked her, remaining composed.

"*What?*" She shook her head in shock.

"She didn't tell you?" I asked when I could see that my suspicion toward how it happened had actually been . . . *wrong*.

"No, I—" she started and then stopped. "My god. No wonder you . . ."

I shouldn't have reacted the way I had over any of this. I thought of what Chandler had said before about being emotionally involved, and . . . he was right. I'd been so caught up in it all, trying to make sense of everything and find something substantial.

How could you find *anything* when *everything* was clouded?

"I suspect I shall forgive her for it someday." I forced a smile onto my face. "She is like a mother to me, after all."

"Maybe something good will come of it that you can't see yet," Amber said thoughtfully.

"Perhaps." I chuckled, though there was no humor in it. "But it has been nothing more or less than horrible so far."

"It's not horrible to have more people you can trust." Her voice was quiet, like trust was a secret. "You met Jas."

The smile on my face was very tight when I informed her, "That is exactly what I meant by horrible."

CHAPTER TWENTY-SIX

COWARDS AND LIARS

URING THE PROCESS, I was still unsure as to how *exactly* Amber convinced me to let her cut my hair properly. Perhaps it was because I felt guilty over the way I'd treated her, knowing now it had not been completely deserved. Perhaps I allowed it because I was sad, and lonely, and confused, and I was so very angry at myself for a great many things. There were several other options I contemplated, but perhaps it was nothing more than the embarrassment of being informed that my hair was now entirely lopsided on my head.

Though the appearance of my hair mattered very little to me, I was quite pleased that the product of my action could possibly be remedied, at least in a sense. I felt foolish, but I couldn't say I regretted it despite knowing what people might possibly say about my mental state.

What might be *thought* of my mental state, said or otherwise. It wasn't as if I could walk out and it be believed that I'd simply made a rational decision to cut my hair.

I *could* make a rational decision to *fix* my hair.

Amber and I did not speak again for a long time, but when I saw her smiling in a way that was unmistakably *content*, I couldn't help trying to discover why the expression was on her face.

"Do you enjoy . . . cutting hair?" It was such a strange thing to enjoy doing, I thought.

"Oh yes," she said. "Some of the other Reapers let me do it for them, but most don't care about it. Reaper women . . . Well, a lot of us aren't very pleasant."

"So I've heard." I pursed my lips for a moment. "What does that even mean?"

"They're pretty heartless," she said. "I don't know if it's because we're always trying to prove we can do the same things as the men—better even, with some things. Or maybe we're just built that way. A lot of the women shave their heads like the men and wear wigs when they go on missions that call for . . ." She did not say anything more.

When I realized she had no intention whatsoever to elaborate, I asked, "Do you not want to be a Reaper?"

Her face drooped a little. "It doesn't really matter what I want. There are rules. Even if your father allowed me to do something different, I still . . ." She stopped speaking again and the smile she'd somehow managed to hold, even through the drooping, tightened where it sat.

"Still what?" I asked curiously.

"Your father and Anders changed a lot of our rules." She was examining my hair as she spoke. "They've made a lot of changes with everything. I know because they make sure we're aware of how different things are in our cities, compared to others." She paused to cut a bit more of it. "But we still have rules about children."

"They still take children?"

"It's not as simple as that, no." She forced her smile wider, but she wouldn't meet my eyes. "I really don't want to talk about it."

I would not remind her how many times I had answered questions for her that I'd not really wanted to. I simply told myself I would discover the answers about the rules from someone it did not upset to such a degree. I sat in silence after that point until Amber stepped several feet in front of me and smiled hugely.

"I like it better this way," she said in a thoughtful tone.

I chuckled a little to myself, thinking she only liked it better because she'd assisted in it, but then she ran off toward the carriage. When she returned, she had a small mirror in her hand.

I looked at my reflection and found my green eyes blinking at me. My hair had always been long and bothersome, but it was hanging down no farther than my chin now. And seeing the way it framed my face, I said, "I'm inclined to agree. Thank you."

She sort of wiggled a bit where she stood, in what I thought was excitement. "You really like it?"

"Very much," I told her honestly with a smile. I would not tell her I liked it because it made me look like an entirely different person, as if I were no longer myself. "You're quite exceptional at that, if it was as horrible as I'm assuming it was before you got ahold of it. I might just ask you to keep it this way for me, if you wouldn't mind."

"Oh, of course I wouldn't! Just let me know any time you want it done."

I stood and began to walk away, but I stopped when she spoke again.

"Aster." Her nose was scrunched when I looked over my shoulder at her. "You *probably* shouldn't try to do it yourself again."

I laughed. "You're probably right about that."

I stopped laughing because she stepped closer and asked, "Why did you do it? Don't get me wrong, I like it better this way, but . . . your hair was so beautiful."

"I did it because Jastin asked me not to."

"Is that why you threw it at him?" she whispered.

I forced a smile at her and responded with, "It's all close enough."

I SAT DOWN NEAR THE FIRE and ignored the sight of the sun beginning to set in the sky, because I could not bear to look at it. When I realized I was unable to ignore it properly, I turned away from it, putting my back to the fire and staring into the trees.

I had only been in my new position for a minute or so when one of my father's Reapers sat down beside me. It was not Roger or the one who had accused me of . . . the thing I did not want to think about. He'd never spoken to me before, and his first words to me were . . .

"I would think a pretty flower would enjoy a pretty sunset."

I blinked at the ground for a moment before taking a deep breath and looking at him. "What did you just say to me?"

He shrugged. "Just a thought."

I nodded my head and, while doing so, searched for my father. When I was certain he was nowhere near, I lunged at the Reaper.

I heard him laugh for a few seconds as he and I were rolling on the ground with one another, but he must not have realized that I'd been fighting with Chandler who was nearly twice his mass. It took me a moment to get accustomed to the weight difference and act accordingly, long enough for me to get hit in the face more than once.

In the end, I was not entirely certain how I managed to get him pinned down, nor was I certain how many times I hit him in his face before I was pulled off him.

He stood up as though he were not the slightest bit fazed or angry and smiled at me. His teeth were red.

"You're better than I would've thought," he said in a way that was unmistakably and confoundingly appreciative. So it had been a setup? "Too much *feeling* for my taste, but I'm sure we can blame part of that on the day. Or perhaps not. One can only work with what they've got, and you've not had near enough time. Still . . . *surprising*. Just got to work on that temper of yours."

I spit blood from my mouth onto his shirt and smiled, which he did not care about at all.

He looked behind my back and asked, "How long did you say you had with her? Just a month?"

There was a slight pause in his speaking while anger built up inside me.

"I think you're right, but if she can't figure out how to control herself, it won't make a damn bit of difference. You can't do anything for that."

I shrugged off the person restraining me, which I knew now to be Chandler, and I rounded on him.

I was able to spout off several of his angry words before he calmly said, "You wanted to be treated like an equal. Didn't you?" He then shook his head and looked away from me. "Congratulations in taking the first step."

I stormed off, spitting blood out of my mouth onto the ground periodically while I waited for the bleeding to stop. I did not know exactly where I was going as I walked, only that I needed to get there. *Somewhere*, wherever that was. The damn hair that had been cut was sticking to my skin and itching horrendously, and part of me wondered how or why such a small thing could make all the larger things seem so much worse. It made no sense.

Nothing seemed to make much sense.

Amber caught up to me after several minutes spent wandering while spitting blood and grumbling numerous unknown obscenities under my breath. I even found myself frustrated, for the first time, over using those words without really knowing what they meant.

"Where are you going?" she asked.

"I don't know," I answered cluelessly. "I just need to move. And I need to get this damned hair off me."

"And wash the blood off your face," she offered apologetically.

"And that," I said under my breath. "If I could just find . . ."

"Find what?" She began trudging forward alongside me rather than just a bit behind.

"That water Jastin brought me to earlier," I grumbled.

"Oh, I know where it is!" she exclaimed happily. "That big lake? Your father showed it to Agatha and me this morning so we could clean ourselves properly. Do you want me to take you there?"

I wanted to say no, but instead I said, "Yes, I suspect it would be a good idea." I did not want to explain to her why I didn't want to go back there. It would be far too difficult and embarrassing, and I didn't even know if I could actually explain it properly if I tried. But I *wouldn't* try, and that was the point.

"We're already going in the right direction." Her tone made it sound as though everything in the world was nothing short of *delightful*. "It's good I'm exceptional at remembering things. I'll be able to find our way back to camp, even if it gets dark."

"I should hope so," I said. I wanted to be frustrated at her excitability, but I found myself grinning a little over it instead. It was a surprisingly nice change, given how unpleasant the entire day had been.

I WOULD'VE BEEN QUITE ASHAMED to admit aloud that I tuned Amber out as we were walking together to a place I desperately wished not to return to, but I had. No matter how nice . . .

It was *a lot*.

"And *then* he sai—"

It was the fact that she'd stopped moving and speaking at once that pulled me out of my own head.

I would've been *more* than quite ashamed to admit that I didn't have a clue who *he* was when I asked, "And then he said what?"

But she was not looking at me.

She was staring off at something in the distance. I followed her line of sight and found . . .

Jastin in the water.

I had only enough time to catch him blinking at me as if he were confused before I averted my vision. I was almost entirely certain he had no clothing on whatsoever.

Of course he's not clothed, you moron, some bit of logic broke through and said. *People don't bathe while wearing clothing, and that's clearly what he's doing.*

I hurriedly began walking away, and I ignored the splashing sounds behind me as I went. Amber had come along with me, but when the splashing stopped, so did she yet again. I glanced at her for an instant and then did a double take when I realized she was staring back in the direction we'd come from with her head tilted.

"*Amber,*" I said in disbelief.

"What?" A sheepish grin took over her face.

"Come along," I urged as I tugged on her arm.

But she was not coming with me, as she stood there grinning like a complete and utter moron. I didn't know that she *could* move.

I made a frustrated sound and began walking on my own.

And I kept walking when I heard Jastin say, "Aster." He attempted to get me to stop moving several times in that very way and none of them worked until he grabbed hold of my hand.

I closed my eyes and took a deep breath. When I opened them and found him in front of me, I saw that he was partially clothed. He had thrown trousers on at least, but that was all. He did not release my hand.

I was torn. It was such a small tearing, only enough to keep me standing still as I analyzed both sides. The larger side wanted me to jerk my hand away and scream at him, just scream in general until he left me alone. But the smaller part was a whisper through all the screaming.

Please let go.

Why was I standing still, letting him touch my hand?

Because there was more.

His voice was quiet when he asked, "Who have you been fighting?"

I wanted to scream at him, so I could not explain why I just as quietly said, "It's nothing. Chandler set me up, trying to make everyone look at me like . . ." I forced a tight smile when I could not force myself to continue.

"Like I do?" he barely said.

I forced another smile at him as I took in a deep breath through my nose. "But I never had to fight someone for you to look at me that way."

Push it down, I told myself.

"Only kill someone." *Too light.* The way he'd said it, paired with his scrunched face, it was . . . too light for so heavy a statement.

I looked down at the ground. "Only that." I felt my eyes beginning to water so I asked, "May I go, please?"

"Aster."

The lightness had dropped away from his voice, and I found myself staring up at him in defiance.

"I changed my mind because it's the best thing for you."

"It's the best thing for you to take away the one person who has *any* sort of faith in me?" I asked him, desperation overriding the defiance. I shook my head and wiped at my eyes with my free hand. Only when doing that did I realize I'd split my knuckles open on the Reaper's face.

I was quite accustomed to bloody knuckles now.

Jastin dropped my hand and grabbed the other, analyzing it. I ignored what he was doing entirely, or I tried very hard to.

I said, "If you're truly using that to explain what you've done, then there are only two options." I would get some sort of productivity from this interaction if he would not allow me to go and would not go himself. "Either Chase is right and you simply cannot care about another living person, or you're a coward."

"Is that what you think?" he asked quietly, his brow furrowing. He did not drop my hand, even when I said nothing in response. "Tell me you don't feel something you shouldn't for me."

"I don't." And my lie wiped every bit of caring from his face.

He tilted his head and grinned at me. "No?"

I shook my head and was in the air with my back pinned against a tree before my mind registered what was happening.

His face was so close to mine when he said, "Your brother told me he was worried Chase was going to ruin you. Chase doesn't have it in him to ruin a person because he'd rather not waste his time with it. *Kill* them? *Sure.*" He shrugged as if it were no large thing and then leaned forward until his mouth was almost against mine. "I *will* ruin you, if you're stupid enough to let me."

I ignored my nose twitching in anger. "You're afraid," I accused.

"You think I'm *afraid* of you?" He sounded so amused. He pressed his body against mine which made me go rigid. "Afraid of being close to you?" His hand squeezed my waist. "Afraid of touching you?" He laughed and said, "I can assure you . . . I'm *not.*"

I smiled when I realized I was correct. He was afraid of something, though it had not been one of the things he'd mentioned.

Jastin was afraid of being in love.

"*Coward*," I said through my teeth.

He smiled, and then . . .

He kissed me.

I'd not anticipated it. I'd not thought he would ever do it. But I would never have thought my body would respond to it if it happened, no matter how I felt about him.

It was brief, only long enough for me to realize he was *extremely* skilled at it and that I was breathing heavily.

He barely pulled his face away, and he was smiling when one word fell off his lips, landing on mine. "*Liar.*"

CHAPTER TWENTY-SEVEN

OPENING EYES

"OW THAT WE UNDERSTAND our predicament . . ." Jastin's voice was bafflingly . . . *happy* as he dropped my feet back onto the ground as though nothing at all had happened. "Let's accept it and move past it."

Something *had* happened, and my head was uncooperative because of it. He'd *kissed* me.

It took me a long time and several attempts to get the word, "What?" to come out of my mouth.

"You and I both have feelings for one another that neither of us want to have." He shrugged. "We need to get past that and proceed forward accordingly."

"I . . ." I started and then stopped. "I don't understand."

"Let me explain this simply to you," he began with an exaggerated sigh. "We met and grew close." He put his hands together dramatically. "Lines became blurred due to the circumstances, and that creates . . ." He rubbed his two hands together and smiled. "*Friction.*"

I narrowed my eyes at him, but he did not seem to mind.

"We've kissed now. And I've realized you're *clearly* too inexperienced to handle me, which is . . ." His face scrunched a bit. "Well, it's very off-putting to be totally honest." He smirked, which very much made me want to punch him in the face as well. My knuckles were already split and bloody anyhow. The damage was already done. What would a little more hurt? "Now we set clear lines and we don't step over them again."

I would not tell him I *very well* knew he liked kissing me, despite what he'd just said, as I believed it would be counterproductive to what he was currently proposing.

I wanted to hear him out, so I ensured my voice was blank to ask, "What are the lines?"

"Whatever little lovey feelings we have for each other need to be squashed." He shrugged again. "I'll do what I can to assist you with that, though I'm sure you can't return the favor properly. I'm much more skilled at breaking things than you are. I suspect they'll start to surface again, likely repeatedly, so we'll do what we can for the other person to ensure they aren't bothered by them. We don't speak about it, not to one another or anyone else. We ignore it and we *pretend* it isn't there at all. Then one day, we'll wake up and it won't be."

"Is that what you think?" I shook my head. "That problems simply . . . *go away*?"

"Oh, good girl," he said in relief as he patted my face. "I'm so glad to know you look at our predicament as a problem, too." He took in a deep breath. "As for your question? I'm sure they will. You'll wake up one day pregnant with Chase's baby, and you'll look over at him and realize how *stupid* you were to feel anything for me."

What a horrible prospect. "And what about your end?"

"I can assure you I already feel stupid." He laughed. "But I'm able to twist and distort my feelings for you. You're my best friend's sister and my leader's daughter. It's only natural for me to want to look out for you, isn't it? It just so happens that we have a *wonderful, trust-filled relationship* with one another, which makes my job *so* much easier to do." He stopped laughing and frowned at me. His voice was not faking excitement when he said, "So I'm going to tell you what this is." He gestured at the space between the two of us. "You and I are friends. I don't have many friends. Your brother is the only one, actually. . . . So I will protect you, and I will trust you. I will do those things because I care about you and also because it's my job. This is *nothing* else."

"Good," I said to the ground. That was all I wanted from him. My voice was very quiet again when I spoke next. "Will you still let me sleep close to you?"

"Of course," he said nonchalantly. "I don't care if you want me around all the time, as long as we're clear on things."

"Don't worry." I barely said the words, and I forced a smile at him. "We're clear as glass."

"Besides." He forced out a small laugh. "I couldn't just leave you alone with all those morons. I mean, I love your brother, but even *he's* an idiot with you."

I spent a moment thinking about it all and realized I currently had no hopes of getting anywhere with it. "So, what do we do now?"

"You're going to do what you set out here to do and let me go back to deal with the barrage of shit from Chase," he replied. "And then, when you get back, you're going to fix things with him."

"But—"

"*Please.*" There was almost desperation in the word when it came out of his mouth.

I took a deep breath and nodded.

"Don't worry," he said. "I'll inform him that he's going to have to learn how to tolerate me. I don't plan on going anywhere."

"No?"

He shook his head.

"What about . . ." I didn't want to ask, but . . . "when we get where we're going?"

He looked away, and the nonchalance had returned when he said, "I haven't made up my mind yet."

"Yes, you have," I whispered.

He grinned and put one of his fingers over my mouth, clearly telling me to be quiet. Hadn't we agreed never to speak of it? I was already failing, and we were still in the very same conversation. How was I supposed to manage this if I couldn't get through the same conversation? How was I supposed to manage it if I couldn't even walk away when I knew I should?

How much trouble was this going to cause?

His hand lingered by my mouth, and he spent a moment trailing his thumb over my bottom lip before taking a deep breath and leaning down to kiss me briefly on the forehead.

I closed my eyes and heard myself ask, "Are we always going to lie to everyone, to each other?"

"It's easier, isn't it?" he asked curiously.

There was a sad smile on his face when I opened my eyes. I realized that I now completely understood what he meant when he'd said that to me before, but then the smile dropped off his face.

He wiped away a tear that had accidentally fallen down my own. "I don't ever want to see you cry over me again. You know I'll have to make you regret it if I do. That will have to be part of our arrangement. If you do it . . . don't let me see it."

No trouble. I already had too much of it. I would not let this cause more.

"And what if I'm crying for some other reason?" I asked impassively. "Or crying simply to cry?"

"I'll always be there." It shouldn't have been so easy for him to say. It shouldn't have sounded so . . . *believable.*

"How can you say that?" I demanded. Trust or not, I hardly thought *always* was—

"Because I love you." He said it as if I should've known. "Remember that because . . ." He shook his head and took a deep breath. "You won't ever hear it from me again."

I opened my mouth.

He quickly covered it with his hand and said, "*Don't.* I don't want that in my head."

I closed my eyes and nodded. I would not tell him that I hadn't almost said it back to him. I would not tell him I'd been going to say something similar to not wanting his words inside my head, either.

He brought his lips to mine when he removed his hand and, before I allowed myself to get lost in it like I wanted to, I pushed against his chest and forced myself to laugh. Both his hands went on my arms.

"Stop kissing me," I told him.

"Well we *could* . . ." He trailed off.

"Go away." I laughed again, but I heard another whisper in my head.

Please let go.

He smiled at me, but I saw it fall away from his face before he'd released my arms and turned all the way around. And as soon as he *had* turned completely, my own smile fell off mine.

I watched him walk away, and he did not look back at me.

"Is that love?" Amber asked quietly from behind me a minute or so later.

I hastily wiped at my eyes before I faced her. "No." I forced a tight smile at her. "I don't know what that is, but . . . it's not love."

I was embarrassed that I'd forgotten both her presence entirely and her tendency to eavesdrop on other people's personal matters.

I tried to conceal my wariness when I asked, "How much did you overhear?"

If not for my current state, I was sure I could've been more successful.

"I wasn't listening, but . . ." she said then stopped. "I . . . *saw* most of it."

I put my hands over my face, which made me realize it was rather tender from being punched.

How was I supposed to pretend that interaction with Jastin had never happened when someone had *seen* it? Was seeing it worse than hearing it? Seeing and hearing were worse than knowing what was felt.

"Are you going to tell Chase?" she asked.

"No," I said through my hands. Then I dropped them and looked at her.

Her face scrunched up in confusion. "Aren't you going to keep seeing Jas?"

"Not how you think." I shook my head. "He and I came to an agreement about the boundaries in our relationship. We're friends and absolutely nothing more."

"But . . ." she started and then stopped again. "He *kissed* you." How could she make it sound so simple? There was always so much more to things, wasn't there?

I heard myself sniffle as I wiped at my stupid eyes. "It won't ever happen again." I couldn't think about it right now. "Are *you* going to tell anyone?"

She shook her head slowly and then looked away. "You *do* love him," she whispered. "Don't you?"

"I'm very glad to say I most certainly do not." I almost could not hold myself together any longer. "If you'll excuse me, I need to get myself cleaned off. If you'll just wait for me here . . . I won't be gone long."

I did not wait for any form of response; I simply walked away, back toward the water. I removed all my clothing and stepped into it, but all I could do was cry.

I DID NOT ALLOW MYSELF THE PROPER TIME to deal with my feelings, as I did not believe they were feelings that could truly be dealt with. I was discovering there were a great many things that could not be dealt with, at least not in the ways I knew how to. Some things were not easy to push down and some things refused to be pushed at all.

Perhaps all the recent events had me overloaded and I would begin to find some purpose to it eventually. Perhaps when I could catch a full breath.

Knowing that time of clarity or relief was not now, I cleaned myself off once I was able to manage it. I was no longer itchy when I stepped out and put a different set of clothing on, which was somewhat relieving.

It was something positive, and I would not complain about a positive, no matter how small.

There was a soft thud as a wrapping of large, waxy leaves fell out of my bag and hit the ground as I was picking it up. Rather than replacing it, I took it in my hand and walked back to where I'd left Amber. She was still there.

"Have you ever had honey?" I asked her with a smile.

"Only once," she said. "Why?"

I unwrapped the honeycomb from the leaves and broke it in half.

"Where did you *get* that?" she exclaimed as I handed one half of it to her.

I had no intention whatsoever of answering her question.

I sat down on the ground and allowed myself a moment to stare at it—thinking there may very well not ever be a time where I *could* enjoy it as instructed, but now was certainly a time where I needed something enjoyable—before sticking it in my mouth.

I had forgotten the taste of it!

"So good," I said, then realized I was giggling in pure happiness. It was nice, for it to be genuine.

Amber did not ask me again where I'd gotten the honeycomb, I assumed because she was so distracted by the taste of it as well.

Bad experiences did not mean you should stop yourself from having good ones, that you should stop yourself from living. It did not take away the bad, but perhaps if you simply permitted yourself a moment to keep trudging forward with a relatively open mind, life would grant you a small happiness in exchange for all your trouble. Perhaps that was where I'd been going wrong.

Was it possible *good* didn't exist to be taken away by *bad*, but to . . . make up for it? Was *good* life's apology for it all—the trouble, the sadness, the pain? Did it exist to keep you moving when it felt you couldn't go on any longer? Was it not something you could have, just . . . be grateful for in the moment or two of it?

Rather than listen to the logic in my head, telling me *life* granted no favors and owed nothing to no one, I ignored it.

I pushed down everything telling me that if life granted any favors at all they would only go to people who were worthy of such, and I enjoyed the moment I'd been given.

The two of us sat there giggling on the ground together until we had expended every drop of honey from each half of the comb, and I enjoyed it. Once we were done, we went to the water to wash all traces of it from our hands.

"Don't tell anyone about that," I warned her, speaking now about the honey. I did not want it to raise questions that I didn't want to be asked.

She tossed her chunk of wax into the water and innocently asked, "Tell who what?" Her response was more than satisfactory, if it was genuine.

I suspected she caught me sneaking my own bit of wax back into my bag rather than tossing it away, but she didn't mention it. I was also relieved about that.

The two of us walked back to the camp holding hands with one another. That had been her doing, and I assumed she'd done it in an attempt to comfort me with physical closeness. It worked a little and I found myself somewhat glad for the events of the day because of it.

How strange.

I wondered if I would ever stop finding it so bizarre to enjoy physical contact of any sort. I had to assume I would, as I did enjoy it occasionally, depending on the person. I supposed my feelings on the matter had always been somewhat inaccurate. Perhaps it had less to do with the people involved and more to do with situations.

Perhaps sometimes it was the situation.

And sometimes it was the person.

I pondered over all that as Amber and I walked together, and when we reached our destination, I kept up my end of the bargain with Jastin.

I went over to Chase and sat down next to him. He narrowed his eyes at me as if he suspected I was going to punch him at a moment's notice, but I had no intention of doing so. I took a deep breath in preparation, forced a smile at him, and then I took his hand in mine.

"What are you doing?" He was wary, and rightfully so, but there was something else I couldn't quite place.

"Fixing things," I said. I wasn't certain what that meant, but he surely knew.

He looked away from me, and I followed his gaze to Jastin, who sat alone a good ways from the fire.

Jastin did not acknowledge me. He looked only at Chase, and all he did was point to his own eye and grin.

Open your eyes. I heard his shouting from when I'd followed them, only spoken calmly.

Then Jastin looked away and Chase and I looked at each other.

CHAPTER TWENTY-EIGHT

FIXING HAIR

THE HESITATION CHASE FELT was apparent when he said, "He told me you would."

He stared at me unblinkingly, and I realized what the thing I couldn't place was.

Suspicion.

"He told me that as soon as you came out of the trees, you would come over and try to fix things with me."

"Are you disappointed?" I asked him, curious. It almost seemed as if he were.

"Of course not," he replied. "Only wary."

I watched him for just an instant before he sucked in a breath and quickly asked his question.

"What did he say to make you do this?"

"He's not as awful as you believe him to be."

"Maybe not," Chase said, seeming to be careful in choosing his words. "But he's not as good as you believe him to be either." Chase couldn't know what was in my head, especially when it came to matters like this. He could only assume.

"We'll have to agree to disagree," I said, my voice successfully blank. "I'm quite certain I know the limits of his goodness, probably better than you."

"Is that so?" A small grin spread on his face. "You finally saw his scars today, didn't you? Do you know why he put them there?"

"Do *you*?"

He looked at the ground and chuckled under his breath quietly for a moment before looking up at me again, and I wondered what he was thinking. "You remember that talk we had before . . . when you told me you hoped I never forgot the things I've done?"

"Of course I remember," I answered, still remaining entirely calm.

"Let me guess. . . . You think he put them there so he wouldn't ever be able to forget what he'd done. Or maybe even because he wanted to scare people away when they saw how big of a *horrible monster* he is."

Chase waited expectantly for a response, though I suspected he very well knew I had no intention of giving him one.

"Both of those are right, but you are *so* wrong about the *why*. He *did it* because that's what he *is*. Why lie about it? I *do* have to commend him for that, given the city he's from." He paused for the briefest instant to smile. "And you're right—he doesn't want to forget, but not because he *feels bad*." He tilted his head the most minuscule amount and gestured to where Jastin had been sitting. "Go ask him if he does, if you're so sure you know him."

"And you believe this to be true, *why*?" I asked as I ignored his gesturing and his challenge. I didn't need to speak with Jastin. "Because it's the way he presents himself?"

Chase leaned a little closer and smiled at me before almost whispering, "Because your brother told me."

"So his best friend believes him to be a monster," I said under my breath, trying to process that and the way it made me feel. "That's so nice."

"Oh no, Ahren would never say that," Chase stated believably. "Think on this for a minute. Your brother has known Jas for a *very* long time. They go on their missions together, they travel together, they kill people together. If there's anyone in this world who knows him . . . it's Ahren." He paused for just an instant. "Would you like to go have a little discussion with your brother about your new best friend? I'm sure he could lay more than a few things to rest for you. Would you like to go have that discussion?"

I smiled. "No."

"You see, Aster," Chase said after releasing an almost satisfied-sounding breath. "When most people get to know you, they think your biggest flaw is that you trust too easily. You don't, do you?" He shook his head at me. "No. Your biggest flaw is that you want to see the good in everyone."

"And that's a flaw?" I asked curiously.

"With *us*?" I thought he wanted to laugh, but he didn't do it. "It most certainly is. You think that one tiny little piece of good mixed into a giant load of bad means a person is good at their core." He raised one of his eyebrows. "It *doesn't*. They're not a good person who does bad things. They're a bad person who does good things. You don't know how to tell the difference between the two."

"Is that so?" I asked as I felt the smile tugging harder at the corners of my mouth.

He nodded his head.

I laughed once beneath my breath. "Agatha told me once that it didn't matter what a person was to me. It mattered what they were to everyone else. That was when I told myself it was all right to love you. Because I realized that, even if Agatha was right . . ." I shook my head. "I didn't care. I didn't care how a person treated anyone else."

Perhaps that *was* a flaw in its way, but not the likes of the one he'd said. Perhaps this sort of thing was all to do with perspective.

I stared at him as he waited for me to make my point.

"I'm curious . . ." I went on, then paused. "If you and Agatha are both correct, which is what you seem to be telling me now . . .? What does that say about you?"

He recoiled as though I'd slapped him, and I found myself satisfied. I did not like him speaking to me that way, as if I were incapable of understanding what was right and what was not, as if he knew better than I did about everything. I did not believe he did.

"They were your own words, weren't they?" I asked. He should not have tossed them away in the way he had.

He stood up then and stared down at me in clear disbelief.

It did not faze me in the slightest.

I shrugged and said, "I tried."

At that, he shook his head and walked away.

I sat there for a short while staring at his back as it went away from me, and when he made his place by his brother, I looked over at Jastin.

I could barely see his eyes narrowed at me when I shrugged once more.

He'd seen that Chase had been the one to walk away from me.

I had done precisely what I'd agreed and intended to do, which was try. Chase had been the one to bring Jastin's name into it, and I'd done what any friend would naturally do. I had defended him.

Besides, I'd never agreed to the amount of effort I would expend on the cause. I wasn't certain what the cause fully was.

Content with that, I stood and walked over to the fire, making a place between Anders and my father.

I WAS VERY HAPPY as I ate the special meal my father had prepared for me, though I likely should not have been. I did not allow myself to think on the madness of the day, nor did I focus on my father as he was now. I thought of honey and of sitting with him eating the very same meal such an incredibly long time ago. It didn't quite taste the way I remembered, but it was very close and I wondered if it had something to do with ingredients.

Or time.

Life.

So I thought about the food while I ate it and simultaneously contemplated over the oddities of memories. I also thought about a few other things, which felt more pertinent than any relationships or bonds I had with people. Far larger than any nonsense with boys. I ensured none of it took away from the moment.

It's all right to smile, Flower. I see it there in your eyes. You love this, and you're happy. It's all right.

When I would look at my father as we ate around the fire, people talking amongst themselves, I would see him searching in my eyes for things he seemed unable to find.

I didn't know if it was him or me. It, in ways, was the most excruciating pain.

It was when I was halfway done with my bowl of stew that Anders laughed from out of nowhere beside me, drawing my attention.

"What is it?" I asked, finding myself wondering about his mental state.

He leaned a bit behind my back. "Can I tell her about the cat?"

I looked at my father to my right. He was shaking his head but laughing quietly as well.

I asked, "What . . . *cat*?"

Given that my father hadn't told him not to say anything, Anders began another of his stories.

"This one time, your mother accompanied me on one of my missions. It was supposed to be an easy thing—just stealing some documents. I decided to go in while they were sleeping so there was no fuss made and no bloodshed. They hadn't actually done anything, only had something we needed. I hadn't wanted to kill them if it wasn't necessary."

Wary, I said, "I don't know if I want to hear this story."

He ignored me and laughed a little again, continuing on. "So, she and I slip in through the window, and out of *nowhere* this cat comes into the room. Your mother was so jumpy that she threw a knife and killed the poor thing dead. Then she starts crying hysterically and wakes *every* person in the house. So I had to grab the cat, grab the documents, grab your mother, and haul the lot of them back out the window before anyone noticed."

I placed the bowl of stew on my lap. "That's not a nice story." It was not nice, nor funny, and I had suddenly lost a great deal of my appetite.

He held his right hand into the air, waving it a bit in what seemed to be an apologetic manner. "Your mother insisted she could *not* leave the family petless, so she and I spent the next several hours tearing up a hostile city in search of a stray cat. When she found one, she insisted she should be responsible for putting it in the house because it was her fault. The devil was feral and scratched her to pieces." He was still laughing heartily. "I told her they would know it wasn't the same cat. It wasn't even the same *color*, but she didn't care. She said she had to do the right thing."

"Is that another of your exaggerated stories?" I asked, curious. It had to be, given how ridiculous it was.

"Oh no," my father said. "Your mother told me that story herself once, but I must admit you just heard a very tame version of it. I accused her of allowing Anders' bad habits to rub off on her, so she showed me the scars to prove it." He shook his head and fought against a chuckle.

Rather than try to discover what had been left out and why my father and Anders both seemed to find it so amusing, I very slowly asked, "How would it be the right thing to put a feral cat inside a person's home that she'd assisted in stealing documents from?"

"I don't have a clue." Anders laughed, shaking his head. "Seemed like adding insult to the injury to me, but . . . it was how she was. Act first and deal with the consequences later." He seemed to think on that for a moment before clearly deciding he'd said it wrong. "Later, during, whenever they chose to come about."

"Very strange, you mean?" I asked.

My father laughed. "No stranger than hacking off your hair and throwing it at a person."

Unhappy, I looked back at my father. "Thank you so much for mentioning that."

He and Anders both laughed again, then Anders said, "I always tried to convince Elena to cut off her hair."

"Why?" I asked, puzzled. Ahren had been the one to inform me that boys liked hair. I'd seen the drawing of her and thought her hair looked quite nice, so I could not understand why he would've wanted her to cut it off.

I hadn't noticed that my father had stopped laughing until he said, "If you answer that question the way you likely want to answer it, we're going to have a problem."

I looked at my father in confusion, who was staring intently over my shoulder at Anders, then I turned my gaze on him.

He had his lips pursed together in unmistakable amusement before he looked at me and nonchalantly answered with, "No reason."

I was very confused because I couldn't fathom how talk of cutting hair could make a person angry. But seeing how angry my father so clearly was . . . I did not press the matter further.

The remainder of the evening passed by in a strained silence from everyone, even the other Reapers who had been talking amongst themselves before the exchange.

When most of them stood with their food in hand and walked far away from the fire to eat their meals elsewhere . . . I began to better understand my father's place.

Or perhaps how he'd found himself there.

I'D BEEN LYING ON THE GROUND for several hours—curled up beneath my blanket at the same distance from Jastin that I always laid now—when I heard a noise. I discreetly looked toward it and saw my father and Anders slipping off into the trees together. Thinking nothing of it, I closed my eyes and went back to sleep. But when I woke the next morning and looked at Anders, he had a blackened eye.

Subject of my mother's hair in relation to Anders wishing for her to cut it off seemed to be a very *sore* thing for my father, who was physically unharmed so far as I could tell.

I was inclined to agree with my father and believe everyone *had* lost their goddamned minds. Perhaps the sun could be blamed in part for that as well, or perhaps there was simply no hope for any of us either way.

CHAPTER TWENTY-NINE

WHAT FRIENDS DO

THOUGH I WAS QUITE TEMPTED to get Anders alone so I could figure out what in the world was going on and why my mother's hair was cause for such strife, I decided against it. I woke up and decided against dwelling in any way on past events. Dwelling on and moving forward from were two entirely different things. Dwelling on something without making use of it was as ignorant as learning and not applying the knowledge.

It was pointless and an utter waste of time. Realizing as much, I woke up feeling I needed to begin making changes.

I went to my father and smiled at him, as genuinely as I could manage. He did not return it, I suspected because he was wary that I would accuse him of blackening Anders' eye. I had no intention of doing so because I did not need to accuse him of it when I already knew he'd done it.

"That Reaper training clothing," I began. "Do you have any of it with you in my size?"

After a moment surely spent thinking on it, my father said, "We've remained here long enough already. We're leaving after breakfast. You can continue your training when we arrive at our city."

Your city, Father, I could've said and didn't. *Not ours. Not mine.*

"No, it's not that." I shook my head. "It's just so un*bearably* hot here. I'm not accustomed to this sort of weather or to being outdoors. I feel as though wearing my current clothing is comparable to being stuck inside a fireplace."

"Aster." He sighed. "It wouldn't be a good idea for us to travel with you wearing that." I realized then that my father had worn only long sleeves since setting out. How he could wear long sleeves in the heat . . .

Only he could've known. I suspected he very much disliked sunburns and for whatever reason felt it was a good exchange. I hadn't the vaguest clue as to how he could bear it, but I supposed what one person found unbearable might hardly faze the next.

"How many people have we seen in these weeks?" I asked, pushing down a sense of exasperation fighting to make its way to the surface. *None.* "I don't wish to wear the bottom, only the top. And also the boots because I prefer them to normal shoes."

He walked away toward the carriage without another word, and I followed him, hoping it was a silent invitation and not an end to the conversation. Shortly after stopping, he held in his hands both things I'd requested, but he did not extend them to me.

"You make a deal with me," he said. "I give you these and you promise to keep your normal shirt ready at all times. If we see *anyone*, you throw your shirt on over this. And you *never* wear this at night unless it is beneath something else."

"That sounds perfectly reasonable," I stated with a nod. Strange, yes, but incredibly reasonable. It would be a slight annoyance, but that was a fair exchange.

"Promise." He was so serious.

I said, "I promise."

Only then did he hand them over to me.

"How long until we eat breakfast?"

"Another half-hour or so."

I nodded and smiled genuinely before saying, "Thank you."

I shoved the shirt into my bag and then walked over to Jastin, who was sitting alone with his back against a tree. He'd been staring off, watching everyone and playing with one of his knives in his hands, but he looked at me when I came close and said, "I require your assistance."

He laughed. "You *what?*"

"Require your assistance." I repeated myself slowly, as if he were inept. He very well might have been, as I didn't believe being a Reaper meant one should play with knives, especially when not paying proper attention.

He was still laughing. "With what exactly?"

"I'm inclined to believe that my father is having his other Reapers take turns following me every time I wander off," I said. "I would like to go do things females need to do without worrying I'm being seen. As my only true friend, it is your responsibility to look out for me, isn't it?"

"What?" Jastin asked. "You believe he's having you followed when you go off to bathe? I'm *pretty* sure he wouldn't want his men seeing you naked. So what makes you think they're getting that close?"

"Something one of them said to me yesterday," I said. "I'm *quite* certain that what I've just told you is true. Will you please?"

"What are these . . . *female* things you need to do?" he asked warily. "Are you asking me to go with you to bathe or is it something else?

"It's nothing for you to be concerned about either way." I smiled. "You won't be looking. You'll be watching my back."

Walking off, I watched gazes. Hitting on me. Jastin. Chase.

My brother, even.

So many glances. So much attention, even if discreet.

I fought against my brow wanting to furrow, and I walked.

THAT WAS PRECISELY HOW I ENDED UP mostly naked, standing at Jastin's back.

"What did you say you were doing?" he asked, seeming distracted.

"Shaving," I replied. "And then possibly bathing again because this hot weather disgusts me."

He shook his head but was silent.

"Don't look at me," I warned him. "This shaver would work just as well as a knife." If not better than.

"Trust me," he said. "You don't need to threaten me with that."

I laughed silently to myself and sat down at the water's edge, putting my legs in. I hated shaving, but only because cutting myself with the long, thin blade was inevitable. My legs were riddled with extremely faint scars from the process. No matter how many times I did it or how often I used my hands in general, they refused to cooperate in such a way.

I'd been doing that for nearly five minutes when I heard Jastin backing up. "Do you have any clothes on at all right now?"

"Not much," I told the back of his head from over my shoulder. "Only my undergarments."

He turned around then, and I watched his gaze briefly touch on my back. In that small space of time, I somehow managed to remain entirely still. It seemed as though he hadn't noticed the scars covering it at all when he quietly said, "Get in the water."

I stood up with no objection whatsoever and walked out into the water, taking my bar of soap with me and leaving the shaver on a nearby rock. I kept walking until the water was just past my collarbone. When I looked back at where we'd been before, he was no longer there. I smiled contentedly as I worked on completing the second part of coming to the water.

Jastin had returned before I was entirely done cleaning myself.

He knelt at the edge of the water, washing redness from one of his hands. There wasn't a lot of it, but there was enough.

I walked back toward him with the smile still on my face. "Do you believe me now?"

He did not respond to me in any way as he checked his hand thoroughly for any lingering traces of redness.

I said, "I trust you only hit him."

"Maybe." He shrugged then stood.

I was unsuccessful at forcing the smile from my face when I saw his eyes trailing up my body in the process.

"Aren't you going to turn around?" Even pursing my lips together could not stop the corners of my mouth from doing what they wanted.

"Aren't you finished?" he asked.

I breathed out dramatically and shook my head. "No, not quite yet." I finally managed to force a frown to say, "Turn around, please."

He did as I'd requested, but he didn't move when I sat back down to finish my first task. I was nearly done by the time he spoke again.

"Is this what friends do?"

"Hmm?" I asked innocently.

"You heard what I said." Unhappiness was clearly distinguishable in his voice.

I *had* heard him.

"Oh, but isn't it for good cause?" I asked, sounding positively gleeful. "Now you know I'm being followed everywhere and you can stop people from seeing me naked when I don't wish for them to. What an amazingly wonderful friend you are."

"I'm trying to figure out why you're doing this," he said in a thoughtful tone.

"What do you mean?" I asked, returning to false innocence. "I've just told you what was going on. I'm quite sure that explains why."

"No," he said assuredly. "You're always thinking and planning. It's what you do. I've known that since I first saw you, and I'll admit I'm a bit concerned about what you might've come up with in your silence. I *do* know you're not ever this obvious. I just haven't figured out your real reason for this little . . . *activity* yet."

"*Activity*?" I stood and began digging around in my bag for the appropriate clothing. "My privacy has been violated. Yours as well, if you didn't figure that out during your . . . *discussion* with that man. I fail to see how this could be considered an *activity*."

"Oh, it's most certainly an activity to you."

I smiled behind his back as I slipped the tight-fitting Reaper shirt on.

"But yes, I gathered that if you're being followed, so am I when I'm with you." He paused. "Are you clothed now?"

"Yes, I am."

He nodded and pulled his shirt over his head, which I'd prepared myself for the possibility of.

My head did not sputter, though it still tried to despite my mental preparation. "What are you doing?"

"Expecting you to return the favor," he said blankly as he turned to me.

I took one of his hands in mine. "I would be *more* than happy to do anything for you that you would do for me." I smiled hugely. "That's what friends are supposed to do, isn't it?"

He returned the expression as he began figuring out why, exactly, I was doing this.

I did not mind if he did.

I dropped his hand when it went downward, taking mine with it.

He narrowed his eyes and said, "I suggest you turn around unless you want to see me naked. Believe me, I don't care if you do or don't, as long as you're watching my back."

I wanted to chuckle at the slightest emphasis he'd placed on the appropriate words, but I turned around instead. I'd barely just done so before he began removing the remainder of his clothing. Then, I sat down and ignored the sounds he made as I did what he expected of me. I listened for out of place sounds and watched for people.

I heard nothing apart from his movements and saw nothing at all. Only once was I tempted to turn, but I pushed that down, as it distracted me from my task.

He didn't take anywhere near as long in the water as I had, but I was not entirely surprised by that. I was quite pleased by it as well because it gave no time for the temptation to possibly return.

"You're good," he said at some point.

I stood and turned, finding him digging around in his bag for a different shirt.

Before he put it on, he tilted his head at me. "How did you convince your father to let you wear that?"

"I told him the truth." I shrugged. "That it was hot out and I don't like it."

He grinned. "Is that the truth?"

His eyes lingered for the briefest moment on my chest before I smiled and said, "Of course it's true." I kept my eyes on his.

He chuckled and finally slipped his shirt on over his head. "It may be true," he said, "but it's not the truth. I think I've been a bad influence on you, and that's worrisome."

"What ever could you *possibly* mean?" I asked him innocently. "Having your friendship in my life is *exactly* what I need."

He shook his head and chuckled a little more before beginning to walk back to the camp. I went with him.

"You know . . ." he started after two or so minutes of silence. "If you wanted to see whether or not I'd look at you, all you had to do was strip down in front of me. You didn't have to go through all this extra trouble."

"I wouldn't have told you to turn around if I wanted you to look at me, would I have?"

"No, you would have." He sounded so sure. "You wanted to see whether I'd look after you told me not to."

"That's preposterous." I laughed when saying as much, which made him shake his head. "I wanted you to come out here to prevent anyone from seeing me."

"See, that's what I'd actually expect from you," he said, the thoughtful tone returning. "Your brother told me how you used to be with men, so I would expect you to not want men to see you. But not with how you're acting right now. So, it stands to reason this is because of something I said to you. You're too tame to—"

He stopped speaking and moving suddenly.

When I stopped with him and looked up at his face, he was smiling hugely.

He nodded his head and said, "I've got it."

"Got *what*?"

He laughed. "If *that's* what you're doing . . . have fun trying to prove me wrong."

"I don't have a clue what you're going on about." I forced my voice to *sound* concerned when I added, "I must say I'm quite concerned about your mental state."

"That's fine." He kept nodding his head. "Keep on doing what you're doing. We'll see how good an idea it is. Or maybe I'll tell your brother you're being inappropriate with me."

"*Inappropriate*?" I pretended to be aghast at the prospect. "Surely I'm not making you uncomfortable, am I? I would *never* want to do that."

"That's it." He grabbed hold of me and tucked me under his arm easily. Then . . . he began walking. "I'm telling your brother you've had a mental break. We all should've known when you hacked your hair off. I'll inform him he needs to restrain you in the carriage for your own good."

It took me a few seconds to gain my bearings, given the world was sideways. When I did, I leaned my face forward and sank my teeth down into his abdomen—hard enough to latch on but not hard enough to really hurt him. Before I knew it, we were both on the ground and his abdomen was still attached to my face.

"Let go," he warned.

I shook my head minutely and did not do as he'd said.

"I'm giving you three—" He stopped mid-sentence when I bit down harder, and he began uttering off a rather impressive stream of profanities. Then his hands slipped up by my face and he pried my mouth off him.

When he had my mouth properly detached, he grabbed both my hands and put them on the ground above my head.

"What did I tell you?" He was trying to sound stern, but he could not get all the amusement to leave his voice.

"Given you'd picked me up, I took it as you asking for me to attack you," I stated. Then I scrunched my face up and whispered. "I'm curious . . . If this is what friends do . . . how many times have you been on top of my brother this way?"

He snorted and said, "Oh, we don't talk about that."

Then we were both laughing loudly until, all at once, he stopped and pulled me to my feet.

It was not ten seconds later that my brother stumbled upon us, his gaze slowly going back and forth between our faces. "What's so funny?"

"Your sister just bit me." Jastin pulled up his shirt to look at the damage.

I smiled in a satisfied sort of way when I saw red teeth marks in the shape of my mouth on his abdomen.

"Why would she do that?" Ahren asked carefully.

"Apparently that's what friends do," was Jastin's response, which caused me to snort and cover my face with my hand.

My brother shook his head and continued on his way to the water.

When I was sure he was properly out of earshot I said, "You like being friends with me."

Jastin laughed. "If this is what our friendship is going to be . . . you have no idea how much I'm going to enjoy it."

"Oh, isn't that wonderful?"

His laughing continued and I thought for a moment that there may be no end to it. "You have no idea how bad it can be for other people when I enjoy myself."

The thing Jastin didn't realize was that, for one of the first times in my life . . .

I was enjoying myself too.

We antagonized one another the remainder of the way back to the camp. I would push him and he would say angry words at me, but then he would playfully nudge me with his arm shortly thereafter.

There was something strangely—yet immensely—satisfying about the harmless bantering. I suspected it was due to the fact that I'd not touched many men in my life, and none of them in such a way. I'd touched Chase in loving ways. I'd touched several men when fighting with them. But I had never touched a man simply to enjoy touching them, to have . . . *fun*.

I'd never had someone want to touch me in such a way.

I wondered now if all the things I had and hadn't done in my life were not truly connected to me as a person. I wondered if I'd only ever done—or not done—things because it was required or expected of me. Had I ever really been free to be who I was?

No. I had never been free enough to even begin *discovering* who I was, or who I would naturally be without all the constraints. I wasn't sure of my potential. How could I be sure of anything when I didn't truly know who I was?

It was time to change that.

CHAPTER THIRTY

IRRESPONSIBLE MONSTERS

I KNEW HOW MY BODY LOOKED in the Reaper training clothes. I'd been stunned over it at the first sight of my reflection when wearing the tight-fitting black fabric. The horror I felt while staring at myself and realizing I'd turned into a woman at some point without my own knowledge or consent was still fresh enough. Fresh or not, I didn't believe I would ever forget it.

Becoming *a woman* had been a rather difficult thing to fully come to terms with, but somewhere along the way, I'd accepted it. I'd accepted that some things were beyond my control. And now I found myself past the acceptance and at some strange point where I was learning how to appreciate it.

I'd been staring straight ahead throughout the entire morning on my horse, but I caught Jastin glancing at me very briefly in my peripherals on several occasions. I kept my lips pursed so I wouldn't smile, but I was not entirely successful in my attempt despite my best—halfhearted—efforts.

We remained silent all morning, which didn't bother me in the slightest. Even when we stopped to eat lunch and stretch our legs, we didn't speak to one another past a very brief conversation as to my qualms with Agatha. He'd asked me the question, I'd answered, and that had been the end of it.

I supposed he must've understood, to have not pressed the matter further.

We'd remained close despite our lack of talking, and I was quite sure we both had our own agendas. After lunch, the riding resumed, and he remained decently close.

I did not ask him why he'd begun riding next to my left side now, rather than my right, though I was tempted to. I wondered if I was correct in my assumption on the matter, but I sincerely doubted he would be honest if I inquired. So, I kept my mouth shut and waited.

For a time, he kept his mouth shut as well and looked at me on occasion, but eventually he must've become fed up with my smiling in amusement at him while pretending to ignore him completely. At that point, he took off his shirt, which forced me to finally look at him directly.

I was only seeing what all the movement was about. That was all.

"It *is* hot, isn't it?" was the first thing he said.

"Indeed, it is." I responded to the redundant statement then grinned.

His action caused a good deal of attention for a while, as various companions periodically looked back at us to see if I was looking at him. At least I assumed that was the reason behind the attention, but I might've easily been wrong and one could never know for certain. I was proud to say I did not do so, if that were the cause of their concern.

At least . . . I did not do so until I noticed the glancing from everyone else stopping. Then I unfortunately could not help myself. And I also unfortunately could not manage to do it as briefly, or discreetly, as he'd done with me.

I told myself I was counting the scars he'd intentionally put on his body to justify it.

There were two separate columns of small horizontal lines that ran from beneath his arm, down his side, and onto his hip. A third was not yet complete.

But in all honesty, I was admiring the way his hips appeared from the angle I was looking and the way his muscles fit together beneath the skin on his abdomen.

Though I'd seen Chase shirtless and had been intimate with him, I'd not allowed myself to fully appreciate his body.

Perhaps I'd simply been so dumbstruck at the time with the

realization that men's bodies looked so much different from women's that I hadn't been *able* to appreciate it fully. Or perhaps I'd been too afraid.

But I was looking, and I was most certainly appreciating. I did not believe there was anything wrong with it. I felt, in a sense, it was like reading a book—focusing your eyes and attention to something you would otherwise not know.

He spoke again eventually. "Are you counting?"

"Yes, that was precisely what I was doing."

"How many are there?" It was apparent he didn't believe I'd done so.

"Sixty-two on your side," I replied. Necessities always came first, and counting had been necessary. I wouldn't forget to dispose of the food twice after learning my lesson from Anders.

"Are you sure about that?"

"Yes, I'm quite sure," I said. "Two rows of twenty-five and one that isn't completed. I can't count the ones on your arm properly with the way you're holding it, so don't ask me about that."

"The rows aren't of twenty-five." His voice was so blank that I momentarily questioned myself.

"I counted," I said assuredly. "They're of twenty-five."

"You can only *see* twenty-five." He grinned. "They go down farther. Would you like to see the rest?"

I could not stop my face from burning when I smiled and said, "No, thank you." I cleared my throat. "How many lines are in each row?"

"Fifty." He hadn't looked directly at me once yet during our talking.

"And, um—" How far down did they go? That didn't matter. I cleared my throat again. "Is that number doubled?"

"Doubled?" he asked. I got a very brief glance from him then.

"Yes, because most the lines have another running the opposite way through them."

He grinned a little again and said, "Those are Reapers." Almost all the ones on his side had been other Reapers he'd killed, then. How in the world had he managed that?

The grin dropped away from his face when he extended his right arm toward me. The lines were not all straight on his arm, though they were still organized in the same way—neat, precise columns.

He pointed to a zigzagged line with a finger from his opposite hand and said, "Women." Then, he pointed to a smaller one that was not the standard length of the others. "Children."

There was a good deal of both those on his arm.

He pulled his arm back to himself. "That was before your father came along."

I looked at him and I waited. I waited for him to ask me if I was afraid of him now, or if I thought him a monster.

I waited for *something*, but he asked me nothing at all.

"Have you killed many female Reapers?" I asked him curiously. He'd not distinguished a different mark for them.

"A Reaper is a Reaper," he said. "It doesn't matter if they're female. They've had the same training and they do the same things. If we had any with us right now, you wouldn't have asked me that question. The fact that we don't when I know your father was informed about your feelings toward men . . . it should tell you something."

We were off topic and I assumed he'd done as much purposely, but I wasn't done. "Chase told me . . ." I started and then stopped.

"Told you what?"

I took a deep breath, preparing myself for it. "That you don't feel bad. About the things you've done."

"Is *that* what happened when you were talking to him?" he asked. "He brings that up and you get in an argument over it?"

"We didn't argue," I told him. "We simply had a disagreement about what sort of person you are and whether or not I'm capable of seeing it."

"Then I'm sorry."

I felt my forehead scrunching. "Sorry why?"

"That you didn't fix things with him on account of me and your stubborn loyalty," he replied. "I'm sorry to tell you that your *disagreement* was unhelpful and pointless." He paused. "You should apologize to him."

"Why would I do that?"

"Because, on this one occasion?" He chuckled beneath his breath. "He was right, and you were wrong."

I decided at that point I'd had enough speaking with Jastin to suit me for a time, but I still thought of him. I thought back on the first conversation I'd had with Stewart, about the number of people he'd killed. He'd told me that because he wanted me to think him a monster.

I did not care what words Jastin said to me, I didn't think of him that way. I did not care what he told me, because I knew he was lying to everyone. I hoped that, eventually, he would stop feeling the need to do so with me. I was unsure if that would ever happen, or if it were even possible, but I could hope so.

He kept his shirt off for the remainder of the day, until the sun began setting, and he rode on my left side all the while. I felt as though he were finally showing himself to me, displaying what he was and seeing whether I would run because of it. I was sure a part of him hoped I would. But I knew he wouldn't show that to me unless a small part of him hoped I would not.

I'd told Stewart that day I would be glad to be the one person who wouldn't think of him as a monster. I trusted Stewart, but I did not truly consider him my friend. Not a close one at least, but perhaps some loose form of the word. I truly did not believe Stewart was *any* sort of monster, though.

Well. Perhaps a small, fluffy sort of one that might poke at your ankles as you walked.

I'd read about something so ridiculous in a book once, if not that precise thing.

If my brother had told Chase that Jastin was a monster, without using those words but still saying the same thing . . . I would be glad to be the one person who didn't look at him as such. Everyone deserved that, I thought, even if they might not deserve it.

What was deserved or not was all down to the standards people chose and held. So, I said he deserved it.

Perhaps everyone was right. Perhaps Jastin was right and he was not lying. But maybe . . . if I showed him that I believed him to be something different, that I believed in *him* . . . perhaps he would wake up one day and realize everyone was wrong. If he didn't, that would be all right. But it was my responsibility as his friend to do that for him. It was what he'd done for me when no one else would, after all. So I would be the one person to do that for him when no one else cared to.

I would stand by him, and I would have his back.

I would do that even when the person standing on my other side might consider him unworthy of it, or if the world might say his actions made him unworthy. I would do that even if he chose to act like he didn't want me to or didn't care either way. He'd done that for me, and it was the only way for me to get out of his debt.

I felt as though that debt would not stop piling up. At the rate we were currently going, I did not know if I would ever be able to repay him for everything.

For some reason . . . it did not seem such a horrible prospect.

WHEN WE STOPPED TO MAKE CAMP for the night, Jastin attempted to slip away into the trees without me as he'd always done before. He was unsuccessful this time, which was immensely satisfying, but I'd never tried to go after him.

He allowed me to trail behind him for a short while before he rounded on me. "Why are you following me?"

"Would you allow me to wander by myself at night?" I asked, sounding curious though I already knew the answer. "Given my brother is not being fair in his partnership with you, I feel it's my responsibility to take up his place for now."

"Trust me, Flower, I don't need you trailing along after me."

I was very calm when I said, "Don't speak to me that way. Either you're going to allow me to come with you or you're going to accompany me back to camp and stay there for the remainder of the night."

He grinned. "Is that so?"

"Yes." I did not return the expression. "It is."

"And if I was coming out here to get away from you?"

"My answer would still be the same," I told him flatly. "You can have all the time you need away from me when we reach your city. Until that point, I consider us all to be in dangerous territory and I'll not allow you wandering alone anymore."

"Why does it matter?" I believed he'd reached the point of realizing I wouldn't rise, and that I was being serious.

"Because it's irresponsible," I answered. "And completely ignorant, to be wholly honest."

"And you believe coming with me would be the responsible thing to do?" he asked very slowly.

"I suspect it would only make me ignorant as well." I gave a stiff shrug of my shoulders. "But if you're going to be stupid, I'll simply have to be stupid with you."

After a moment, a small smile stretched across his face. "Come along, then."

Chapter Thirty-One

Having Dreams

KNEW JASTIN HAD NO INTENTION whatsoever of speaking to me as I trailed along behind him in the darkness.

I was careful in trying not to trip on stones and undergrowth, and I attempted as best I could not to get hung up on low-hanging branches. The stray prickly bush grabbed hold of my skin and clothing on occasion, which was more irritating than anything else.

Though I had a separate purpose or two in what I was doing, I couldn't help looking at this as a learning opportunity of sorts. So I spent a bit more time than what I'd initially anticipated following after him, observing and doing my best to be silent enough that he might forget my presence entirely.

I gave him his time, hoping I might learn a few things as it passed.

He seemed to be looking for something and nothing at once, like perhaps he wouldn't know what it was until he found it. He told me before that he'd gone out into the trees thinking and looking. I suspected since he seemed to have found what he'd been looking for with the surprise he'd given me, now he was simply thinking and pretending very hard to look.

When I'd learned enough from that particular exercise, I jogged up beside him and stared up at his face as we walked at a brisk pace.

He did not return my gaze.

One thing I'd learned was I hadn't the faintest hope of navigating the terrain in a satisfactory manner, even through observing the way he did as much. So I stared at him as we walked together in our silence and he stared straight ahead.

I gave him quite a bit more time before I said, "My brother."

He sighed, making his frustration at my presence known. It was not needed, as I was already aware of as much. It didn't bother me in the slightest. "What about him?"

"You said he's your only friend," I stated.

"Was." He clarified blankly with the word because I was his friend now, too. I wondered if that frustrated him. "What of it?"

"I was simply curious how long the two of you have been working together." I shrugged. I knew he could see it, even if he wasn't looking directly at me.

"Quite a while." When I continued staring at him expectantly, he sighed again and said, "Four years."

"That's all?" I'd thought it would've been a good deal longer than that from the things I'd learned. Four years was enough time to get the proper measure of a person only if they let you.

"It took a while after your father came into his position for things to get changed the way he wanted them. When they instated the rule that we had to go out in pairs, it didn't—" He paused, seeming to rearrange his thoughts. "It didn't work out very well. I went through quite a few *partners* before they assigned me to your brother."

"You sound as though you weren't happy about it," I said. He'd sounded unhappy both at his previous partners and his assignment to my brother, but especially so with the latter.

"Oh, I wasn't." He chuckled. "Your brother is too pretty."

"*What*?" I laughed. What a strange thing to say. "You're very pretty. You have no room to talk."

"Am I?" For a moment, he grinned at the blank space in front of us. Then he shook his head before I could reiterate and went on. "I didn't mean it that way. I knew the things he'd done, but I also knew about what happened with Evelyn's family. I didn't think he had it in him to do what was necessary, which meant I couldn't depend on him in the field. I just . . . didn't like him in general." Before I could say anything on the matter, he glanced over at me with a grin and said, "He won't like me telling you this, but I'd imagine females find him *pretty* in the way you thought I meant, with how much he gets around. You should *probably* keep that to yourself."

"But you came to like him," I said, getting back to something of importance. "Why is that?"

"We'd gone on five missions together." He chuckled quietly again. "Five of them and I was miserable every single *second* I had to be around him. God, I couldn't *stand* him." He paused, clenching his jaw. "And then he saved my ass."

"Did he?"

"Oh yeah, he did." He nodded. "I didn't even care so much about that. I cared about what happened when we went back to the city." He glanced over at the puzzled expression on my face and then smiled. "He lied. He lied about absolutely *everything* that happened. It was my fault the mission almost got messed up, and I expected that to be the first thing he did when we got back—tell his daddy all about it. But he didn't. And he never said a word to me about it. Still hasn't."

"Why didn't he?" I asked curiously.

"I don't have a clue, because I know he couldn't stand me either." He shook his head. "But that started our little bubble of trust. Then, after going on more missions with him and seeing how good he was . . . trust turned into respect. It was a long time, but eventually that respect turned into friendship."

"My brother is good?" I asked in disbelief. "At *killing people*?" I knew certain things were not past him, but . . .

"Doesn't strike you that way, does he?" Jastin laughed. "Didn't strike me that way either. But yes, he's very good at it. So is your father. It's like I told you—it's the ones you wouldn't expect that you need to look out for."

Because I didn't want to do more thinking on my father killing people, I guiltily admitted, "I feel bad saying this, but Ahren . . . I didn't think he would be."

"So you assumed I was the one who always did the killing when we went on missions together?"

"Well, to be wholly honest with you . . ." I started quietly, "until I learned the two of you worked as partners, I'd assumed my father didn't ask him to go on missions. But then . . . yes." I nodded. "I did assume you did most of them."

He grinned at me. "I won't tell him you said that."

I nodded, finding I was glad he wouldn't. It likely would've offended my brother immensely.

"Why is it you thought that?" he asked after a moment. "Just because of how he is?"

"Because he loses his cool so often," I replied. "Everyone else seems very well able to control themselves, for the most part. The big fight with you all happened because he was angry, didn't it?" I already knew the answer to that question.

"I never *once* saw your brother lose his head until you came into the picture." He paused, seeming to think on it. "Well, apart from that one time. But there were extenuating circumstances."

Who knew what *that one time* actually was?

"So the two of you are opposites," I said in understanding.

I caught him tilting his head at me.

I clarified with, "He plays himself off better than he is, and you play yourself off as worse."

"If that's what you want to think." He shrugged. "I see now that nobody can say anything to make you get an idea out of your head. Put new ideas in there? Sure. But not take them away. I won't bother trying."

"If that's what you want to think," I told him with a small grin.

He shook his head but did not respond to me in any way.

It was quite a while before I broke the next long stretch of silence. "The whistling," I said. "Do the two of you have all sorts of little things like that worked out with one another?"

"Yes," he answered blankly.

"Well, I suppose that would be the only way to work efficiently as a pair."

"I hate it." He was shaking his head when I looked directly at him.

"Why?" I asked. It was such a strange thing to hate, but . . . "Because you're forced to share something with a person?"

He stopped moving and smiled, trying to hide his discomfort. He was unsuccessful. "That's not why I hate it." He shook his head. "I just wish we hadn't had to sit down and come up with all of them."

"Ah." I looked down at the ground and nodded. "You wish you had someone who could understand you without having to tell them something directly for them to know what you mean."

"Is that what it is?"

"I'm quite certain it is." I shrugged. "It's understandable—putting your life in a person's hands and wanting them to know you. Even if you won't tell them as much. I'm speaking you as a generalization, not you specifically."

He stared at me for a very long time before saying, "I'm ready to go back now."

I shrugged again. "Then let's go back."

He did not speak to me any more as we made our way back to the camp. Satisfied at all I'd learned and that I'd gotten underneath his skin, causing him to return as I'd intended . . . I did not bother speaking to him either.

MY FATHER WAS NOT HAPPY when we made our way through the trees, but he was not as angry as he had been on the day I'd gone hunting with Anders. "Didn't I ask you to tell me before you wandered off?"

"Well, given you've had your Reapers following me every time I have, I don't see why it should matter," I told him. "And by the way, if I ever personally catch one of them watching me while I bathe, I'll do *far* more than punch them."

He shook his head at me as I smiled at him, like he thought I was completely ridiculous. I was not being ridiculous. I was telling him the truth.

I informed him, "You should *probably* advise them against doing that."

He was still shaking his head when he said, "Get ready to pull your shift. And didn't I ask you to wear a normal shirt at night? I'm certain you promised me you would."

I sighed as I pulled my normal shirt out and threw it on over the Reaper one, but I'd been so otherwise focused I truly had forgotten.

I spent the next several hours being only as useful as they would allow me to be, but I noticed for the first time that more of them fell asleep while I was on my shift than they'd done initially. I watched nearly half of them twitching and jerking beneath their blankets as I quietly walked my half of the perimeter. I tried as best I could to ignore the Reaper I'd scuffled with as he walked the opposite side.

When my shift was over, I spent a few minutes sitting on top of my blankets, watching Jastin twitching in his sleep. His movements began happening more frequently and I knew he was dreaming of something awful. It was easy to discover things when you paid attention. I worried he would stab me if I attempted to wake him, but all I could think about was him promising to pay attention to my dreams and that he would wake me if they became unpleasant.

Friendships were supposed to be equal.

I moved until I was sitting directly behind him, and I was wary as I reached my hand out. I held it just behind his back for a moment, hesitating.

They were supposed to be equal, so I touched him.

He instantaneously jolted upright and grabbed hold of a knife from somewhere on his body. He looked around, looked at me, blinked, and then shook his head. Then, anger took over his face.

"I could have *killed* you," he whispered loudly.

"You wouldn't hurt me," I whispered in assurance. "I was at your back." And he had looked around before looking at me because he'd known I was at his back.

He could've killed me.

"Don't wake me up like that again," he said before he laid down again with his back facing me. "Just let me have the dreams."

He knew that was all I'd been wanting when waking him, without me having to say as much.

I reached my hand out once more and touched his wavy hair, feeling a frown on my face. I leaned down close to his ear and whispered, "You have to think about happy things. Remember?" I sighed quietly. "I hope you have good dreams, for once."

Then I kissed his ear. I could not explain why I'd done it. I only wished him to know I was there for him. Still, it was a strange thing to have done.

Was it inappropriate?

It didn't feel that way.

I felt it couldn't have been.

I moved and looked at my own blankets for a moment. I adjusted them slightly, bringing them another two inches closer to him. Then, I did the same thing I did every night now.

I put my back to Jastin, closed my eyes, and forced myself to think of happy things until I fell asleep.

CHAPTER THIRTY-TWO

FORCES OF NATURE

JASTIN DID NOT SPEAK TO ME at all as we rode together the next day, and he kept his shirt on. He didn't look at me either, not even discreetly. I suspected his coldness toward me had a great deal to do with the manner in which I'd woken him the previous night. He did not necessarily seem angry about it, only cold.

I could've easily been mistaken, as his coldness might have stemmed from a great number of things.

He might've had more of a problem with my having followed him than what he had initially. Possibly for realizing why I'd done it or perhaps being struck that he would have no more time wandering alone while we traveled.

For a little while during and after lunch, I wondered if his mood mightn't have had anything at all to do with me.

He avoided my brother while we were stopped, but he stayed relatively close to me. Not close, but closer than he got to Ahren. So I spent some time while riding thinking I'd been horribly presumptuous and that I'd gotten the wrong impression from the air he was putting off.

As the day passed, I knew I'd not been mistaken. I couldn't be sure as to the reasons behind his behavior, but I knew I was the cause of it, in whatever way I was. It made me both uncomfortable and uneasy, but I could do nothing for that.

I did not inform my father when I snuck off after Jastin into the trees that night, as I'd never told him I would, only known he'd asked and expected it of me. I did not believe anyone had noticed me doing it, apart from an unhappy Jastin. I could've been mistaken.

After several minutes of listening to my footsteps trailing along behind him, he spoke in an exasperated tone. "Can I be ignorant alone tonight?"

"Of course not," I told him.

He did not speak to me again and I didn't want to push him farther than necessary when he was in such a mood. I had no intention of pushing him at all tonight, apart from with my presence alone. With the way the day had gone, I assumed that would be enough.

I walked behind him and listened to the noises that happen naturally in the trees—animals skittering away, branches breaking far off in the distance. Once, I thought I heard a misplaced footstep behind us, obviously one of my father's Reapers who had caught up and was just doing their job.

I took a different approach to my attempts at stealth than what I had the previous night. I kept my eyes on Jastin, but I didn't try to mimic his movements. I didn't focus so much on him past watching, instead letting the natural sounds invade my head. Reapers never focused so much on what they were doing; they just did it.

It only took me a few minutes to realize that my new efforts had done nothing but worsen my abilities. So I tuned out the pleasant humming of insects and focused on putting one foot in front of the other, with only the pale glow of what moonlight could touch through the trees and my friend walking fast to guide me.

I tried to ignore the obvious fact that he wanted to be away from me, though it did sting. But necessities came first.

It wasn't until we'd been walking for quite some time that I began to get a strange feeling, like invisible hands grasping up and down my back.

I attempted to shake it off, attributing it to an overactive mind after a day spent trying to discover things by analyzing energies. Given the practice had gotten me nowhere despite all the effort put into it, I knew it was not the way to yield results.

But the unpleasant feeling wouldn't go away no matter how I tried to disregard it.

It was simply one of my father's Reapers as it always was. That was all it was.

That was all.

Was that all?

I hurried to catch up with Jastin and, when I got near enough, took his hand in mine.

Before he could pull his own away or act horribly to me, which he would surely do, I asked, "Do you remember when I made you go to the water with me?" I ensured my voice was entirely calm and tinged with an air of believably fake contentedness—something he would find out of place even more so than me holding his hand. "Do you remember why I wanted to you to go?"

He stopped so suddenly that I took a step past him.

And there it was—another misplaced footstep in the distance behind us as whoever it was struggled to stop at the same time.

Jastin tilted his head for an instant before he pulled me close to him. Then he grabbed either side of my face with both of his hands and put his mouth against mine.

"Heard." He whispered the word so quietly against my lips before touching them with his.

I knew it was *not* one of my father's Reapers when a few seconds later he stopped kissing me and whispered, "Sonofabitch."

Then he kissed me again, but I knew neither of us was paying any attention to the action. We were both listening.

If it was not one of my father's Reapers, I did not know what to do. I was not trained despite my arguments on the matter, not well enough.

We'd been tracked. Only a Reaper would track a Reaper away from their party. Had they followed the sound of my footsteps?

I would get us both killed, if I hadn't already.

What had I done?

My body began shaking, but when Jastin put his hand on my right arm and tapped his finger on it twice, that took part of my fear away. He wanted me to go that way when he released me, so I would go that way. It was something to do and I could do what was needed of me. I had always been very good at that.

I could move when I needed to move, even if I was afraid.

As soon as his face left mine again, I took a quick step in the appropriate direction and then heard several wet-sounding *thunks* in only a few short seconds. I knew the sound of knives being thrown into bodies. It was not something one forgot.

The world seemed fuzzy, like everything was not real but was also *too real* at once. My head struggled to keep up.

Jastin calmly walked toward our pursuer, but while he was in the process of doing so . . . I realized how mistaken I'd been about the way Reapers operated.

On my shifts, I'd always assumed they would come for me first if I was awake. I was the easiest target by far, after all. Wouldn't they take out the easiest target first? At least at the same time?

Why had I thought that? It seemed so foolish now.

Scenarios. There could be *so many* scenarios.

When a second Reaper stepped through from the opposite direction, he did not even look at me as he strode silently toward Jastin, whose attention was elsewhere. Not a predatory smile, not an acknowledgement, not a glance. I was insignificant. Invisible. I was not a threat.

I was not even a target.

Invisible. I was invisible.

Time seemed to distort itself in the strangeness this scenario had inflicted upon the world. In one instant it seemed to disappear, only to reappear in the briefest yet most vivid of flashes. In that minuscule moment of clarity, I knew I was moving, but I didn't know to where or what I was doing.

Time flashed out then in so many times in the shortness of the moment, and somehow . . . it felt like an entire lifetime passed in the brevity of it.

And that was how I ended up on the back of the second Reaper with my knife in the base of his neck, not fully understanding how I got there. I stabbed him repeatedly—*so difficult*—as fast as I could until his body went limp and sent us both to the ground. Right next to Jastin, knelt down by the other Reaper who was splayed out.

Jastin didn't so much as turn around to see what had happened. He rolled the other Reaper over and stabbed him somewhere in the middle of his back.

The scream that followed seemed to bounce off the trees and inside my head as the bottom half of his body went limp.

263

Jastin rolled him back over and I was unable to tear my gaze from the Reaper's face, contorted in such pain.

"You cooperate and I'll make it fast," Jastin said in a tone I'd not ever heard from him. It went past the point of blankness. I couldn't . . . "If not, you're going to spend a very long time bleeding out on the ground. Name?"

Business.

He was . . . He was *working*.

The Reaper was breathing so hard. I could see his chest rising and falling rapidly as he struggled to form a word that slipped through between his teeth. "*Dray.*"

"City?" Jastin asked.

"*Bethel*," he responded, his voice shaking.

Not New Bethel, but Bethel? I'd never heard of it, not even in the books of the library in the Valdour House, but I shouldn't have been surprised by that.

Even with the Reaper's strained speaking, I'd never heard such an accent before. It wasn't that I thought I knew all the ways people spoke. I didn't. I just hadn't known a voice could sound in such a way. Where was this Bethel located and why was he here following us in the woods? Were they trying to take out our party slowly to have a better chance at success? Surely they were here to eliminate my father.

"Mark?" Jastin asked calmly.

The Reaper pointed a shaking finger in my direction, but Jastin did not look back at me to see my eyes widen to what felt like their breaking point.

"Kill order?" I hardly heard Jastin ask the question.

"*Abduction*," the Reaper said. "*Leverage*. It's—" His words cut off as he sucked in a breath. "*All I know.*"

Jastin nodded and said, "Thank you for your cooperation," before leaning forward and snapping the man's neck.

And then I bent over and threw up everywhere, next to the body of the second man I had stabbed to death in a matter of weeks.

My thoughts were jumbled and incoherent as my head tried to make everything fall into its proper place. Little bits popped through, somehow so clear despite all the madness.

My hand is wet.

Sticky.

Reapers.
We should be dead.
My fault.

I was reeling and lightheaded when Jastin pulled me to my feet, putting his forehead against mine. He must've been leaning over.

"You did good," he said quietly several times.

I struggled to listen to his words. I could hardly hear them over my own labored breathing.

"You're okay," he said. "It's okay. They can't take you."

I nodded after a time and, seeming to be satisfied, he went over to the Reaper he'd killed. He bent down next to the man and stared at his face.

"Wha—" I started and then stopped because my brain did not want to function. I spent a moment silently pleading for it to work. "What are you doing?"

"I never get to look at their faces for very long anymore," he said. "I never wanted your brother to see me do it."

I wiped away tears that were making their way down my face with my hand. I only distantly noticed the wet smearing.

I should not have been thinking of it now, but it was right there in front of me and was so much better than thinking of what had just happened. It felt I had no say in what would come through and what wouldn't though, and my head made whatever connections it wanted to make.

I had been right about Jastin and everyone else had been wrong.

I could not explain why I did it because I wasn't thinking clearly, but I wiped my knife off on my trousers and cut a line near my left hand on the side opposite my wrist.

Jastin had stepped over to me at some point shaking his head, but he did not try to stop me. He was still shaking his head when he gently grabbed my newly cut arm.

"Second," he said as he cut a new line next to the one I'd put there, precisely the same distance apart from it as all his own. Then, he cut another line through it. "Reaper."

I'd not felt the pain of it at all in my state, though I was sure I would feel it later. I would feel all of this later.

He extended his knife toward me and stood there staring at me what seemed to be expectantly. It took me a moment to realize what he wanted.

I replaced my knife where it belonged and took his. I did not lift his shirt to put it in what he likely assumed would be its proper place. I took his left arm by my shaky left hand and, in the exact same place he'd put it on me, cut one line with another running through it. I handed his knife back to him and he smiled sadly at me.

He said, "We need to go."

I nodded. "We should—" I cleared my throat. "We should take them to camp, shouldn't we?"

"I can't." He looked away.

I shook my head at him in confusion.

"I don't think I can carry one body," he said, "let alone two."

"I'll carry one," I told him. I could probably manage the smaller one.

"No," he said. "I'm telling you I *can't.*" And then he swayed slightly on his feet.

I grabbed hold of him before the sinking feeling had time to make its way to the appropriate place in my stomach.

"Where are you injured?" I demanded as I hurriedly began checking over his body for injuries. And then I found it—a long cut in his shirt—just in time for him to fall to the ground.

I rushed to get the fabric over his head, and I tossed it aside. I pulled my own shirt over mine, followed by the tight-fitting Reaper training shirt underneath. I held my normal clothing over the long gash on his left side with my knee and began slicing the top off the Reaper shirt with my knife.

I fumbled several times and misjudged the amount of slicing needed to get it over his head and around his body, but eventually . . . I got it there. That would keep the blood from leaving too quickly, I hoped—possibly enough to get him back to the camp. I did not know how much of it he'd lost, but it seemed to be everywhere.

How had I missed it? How had I missed his blood in all the rest?

Damn my eyes for never seeing what they needed to see.

Why hadn't he *said* anything?

"Jastin, *Jastin,*" I said several times as I shook him. I had to smack him in the face to get him to wake back up because the shaking had done nothing at all. "I have to get you back. I need you to stand up and point me in the right direction. *Please.*"

Was my voice hysterical? I did not know. I just knew I had to get him back so they could fix him.

I somehow managed to pull him to his feet and get myself tucked under his right arm. He began walking, so I assumed it to be the correct direction. It *seemed* to be the direction we'd come from, though nothing seemed to be in the appropriate place and the world was spinning so fast.

Had I seen that tree before? Why did they all start looking the same when you saw more of them? Even the striking ones. . . .

I told myself I needed to calm down so I could ensure we kept going the correct way. I distantly knew I was speaking to him, that I was begging him to keep moving. But it was not long before I realized how small and weak I was when his body began slackening over mine.

I felt as though we'd only been walking for an instant when his body gave out altogether. I tried so hard to keep him upright, but I could not do it. The tears of weakness and desperation fell down my face as I shook him and shook him and begged him to wake up and keep walking.

He didn't.

I was certain it was some unknown force of nature hearing my desperation that gave me the strength to get his body over my shoulders and walk with it. A bit of logic appeared somewhere in my head. It told me I wasn't strong enough to do this, but I did not care. I just needed to get him to people who could fix him. It was the only thing that mattered, not the how.

So I cried and I walked.

I was certain I stumbled more than once, though I was only aware of it distantly. I only cared about falling because it kept me from keeping him alive. But every time we both hit the ground, I somehow managed to pick him back up again.

I cried, and I kept crying.

Whatever force of nature that gave me the strength to keep moving must have been listening to the silent pleas I was sending up to all the stars in the sky above, because eventually . . .

I heard shouting.

CHAPTER THIRTY-THREE

STOLEN HEART BEATS

I COULD NOT RESPOND to the shouting when I heard it, though some part of me knew I should. I couldn't even try. I could not do anything more than continue on in whatever way I was.

The sound came closer, and suddenly Jastin's weight was gone from my shoulders. And I screamed. I screamed and screamed until Anders was in my face, shaking my body at my arms. Had I already been screaming?

I distantly heard him saying my name.

I came out of it in enough time to see my father walking with Jastin over his shoulders, and I ran after them.

"What happened?" my father asked.

I did not respond because I did not care what had happened.

"Who did this?"

I did not care about that either, but then he finally asked me the appropriate question.

"What injuries does he have?"

"He's cut open on his left side," I answered through my tears. I would say nothing else because nothing else mattered.

"I'll run ahead and inform them what happened," Anders said from my right, and then he was gone.

It felt like forever that I spent following hurriedly—still too slow—after my father, fighting the irrational urge to pull Jastin from his shoulders and carry him myself.

How had I carried him at all? I didn't know.

Was this even happening? Was it happening or was it another horrible, vivid dream brought on by the heat?

No matter the impossibilities of it, I knew it was real. I couldn't wake up from it, but I kept trying.

I walked behind my father, staring at Jastin's limp body, and I cried, trying *so hard* to wake up.

When we made it back to the camp, there were so many candles and lanterns lit near the fire, lined up and waiting.

My father dropped Jastin's body onto the ground and, as he was cutting off the fabric I'd wrapped around him, calmly said, "Get her away from here."

Someone grabbed my arm, gentle even in the attempt at pulling, but it felt like knives.

I rounded on them, finding myself face to face with Anders again.

"I will kill you," I heard myself say. Was my voice calm? All I heard was screaming inside my head. "If you try to make me move. I will kill you."

He looked down at my left arm held in his hand, and I could see the blood in my peripherals though I didn't move my gaze away from his eyes. Then he looked at my face.

"I won't take her away from him," Anders said, our gazes still met. "Your daughter killed a Reaper and then carried one of your own for who knows how long. She deserves to stay with him and make sure he doesn't die."

He released my arm and I brought my attention back to the fire and what was near it.

My father had been spouting off obscenities as he inspected Jastin's injury. He did not look up to say, "At least make her put a shirt on."

Anders removed his own shirt and extended it to me. I did not care that I was standing around with only my top undergarment covering me. I simply did not care.

"Put it on," Anders said quietly as I stared at Jastin's body. "And then you can go sit there if you promise not to get in the way."

I did not put it on, but I covered the front of myself with it and went to watch my father.

I sat a good distance away but close enough to see what was happening. I was close enough to see the inside of Jastin's body when my father inspected it for deeper damage.

Anders sat down beside me at some point and whispered, "He'll be all right. It missed his kidney."

I did not know what a kidney was, nor did I care, so long as it hadn't been harmed if it was something important.

I realized I was not as hysterical on the outside as I believed myself to be.

I was crying silently and fidgeting with my legs, the latter of which I never did. My hands were shaking. But I was making no sound at all, apart from my uneven breathing and my legs moving against the grass. I listened, and I sat there for what felt like forever while my father cleaned and sewed up the wound.

"He's lost too much blood." My father was shaking his head, but he hadn't looked away from Jastin. Then he glanced up and around. "*Ahren*? Where's Ahren?"

"I've already got it," Ahren said as he held out some strange-looking thing in his hand.

"What are they doing?" I demanded quietly.

"Your brother has to give him some blood," Anders replied.

"No," I said, not realizing I'd stood up from my spot on the ground. "*No*."

Anders shook his head at me in confusion, but I stormed over to my brother.

"It's *my* responsibility," I said firmly. "It's *my* fault."

"Your fault?" Ahren asked.

"He got cut open because I didn't kill the other Reaper fast enough!" I yelled. "So you get out of the way and let me take care of him because it's *my* fault!"

I was restrained when I attempted to grab the strange thing from my brother's hand.

"Aster," Anders said in my ear. He ignored the obscenities I was shouting at him. "You don't know if your blood would be compatible with his. Testing compatibility is dangerous even under normal circumstances. It could kill him. Let your brother do it. You're not helping in delaying him from getting it."

I knew that what he was saying was entirely reasonable, but my head could not listen to reason.

I was shouting and struggling against the hold Anders had on me when my father said, "I want him awake." He had several of his fingers at the pulse point on Jastin's neck. "I'm worried he'll go into shock. Feels like he's close to it now."

I screamed at everyone when my father began flicking Jastin on one of his closed eyes.

What was he *doing*?

Someone came up and handed my father a glass of a very thick, brownish-green drink.

Fandir root.

Jastin's eyes were open when I looked back at his face.

My father said, "You have to drink it."

I did not know how Jastin was awake, nor did I know how they got the Fandir root down his throat, but I stopped shouting at the sight of it. It was not long before a glazed look took over his face.

I watched with wide eyes as my brother began giving Jastin blood. I did not entirely understand how it worked, even when witnessing it.

Time seemed infinite in that space, watching the fire illuminating parts of Jastin's face in waves. It popped, he blinked. His eyes seemed to search for everything and focus on nothing in the silence.

But it was not silent. The bugs still hummed, the fire still crackled, people spoke in hushed tones. But in that moment, that seemingly infinite moment where I watched his eyes moving . . . there was *absolute silence* in my head.

Then it was over and I discovered what the other side of Fandir root looked like.

"Where is she?" Jastin's words slurred together. He did not move at all, apart from a blinking of his eyes and a slight opening and closing of his mouth.

No one responded to him in any way, all of them standing around and watching.

"Where's the flower? She saved my life, you know. How am I here? Did she do that? I'm not surprised. Are you surprised? I bet you are."

I looked around hurriedly at the crowd of Reapers, and my stomach sank.

I would not allow them to hear him rambling when he had no control of his tongue. I should have made them leave as soon as I'd realized what they were giving him. . . . I just hadn't believed he could be conscious.

I threw Anders' shirt on over me and was just getting ready to make them move when I heard something come from Jastin's mouth that stopped me in my tracks.

"Where's Aston? I need to see my son. I need to tell him I was wrong. He's so young. I don't want my poison in his head. I don't want him to be like me."

I took a deep breath and allowed myself the briefest moment to understand what he'd actually just said before turning on everyone. I tried *so hard* to tune him out.

"Get away," I said through my teeth.

Most of them filed off without any objection whatsoever, but some pretended as though I wasn't there at all. I'd expected nothing more.

I pushed the closest non-leaving person to the ground. He mustn't have been expecting it, either due to his focus on Jastin or due to me as a person. I kicked him once he fell. And I kept kicking him until I was restrained again.

"It's just a little Fandir root," my father's Reaper said when he stood.

I screamed at him and, though the yelling was intentional, I did not know what I was saying.

"And what would you do for your partner if he was given some?" Anders asked from behind me.

"She's acting like this because she's in love with him," the Reaper said. "It has *nothing* to do with partnering. She's not even a Reaper."

"I can assure you this has *everything* to do with partnering," Anders said firmly. "And you don't need to be a Reaper to kill one, clearly, as she has already done that tonight. You should hope she doesn't slit your throat in your sleep."

"She couldn't." The Reaper chuckled. "And even if she had the training, she doesn't have it in her. Not unless—"

He was interrupted then as another Reaper came up and pushed him.

He frowned then and walked away without another word said.

"I tried to tell him the other day what their relationship is, but . . . he's ignorant." The pusher shook his head and looked at me in a way that appeared to be embarrassed. "I'm sorry for my partner. As I said, he's ignorant." Then he walked away as well, in the same direction.

"The sensible man is the one Jastin had his way with for following you several days ago," Anders said as he released me. "You probably couldn't recognize his face now that it's had a bit of time to heal. You should've seen it immediately after Jastin got done with him. Now, if you're done causing your distraction—"

I did not wait for him to continue as I made my way back over to Jastin. I stayed far enough away that I could not hear his words, but it prevented me from doing anything more than seeing he was still alive. It was good enough.

"Aren't you curious?" Anders asked shortly after I'd found a suitable location.

I did not acknowledge him as I stared at the only sight that I currently cared about seeing.

"What he's saying," he said. "Aren't you curious?"

"I don't want to hear anything he doesn't want to tell me." I stood there, rigid, breathing deeply and holding my head high. "And I don't want anyone else to hear either."

"This truly has nothing at all to do with love, does it?"

I shook my head and barely said, "He's done too much for me." Then I shook my head again. "I don't want to talk about it."

My father came and stood in front of me not a minute later, and his voice was even when he spoke. "You killed a Reaper."

I did not respond to him; I simply moved so that I could see Jastin again.

"Did you learn anything?"

I still said nothing.

He sighed. "Aster, you need to tell me these things. I need to know if we're in further danger. How many Reapers were there?"

"Two." I answered without looking at him. "Dray from Bethel. They were sent to abduct me for leverage. That's all I know. Leave me alone."

My father began walking away hurriedly at that and said, "That's enough blood. We need to go. Put him in the carriage. Agatha will take care of him."

"*I* will take care of him," I said firmly as I followed after.

"You just attacked one of my men," my father said, clearly exhausted. "How are you going to take care of him if you don't have control of yourself?"

"Garin," Anders said with a deep sigh. "She did that to draw attention away from his words. She had the utmost control over herself, I can assure you."

"You *will* let me take care of him," I demanded as I ignored Anders.

"We don't have time for this." My father glanced over his shoulder.

"Garin," Anders said again, only it was infinitely more frustrated. "If not for her, he would be lying dead in the trees. And if not for him, your daughter would be gone and used against you."

"And if not for him wandering off and her following around after him, this would never have *happened*." My father almost shouted at him.

"Because they never would've tried at the next opportunity, would they have?" Anders said, his volume also rising. "He's the one who's keeping that sort of thing from happening to her, wandering or not, as you well know. And I *suggest* you don't give her reason to *want* to use herself against you. Let her do what she wants and be glad they're both alive after being ambushed."

I ignored the both of them as I followed my brother carrying Jastin's body to the carriage. He got him inside it easily, and I stood there for a moment until my brother reemerged.

He stared at me for a moment, frowning. "You haven't accused me once of not being there for him."

I got inside it then and sat down next to Jastin's body.

"Why?" my brother asked from the door.

I patted down Jastin's hair and calmly said, "Because he's my responsibility."

"You've stolen my partner from me," Ahren accused. I did not know whether he sounded amused or angry, nor did I care in the slightest how he felt about it.

I laid down next to Jastin. "I'll take care of him." I scooted my body as close as I could to his back, leaving my own exposed. I did not really notice my brother closing the door.

"I'll take care of you," I whispered then kissed Jastin's shoulder. I tucked my arm underneath his, ensuring it was nowhere near his injury, and put my hand across his chest.

I stayed awake as the carriage began moving, and I kept my hand there so I could know with certainty that he was alive. I kept my hand there so I could feel his heart beating inside his chest, knowing how close I'd come to never being able to do as much. And I *could* feel his heartbeat there.

It was the only thing that mattered.

CHAPTER THIRTY-FOUR

INARGUABLY LESS MAGICAL

DID NOT REALIZE THAT I'D FALLEN asleep until Jastin moved, putting his hand over mine where it still rested over his chest. Our fingers twined together and I breathed in deeply, inhaling until I thought my chest might burst.

Blood, sweat, and tears. It was only pleasant because we were both here. *Alive.* And for one glorious moment, I somehow convinced myself I was dreaming.

"Aster?" he whispered. His voice made it clear I was not dreaming.

I moved involuntarily, the tip of my nose bumping against the skin on the middle of his back. When I found the mind to, I squeezed his hand in response.

"Will you come over here?"

"I'm right here," I whispered. Was I dreaming? Had my mind finally broken the cycle? Perhaps it had simply broken.

"No," he said. "I want you here." He touched both our hands on the space in front of him.

"Who's going to watch your back?" I asked as I put my forehead there. *Too real.* He was too substantial, but still . . . I didn't want to wake from this.

"Just for a few minutes."

And he sounded so pitiful that I could not help myself from doing what he wanted, despite knowing I shouldn't and not wanting to jar myself awake.

I paid great mind to my movements as I crawled over the top of him, each second bringing me closer to reality. I took his hand in mine again once I got settled and saw that his eyes were watering.

"How did I get back?"

"I carried you," I whispered with a sad smile.

He looked away and nodded his head as a tear fell from his eye, rolling over the bridge of his nose and disappearing.

Trying to lighten everything, I added, "I dropped you quite a lot, I'm afraid."

He had already noticed the proof of my falling, it seemed, because his eyes had found scrapes and scratches all along both my arms that I hadn't known existed until following his gaze. I watched as he ran a finger over a bit of redness near my right elbow. It had already scabbed, but by the looks of it, it appeared quite deep. His finger trailed a little down my arm, and I looked up, finding his gaze on my face.

I forced a smile at him and felt a tear fall from my own eye. "That was my fault," I told him. "I'm so sorry. It was the Reaper I killed who cut you, wasn't it?"

"That was *my* fault," he said—it was almost not a whisper. "If I hadn't been wandering . . ."

"Perhaps it should be both our fault or no one's," I said. "If you hadn't been wandering and if I'd been faster . . ." If I was better trained. If I was quieter. If my mind was faster. If I'd been smarter. I shook my head. "It doesn't matter. We're both alive."

He said nothing.

I looked down at our hands and admitted, "I was so afraid."

"You did good." His hand pushed some of my hair back. It got in my face more often than it used to now that it was short. It could not be tucked behind my ears and stay or tied up, had I something to tie it with.

I shook my head and clarified. "I was so afraid I'd lost you." That had been so much more frightening to me than the prospect of two Reapers. The thought of taking life was so much easier to think of than losing life.

Was that wrong?

"I'm right here," he said, drawing me from my thoughts. "Because of you."

I could not fully explain why I leaned forward and pressed my lips against his. I'd expected for him to stop me. I'd expected for him to tell me not to, for any number of reasons. He did neither.

He kissed me back.

It was not like the way our kisses had been before. There was no tension to it; it was pure relief and happiness. Like hugging my father when he'd returned home from his hunting trips or curling up next to Agatha to go to sleep at night when it felt as though there was no one else in the world. It felt like telling him what I felt and couldn't put words to.

I was so glad he was alive.

His left hand touched my face, his thumb running over my cheek bone. His mouth parted and mine followed, or perhaps it was the other way around. His tongue found mine, or perhaps that was the other way around. I wanted to get lost in it. It was so tempting, but . . . that was not the purpose of it.

When I realized the kiss had gone past the point of showing him what I wanted him to see, I pulled away and quickly said, "I'm so sorry. I shouldn't have done that."

"I'm not," he told me. "We can be the way we should be when the sun comes back up, but for now . . . I don't care." His lack of caring sounded so sincere.

I reached my hand out and touched his face. If he would let me, it was something I wanted to do.

Warily, he spoke again. "They gave me Fandir root. I can taste it."

"Yes," I confirmed.

He watched my face as I touched his and, for a long time, he said nothing. But eventually, he did. "Aren't you going to bring up anything I said?"

I almost felt as though, for now, he would not mind if I did.

"No." I gave him another sad smile. "The other day when I told you I would be happy to do anything for you that you would do for me . . . I wasn't being malicious."

"I'd bring up things you said," he stated.

"No, you wouldn't."

He would've done the exact same things I had, I was sure, only better.

I could not ensure that my tongue would stay silent if pressed much further by him on the matter, so I hastily said, "Let's not talk about it."

"Let's talk about why you fought so hard to save me instead," he said. "Adrenaline or not, I don't know how the hell you got me back. I'm twice your size. How many times did you fall and have my weight on you? Do you even realize how much shit you have stuck in your skin right now?"

I only flinched a little when he moved and pulled something from my arm, mostly because I hadn't expected it. He held a bit of a stick in front of my face before dropping it between us.

I was struggling against more tears when I said, "I was just returning the favor."

"I haven't saved your life."

Technically, he had not. And yet . . .

I swallowed and whispered, "Yes, you have."

He did not smile and tell me he was concerned about my mental state. He kissed me again.

I did not allow sensible thought into my head. I did not let myself think about how it was wrong to kiss him or touch him in such a way. So I did both those things.

His hand went to the back of my head, pulling my face closer to his. Closer was not close enough, but in a way . . . it was. My hand went to the side of his neck, and I knew I shouldn't have, that I should've been gentle with him, but I could feel his pulse quickening and I pulled back. Both our breathing sped and his hand moved.

I thought for a moment that I'd done something wrong, but he kept kissing me and his hand went down my side, from my waist to my hip. And . . . I was lost.

I did not allow myself to think about anything more than the fact that he was alive and that we were both here. When thinking about that, there did not seem to be such a distinguishable line between wrong and right with it. Or perhaps I was incorrect about which of the two were which.

Where was the line?

But eventually he pulled away and closed his eyes. "I'm so pissed off."

I shook my head and was about to ask him if he was angry with me, but he clarified.

"I can't feel anything because of the damn Fandir root. The one time I'm not listening to my brain and . . ." He finally opened his eyes to smile sadly at me and sigh. "I guess that's what I get."

"Get for what?" I was so confused as I tried to process what had just happened and the responses to it. I didn't know if my head could catch up.

He said, "Doing the wrong thing."

It caught up.

I felt all the air rush out of my lungs at once, and I struggled to take in another breath while wiping at my eyes.

There was the line.

"We're simply sharing our relief with one another," I said quickly. "It was nothing more than that. I don't see anything wrong with it. We're friends."

"Is this what friends do, Aster?" he asked me again.

"It's what *we* do, it seems," I said to the space between us, unable to meet his eyes. "We just won't speak of it again. It's no big deal."

"You sounded just like me then." He did not seem pleased about it.

I laughed quietly on a breath. "The first night I ever spoke to Chase . . ." I began, being deliberate with my words. "He told me that he and I weren't so different. I thought he was right for a time, but I can see now that he wasn't. I'm so much more like you than I am him."

"You're nothing like me."

"Not exactly, no," I conceded. "But closer to."

"And what makes you say that?"

"You're very smart," I told him. "I'm sure you can figure it out." Then I kissed him on the forehead and carefully crawled back over his body, curling up close. Some part of me wished I could take back what had just happened, but the rest of me couldn't agree with it, no matter how I currently felt.

"I want you to fix things with him," Jastin said after a moment. "Not try to, but *do*. I need you to do that for me."

"I had every intention of doing just that."

I ignored him when he called me a liar and I snaked my arm underneath his once more to put my hand over his heart. Then I allowed sensible thought into my head, letting it override all the intense and unfathomable emotions swirling inside me and threatening to tear me apart.

I thought about the fight they had all gotten into before and the words he'd said to Chase afterward.

Will you get married and have little babies together? Maybe he'll even let you keep them. What would it be like not to have little Reaper children, I wonder. What would it be like to have a family?

It made so much more sense to me, now that I knew Jastin had a child. And I understood so clearly why he would not allow himself to be in love. He knew there was no point to it. Being in love did not change what he was allowed in his life. It did not change the fact that he could not have the things people should be allowed to have when they're in love. He knew that because he'd already had a child—a little Reaper child.

I wondered about the mother of his child, which was not a sensible thing to do, but I couldn't help myself. I wondered who she was and if he had loved her. I wondered if he *still* loved her. I did not expect that, if he had made a child with a person, he would love me more than the mother of his son.

So it had not been a lie to tell him that I had every intention of working things out with Chase. There may not even be a point to love Chase in a world such as ours, but there certainly was no point in loving a man who loved another woman, even if he claimed to love me as well. I refused to put myself through such a thing. It could only end in heartbreak—loving a man who couldn't love you in return.

And that was when the world fell into place for me, at least in that respect. I could not complain about anything becoming clear, no matter where it sat on my list of priorities.

I would love Jastin, but I would not allow myself to be in love with him. I would take care of him and I would train so I could protect him. I would be his friend. I would keep his confidence.

I would trust him.

I could not complain about anything becoming clear . . . even if it hurt.

I let the tears fall from my eyes and did not bother wiping them away as I repeated the words Anders had said inside my head until I fell asleep.

Love can be destroyed by a great many things. It is still special in its way of course, but inarguably less magical.

And every time I woke to Jastin rubbing my arms or bringing my hand to his lips, I pretended I was fast asleep. My heart already felt like it was breaking, regardless of where it would inevitably lead should I not stop it. Wasn't it a good thing to be reminded it was still in there somewhere?

Why could I only feel the breaking and not the beating?

CHAPTER THIRTY-FIVE

THOUGHTLESS

I WOKE TO JASTIN MOVING ABOUT and realized the carriage had stopped.

Surely he shouldn't be doing such a thing right now—*moving*. He needed time to heal.

"What are you doing?" I asked as I struggled to wake up entirely. My body felt exhausted, completely worn down, and my head was not in much better of a state.

"I need to move." Though his voice was blank, there was something about him that set me on edge and woke me enough that it felt like the world was crashing down on me.

"You need to lie still," I stated.

"I need to *move*," he said firmly.

I got out of his way to let him pass, but I could not stop myself from saying, "Take mind to your injury."

"This isn't the first time I've been sewn up, Aster." His voice had gone so harsh so fast, and I tried very hard to act unfazed by it. "I'm *pretty sure* I can manage not to blow it out."

"If being an asshole to me is what will make you feel better, that's fine." I was pleased the words had been delivered the way I'd intended. Calm, indifferent, entirely unfazed.

"Sorry," he grumbled before opening the door to the carriage and stepping outside.

I closed my eyes against the bright light rushing in, thinking on how different things could be and how quickly they could change.

I sniffled a little, but I was determined to be all right. We were both here, *alive*, and that was what mattered. Everything else was irrelevant, at least where this was concerned.

I spent a very brief moment looking around the inside of the carriage, trying to gain my bearings. And then I saw it.

A piece of wood, about two inches long, darkened by blood halfway up.

I leaned over to grab it, paying no mind to the soreness of my body. I didn't exactly know why, but I slipped the wood inside my pocket before stepping out into the sun.

I ignored the sight of Jastin walking away as best I could. He was trying to conceal the fact that he was injured. I thought it was slightly ridiculous, given everyone already knew and could easily see the dark line—nearly a foot long—on his exposed skin. His gait was not as perfect as it always was despite how hard I could tell he was trying to make it so.

I went into the trees to take care of whatever business I needed to do and then, upon coming back out, took several long moments to stare around at the normalcy in front of me. Jastin, now wearing a shirt, speaking to my brother. People sitting around a fire or napping on the ground while they could. Chase standing next to Chandler. Everyone looked tired, but so . . . *normal.*

Was this life? Everyone living and not caring at all for the things going on around them? No one caring at all for the people next to them, even if they were hurting?

Of course. This was life, and people *never* cared, not unless it benefitted them.

I walked over to Chase.

It took quite a while that the two of us spent staring at one another in silence for Chandler to leave.

It took even longer for Chase to say, "You're in love with him."

Before, I wouldn't have even known what he was talking about, or who. I likely would've assumed before that he'd meant Chandler if he'd just walked away. I likely would've assumed he'd meant Chandler if he'd said it at all. But I knew very well who he meant.

Everything was blank when I said, "I'm not."

He looked away and forced a smile. "I saw your face last night," he said, his voice quiet. "Yes, you are."

"*Understand* something," I began firmly. "I was walking with my friend in the woods and got ambushed by two Reapers. I'm not trained like you are, Chase. I don't know what to do in *any* situation, let alone *all* of them. Still, I managed to kill one of those Reapers because they didn't even look at me. And then I discover my friend is bleeding out everywhere. I had to carry someone twice my size for . . . I don't even *know* how long, all the while thinking my friend was going to die and that it would all be my fault for being too *weak*."

I took a breath and added, "I was understandably distraught when you saw my face last night."

"Oh, it's entirely understandable." He nodded his head. "And yet the two of you still had the time to cut the little shared memories of it into your arms, didn't you?" He gestured to my left arm.

"I didn't know he was injured," I barely said.

"So you did it yourself?" he asked. "I figured you'd done it to each other to make it *that* much more special. I'm just curious about the why. Is that what you're aspiring to be? Some thoughtless murderer who literally wears their kills on their sleeves? I thought I knew who you were, but I'm wondering now how wrong I've been all this time."

And then I punched him in the face. I knew he allowed me to do it. I knew he could've stopped me, but I didn't care. I did not punch him as hard as I could have, only hard enough to make a point.

"All that time you saw an animal dying in a cage," I told him through gritted teeth. "I'll not have you speak to me that way."

He licked a bit of blood from the corner of his mouth, then spit red onto the ground. "And I'll not have you hitting me." He seemed unperturbed, apart from his tone. "Do you think that's a better thing to do to a person?"

"Better than stabbing them in the heart." I wiped at my eyes. "Better than someone hearing the person they love call them a thoughtless murderer." I heard my breathing coming in ragged spurts when I whispered, "Do you know me?"

His eyes narrowed. "Do you *love* me?"

"Of course I do."

"But you love him too."

"I love you, I love my brother, I love Chandler, I love Anders, I love Stanley and Stewart, and Agatha, and *yes* I love Jastin," I said quickly. "And every one of those loves is different from the other. I am not in love with him. But do you believe it wrong of me to love a person who would never call me a thoughtless murderer? Is that love, Chase? Is it *really*? Because I'm beginning to discover I don't like it very much, if that's the way it is."

"Listen to what she's saying, baby brother," Chandler said from behind me. "Because I'm about *this* close to knocking some sense into you."

I did not look to see how close Chandler was to knocking some sense into him, if he were gesturing it.

Slowly Chandler added, "And I'm about *this* close to convincing her to stop trying."

Chase shook his head at his brother and then walked away without another word. It felt like I was watching his retreating form forever before Chandler spoke again.

"You really need to have someone pull all that from your skin and clean it off."

I didn't acknowledge that he'd spoken.

Chandler sighed. "Fine. If you don't want to listen to me right now . . . that's fine. We'll just talk, then. Is that all right with you?"

When I didn't walk away, he continued with what he wanted to talk about.

"Why *did* you cut your arm?"

It took me a moment to ensure something similar to not leaving the plate of food behind pertaining to my face, but I couldn't help glancing to see who might be looking when I turned around to face him. I responded with, "It seemed like a good idea at the time."

"And would you do it again if you were thinking clearly?"

"I would," I admitted.

"I'll not tell my brother that Jas cut the second mark in your arm," Chandler said. "If he wasn't blinded by everything, he would've noticed they were done with two different knives. You may want to keep your arm concealed from him until it's had a few days to heal properly, if you don't want him to be aware of it. But I'm sure he'll know what happened if he gets a good look at what you did to Jas."

"What—"

"Things you do in the dark never look the same in the light," Chandler said. "That second cut on your arm is perfect. The one on his arm?" He paused for just an instant to shake his head. "It's not. Almost maybe, but not quite. And every single cut he's ever made on himself is absolutely perfect, or perfect for him. Maybe by the time my brother figures out the relationship the two of you have and deals with it . . . maybe it won't matter so much to him that you're sharing your kills. It's understandable. You killed people together last night."

I tried to find it there on his face, the conveyance of the emotion I'd anticipated from him, but I still hadn't found it when he said, "If you didn't share something with him before . . . you do now."

I still didn't see or hear it there. "You're not angry?"

"I'm not angry you have something good in your life," Chandler said believably. "Dealing with this sort of shit is hard, Aster. Why should I be angry about my friend not having to go it alone?"

It was hard not to let the unexpected statement faze me, but it also wasn't. Of course I was his friend. Him saying it didn't change what I already knew. I might've smiled if he'd said it at another point in time, but I couldn't now, so I answered his question without a beat. "Because it upsets your brother."

"My brother is being ignorant," he said. "He doesn't like it that you're sharing something special with a person that isn't him. I'm not going to lie; I don't like Jas. I think he's an asshole. But I bet he's not that way with you, is he? Not all the time, at least."

When I said nothing in response he nodded.

"I thought so. One day I'll figure out how you get everyone to show who they really are to you."

"They don't," I barely said.

"Oh yes, they do." He sounded so sure, but he had no idea. "Maybe it's just that everyone knows you can see through them and they decide there's really no point in trying to hide. Or maybe it's because they know they can trust you. You would never tell someone another person's secrets, would you? That's why you made that big scene last night with your father's Reaper, so they couldn't hear his secrets. And then you went and stood far enough away that you wouldn't hear them either. Who *does* that?" He paused before answering his own question, in a sense. "*We* don't."

Chandler tilted his head before very slowly adding, "And I *bet* you didn't say a single word to him about his son, did you? Probably have no intention of ever doing so until he decides to tell you about it while in his right mind, if he ever does."

I looked away.

A few seconds passed before he asked, "Does it upset you?"

"What?" I asked.

"That he has a son," he said. "Does it upset you?"

"Why would it?"

"Because he has a child and didn't bother telling you," Chandler said nonchalantly. "Or simply because he has a child. Or maybe even because he shares something special with a woman that isn't you." I caught him shrugging.

I looked into his eyes and said, "No."

He grinned and pointed a finger in the air. "I almost believed that." He turned and—

"Chandler."

He halted and looked back at me.

I barely shook my head. "I would never lie to you."

He turned all the way back, raising both his eyebrows. Clearly asking me . . .

I told him, "It's the wrong word." *Upset* wasn't the word I would call it.

He looked into my eyes for only a few seconds before nodding.

As he nodded, someone walking past somewhat nearby caught my attention for an instant.

I was unsure what Chandler might've seen in my eyes, but his were narrowed at me when we met gazes.

Only a few seconds passed after, and I wondered if he could see all the things I couldn't say.

If he could see any of it. If he knew . . .

I miss you.

His brow furrowed, and he turned and walked away.

Tears fought to well, though they lost.

To move on from the interaction, I assessed my surroundings, and I realized I now felt as though I had nowhere at all to fit.

I belonged nowhere, next to no one. I was simply . . . *here.*

I stepped back into the trees—realizing distantly that they were beginning to thin out somewhat—and decided I would practice being quiet on an uneven, cluttered surface alone as I'd intended to do before.

I did not go far. I ensured I could always see at least one person from wherever I was, just in case. I knew safety was only a word, an *illusion*, but I tried to tell myself that having eyes on another living person might make some sort of difference.

I quickly became frustrated at the difficulty of what I was attempting to do. I did not focus on my breathing. My breathing was irrelevant if my feet made noise. So I cried frustrated tears as I attempted to place my boots silently on the ground.

No one came to help or give me any advice on how to make it work, but I didn't care. I did not want anyone to see me failing so horribly at such a simple task. I did not want anyone to see that I'd led the Reapers from Bethel straight to us with my racket. I'd almost gotten Jastin killed because I could not *walk*.

I felt as though my feet were giant boulders and every step that I made was those giant boulders being tossed down from a great height and breaking apart. I could not make the noise stop no matter how carefully I moved or how hard I tried, even in the daylight.

My face was soaked with tears when Anders found me and said, "You need to eat so we can leave."

"I'm not hungry," I told him dismissively.

"I don't care." His voice was unyielding. "You're *going* to eat. And before all that, you're going to have someone get this shit out of your skin." He gestured at me.

"And why should I?" I demanded, holding my head up and staring at him through my blurry vision.

"Because I said so," was his response.

I huffed and grumbled as I followed him back out of the trees. I did not tell him that I didn't have to listen to him. He was not my father, after all. But I did not have to listen to my father, either. So I allowed some bit of reason to come through from where it was scratching at the surface of all the madness. And I listened to Anders because all he ever did was try to help me.

Even if I had no idea what to do or how to help myself . . . listening to Anders seemed a good direction to travel.

That did not mean I wanted to.

CHAPTER THIRTY-SIX

LOYALTY AND JEALOUSY

OST EVERYONE WAS STILL NAPPING on the ground while the damage to my body was tended to. I'd asked Stanley to do it and he'd walked to the back of the carriage without a word. I followed and watched him pull out a bag of instruments.

His voice was so quiet when he gestured at my arms and said, "This isn't it, is it?"

I fidgeted a bit, looking away from his face and off toward the trees to shake my head.

He said nothing and I eventually brought my gaze back to him. His eyes were on mine, but I saw his hand move. Palm up, he crooked his finger.

I sniffled in hard and partially lifted my shirt, exposing quite a lot of random things stuck in and embedded into my skin, including a piece of wood—well over six inches long—running lengthwise in my side. Only a small bit of brown could be seen, tinged with red, but its length and width were easily detectable by the bulge it made.

Stanley gestured for me to pull my shirt back down. "At least you didn't try doing that yourself. I'll get your arms first." He then walked to the other side of the carriage, putting it between us and everyone else.

I watched as he laid everything out neatly onto the ground then sat down next to it. I sat when and where he gestured for me to. I watched as he sterilized several things with a clear liquid that he then extended to me. I shook my head, he shook his, then got to work.

Despite all the wounds I'd sustained in my life, I'd never felt anything quite like this before.

It was another new sort of pain, worse than sunburns, but nowhere near as bad as some other things. Some parts were worse than others.

I supposed that was life.

Stanley was silent as he worked, focused on the task. He only spoke twice for quite a while. Once, when I pulled my shirt over my head. A few very quiet obscenities fell out of his mouth when he saw the old scars on my back. The second time was when someone coughed. He said, "Put that back on," and then left.

He wasn't gone long and he didn't say a word when he returned despite me asking what was going on. He just shook his head, I removed my shirt again, and he set off to work once more. All the bits of objects were removed from my arms, my torso and back, then the few things that had somehow managed to get themselves in my legs and my hips.

He saved the large piece of wood in my side for last, and he spoke again then in a hushed tone.

"If I could manage to get hold of this and pull it out, it would splinter and leave slivers in your side. It's the type of wood. I have to cut it out. Sometimes the only way to get things out is to cut them open."

"That's not the only way," I informed him.

He raised an eyebrow at me, so I explained.

"Best doesn't mean only."

He smiled a little. "Sometimes *best* is the only thing worth mentioning."

I declined the clear liquid when he offered it again, and I let him cut my side open.

Despite being partially numbed from being poked and cut at for an hour or so . . . this was not like the rest. I gritted my teeth and fought so hard against the sound building up in my chest, demanding to be released. I was silent and, after a few seconds, I felt the wood being removed.

"This is just deep enough that it can either be sewn up or not," he said. "You'll be fine regardless, but you'll be less likely to get an infection if you let me close it properly. Given our current situation, I suggest you let me do it, but the choice is yours."

"Sew it up."

I almost screamed when he poured the liquid on my side, but I managed not to. I'd had enough practice, I supposed. I gritted my teeth again and closed my eyes so tightly it was almost as painful as my side. There was poking, tugging, and tightness, but like all things . . . it passed.

"I know you've been having Bryon tea," Stanley said as he was cleaning the instruments again. "You should be safe to cut those stitches out in about two days."

"Will—" I stopped speaking and he turned to look at me. "Will you do it, please?"

He analyzed my face for a moment, nodded his head, and did not ask me why, for which I was grateful. I did not want to explain to him that, with my hands refusing to cooperate in such a way . . . I wouldn't have been able to do it, not without likely cutting myself up far worse.

I replaced my shirt. When Stanley wasn't looking, I grabbed the stick that had been in my side from off the ground, where it was resting amid a pile of twigs, rocks, and the like. Then I walked the opposite way of what he'd gone, shoving it inside my bag before I made my way around the carriage. I found Stewart halfway between my position and the fire, just sitting there. I stopped moving for a moment, realizing . . . he'd been guarding me.

I resumed my walking, not knowing what I should say to him, if anything. I'd come up with nothing by the point I reached him, but he'd stood and was looking at me. All I did was nudge him with my right arm as I passed.

He almost seemed embarrassed, which made the moment all the more awkward. But he went one way, I went another, and the moment was over.

I sat down near the fire and ate alone, despite not being the slightest bit hungry. As I ate the unwanted food, I watched my father and Anders speaking alone a good ways off, both of them occasionally stealing glances at me. They didn't even bother trying to be discreet about it.

The instant I was finished eating, the nappers on the ground were roused.

There was a bit of an argument—which I was not involved in—before we set off. Jastin refused to ride in the carriage any longer. My father spent a short time arguing with him on the matter and informing him that he needed to allow his body to heal properly, which I agreed with. Then my father gave up and told Jastin that he could be an imbecile if he insisted on it, which I also agreed with.

Jastin's response had been a very down-sounding, "It's what I've always been good at, Sir."

Jastin did not ride next to me, instead remaining next to my brother. I rode entirely alone for the very first time since leaving my life of confinement in New Bethel. I likely would've been happy about it, if not for the circumstances. I watched Jastin from a distance throughout the day, worried he would injure himself further. He never once looked back at me, nor did my brother.

It was a very lonely day.

When we stopped for the night, there were not only two Reapers taking shifts together. Half of them were awake at once and the other half would take up their place in the middle of the night.

I was no longer allowed to participate at all.

My brother took up my position next to Jastin. I only allowed myself a moment to stare at the two of them lying back to back before settling myself down in the middle of the circle.

It was a very lonely night.

I was not ashamed that I cried a little. I was not ashamed that I was afraid of how stranded I felt in the middle of that double circle of Reapers. I was not ashamed to admit that I was humiliated for being considered too weak to help, and even more so for knowing I was. I was not ashamed that I missed the safety of knowing Jastin was just behind me. I was not ashamed that I missed feeling as though I were taking care of him.

But I *was* ashamed that I wanted to go punch both he and my brother in their respective faces.

The next day was exactly the same, at least in its ways. I attempted to be silent in the thinning trees while we were stopped and the sun was in the sky, and no one spoke a word to me then or otherwise. No one acted as though I were there at all. Not my father. Not Chandler or Chase. Stanley or Stewart. Ahren. Agatha or Amber. Not even

Anders. And certainly not Jastin. I should've expected nothing more and could only blame myself.

But it was on the evening after that second silent day when my brother came and sat down beside me on the grass. No one was anywhere near us because it was painfully clear that no one wanted me near.

Ahren said, "He's embarrassed."

I looked over and blinked at him.

"Embarrassed about messing up and endangering your safety," he said. "Embarrassed about you having to carry him back. Embarrassed about all you had to do afterward. And embarrassed about what you overheard. I believe he's upset you didn't mention it to him."

I brought my gaze to the ground. "That's ridiculous."

"Maybe so." Ahren shrugged. "But it's why he's behaving this way. He didn't tell me any of those things of course, but I've known him a very long time."

"He's embarrassed about those things because I'm female and untrained." It was why anyone would be embarrassed about those things, I thought.

"He's embarrassed about them because he's in love with you," he said. "He's very torn. Part of him feels he should have told you about his son, but the other part is telling him it doesn't matter either way. That's the part he listens to most often."

I said nothing and continued staring at the ground.

"There are a lot of things a lot of people should have told you," Ahren continued. "I should have told you I was your brother. I should have told you about our father. I should have told you we have different rules concerning children than most other cities. So I'm going to willingly tell you now that I have a daughter."

I looked over at him then with wide eyes. "I'm an aunt?" I had never even contemplated. . . .

"Only by blood," he said. "Just as I'm only a father by blood. The word and everything it's supposed to mean?" He shook his head. "I'm not."

"I don't understand." That made no sense.

"We don't necessarily have our children taken from us the same as they do in other cities." Very slowly he added, "But we're required to reproduce."

When I sat there gaping at him and said nothing, he went on.

"The rules are lengthy and frustrating. I won't burden you with them right now. I'll simply tell you we're required to produce Reapers to keep our numbers up."

I said nothing.

He narrowed his eyes after an extended time of silence and said, "Your loyalty to him is . . . Well, it's quite astounding."

"I don't know what you mean," I told him.

"I know you want to ask me whether he loved the mother of his child." His head tilted slightly. "And if he still does. I know you do. But you're not going to ask me that, are you, no matter how badly you want to?"

I looked back at the ground. "I don't care if he does."

"Oh, you are such a liar now, baby sister." The taunting in his voice was undeniable. "Or perhaps you won't ask me simply because you know I'll inform you it's not my business to tell. Believe it or not, I *do* know the answer, but I *won't* tell you. And you *do* care."

"I don't."

"And if I didn't know you, I would believe every lie you tell." He nodded his head thoughtfully for a moment before adding, "You know . . . it's almost a shame you didn't spend your life training. I'm inclined to believe you would have made an impeccable Reaper."

Then, he stood and walked away.

I did not bother trying to conceal my crying once he'd gone. No one was close and no one would notice me doing it. No one would know about the slap in the face I'd just received from my brother.

WHEN ALL THE SHAME AND SADNESS washed down my face through my tears, I was left with absolutely nothing but anger. Anger and determination. I knew there could only a select few reasons as to why my brother had behaved that way toward me. He had never once treated me in such a way before. I would find out which of those reasons was the cause of it, and then, I would feel better.

I stormed over to where my brother and Jastin were sitting far away from everyone else on the opposite side of the camp.

"Did he put you up to it?" I demanded of Ahren.

"Up to what, baby sister?" he asked, sounding baffled as to what I could be inquiring about. But there was a note of innocence in his tone, implying he couldn't possibly hold any guilt in whatever it was.

"You know damn well what I'm talking about, Ahren," I said firmly. "Either he put you up to it, or you did it for your own reasons. Either loyalty because he wishes to be away from me, or jealousy because you wish for me to be away from him. Which is it?"

"What is she talking about?" Jastin's voice was quiet and directed at my brother.

"And what is your reason for asking while I'm with him?" Ahren's left eyebrow rose. "To see if he'll become angry with me and take your side?"

"You've been with him constantly for the past three days, so when in the world could I ask you alone?" I asked in disbelief. "And I'm asking to know the reasoning behind why my brother was intentionally hurtful to me for the very first time in my life."

"What did you say to her?" Jastin asked him calmly. He still had not looked at me once.

"Clearly you don't know," I said to him without taking my eyes off my brother. And then, to Ahren I asked, "So was it loyalty or jealousy, then?"

"*What* did you say to her?" Jastin repeated. I could tell he was losing his patience.

Distantly I knew I shouldn't be burdening him while he was healing, but it would not physically harm him.

When my brother did nothing more than stare back at me, Jastin finally looked at me. "What did he say to you?"

"You tell me which of those reasons it was," I told my brother. "And I won't tell him the two things you taunted me over. Then you can know without a doubt my reason for doing this was not to harm your relationship, only to understand why my brother would say such intentionally hurtful things to me."

Ahren stood and leaned down into my face. The word, "*Both*," slipped out from between his teeth.

"Well . . . I hope it was worth it." I nodded. "I would've *never* done that to you." Then I walked away.

I did not feel any better after receiving my answer. I did not feel any better because it didn't change the hidden messages in my brother's taunting.

It did not change the fact that he had basically called me worthless, making it very clear I could never protect Jastin the way he could. It did not change the fact that he'd told me Jastin was still in love with the mother of his child. I knew he was because, if he *wasn't* . . . my brother would not have mentioned it to hurt me. And that felt, in some ways, as if being told he truly didn't care for me at all.

It was irrational and it made absolutely no sense, given what had happened and my feelings about everything, but I went over to Chase. I grabbed his hand, jerked him to his feet, and pulled him into the trees.

He asked me several questions as I dragged him along behind me, but I didn't answer any of them because I did not care to talk to him. When I could no longer see or hear anyone back at the camp, I grabbed his face and kissed him.

At first he was—rightfully—hesitant, but then he gave into it as I thought he might. But it wasn't long before he pulled away and narrowed his eyes at me. "Have you slept with him?"

"You know I've slept next to him," I stated.

"No," he said. "Have you been intimate with him?"

My face scrunched. "Of course not."

Chase analyzed my face in the darkness, looking for a sign of deception that would not be there. When he seemed to be satisfied that I'd not done so, he kissed me again.

I did not mind that he could tell I'd kissed Jastin since he'd kissed me last. I knew he was aware of it, given I felt a bit more experienced at kissing than I had before. I did not care for a great many reasons. He mustn't have cared either, because he didn't ask me that particular question. I was certain that, if he *had* asked, I wouldn't have cared to give him the truthful answer.

In that moment, I almost felt more out of control than I had when I'd been carrying Jastin's limp body back to the camp, only it was anger I felt inside me instead of everything else. Only anger and nothing.

CHAPTER THIRTY-SEVEN

PROMOTION

THAT WAS HOW MY FATHER FOUND US—with Chase's arms around me and our faces together.

"What are the two of you *doing* out here?" he demanded. He sounded, and appeared, shocked. I had to admit it was somewhat satisfying.

"Kissing," I answered innocently, watching my father's gaze dart from my face, to Chase's, then to Chase's hands which were on either side of my hips.

Those hands moved away when my father's focus remained on them.

Truly, kissing was all the two of us had been doing, apart from a very small and insignificant bit of touching on Chase's part.

"Time to stop and go to sleep." My father was clearly unhappy, but I believed he was trying quite hard not to show as much. I started walking, and my father seemed unable to stop himself from saying, "And I don't want to catch the two of you doing . . . *that* again."

I stepped past him. "Then don't be the one to look for us if we leave together."

Chase was walking behind me, but my father said his name which caused us both to stop.

"A word?" my father asked. It was not a true question but an order. Even I could tell as much.

I shrugged and went back to camp, leaving the two of them alone together. I did not care what my father wanted to say to him or that he was ordering him around. I also did not care that I very well might've gotten Chase a bit of trouble from my father, though I likely should have.

I hadn't *forced* him to accompany me. He could've said no or otherwise stopped it from happening, but he hadn't. He'd made his decision.

I had absolutely no intention of sleeping so I went and sat next to the fire, which was quite far away from where everyone else was. I did wonder for a moment how it always seemed to work out that no one was ever where I wanted to be. Then I remembered that was often my own doing.

It was not three minutes before Jastin came and sat down beside me, gingerly placing himself onto the ground. Even with the clear drink, he did not seem to be healing very fast. My father and Chase still had not returned by that point, meaning it had clearly been more than *a* word.

I didn't want to look over at Jastin, but I simply could not help myself. An entire silent conversation passed between the two of us, at least inside my head.

A conversation where he accused me of dragging Chase into the woods either because of the feelings he held for the mother of his child or because he had told me to fix things—either way, because of him for one reason or another.

A conversation where he accused me of wording things in the way I had in front of him because I knew he would demand my brother inform him of what had happened once I'd gone.

A conversation where I accused him of treating me as though I were in love with him when I wasn't and declared I did not give a damn about the mother of his child or his feelings for her.

I was not entirely surprised when I realized neither of us would accuse the other of anything. I supposed there truly was no point to it after all, not when we could see one another so clearly.

It was several minutes later when he nonchalantly asked, "Will you be sleeping next to me again?"

"Are you finding yourself wanting me to now?" I spoke in the same tone he'd just used with me.

"I always wanted you to," he said. "But your father and brother had a very convincing conversation with me about how you would be safer in the middle, given that I was injured. All of it was very . . ." He picked up a very small stick and tossed it into the fire. "*Reasonable.*"

"So what made you change your mind?"

He grinned a little. "I'm finding myself very tired of spending my life listening to other people." He looked at the ground to add, "It seems both of us are rubbing off on one another. Doesn't it?"

I returned his grin. "If it makes you feel better to tell yourself that."

He nudged me playfully with his arm, which made us both smile. I imagined the both of us were thinking that his words were better than admitting that the only time we were ourselves was while we were in one another's company. Or perhaps the closest we came to it. Being near him felt like releasing strain and rigidity.

Sometimes.

"It would make me feel better for you to agree to handle your father and brother if they give us grief about it." He chuckled. "I'm feeling too tired to handle them myself."

"Is that your discreet way of telling me to come to bed?"

"I'm also feeling too tired for you to tease me right now." He frowned at me, but it was certainly faked.

"Not teasing." I laughed. "I'll go to bed with you anytime you'd like. All you have to do is say so."

"Come to bed with me, then." His frown was now replaced with a mischievous grin, and my stomach threatened to flop a bit.

I sighed dramatically. "Only if you'll allow me to check your injury first. No one's looking."

"But you just said . . ." He trailed off purposely and narrowed his eyes.

"Only for my own mental well-being," I said. "It will take me two seconds, and I've been worried about you, given you've been avoiding me."

His head tilted a very small amount. "Are we going there?"

"No," I said. "I care more about your health than your reasons for doing what you do. Be quiet and don't move." I checked again to ensure no one was paying us any attention before leaning over and pulling up the left side of his shirt. "Oh, that's healing quite nicely, it seems." It was scabbed and . . . quite disgusting-looking if I was being wholly honest, but it did not seem to be infected.

"If you're done looking at my body, let's go to sleep." He laughed, then raised an eyebrow. He seemed unable to stop himself from adding, "Unless you're going to let me return the favor."

I snorted when I stood up in front of him, positioning my body so no one behind us would see, then I extended my hand toward him.

He stared at it for what felt like a very long time before taking it in his own and allowing me to pull him up from the ground.

I pretended to ignore the way his face flinched from the movement, and I definitely ignored the slight pulling sensation on my right side. I either did a satisfactory job or he was too preoccupied because he gave no indication of noticing.

I began walking but had only made it one step before he tugged backward on my hand that he still had in his. When he'd properly gotten my attention, he dropped it. I expected to be proven wrong on what he'd possibly noticed, but he said, "Thank you."

I felt my forehead scrunching. "What for?"

I thought he would say for one specific, unknown thing, but he responded with, "Everything." He looked away for a moment and nodded his head thoughtfully. "I haven't been as good a friend to you as you've been to me. I know you think I have, but . . . I haven't. You may be able to say I've been there for you when no one else was, but you can't say I've been there every time you've needed me. But you've been there for me all the time, even though I don't deserve it."

I hadn't been. I didn't really know how, especially when he wouldn't let me be. Before I could think of a way to say as much, he took a deep breath and continued on.

"*You* deserve it," he said. "I think I've spent too much of my time trying to figure out why you want me around, but I already know why and just pretend I don't. So I'm going to stop doing that."

"What are you saying?" I asked. This was so very unlike him that I didn't know what to think about it. I did not feel as though he were playing some sort of a game with me, which was likely what made it so disturbing. "I'm already too far in your debt, Jastin. If you do more for me, I won't ever be able to repay you for it all."

"That's the thing," he said quietly. "You don't owe me anything. And I'm beginning to see I don't owe you anything either. But I know both of us will keep feeling that way, which is sort of my point. If you always feel like you owe me something, you'll always have use for me. Won't you?" He tilted his head. "You deserve so much more than I could ever give you, but as long as you're stupid enough to want me around, I'll be around."

"When the sun is down," I said playfully.

"No." He did not share my smile nor my playfulness. He was being completely serious, and I could see that no words of mine would bring him out of it.

I pursed my lips together because the seriousness was so much more difficult than the playing. What was I supposed to say to this? How could I say anything at all when I didn't even understand what was happening? Was he talking about going back on our arrangement? He wouldn't.

"I've never made a single decision in my life." He shook his head. "Not an important one, at least. I've followed orders. I've done what other people have told me to do." He paused before saying, "I've finally made one."

"And what is that?" Why did I feel so wary?

"I'm yours," he said evenly, as if it was not a difficult thing to say. I knew it was. It was such a difficult thing to say that it should not have come out of his mouth. "You told me I'd already made my decision about what I was going to do when we got back to the city. I'm going to be in charge of your safety when we get there."

I blinked hard at him. That was . . . *unexpected*. "How do you think that will work? What about my brother?"

"That will work because your brother and I are going to talk to your father," he said. "He and I had a very serious discussion about the future and what was important while you were in the trees. I want you to know I'm not doing this because I think you're a little flower who needs protection. I'm doing it because it's the closest you and I will ever get to being partners. That's what I'm going to tell anyone who asks—no jokes, no smartass remarks."

"But I like your jokes and remarks," I told him quietly. They always seemed to make the days a bit brighter somehow, no matter how infuriating they often were.

He smiled and shook his head a little. "And I'll keep making them to you. But I need to change. I can't keep living my life the way I have been. You'll support me in making those changes, won't you?"

"Of course," I said easily. I was unsure how I felt about this or that it could even happen at all, but . . . "I'd support you in anything you felt you needed to do."

"Which is why I have to do it."

I could feel my brow furrowing as I waited for the joke. I waited and waited for some sort of snarky remark.

But then my father stepped out and asked, "Is all that true?"

And when Jastin straightened himself up and said, "It is, Sir," I knew there would be no remark. Jastin ignored Chase's presence beside my father.

"So, you want to trade out my son for my daughter?" he asked blankly. "Why is that, I wonder? Is it because you're in love with her?"

"I won't deny that I am any longer, Sir," Jastin said, which made my eyes widen in shock. "But you can ask your daughter how much stock I put into love, though I'm sure your son has already told you as much. I don't care for it. It's entirely irrelevant to me."

My father turned to me and, in an almost taunting way asked, "Is that true, Aster?"

I looked around at the three of them uncomfortably, feeling uncertain of what I should do or how this would best be handled. Jastin had not once taken his eyes off my father. I decided to be completely honest for now, as I believed that was currently the best approach to take.

"He doesn't care for love at all," I said. "And our relationship with one another has nothing whatsoever to do with it."

My father turned back to Jastin. "So why is it, then," he started slowly, "that if you could, you would want to trade out your thoroughly trained partner for her?"

"If you had seen the way we operate together, Sir, you would not be asking me that question," Jastin replied.

"Her lack of training almost got you killed," my father stated.

I expected my father's remark about me to set Jastin off, but it did not. I suspected that was why he'd said it in the tone he had—waiting for Jastin's temper.

Coolly, Jastin said, "You cannot train instinct and intuition into a person, Sir. She knew we were being followed before I did. She might not be thoroughly trained, but she still saved my life in several ways that night."

"And has my son never saved your life?" My father was still speaking in a blank tone that was not *entirely* blank. Falsely void. Empty, but with spurs.

"He has many times, Sir," Jastin said. "I love your son, but your daughter is the only person I've ever met in my life who can see through me."

"I'm curious how serious you are about this," my father said after a pause. "Your words sound believable, but I've known you for quite a long time, haven't I? You'll forgive me if I'm not inclined to believe you to be telling the truth. Do you even know how?"

"I'll give you a truth, Sir." Jastin clenched his jaw for a moment. "I cut my kills into my body because I'm ashamed of what I've done. I cry about it sometimes when no one is around. I cry about the women and the children I was forced to murder before you came. And sometimes I cry just because I'm relieved your presence means I don't have to do that anymore. I always lied about it because that's what we're trained to do—never feel anything that would get in the way."

He did not look away from my father to say, "She's the only person who's ever looked past my lies and seen the truth. She's the only one who's ever cared to look that far. And it's not just me she does that for. It's everyone. Haven't you heard them all talking about her? Even with our training, we're not half the person your daughter is, and we don't have half her potential. Don't you see that?"

My father stared at Jastin with narrowed eyes for a very long time before asking, "You said Ahren was going to speak to me about this?"

"He and I had a discussion, Sir," Jastin said. "He was going to ask you if we could both be assigned to her when we return to the city. I'm not asking."

"No?"

"No." Jastin's voice was so blank. "I've spent my entire life letting people down, Sir. I don't need to name off the list of them. I'm sure you have it repeating in your head as we speak. You can punish me for insubordination every day, Sir, but I will not let your daughter down no matter what you tell me to do."

"I'm curious . . ." My father paused for effect. "Would you lay down your life for her? I'm not strictly talking about situations like the one you just survived."

Though I did not know what other sort of situation my father could possibly be asking about, Jastin answered his question. "Willingly, Sir."

My father lazily rubbed at the stubble on his chin as he studied Jastin. "Consider yourself on a probationary period," he said eventually. "I'll see how you handle her and her safety for the remainder of our journey, and if you're satisfactory, I'll sign off on your transfer."

A few seconds of silence passed.

"You're used to killing people, aren't you?" my father asked. "I wonder if you're capable of keeping them in line. If you're to be in charge, you'll be in control of . . . How many Reapers will be watching after her directly? *Six*, including yourself. You don't have the vaguest idea how different that is." My father paused. "Your injury is irrelevant now. You may as well pretend it's not there at all."

Jastin nodded and said, "I don't suggest you try to test me while we sleep. From this point forward, I no longer belong to your city. I belong to your daughter. And if anyone gets close to her while she sleeps, I'll kill them. I don't care if it's your men. I can guarantee you I wouldn't feel the slightest bit badly about it."

Chase quietly asked, "Aren't you worried this is about a promotion?"

"Jastin has never cared about promotions." My father smiled. "He's never even cared about his own life. I've never seen him willingly show that he cares about anything other than my daughter." He paused again, staring down at Chase's face. "Perhaps you should take a moment to get better acquainted. You *are* staring at your new superior, after all. I hope you all have a wonderful night."

I was almost entirely certain my father was chuckling silently to himself as he walked away, but I could've been mistaken.

CHAPTER THIRTY-EIGHT

TAKE LOVE AWAY

I TOOK TURNS looking awkwardly between Chase and Jastin during the absolute silence that followed in my father's wake. I'd been concerned about how to handle being asked a direct question in a situation I was unsure of, but seeing the two of them standing there staring at one another intently . . . I hadn't the vaguest clue what to do. Were they going to kill each other?

Surely not, but another fight seemed possible and they *were* Reapers. . . .

"I . . ." I started and then stopped.

Jastin brought his attention to me, but Chase did not take his eyes off him.

"I'm ready to go to sleep, I think." It was an utter lie, and I was sure they were both aware of that fact, but I didn't know what else to do and I'd needed to do *something*. If going to sleep got them away from one another . . .

Wanting to wasn't *technically* a lie. Not a full one.

Jastin nodded. "I'm not happy with the sleeping arrangement. I want our group to tighten the circle."

"Tighten the circle," Chase said slowly as he nodded his own head. "So you want us all sleeping on top of one another when half of us don't trust the other half and she doesn't trust anyone other than you."

"The six of us?" Jastin asked. "We may not trust or *like* one another, but that's irrelevant. Everyone wants her kept safe, so that's going to have to be good enough to suffice. So yes, we're tightening the circle."

"Because she's not trained?" Chase asked, his voice blank. "I thought you believed her capable of protecting herself? I thought her lack of thorough training didn't matter?"

Jastin brought his attention to me, his brow furrowed. "Did you not tell anyone what those Reapers were after?"

"I told my father," I replied. "And Anders was there when I did. I assumed they'd told everyone else."

"Apparently not."

"You *interrogated* them?" Chase asked. "No wonder you almost bled out. Interrogations and cutting kills into your arms. . . . How long did you hide that you were cut up before she realized?"

Jastin somehow kept his cool and said, "You clearly don't know they were sent to abduct her."

Chase's gaze shot to me. I could've imagined he'd forgotten my existence in the world entirely, if not for how quickly his eyes had found mine and that he'd just mentioned me. "Why didn't you *tell* me?"

"You didn't ask," I told him, unruffled. "You were more concerned about who I'd had the experience *with*, rather than the experience itself, weren't you? You've been looking at the wrong things and asking the wrong questions all this time."

Chase muttered off a rather impressive string of profanities as he stood there shaking his head.

"I want you on the other side of her while she sleeps." Jastin said it as if Chase were not throwing a small tantrum.

"*Really*?" Chase asked. I could not tell if he was being hostile because Jastin seemed to be giving him permission to sleep next to me or simply because he was ordering him around.

"Yes." Jastin's voice was still calm. "Given that her brother was extremely unkind to her earlier and the reasons he had for doing so, you're the only person I currently trust at her front. But you *will* put your back to her like you should and you *will* deal with the fact that I'll have one hand on her at all times while she and I are both sleeping. At least until we get where we're going."

"You expect me to be fine with you touching her after you just openly declared you're in love with her?" Chase demanded.

Jastin still was not angry, but I heard him sigh loudly. "Do you listen?"

"What?" Chase chuckled. "That you don't *care* about love? Correct me if I'm wrong, but your entire argument for protecting her is a lie. You wouldn't have been rattling off about your son for everyone to hear before she could get them all away from you if that was true. You *do* care. You just want everyone to think you don't."

I had several choice harsh words preparing themselves in my throat, but they died there when Jastin stepped directly in front of Chase and stared down at his face.

"Do you have a child?" Jastin asked impassively. "I know you don't. So I'm going to explain something very important to you. I want you to ignore her standing behind me and *listen*."

He waited to say anything more.

I wasn't sure if he was hoping Chase would listen harder, if he didn't want to say what he was about to, or if he waited simply because he could.

"I love my son." Jastin said that slowly. "Before I say anything else, get that much through your head." He paused. "You know about our rules, don't you? I'm sure Ahren told you about them at some point or another. So you understand I was assigned to procreate with his mother, and just like the rest of them she got reimbursed *unbelievably* well for her services to our city."

I felt my eyes widening in shock, but I did not move an inch and I did not open my mouth. *Assigned to procreate. . . .*

"A lot of our Reapers, her *brother* included," Jastin went on, briefly pointing a finger back in my direction, "get their assigned female pregnant and leave them alone. Our female Reapers are the same with the fathers when they get pregnant. They have no more contact because they've done what they were required to do and they don't care." He shook his head. "I didn't do that. Cherise didn't want me to be there." Jastin laughed. "She wanted me to leave her alone and just let her have the baby, but I couldn't. And eventually . . . she wanted me there. So I spent months and months watching the little thing she and I had made together growing inside her. I was there when she had him. She even let me name him. They used to take the babies from the mothers right after they had them. They don't do that anymore.

"Six months," Jastin went on. "Six months, I saw him *every day* I wasn't on a mission. I got to hear him laugh and see him smile and watch his little hands grow. And then, when I come back from a mission . . . he's *gone*. And *Cherise*?" Jastin paused to shake his head again. "She doesn't even *care*. She told me he wasn't our child. Can you believe that?" He laughed humorlessly once. "Whose child was he, then? He might not be her child, but he is *my* child. I get to talk to him once a year. He doesn't even *know* who I *am*. I'm not allowed to tell him I'm his father. I would imagine he'll figure it out one day, but who knows when that'll be? Long after I'm dead, I'm sure." He paused. "Do you know how many of our Reapers go to see their children? Would you like to take a guess?"

Chase remained silent with his jaw clenched.

"*Five*," Jastin said. "And don't you know how many we have?"

Chase nodded. "So, you're telling me this to make me see you're *so much better* than you play yourself off to be."

"I'm telling you this so you understand why I don't care about love," Jastin corrected him. "What does loving my son matter? It doesn't give him to me. I can't go in there and demand to have him because I *love* him. He doesn't belong to me." He paused again. "I don't care about love because loving a person changes nothing. Loving her brother didn't stop him from hurting her, did it?

"And if you *think*," Jastin went on quietly after a moment of silence, "that I give a *shit* about loving her . . .? You're *wrong*. Look at her face and see if hearing me say that surprises her. And, while you're at it . . . ask her why she doesn't care. You think she's in love with me, don't you?" Jastin laughed a little. "I think you're right. Ask her why she doesn't care. Please."

Chase did not look at me, though I'd known he wouldn't.

"Love hurts," I barely heard myself say.

It got Chase's attention on me—his jaw unclenched and he tilted his head.

"Trust doesn't."

"There you have it," Jastin said, his calmness returning. "I would never risk losing what I have with her. So you should stop worrying about . . ." He shook his head. "Whatever it is you're worried about. Because I can guarantee you . . . it will *never* happen."

I felt as though I should not have been present for this conversation when Chase asked, "You're saying you're not going to have a problem with the two of us being together when we get to your city? You're just going to sit back and let us sleep together when you're in love with her?" He shook his head then. "I have a hard time believing that. It's easy to say things, isn't it?"

"That's exactly what I'm saying, and I mean every word of it." Jastin's voice had been blank, but I could hear the smile growing on his face when he added, "If she'll still have you."

"What's that supposed to mean?" Chase demanded.

"She and I are very alike in some ways. Not many, but some," Jastin said. "It's defense. You only let yourself be hurt by something so many times until you numb yourself to it. That's why she kept doing what she wanted that caused her to get those scars on her back, not because she's stubborn. She *is*, but that's not why." Jastin paused, and his tone was thoughtful when he spoke again. "I'm *pretty sure* she's just about had it with love. I suggest you try to change her mind if you don't want that to happen. I'd say you're on your last chance."

"Is that so?" Chase asked.

"I'd say it is," Jastin said. "And I know that because she's already tried to fix things with you twice now, am I correct? Dragging you into the woods like her little love slave doesn't count. I gave Cherise three tries to get some sense into her head before I gave up."

Chase laughed. "Sense to be with you?"

"She and I *were* together," Jastin said firmly. "She even wanted to have another child with me. For the payment of course, which is the reason I wouldn't agree to it. Don't ask me why the girl wanted to marry me when she wouldn't have gotten anything from it. And you want to be with Aster why?"

"What do you mean, *why*?" The harsh humor was gone from Chase's voice, leaving nothing but confusion.

"*Why*," Jastin said. "Don't tell me about your little backstory. I already know all about it. Her brother has a *very* difficult time keeping other people's personal information to himself, if you hadn't noticed. And don't tell me it's because you fell in love with her. I'm asking *why*. Take the love away and . . . what is there? What reasons do you have? What does she offer you and you her? What is it about her that makes you feel you can't live without her? It's got to be something or else you wouldn't still be here putting up with me. So what is it?"

Chase's mouth had parted slightly, but nothing came out of it.

"You think on that," Jastin told him, "and get back to her with it."

"You asked the question," Chase stated.

"But she's the one who would care about the answer." Jastin shrugged. "I don't."

"No," Chase said carefully. "You *do* care. You care about everything that has to do with her."

"Think about it." Jastin smiled. "Every time she gets upset with you, every time she's hurt by your lack of faith in her, every time she has *anything* she can't go to you with . . ." He paused and tilted his head before very slowly asking, "Who's she going to come to?"

Chase took a step back and nodded his head in what seemed to be understanding. "*That's* what you're doing," Chase said. "You manipulative bastard."

"You think I'm competing with you or something?" Jastin laughed. "I can't say I'm surprised, but this is what I'm saying about you needing to listen. This isn't *about* me and her. I've already got what I want from her, same as you. Thing is . . . you're breaking what you have. Tell me why you think I'd feel the need to compete. This is all on you."

"Are you *listening* to him?" Chase asked me, his eyes wide.

"I am," I answered. I'd heard every word of it.

"Just listen to me and ask her why she doesn't care." Jastin sounded almost gleeful when he made his request. "*Please.*"

Chase clenched his jaw for a moment before he asked the question. "Why don't you care?"

I frowned and gave him the only response I could. "Because it's the truth."

It was true, and it was the truth.

I hadn't truly been tired before, but I felt as though their conversation had drained me of absolutely everything. I stepped forward, tugged on Jastin's arm, and whispered my own request. "Let's go to bed."

"Yes ma'am," was his response, but I did not miss the smile he shot Chase.

So I said, "Stop smiling at him that way."

The smile did not leave Jastin's face; he simply turned it to me instead. "If you insist."

On this occasion, I *did* insist, but I did not have to say so. Jastin walked away with me, no further words or tugging required.

We'd only made it a few steps away before Chase said, "Aster."

I stopped and turned to him, finding him staring at me with his head tilted.

"How did he see the scars on your back?"

"He was the only person I trusted to watch my back while I bathed," I answered blankly.

"But you knew he would look," Chase said. "Did you trust him to do that?"

"He looked to tell me to get in the water because I'd been followed," I stated. "He's seen less of me than most my father's Reapers, I would imagine. Perhaps you should be angry with them instead." I felt my own head tilting slightly when I asked, "Are you satisfied?"

Chase did not respond to me, so I resumed walking.

We'd made it halfway to the bedding area when Jastin said, "You know I looked more than that."

I frowned before informing him, "I'm far too tired to go there."

But he smiled because he knew my expression was halfhearted.

CHAPTER THIRTY-NINE

SOMETHING TO THINK OVER

E HADN'T EVEN MADE IT all the way to the bedding area when Jastin said, "I'm not going to give you my back."

I stopped walking, he stopped, and I frowned at him, genuinely then. That was the *point* of it.

"I'm trying to show your father I'm going to take care of you, not that I expect you to take care of me," he said. "We have to be sensible about the way we handle things until we get where we're going. And then when we get there, you and I are going to have to be even more sensible in many more ways. If we're not, he'll put your brother in charge of you which ultimately means *he* will be in charge of you."

I understood what he was saying, but I didn't like it. Rather than focus on things that seemed so petty in comparison, I asked, "Is that how it would be?"

"You have no idea." He shook his head as if internally lost in the possibility of it. "I've only ever seen Ahren disobey your father once, which was . . ." He glanced over his shoulder for a moment. "You know what. He won't directly disobey him when he's under his nose, especially with something like this. I can promise you that."

"But you like my father," I said, my voice quiet. I could see now that he did, and I couldn't understand why he would go against his wishes.

When realizing the way Jastin felt about my father and why he felt that way . . . I didn't believe it was comparable.

"I like your father being in control of the city," he said. "But you don't want him in control of you and there's a big difference between those two things. I'm trying to help you. If that means straightening up and kissing a lot of ass . . . so be it. You and I always need to be on the same page."

"We are," I whispered. Then I nudged his arm with mine, thinking of what he'd said to Chase about sleeping arrangements. "If you wanted to put a hand on me, you just had to say so."

"I don't have a clue what you're talking about," he said innocently.

I shook my head at him as we walked the remainder of the way to our destination. I ignored the talk of strategy shortly after that as I laid down and buried myself between my two blankets, but I did gather that they would be pulling their own half-awake, half-asleep shifts. Chandler, Stanley, and Stewart would be sleeping during the last half of the night, but for now it would be Ahren lying with his back near the tops of our heads.

Chase had not yet come over to us. When I made a remark about it, Jastin said, "It's his choice whether he wants to sleep or not."

My brother put his back to me until Chase would come, if he came at all. Ahren had not looked at me once.

I hoped Chase would come and do what Jastin had instructed. If a plan for my safety was being implemented and he refused to take part in it . . . I didn't know that I could keep him safe. I didn't even know if I could keep him *here*.

If he refused to cooperate, would that nullify the deal I'd made with my father? Would that automatically endanger Chandler as well?

Even if they were in no direct danger from my father and his Reapers . . . they had nowhere else to go. If Chase was run off, Chandler would leave. I couldn't lose one of them, let alone *both*.

I decided not to think on it, as I couldn't control anyone's decisions.

So I laid there, rigid under my blanket as I waited for the contact I knew would come. I expected only a hand, as that was all Jastin had said, but he scooted himself close to my back, draping his left arm over me. He did not hold me tightly.

I felt very strange as I realized there was something quite perfect about lying with him in this way, almost like our bodies were made to fit with one another while we slept.

That was ridiculous.

If our bodies were made for anything it was protecting each other.

He should not have been lying with me like this.

My heart and head waged war with one another. One of them told the other that Jastin and I should've been lying back to back. The other responded with something along the lines of . . . *This is nice.*

I did not know which of them won out when I moved my blanket a bit and took Jastin's hand in mine beneath his own, which was covering part of my top half, concealing his arm. My head said I was doing it because I would know more quickly if something was happening and I had my hand on him. My heart said I'd done it simply because I wanted to.

I did not sleep for a long time while I laid there feeling his even breathing on my neck. I pretended I was sleeping, but I was still awake when Chase came and laid down in front of me sometime later, taking Ahren's place. I knew Jastin had been pretending to as well, but when his breathing came more slowly after Chase's arrival, I understood he'd only been waiting for the last member of our party to arrive, because it would be safer.

I lied and told myself that my head had won the war. I lied and convinced myself I'd been staying awake for the exact same reason Jastin had and that it had absolutely nothing to do with wanting to enjoy the contact for as long as I could.

I WOKE HALFWAY THROUGH THE NIGHT when they switched positions. I no longer felt a body behind me, and I heard Chandler whisper.

"I'm not comfortable with that."

"Aster," Jastin said from behind me. I knew he'd knelt down close to my head.

"Hmm?" was my sleepy response.

"Do you have any issues with Chandler lying with you the same way I just was?"

It took me a moment to force out a mumble of, "No." I did it as quickly as I could.

"Just business," Jastin said as he stood.

I heard him suck in a quiet breath from the pain of his injury, but I pretended I hadn't.

Chandler was nowhere near as relaxed as Jastin had been when he laid down behind me. He was infinitely less relaxed when he draped his arm over me. I thought back on my first impression of him—a wall. It felt like I had a wall at my back.

I was not fully in control of myself when I whispered, "Will you hold my hand?"

I almost thought he was chuckling when he did what I asked him to, where I then covered it with blanket. It took away a great deal of his rigidity, which felt nice.

I was *certain* he was chuckling when he said, "I think I spoiled you with that before."

I breathed out and admitted, "I believe I enjoy being spoiled." I squeezed his hand and whispered. "Please sleep well." Then I used my other hand to pat whoever was in front of me so they knew the message was for them as well. I did not care who it was, as either option was all right with me.

And I laid there, perhaps more awake than I'd ever been in all my life, tears threatening to spill if I were to open my eyes.

For how long I was unsure before I barely heard, "I know you're still awake."

I said nothing.

"I can get one of them to switch with me."

I squeezed Chandler's hand.

"What will get you to sleep?"

I said, barely, "You're uncomfortable."

I felt him take in a deep breath behind me. I felt it released. I felt another deep breath.

He pulled me even closer to him, tightening his grip with his arm.

I laid there.

He whispered, "*You're* uncomfortable."

Though my body felt rigid, I told him, "I'm not."

It was the wrong word.

A few seconds passed before . . . "Do you promise?"

I nodded.

He must've seen it. "Would it help if I tell you that I'm not?"

"Do you promise?"

He said, barely, "I promise."

I took in a deep breath and tried as hard as I could to not let a smile pull at my face. "Goodnight."

He whispered, "Goodnight."

I ONLY WOKE AGAIN when the sun was just barely rising in the sky. Even the stray sounds of Reapers in the night hadn't pulled me from sleep. In my grogginess, I wondered how much sway illusions were capable of.

Chandler had hastily stood and made a fast retreat, and the movement had startled me. I looked around, feeling quite well-rested, and found Jastin sitting nearby with an amused sort of expression on his face.

"What's so funny?" I asked as I went over to him.

"We've been gone for weeks now and I *think* that's the first time I've ever seen Chandler sleep well." He was watching Chandler as he spoke.

"You didn't answer my question," I told him with another yawn.

He just shrugged and smiled so I decided to give up because I sincerely doubted it was important. I was just glad to know he might've slept well.

I went and took care of whatever morning business I needed to take care of. When I was done with that, I hadn't made it halfway to the fire when Chase stepped in front of me.

"Can we talk?" he asked, sounding wary.

I sighed and decided against informing him that I'd just woken—which he already knew—and did not feel like talking about much of anything to anyone. I hadn't known what had been going on with him the several times I'd instigated speaking. He'd always spoken to me whenever I'd wanted him to. I could return the favor.

"Sure," I said. I followed him a good distance away from everyone else, and I stood there awkwardly when he stopped, bracing myself for it.

He said, "Let's fix this."

I nodded my head slowly and took a deep breath. "Are you saying that because you genuinely want to or because of what Jastin said to you last night?"

I had to commend his truthfulness when he answered blankly with, "Both." He took his own deep breath then released it. "The only way we can do that is if we're honest with one another. So I'm going to ask you again." He paused, either bracing himself or giving me time to process his words. "Are you in love with him?"

"Not in the same way I'm in love with you," I replied. "Which I'm assuming is what you're asking."

"Aster," Chase said firmly. "You know that's not what I asked you. Are you in love with him?"

I narrowed my eyes as I tried to work through what he meant if not that. If he meant love existing between people . . . "Yes."

He looked away and nodded. There was a very uncomfortable silence before he spoke again, like an unpleasant sound grating at your ears or a crawling sensation across your back. "Do you still want to be with me?"

"Nothing has anything to do with me wanting to *be* with someone else."

He held his hands up in front of him and closed his eyes. "Please stop talking in circles around me." It almost sounded as though he were begging me for as much, but he could've just been frustrated and exhausted.

I felt I was being straight.

He opened his eyes. "Do you want to be with me?"

I clenched my jaw for a moment. "I'm not entirely sure. I love you. I cannot deny what you've done for me and have been *willing* to do for me, but I also cannot ignore the way things are. I don't feel as though you understand me, nor do I feel like I can go to you with things. I worry now that you wouldn't accept the person I truly am." I paused to purse my lips before stating, "I'd say that's problematic to a relationship, wouldn't you?"

We stood there staring at one another for quite a while before I decided to continue on.

He clearly was not yet prepared to say anything more.

"You and I love one another and we've done things that people who are in love do. But I don't feel as though I know you, either. I didn't know you could be such a jealous person, and I didn't know you behaved like a child when you felt threatened."

"You think I'm behaving like a child. . . ." He said it slowly, as if he were trying to work it all out inside his head.

"I've come to you several times, attempting to explain things to you," I began. "But you didn't listen to me. You saw and heard only what you wanted. I'm sure you feel I've done you some great injustice by having feelings for another man and, in all honesty . . . you would be right. You don't deserve that and I'm very sorry it hurts you. But I also can't feel it was wrong for me to have developed those feelings. I believe it was only natural, given the situation."

I could tell he was trying very hard to remain calm, and it only proved to me that he truly did want to work on this. "So you're essentially saying this is my fault."

"I don't believe this is anyone's fault," I told him. "I hate to say this, but it's simply the way things played out."

His eyes narrowed. "Are you sure about that?"

I nodded.

"How many times has he asked you to fix things with me?"

Though he still did not understand . . .

I answered his question. "Several."

"Every time you've tried, right?"

I did not give him any sort of response for that particular question, but I didn't believe he truly expected one.

"Let me ask you this," he started. "Are you *completely* positive he's not playing you? Hasn't it crossed your mind that he might really be working for your father? We go undercover all the time, Aster. I can assure you that we've all done more difficult tasks than what he's done with you. Are you *positive*?"

"I *have* thought about it," I admitted, my voice blank. "Especially after the events of last night and their peculiarity. Does it make you feel better to hear as much?"

"And you're so loyal to him, you have *so much faith* in him, that you don't believe he's on a mission?"

I sighed and stood there blinking as I attempted to formulate the correct response.

I felt as though I needed to choose my words very carefully. "I will admit that every interaction he and I have ever had with one another could be false on his part." It all could've been false. "He would have to be unbelievably good at his job, which I don't deny could be a possibility. As of right now, I don't believe it *has* been false. But I also won't deny that, even if it's all been true . . . he's untouchable by my father."

"But he doesn't care about anything other than you," Chase said. I got the distinct impression he was mocking, either the situation in general or just me. "Your father said so last night."

"I believe my father said that for me to hear because he believes me to be ignorant," I stated. Partial truths worded in ways to make people believe what you wanted them to. "I'm quite certain if Jastin truly is on my side, my father will attempt to sway him with the one thing he wants."

"Which is you."

"He doesn't want me." My voice finally rose a level from the composure I'd thus far been able to maintain. "He wants his *son*."

Chase's eyes narrowed. "You think your father would give him his son."

"I think he would offer it, yes, if he hasn't already." I nodded. "You want to know why I believe all this is true, don't you?" I paused. "Jastin loves my brother and, if he were playing me, it would not only be a betrayal to me but to my brother as well. Depending on the depth to which this hypothetical scenario runs. The *only* way I believe he would betray my brother is if he received his son in exchange for it."

When seeing the expression on Chase's face . . .

I tilted my head and said, "You seem astounded I would think about that."

"You're in love with him." He shook his head. "People see what they want to see when they're in love."

"Perhaps," I conceded. "You may take offense to this, but love is nearly as irrelevant a thing to me as it is to him. Love didn't keep my father from abandoning me, did it? Love doesn't make something inherently yours. And if you're stunned by my ability to think properly . . . I'm very sorry to hear that."

He smiled sadly at the ground. "You weren't going to run away with me because you were in love with me, were you? You loved me, yes, but that wasn't why, was it?"

"I don't suspect you'd like to hear the answer to that question," I told him. "But I will tell you that I would never make any decision in my life based solely on feelings."

"And what about you testing my food?"

"Only logical, and only right," I told him. "From my perspective."

He took a deep breath and continued to stare at the ground for quite some time. "What do you think he would do?" He finally looked up. "If all this is true, his feelings for you, the things he says . . .? What would he do if his son was offered to him?"

"If it were anything else, I believe I would be able to tell you the answer to that question correctly and without any hesitation," I said. "I've never had a child, clearly, but I know they can make you do things you wouldn't normally do. If I had one, I'm sure I *would* make decisions based on feelings and love. So, if it were *me* . . . I would take my child. I suppose that's likely the answer for what he would do."

"Because it's what you would do?"

"Yes," I answered blankly. I did not feel like talking on the subject any longer, so I began to walk away. The conversation on fixing things truly hadn't gotten us anywhere, yet again.

So . . . *pointless.*

I had only made it a few steps away when Chase spoke again, stopping me.

"Your brother told me . . . Jas is *very* good at his job. Did you ever think the way I was acting was because of that and not your feelings for him? Maybe *you're* the one who's been blinded." He paused to tilt his head at me from where I was staring at him over my shoulder. "It's just something to think over."

CHAPTER
FORTY

HEARD

I DID NOT MISS THE FACT that Jastin, Ahren, Anders, and my father were not anywhere within sight when I sat down next to the fire. I did a great deal of thinking as I watched the flames licking at the wood and reaching into the air, and I forced myself to periodically take bites of my breakfast.

I was in the middle of a game, I knew, and I was being played. The problem was that I did not know by whom. None of this was so simple as my father wanting me back with him and kept safe. It was such a shame that it wasn't.

I wondered if Reapers felt this way all the time. I knew they constantly looked over their shoulders to watch for someone coming to stab them in the back or slit their throats, but . . . if you could not trust the people you trusted, whom could you trust?

That was the question, and I could find no way around the truth. There was only one answer.

It was only a matter of time before my father dangled Jastin's child in front of his face, if he'd not done so already. If Jastin told me about it when it happened, would that mean he was truly on my side?

Was my *brother* even on my side? Perhaps he'd known all along that my father was coming to get me. Perhaps the shock on his face in seeing him standing in the doorway had been part of the plan. I didn't know what to think about the realization that my brother could likely fool me better than Jastin, but I did not doubt he could.

Who had more reasoning, the most motivation? That was the next question.

I did not know now why Chase was behaving the way he was. Was it feelings or rightfully placed wariness and suspicion? Had he only said that bit at the end to purposely create doubt inside me? Given the way Jastin was playing—and he *was* in some sense, though I did not know in what sense exactly—I could not put it past Chase to play the same game or to use whatever advantages he could.

And when Anders came back before the other three looking particularly distracted, I did not know if he was truly feeling that way or only pretending to for me to see. Had he been part of something or eavesdropping? Was I to think it was one and not the other?

I tilted my head where I stared at him from across the fire.

When he looked up and met my eyes, he blinked as though he were startled and moved his gaze away.

I followed it.

I looked over at Amber where she was sitting on the grass, talking happily with Agatha. When she met my eyes, she smiled widely as though we were the very best of friends. Did she truly feel that way, or was she like most of the female Reapers as they'd been presented to me? Always trying to prove they could do what the men could. Heartless.

I looked over at Stanley and Stewart next, who were sitting relatively close to me. They were talking about something, but I couldn't quite make out what it was. I heard Stewart snort once. They both met my eyes and the humor dropped away from their faces for the remainder of the time I was watching them, while their eyes stole glances at me.

I looked over at Chase and Chandler, who were a good distance away from the fire. Chase was standing, but Chandler was sitting on the ground with his head in his hands. He shook his head at Chase, looked at me, and said something that caused Chase to turn his attention to me as well. Then Chandler stood and they both walked into the trees.

I looked over at the group of my father's Reapers. They were all distinctly looking away from me—all of them, apart from one.

He smiled at me and I had the instinct to avert my gaze, but I did not. I held his gaze with mine until he said something to the others with a visible chuckle. He did not look at me again.

Sharks in the water, Reapers, I heard Agatha's voice say inside my head.

All this time I'd allowed myself to forget what they were because of how I felt about them as people. Being a person did not change what they were or what they'd been trained to be. They were people, yes, but not normal ones. They were *more.* I had blinded myself to that knowledge out of . . .

Feelings.

I did not fully realize what I was doing until I was standing over Agatha and Amber.

"May I speak with you alone?" I asked Agatha.

She seemed downright ecstatic that I was finally appearing as though I wanted to fix things with her, as did Amber, though she also seemed stunned where Amber did not. She pushed herself to her feet and began walking toward the trees.

I shook my head and said, "I'm quite sick of seeing those trees. Would you walk with me into the clearing a ways?"

She said, "Of course."

I turned back once and pretended as though my only intention was to smile at Amber as she watched us, but in truth, I was checking to see whether or not I'd been noticed.

I *had*, by a great many people. They watched, almost in turns. If they were normal, I would think they were only curious about what I was doing. They *were* curious, and I could tell as much by their faces, but they were *not* normal.

When we'd made it a far enough distance to suit me, I stopped. I had to be very careful with my words, and I'd not planned this. "I am sorry to speak to you in this way when I've not spoken to you in such a very long time, but I need to ask you a question." I paused. "What have you told them about me?"

A confused frown took over her face. "Who?"

"All of them," I said quickly. "Any of them. What have you told them about me?"

She continued frowning at me for quite a while before saying, "Well, when they ask, I tell them." She seemed to be thinking hard on it, her brow furrowing and her lips momentarily pursing. "But they ask very strange questions. Nothing I think you'd have any issues with me saying."

"Very strange how?" I realized my hands were shaking and pretended as if I needed to rub my mouth in an attempt to conceal it. I'd been so ignorant, so careless.

"Just about the sort of person you are, comparing habits and mannerisms to your father. They find it interesting how much of him you inherited. Even more so for the few who knew your mother. They say you've got quite a bit of both of them, somehow." Her tone was nonchalant, as if she thought nothing at all of it, but she knew me well. She narrowed her eyes at me ever so slightly and asked, "What is this about?"

"You probably think I have no right to ask you this, but I need you to do something for me," I said to the ground. "If any of them, I don't care who it is—my father, Chase, I don't care . . .? If they ever ask you a question you haven't already answered . . .? I need you to lie to them. I don't care what you say, so long as it is not the truth."

"Aster, most of these people here care so much about you—"

"That might be true." I conceded the possibility of it with my interruption. "But it might not. You think that because a person is blood or because they say so means they care?" I shook my head. "It doesn't."

"They just want to know you," she said exasperatedly.

"*No*," I said. "They want to know my weaknesses. They're predators, Aggie. You and I have both allowed ourselves to forget as much." It was *so easy* to forget.

She seemed to contemplate over that for a long while, and rather than tell me I was wrong, she said, "I am not a liar."

"I don't care." I fought against the urge to shake my head. "You may not feel as though I have the right to ask this of you, but I do. You have put me in a horrible situation with these people, so if they ask you a question that has something even *remotely* to do with me, even if it's about our relationship with one another . . . You *will* lie, even if only minutely. I cannot ever fix things with you if you don't. If you don't, then you truly care nothing at all for my safety."

Agatha analyzed me, from my face down to my shaking hands. When her gaze met mine again, she spoke in a disbelieving tone. "You're afraid."

"I am," I admitted. "I am very afraid."

"I haven't seen you afraid of anything since you were a child," she said. "Not of anything but men and Reapers." Almost all of them in our party were men, but they were *all* Reapers, apart from the two of us standing here.

I took a deep breath and forced my voice not to shake when I spoke. "Please trust me. You don't know how important my request is. I will never ask you for anything again in my life if you do this for me."

She frowned. "You've only ever asked me to do one thing for you—to watch Chase's food as it was being prepared."

"I'm essentially asking you the same thing now," I told her. "Only for me." I couldn't stop my voice from shaking on those three words.

She smiled sadly and cupped her hand over my face. "I will do this for you."

"Don't ever let them know." I spoke under my breath then hugged her tightly.

"Who are you afraid of?" she whispered in my ear.

"*All* of them," I whispered back, unable to stop my body from trembling, even with her familiar touch, which had been such a comfort to me so many times in my life. Safety, security, comfort . . . it was *all* an illusion. Was it only ever as real as your mind made it? "You should be, too."

AGATHA AND I STOOD THERE HUGGING one another tightly until Jastin came up behind her and said, "Time to go."

She smiled and patted me on the face before walking away.

I stood there with my arms crossed in front of me as I stared down at the ground, listening to her footsteps. I knew I could not hide my feelings from Jastin, though I was sure I could manage it with everyone else. There was no point in trying with him.

"Well, you're making steps towards fixing things with everyone today, aren't you?"

"Seems that way," I said. If speaking was fixing.

"Are you going to tell me what's wrong?" he asked. "Or no?"

"Are you going to tell me what you and my brother were speaking to my father about?" I looked up at him then.

"Strategy," he said. "We're coming close to another city now. We also discussed how things will be with you once we reach our destination." He'd unintentionally said so much in saying so little.

"Has he offered you your son?"

Jastin blinked hard at me in shock for a moment before saying, "No." The expression on his face transformed and, when it had settled, it clearly said he would kill for the prospect of my query. But was it real? "Not yet at least. You think he will."

When I said nothing, he took a good look at my face.

"Or that he already has. You think I'm that good?"

"I think you could be, yes," I told him. He could be *very* good. That much was so much more obvious than he realized.

"I love your faith in me." He stared off for a moment. "Maybe I could be that good, but I've never tried to see. And I do have faith you would know if that was what I'd been doing this entire time." He nodded his head and said, "You'll be the first and only person I'll tell if he makes me that offer."

"How can I know that?" I almost whispered.

"Because if he gives me my son . . . I'll be gone as soon as he turns his head." It sounded so believable.

"That's what I'd expect to hear from you," I said to the ground. I forced myself to look back at his eyes. "It's what I would do."

"I'd take you with me," he said. "I'd drag you kicking and screaming if I had to. And if you refused to go without your merry little group, I'd take them too. All you'd have to do is open your mouth and they'd go. But I'm not going *anywhere* without you. Not ever."

"And that's what I'd *want* to hear from you." I clenched my jaw.

"I can see that your trust in me is bending for some reason . . ." he started slowly. "But it's not broken. You and I wouldn't be having this conversation right now if it was. Bends are understandable. I'm telling you right now that there's going to be a point in time where everything will be thrown out into the open and you're going to see that your trust in me isn't misplaced. You're going to have to wait for that time, just like I am. I can tell you now that it will be a very happy day for me when that happens."

"Why is that?"

"Because I'll never have to see you looking at me the way you're looking at me right now again. But for now . . . wipe that look off your face. Don't let anyone else know you're having doubts about anything. You smile and you laugh like nothing at all is going on in your head. At least nothing like this." He leaned down close to my face to say, "And you listen to me when I tell you not to trust your brother with *anything* you wouldn't want your father to know. Are you hearing me?"

"Heard." The word fell out beneath my breath.

There was no playfulness on his face or in his voice when he said, "Good girl."

CHAPTER FORTY-ONE

PARTNERSHIP

I WAS PUTTING THE SADDLE ON MY HORSE when my brother came up beside me. I glanced over at him briefly then resumed what I was doing.

"I need to apologize." He sounded so believable, but he always did and he always had.

I did not ask him whether our father had put him up to this, though I was tempted to, if only to hear what he would say. I didn't ask him that and I didn't turn to him, continuing on about my business. "You were upset. I've never apologized to you for things I've said when I was upset."

"Yes, but you've never said any of those things to intentionally hurt me," he said. "It was wrong of me, and I shouldn't have done it."

I had two questions—two paths to take—and I asked him what I thought would be the more difficult for him to answer. "Why did you taunt me over Cherise? Out of all things, why that?" There had been so many other paths he could've taken.

His voice was impassive when he said, "Because I was upset and I knew it would hurt you."

Weaknesses, the word repeated inside my head. It wasn't only weaknesses. It was discovering the depths to which they ran.

Prick a person once to see how much they bleed, how much pain can be caused there, and learn if it's a worthwhile place to stab later.

Sharks in the water, Reapers.

I could never let them see me bleed. But perhaps . . .

I heard myself laugh once on a breath. "The first night I spoke to Chase, he asked me a question because I'd apologized to him about something." I finally turned to Ahren before continuing on. "*Do you feel bad*? I asked him *what* because I didn't know how else to respond, and he asked me if I truly felt bad. I didn't, but making insincere apologies was beaten into me. I didn't feel badly at all. Not even a little. When I feel as though your apology is sincere, I will accept it gladly."

"Aster, what do you want me to say?" he nearly begged.

"I don't want you to *say* anything," I told him. "It was your words that hurt me intentionally, wasn't it? I don't want more of those." I shook my head. "You told me once that you were expected to destroy my heart, didn't you? You acted as if the very thought of it was some horrible thing you could *never* possibly take part in." I paused to frown at him. "And yet you could come and make little scratches on it for no reason apart from . . . *wanting* to. Did it make you feel better?"

"No."

I did not tell him that I was almost positive he was lying to me. It *had* made him feel better, at least at the time. If I didn't know him, I would believe every lie he told.

We both stood there waiting for our own respective things. I could not get inside my brother's head, not to anticipate his next move. So I waited for him to move and I would go from there.

Sometimes the best way to learn was to not attack when attacking seemed the sensible thing to do.

Eventually he asked, "What do you want me to do?"

I smiled a little at the ground before looking back at his face. "I would like for you to take me to meet my niece."

"*Aster.*" He gaped. "I can't do that."

I tilted my head. "Can't you?" I shrugged. "You asked me what I wanted and I gave you an answer. Until you take me to meet my niece, you should consider your apology not-accepted."

"You're trying to hurt me." He sounded shocked.

"Why would seeing your child hurt you?" I asked curiously. "You made it, didn't you? It's our blood. Why would it hurt you to see your own blood? That's ridiculous, Ahren."

"Then why that?" he demanded. "Of *all* things, why *that*?"

Out of all things indeed.

"Our blood is tainted," I stated, my voice impassive. "I should like to see the one bit of it left in this world that isn't yet. And if you don't care to see it too . . . then perhaps you're not the person I believe you to be."

He shook his head and began to walk away, but I said, "Ahren," which made him turn back to me.

He was angry, far angrier than I'd ever seen him before by far.

"If I wanted to hurt you, I would've asked you to introduce me to the mother of your child, not the child." I paused. "As you well know, I would never intentionally do *anything* to hurt you."

JASTIN SEEMED AMUSED for a good while as we rode together, but given there were more people closely around us than what we were accustomed to, he said nothing to me at all. Sometimes when I looked at him the small grin was gone, but it was in place for most of the day. But later, when we'd stopped for the evening and he was walking with me to a nearby river so we could both bathe—separately, of course—I asked, "What's been so funny to you all day?"

He chuckled quietly. "You're very cold."

"Am I?" I asked. "I presume you're speaking of the request I made to my brother. I'm curious if you can tell me why I asked him for that."

"He's convinced it's you trying to hurt him, but it isn't," Jastin said. "You didn't mind him thinking that was your intention, but you really asked because you know it's the *one* thing in the world he wouldn't want to do. He'd have to do something difficult to show you he was truly sorry." The humor dropped out of his voice when he spoke next. "Sometimes you have to do difficult things to show a person something."

I laughed a little. "What's with your tone?"

When he said nothing, I stopped moving and frowned.

"It must be serious."

"I've been thinking," he said as he stopped and turned back to me. "When I was forcing that stupid smile on my face today, I was thinking about the conversation we had this morning about trust. I can't completely prove to you that you can trust me, but . . ."

"*But*?" I pressed when he did not immediately continue.

"I'm going to ask you something. And then I'm going to tell you all my reasons for asking. I know I don't have to tell you to keep this between us."

"Of course not."

"I get to see my son again soon." I watched his shoulders rise then fall as he took in then released a deep breath. Very slowly, he said, "I want you to go with me when I do."

I felt my eyes widen and I was nearly certain my mouth had dropped open. Had it dropped? I did not know what to say. All I could formulate and get out of my mouth was, "Why?"

"He's five," Jastin said. "And last year when I went, he asked me so many questions that I just—" He stopped to take another deep breath. He could not even look at me. "It's hard for me. I can't even *begin* to tell you how hard it is. I want you to go because I feel like . . . I need you there."

I wondered then if he had ever asked anyone for anything in his entire life; it almost seemed as though he hadn't. I still could not think of anything to say, nor could I understand why he believed my presence there would be beneficial or helpful in any way.

"Your brother offered to go with me last year because he knows how difficult it is for me," he went on. "I never told him of course, but he knows. I wouldn't let him go. There's not another person in this world I would let go with me." He finally looked at me again. "So, I want you to go for that reason. Also because I think it will show you I'm telling you the truth about everything. And I want you to go because I know you don't want to see him."

"Why would you say that?" I asked quietly.

"Because he's not yours," he answered with a sad smile. "But you have to understand that even if I can't have him . . . he's still a part of me. I need you to accept that, and you can't until you see him. So, you need to go with me because I need you to, and also so we can both show each other what we're willing to do for one another." He shook his head a little. "I'm going to let you see the one part of me that I won't allow anyone to see."

"You don't allow anyone to see any part of you."

"You know that's not true. It's just that no one's cared to look," he said. "So, we're going to do that together. Until that day comes, I want you to think on something. I want you to figure out one thing about yourself that you've never let anyone see. And on that day, you can decide whether or not you want to show me after you've seen mine."

"What if you change your mind?" I almost whispered.

"I won't." He sounded so sure. "But it's like that other thing we talked about. You're just going to have to wait and see." He smiled a little at the ground. "I told your father I would die for you. I'd willingly die for your brother too, but I would never take him with me to see my son. This is me showing you what I'm willing to do for you and share with you."

"Why don't you want me to tell anyone?"

"Because it's not a game to me no matter what you or anyone else thinks," he replied. "I don't want this turned into something it's not. Some people would think it's me trying to buy your trust and other people would think it's me trying to buy your love. I'm not buying and I'm not playing, but they would think that wouldn't they?" He shook his head again and sighed quietly. "I already have both those things and we don't need to share our personal business with anyone. That's why."

I smiled a little to myself before saying, "I've never told you I love you."

"You didn't have to," he said. "And I still don't want to hear it."

"And I still wasn't going to say it." A small chuckle was all I could manage.

He was smiling, but I knew how nervous and uncomfortable he was when he asked, "Will you go?"

I forced a smile back at him and nodded. "If the time comes and you still wish for me to, then yes. I won't tell anyone and I'll think about what you asked me to think about." I frowned when I spent another moment contemplating it. "This is only about partnership, isn't it?"

"This is entirely about partnership."

I forced another smile at him before saying, "That's a very good thing."

CHAPTER FORTY-TWO

HAVING FAITH

IT WAS TWO NIGHTS LATER when our camp was ambushed. I was still lying on the ground but circled protectively by the time I even realized what was happening. My head tried in vain to distinguish the sounds I'd heard from what I'd been dreaming about. Before I'd properly stood, it was all over and my father was chuckling quietly.

"What did they know?" I heard him ask.

I shoved myself between two of the bodies surrounding me and stormed toward the sound of my father's carrying voice. I ignored the four dead bodies on the ground as I went. Even with half our party sleeping . . . it made no sense for them to have attacked when they were so outnumbered.

"Nothing useful," someone said. I was certain I'd never heard that voice before. "They had word you'd left Jarsil to retrieve something important to you, but they didn't know what it was. They didn't even know that much until a few days ago when we were sent here to observe. At least not to my knowledge, but you know how he is. I don't believe any of your men have been giving up your secrets, Sir." There was a short pause before, "Ah, I take it that's her?"

My father sighed and he did not turn around to face me to say, "Go back to sleep, Aster."

"Don't patronize me, Father," I told him firmly. "Who is this man?"

The newcomer was a man—a young one, but still a man.

"Feisty." The Reaper looked from my direction back to my father. "She must've inherited that trait from her mother. I know she didn't get it from you, Sir."

My father turned to me and sighed again. "We're discussing business. It's nothing for you to be concerned over."

"Our camp was just *ambushed* and you're telling me not to be *concerned*?" I nearly shouted at him over the preposterousness of his words. "*Who* is this man?"

"Stelin." The Reaper took several steps toward me.

I felt my face contorting when he extended a hand in my direction.

"Don't touch me," I told him through my teeth.

He smiled.

I did not care that he was remarkably beautiful.

I did not care.

"Who is he?" I demanded once more of my father.

"This is Hasting's son," was my father's response, as if it should've meant anything in the world to me at all. It did not. Why did they always act like I should know?

"Who?" I asked.

Quietly, near to my ear, Jastin said, "The Reaper in control of Bethel."

I felt as if I'd received some horrible sort of jolt throughout my entire body. "What is he *doing* here?" Were they *mad*?

"How does she know of Bethel?" Stelin asked curiously. If he was from Bethel, why did he not have the same dirty accent of the Reaper Jastin had killed? "I thought you said they had her locked away in an isolated House?"

Jastin gently put a hand on my back, and I knew he was telling me to calm down. I took several deep breaths and kept my mouth shut. I did not tell Stelin that I'd killed a Reaper from his city a week ago, despite how badly I wanted to.

"That's all the information I know, Sir," Stelin said to my father when no one made an effort to answer his questions. "If you're ready to send me back, let's get on with it."

"On with what?" I heard myself ask.

"Nosy as well." Stelin was looking at my father, but then he turned to me. "On with the proof that I fought valiantly for my new city and somehow managed to slip away with only minor injuries while the others in my party were killed. I'm sure Bren can overlook the deaths of his Reapers when I return with word of *you*. He'll be so intrigued he very well may forget them entirely."

"You're a traitor," I said on a breath.

"Only to my father." Stelin grinned. "Which has brought us here, with me leading a team of Reapers from Maldir to their deaths. So yes, I suppose you could say as much. It's remarkable the things a person will do when they despise their own parentage." He turned his grin to my father to say, "Shame, given all the trouble you've gone through to get her."

My father did not react to his taunting in any way. He said, "I don't wish to send you back to Maldir. If your information is correct, they're of no consequence. And Bren is far too intelligent to cause problems for me past sending his men to be the occasional thorn in my side. Still, I don't need the worry of what he would do if I gave him something so substantial."

Stelin frowned deeply at him.

"Hasting is the one causing me all the trouble," my father continued. "It would be in my daughter's best interests for her to have another Reaper at her side, one who knows him better than most, at that."

"Oh Father," I said quietly when I realized the point he was making. "You are either incredibly ignorant or incredibly intelligent."

"You wish to be trained, don't you?" My father's voice was impassive. "Why would you complain about one more person assisting you with your goals?"

I ignored the way Stelin was analyzing me, and I continued to ignore him when he said, "I can work with that."

"You are a liar." I stared straight into my father's eyes. "And I shall never forget it." I hardly registered both Jastin and Chase tugging backward on my arms.

"Two of them?" Stelin laughed. "My god, she *is* a handful, isn't she?"

And I barely heard my father quietly say, "She's just like her mother," before I was out of earshot.

My entire body was shaking where the two of them had righted me and held on to either arm, keeping me moving forward.

"That's easier than bribing you, isn't it?" I asked Jastin the question, but I said it to the ground with wide eyes.

"Oh yes," Jastin said. "That's much easier by far. Now he'll have—" Jastin stopped moving and speaking suddenly. Then he put his face in his hands. "Sonofabitch." When he removed his hands, one of them lingered by his mouth as he stared off distantly. He seemed to be thinking very hard.

"You *are* on her side," Chase said, his voice quiet and contemplative. "Unless you're acting right now."

Jastin ignored Chase's obviously questioning statement but was looking at him when he said, "Get your brother. They're going to notice we're off by ourselves, but they're distracted with strategy right now. Get your brother and meet us down there." He pointed off into the dark open space of the clearing. "You know we won't have long."

"What about—"

Jastin interrupted Chase with a very firm, "*No.*"

He'd been going to ask about Ahren, I knew. I felt as though some sort of understanding finally got through to Chase as he stared at Jastin.

"Only your brother," Jastin said. "Go now."

And Chase did as he'd been told.

Jastin immediately began dragging me through the tall grass, muttering random things and profanities under his breath all the while. Most of what he said was unintelligible, but a few bits came through. One of the larger points I gathered was that he thought it ignorant to kill those four Reapers when so close to their city and so short on men, more or less. I was inclined to agree with everything he said that made the slightest bit of sense.

Some of it didn't.

It surely did to him.

It was not long after we stopped that Chase and Chandler caught up to us. Jastin had quieted himself by that point.

Chandler said, "They're going to notice we're talking amongst ourselves."

"Irrelevant," Jastin said dismissively. "All they know is that we're talking. They won't know what we're saying."

"But they'll know—" Chandler started.

"Her father already knows who's most loyal to her. Him and everyone here," Jastin said. "The three of us and Stanley. But Stanley is more loyal to Stewart than he is to her and Stewart is more loyal to his city."

Chandler and I exchanged a short glance in the darkness as Chase said, "And Ahren."

"Ahren is loyal to his father," Jastin said. "He loves his sister as much as he can, but his loyalties lie with his father and his city. Love and loyalty don't always align."

Chase blinked hard at Jastin in the darkness for a moment. "You think he told his father about our plan."

"Agatha told about the plan, didn't she?" Jastin asked. "But how did she get message to him? Did she know there were other Reapers in the House? If she did, Ahren was the one who told her. *You* didn't, did you?"

Chase said nothing, but still . . .

Jastin shook his head. "I didn't think so."

"I've known Ahren a very long time," Chase said slowly. "I've never gotten that impression from him."

"Ahren is very good at giving people the impressions he wants them to receive," Jastin said. "You might know him, but nowhere *near* as well as I do."

"He's your partner," Chandler said. "With what you've just said . . . Wouldn't you know?"

"I wish I did." Jastin's voice was distant. "And I very much hope I'm wrong because, if I'm not . . . he was playing with my life in your escape."

Quiet, I said, "Because of the rope."

Jastin nodded.

"If you're the only other Reaper who knew of our plan to escape . . ." Chase began, being very deliberate with his words. "How do we know *you* weren't the one to inform her father? That's her brother you're speculating about, and I have a hard time believing it was him instead of you."

"You may not believe this, but I don't care about my city," Jastin said. "I used to. For a time after her father came, I was quite happy. But then I spent the last several years of my life watching my son turn into me from a distance. Into you." He nodded at the two of them.

"Into them." He nodded back toward the camp. "So yes, if I were loyal to my city, it would stand to reason I was the one who told. But go ask Agatha if I was the one she gave message to, and that'll put a quick end to *your* speculation. I already knew about your plan, and I can assure you . . . I didn't give a damn about it. I'd never really met any of you, so why should I have cared? Please tell me that."

Chase's eyes were narrowed at Jastin. "That sounds perfect, doesn't it?"

"We don't have the time to talk about this," Jastin said, his anxiousness clearly growing. "For now, you're just going to have to trust her judgment. We need to figure this out."

"Stelin?" Chandler asked in a businesslike tone.

Jastin nodded. "Two reasons. There are only two reasons for her father doing what he just did. Either he couldn't trust Ahren to be entirely objective with his sister, or he trusts in Aster far more than any of us realize."

"To see if he's a spy for his own father?" Chandler asked.

"Yes," Jastin answered.

"Either way he's a spy, but for whom is what we need to discover." I paused, knowing I needed to say something I did not want to say. But necessities always overruled everything. "I don't think I will be able to assist you in it."

Chandler shook his head in confusion. "Why?"

"I know you all believe I have some uncanny ability to see through people . . ." I started slowly, "but if I can do that at all, it's only with people who allow me to look. I only see what people want another person to see. He won't do that, I can assure you."

"How do you know?" Chase asked.

I felt ridiculously silly when I responded with, "Because of the air around him."

Chandler said, "I don't know what that means."

"You remember what you told me before when we talked about being friends?" I looked to Chandler. "You said getting emotionally involved with anything takes away your head, that it makes you think with your heart and not your brain."

"Yes, I remember," Chandler said. "What does that have to do with air?"

They were all going to think I was mad, but I'd seen so many Reapers, so many people.

I thought on something Stewart had told me before I'd ever killed a man, about seeing who people truly were behind the eyes. Perhaps that had less to do with the amount of killing you'd done and more to do with . . .

I didn't know what.

But I'd seen something in Stelin in that short span of looking, something unmistakable.

"His heart isn't beating inside his chest for him to think with it," I said quietly. "He wouldn't let me in no matter what I tried to do. If he won't let me in . . . I cannot discover anything. And if I get close, he'll discover things about me. Then . . . it's only me who's weakened for it."

"You're going to have to try." Chandler's tone was softer than usual, but it was still unyielding. He was really saying something else, though I doubted he knew as much.

You're going to have to bleed.

"I have an idea," Chase said quickly. When I looked over at him, he smiled at me. "You remember that game your brother told you about before? He told you about playing *hard to get*."

"Yes, what about it?" I asked. How was that relevant?

Jastin chuckled and, for the first time ever, Chase's smile for me lingered and carried over to Jastin.

"He would never be expecting it," Jastin said appreciatively. "He knows she's not trained."

"What does training have to do with playing that ridiculous game?" I still didn't even understand the logic behind it.

"As you well know, men can become very stupid over women," Chandler said with a small grin. "Female Reapers are thoroughly trained for that specific purpose. It's one of the many ways they're more useful than men by far."

I felt my face contorting as I thought back to Anders telling me about my mother's first mission, how she'd been sent to . . . "You want me to . . . *seduce* him?"

Chase said, "Discreetly."

"I can't *do* that!" I was somehow able to keep my exclamation much quieter than I'd anticipated it would be when leaving my mouth. "I don't have a clue in the world how!"

"Trust me." Jastin chuckled. "Yes, you do." I felt my face burning until he said, "Congratulations. Consider this your first mission."

I spent a moment contemplating that, letting the excitement—which was tinged with anxiety—beat down the appalled and disgusted feelings swirling around inside me at the prospect of their plan.

"And do you think I can do it?" I asked. "Do you really?"

Chandler said, "We all know you can."

"And now you have three people watching your back." Jastin smiled warmly at me. "So you have nothing to worry about. We'll keep you safe while you're in the field."

"Speaking of," Chase said, which brought my attention to him. His nose was scrunched a bit and he nodded in the direction of the trees. "Got to love the smell of burning bodies."

CHAPTER FORTY-THREE

SO COLD

FTER A BRIEF DISCUSSION about how the dynamics of our relationships with one another needed a very swift and firm shifting, the four of us walked back to the camp together. I tried very hard to ignore the smell that Chase had mentioned, but despite a new fire being made for that specific purpose quite a ways from camp . . . I couldn't manage it. I didn't know that I would ever look at fire the same way again.

I was glad for the darkness though, as the pools of blood on the ground simply appeared to be darkened spots rather than what I knew them to be.

Stelin was sitting with the other three in our group when we arrived, and he was the only one who did not seem uncomfortable and wary.

"Have a nice little chat about me? Trying to figure out my intentions?" He shrugged. "I'm just following orders."

For my part, I pretended as though he was not there at all. I repeated their words inside my head for encouragement.

Don't rush anything. We have time. Ignore his presence more often than you acknowledge it.

"I'm ready to go back to sleep," I told three of the people on the ground.

Stelin stood and looked at Jastin. "Where do you want me?"

"You see that tree over there?" I pointed far off in the distance. "Over *there*."

He said, "I didn't ask you."

"I don't care," I informed him. "I don't know you at all. If you're sleeping while I am, you will be away from me. And if you're awake while I'm asleep, you will be much farther."

"Your father informed me *he* was in charge." Stelin gestured to Jastin.

"Yes, he is in charge of my safety," I said with a tight smile. "Please ask him who he works for."

Stelin narrowed his eyes at me and did not do what I asked.

I turned to Jastin. "Where would you have him?"

"Wherever you say," Jastin replied.

I looked back to Stelin. "Are you clear on the dynamic?"

"Servant, huh?" Stelin's eyes were still narrowed at me, but he seemed to be quite amused.

I took in a breath and forced it to sound happy when it came out of my mouth. "Yes, that is precisely what I am." I nodded. "I *do* hope you're pleased with your change in occupation, Sir." I turned and, after taking only one step toward my bedding area, said, "Kill him if he gets anywhere near me."

I barely heard him say, "Oh, my father would love her." But I did hear it, as I was sure he'd intended me to.

It was not long after lying down before Chandler scooted close behind and draped his arm over me.

He whispered four words in my ear. "I've got your back."

Part of me wanted to tell him I was glad, but instead I said, "I know." I felt it said so much more.

IT WAS NOT LONG INTO THE NEXT DAY when Stelin rode up to my left side on his horse. He did not say anything at all for a time and I did not look at him. But eventually he asked, "What did you do to receive the scars on your back?"

I kept staring straight ahead as though no one was beside me at all.

I heard him breathe out one breath that was just a bit louder than his others when he realized I had no intention whatsoever of responding to him.

"They come up past your collar," he said. "I'm just curious."

I brought my left hand up by my face to bite off my fingernails as Chandler had insisted I do.

When I spit one of them out of my mouth in Stelin's direction, I pretended to be startled when I saw him there. "Oh, were you speaking to me?"

His gaze lingered briefly over the cuts on my arm that had been intentionally placed—which the Bryon tea had already turned to scars—while I blinked innocently at him, as I had intended for it to.

Then he smiled at me and, when he did, I was certain Chandler was wrong about men not being as useful as women in the ways they were currently expecting of me. Stelin's smile clearly told me it worked wonders on females, as there was no uncertainty in it.

It had no effect on me, nor did his dark brown eyes and dark hair. They were nothing more than a mask.

His smile wavered only slightly when I asked, "May I help you?"

"I asked you a question."

"Did you?" I asked. "It's a shame. I mustn't have heard it."

His eyes narrowed. "Are you going to tell me?"

"The only thing I will tell you for now is that if you insist on riding next to me, I'll insist you be quiet while you do."

"Why is that?" His tone was curious, but it was tinged with something similar to mockery. "Don't want to speak to me and get close to another Reaper?"

"I don't want to speak to you because I prefer the silence," I informed him.

"No woman in this world prefers silence to speaking." A quiet chuckle followed his ridiculous statement.

I continued staring straight ahead and biting off my fingernails. Though I spit all ten pieces of them in his direction, he still rode next to me.

He continued to do so after lunch as well, and he remained quiet for most of the day. I suspected he'd been waiting that entire time for me to break the silence because I was a woman. I did not, nor would I ever unless I meant to. It was as the sky was darkening that he broke it, as I knew he would.

"I expected a million questions," he said. "You clearly run the show with your little group. It would be your job to ask questions then, wouldn't it? For their safety."

Very slowly I said, "I *believe* I insisted on your silence."

"Come on, little flower." He laughed. "Don't you want another friend?"

Loudly, I whistled once high and once low. It was not long before my brother rode up on my other side. I *did* look at him.

"I've been very patient today," I told Ahren. "I told this boy he could ride beside me if he could keep his mouth shut. So I've sat here for an entire day having his breathing taking up space inside my head. My patience is finally depleted and now I'll insist you remove him from my immediate vicinity."

"And if I'm quiet?" Stelin asked from my other side.

I finally looked at him then, offering him another tight smile. "Then you're more than welcome to resume riding beside me tomorrow."

"You heard her," Ahren said, his voice both blank and yet firm at once.

Stelin chuckled and trotted his horse ahead of us.

Once he was gone, my brother stopped watching his retreating back and brought his attention to me. "What did he say to you?"

"Nothing of consequence," I answered. "Thank you for helping me."

"Do you want me to ride with you?"

"If you'll be quiet," I told him.

Ahren said, "I never thought you preferred the quiet."

"It's unfortunate that you truly don't know me at all, big brother." I did not have to fake any sadness in my voice to say as much.

Ahren continued riding next to me until we stopped, and he did not say another word to me.

I COULD NOT HELP MYSELF when we stopped for the evening. I didn't do it as part of the mission. I did it because I was angry at my father.

I found Anders as he was removing the saddle from his horse, and I ensured my father would be within hearing distance when I said, "About the hair."

Anders looked over at me with a curious expression, and when he understood what I was speaking to him about he said, "Oh, Aster. Please don't bring that up again. I don't feel like getting punched by your father this evening."

"You see . . ." I grinned. "Why should a woman's hair make a man want to hit another man? Even if you would've preferred it short, that's no reason to make my father angry so many years later. I believe I've discovered at least part of the cause for it." He closed his eyes an instant before I said, "It has something to do with the two of you being intimate with one another, doesn't it? But what, I wonder, could it be?"

"*Aster*!" My father's voice rang out in disbelief from behind me.

"Oh, Father," I said in a stunned tone. "Were you standing just there? I'm dreadfully sorry."

His eyes were widened in absolute shock as I blinked at him.

"You *see*!" he exclaimed several extended moments later to Anders. "I told you she wouldn't drop it. I cannot believe you, tarnishing her mother's memory."

"I have no memory of my mother." I shrugged my shoulders and shook my head at once, feeling a frown attempting—and failing—to tug both corners of my mouth down. "You never said a word of her to me for me to have put any together. And Anders has ever only told me things that have made me find her quite . . . *interesting*. But you see, Father, *you're* the one who's insulted her memory to me." To me and in front of so many people.

"*What*?" Bewilderment took over his face, dulling out a bit of his anger. "What are you talking about?"

"You told a perfect stranger last night that I was just like my mother for two people loving me, didn't you?" I asked him innocently. "I know you didn't mean it as a compliment, clearly. So perhaps you should be angry at yourself for insulting both the daughter you abandoned and her dead mother at once."

"You are exhausting," my father said to me. Indeed, he did sound quite exhausted.

"And you are an overbearing liar." The smile on my face then was not even partially faked.

He'd begun to walk away, but I stopped him by speaking again.

"Anders has no control over what I say. If you punch him again, I'll do the same to you."

"Are you . . . Are you *threatening* me?" My father's mouth had dropped open in shock, but I could see a bit of the anger returning, though it might have been a different sort.

"Promising," I told him with the same smile.

My father looked back at Anders. "*Just* like her."

"Not quite, as I'm sure you remember," Anders said blankly.

My father shook his head and walked away. As soon as his back was turned again, Anders concealed his smile by rubbing at his mouth with several of his fingers.

"I let your father hit me once when we were young," he said. "I taunted him for *weeks* on end to get him to. I knew your mother would come to my defense and be angry with him for it, even though the entire situation was essentially my fault. She told him she would castrate him in his sleep if he touched me again."

My brow furrowed. "That she would what?"

Anders snorted. "Take away his ability to have children."

"Chase talked to me about kneeing people."

"She meant with a knife," Anders clarified. "It's a bit more . . . *foolproof.*"

"Oh." The word was quiet when it fell out of my mouth. I did not want the details of how, *exactly*, that worked, so I stood there awkwardly for a moment while I imagined my mother saying those words to my father.

I did not want to.

I'd almost begun to walk away when Anders said, "I know you only did that to make your father angry. But I'm going to answer your question anyway, to show you what you get for asking questions you shouldn't know the answers to. And also to make you think harder on what I told you before about journeys."

I tilted my head at him.

He smiled. "I told her I wanted her to cut her hair because it occasionally got in my mouth when we were doing *precisely* what you mentioned. I didn't truly want her to, but that's what I always said as a joke."

"That's . . ." I paused as I attempted to discover the appropriate word inside of my head. "Disgusting."

He shrugged. "To you, I'm sure."

And then I heard myself snort loudly as I stood there shaking my head. I could not figure out what was funny to me about it because it *was* quite disgusting, but there was something undeniably humorous to it as well.

"I'm curious . . ." I started after my laughter had died down. "How did you never get her pregnant?"

He tapped on his nose twice with the side of his pointer finger and then pointed off somewhere in the distance with it. I did not know what that signal meant exactly, but the message of it was quite clear.

Go away. So I went away.

As I went, I distantly registered Stelin watching me with narrowed yet amused eyes.

And when I sat down next to Jastin, he grinned and, under his breath, said, "So cold."

"He deserved it." I shrugged. "My father is a proper asshole."

My comment caused several snorts around me for some reason, from Chase on my other side and Chandler next to him. Jastin just smiled.

I wondered what was so funny about my statement until Chandler informed me, "You can't use *proper* and *asshole* in the same sentence."

"Are there rules for using improper language?" I raised my eyebrows at him. "Clearly you're not well-informed of them, given you combine half those words with normal ones every time you stub your toe."

Jastin laughed. "Be quiet."

"You're *all* proper assholes," I muttered under my breath.

"That's it." Chandler stood up. I did not know what he was talking about, so I was not expecting for him to grab hold of me and haul me up over his shoulder.

It was much like being thrown into a tub of freezing water—a shock to the system.

I heard myself laughing until he said, "I'm going to go teach her what the words she's saying actually mean."

Then I was wailing and beating halfheartedly at his back. "Put me down!" I told him through tears of laughter.

"What am I?" he asked.

"A perfectly exceptional and remarkably intelligent man!" I replied. "And you're *far* too amazing and self-aware to ever stub your toe. That's what I just said before, wasn't it?"

He did not let me down, but as he was no longer hauling me off to some unknown location to teach me something I *likely* did not want to learn, I simply enjoyed the ride and stopped beating at his back. When we were back in front of Chase and Jastin, he stopped moving and told me to get down.

"I don't think I will," I informed him through my giggles. "I'm contemplating exchanging you for my horse. Will you carry me to the food? You know . . . I don't believe I'll ever feel the need to walk again, given this is much more preferable. Who could ever have known that having a man beneath you could be such an enjoyable experience? You truly should try it sometime, Chandler. It may do wonders for your mood."

Chandler snorted and forcibly removed me from his shoulder, setting my feet back on the ground. I faked an exaggerated frown at him.

"Is that how she is with you?" Chase asked. He almost sounded confused.

When I turned around to glance at Jastin, he was simply smiling at me.

CHAPTER FORTY-FOUR

QUESTIONS AND FLOWERS

THE NEXT DAY, Stelin rode beside me again. Though he said nothing, I could tell he was simply itching to. He did not fidget, but I could feel his gaze on me, almost as if he were begging me to look at him so he could initiate conversation.

I did not.

It was on the evening of the day after that when I looked at him and tilted my head. "Do you find me beautiful?"

He blinked at me several times before answering with, "Not particularly."

"Then given you have no comprehensible reason to be staring at me, I'll have to ask that you stop." I smiled to add, "It's quite bothersome."

"You don't enjoy being looked at?" His tone was both curious and disbelieving. "You *are* a woman, after all."

I kept the smile on my face to say, "Not by you."

He analyzed me for several seconds before speaking again. "You're very strange."

I shrugged because it was nothing I'd never heard before. Then I resumed staring forward.

THE FOLLOWING DAY, Stelin continued staring at me as I knew he would. And he did not speak to me because he knew that I would fetch my brother if he did, who would then force him to leave.

I made him wait nearly the entire day before I looked at him. "One question."

"What is it?" he asked.

"No," I said. "I'll allow you to ask me one question, so long as you promise to stop staring at me for the remainder of the evening. And by the remainder of the evening, I mean you are not allowed to even glance at me once until tomorrow." I paused for a moment, letting him think about it. "Do you agree to my terms?"

He nodded after another instant spent thinking over it. "Don't you want to ask me something?"

"Oh," I said thoughtfully. "I'm sorry to tell you that you've already expended your allowance for today by asking me what one question I wanted to ask you. Now I'll have to ask you to keep your eyes forward."

He looked straight ahead as promised, but I saw him shaking his head in my peripherals for quite a while before saying, "Well played."

I did not respond to his comment outwardly at all, but I smiled in a pleased sort of way about it on the inside.

I made him wait again the next day, though not quite as long as I had the previous. He stared at me until I looked at him and raised an eyebrow in his direction.

He asked, "Is this an ongoing thing?"

"I don't care." Then I smiled to say, "Eyes forward."

We'd barely been on our horses for five minutes the next day when he spoke. "No matter what I ask you, will you tell me the truth?"

"Perhaps," I said. "But perhaps not. You're trained to detect deception, are you not? You should have enough faith in your own skills to know when a servant is telling you the truth, shouldn't you? I'll not make you promises that carry over to some unknown time with some unknown result to myself. Eyes forward."

The following day, the trees had all but disappeared. There were small smatterings of them periodically, but there was no longer a full forest to our left. I felt extremely exposed, which made me very uncomfortable, but I attempted to not show as much to Stelin. Besides, if we were ambushed now, we would certainly see it coming. That knowledge alone should've made me feel better, but it didn't really.

Midway through the day, Stelin made his next query. "Do you love your father?"

"I do."

"That's a lie," he accused.

I looked over at him and raised an eyebrow to blankly ask, "Is it?"

He narrowed his eyes as he analyzed my face. I knew he believed I didn't love my father, but . . .

I did. I loved the man who had raised me, but that did not necessarily mean I loved the man currently leading our procession.

I was sure that, given the way my words did not match my actions, I had confused him. I was very pleased about it.

"Eyes forward," I instructed.

The next question he asked me was, "Which of your boys do you love more?"

My response was, "I love them both in different ways, so there is no answer for that particular question."

He grinned. "Do I get another, then?"

"Perhaps you should better think your questions for me if you plan on doing this for the remainder of our journey," I told him. "Eyes forward."

I ENSURED STELIN SAW ME talking and laughing with Chandler, Chase, and Jastin that evening, just like I did every night now. I pretended not to notice when he broke his part of the bargain and glanced at me periodically, watching my reactions to things they said or jokes they would tell. I pretended not to notice him at all and was sure I was successful.

"You said yesterday there was no answer for my question," he stated midway through the next day. "I've thought of a better way to ask. Which of the two would you rather have children with?"

"I'm not sure that *is* better." I couldn't help the small chuckle that escaped from my mouth. I looked over at him to say, "I wish to never have children with anyone."

"But you're a woman." His voice was almost entirely blank, apart from a small bit of confusion. "It's . . . in your *blood* to want children."

"Is it?" I tilted my head. "I believe I've had just about enough of your sexist remarks. Clearly not all women prefer speaking to silence, nor do they all enjoy being stared at by every man passing, nor do they all want to bring children into a horrible world. And now I've answered an unasked question for you, as to why I don't want them. I'll answer a third and tell you it was free and does not carry over to tomorrow." I let him analyze my face for nearly fifteen seconds before saying, "Eyes forward."

The next day left me with a satisfied feeling.

"Why haven't you asked me anything?" was his question.

"Why do you believe I would need to ask you anything?" I asked him curiously as I stared at my horse's ears.

"Because you think I'm a threat," he stated.

"Do I?" I chuckled. "The answer is still the same." I looked over at him to repeat myself very slowly. "Why do you believe I would need to ask you anything?"

"You can't answer a question with a question."

"But if it's the only answer, what else do you want me to say to you?" I asked. "Eyes forward."

The day after was frustrating, and I assumed he made it that way intentionally because I'd insulted his relevance.

"You said you wouldn't have children because of the way the world is," he stated. "If the world was different, which of the two would you rather have children with?"

"The world *isn't* different," I said. "There's no answer to that question inside my head because I'll not allow myself to think about what things would be *if*. Now you have a better understanding of my person, but given I wasn't able to answer your question at all, I'll allow you another. Only if you agree to stop asking me questions about childbearing. It's becoming quite . . . *uncomfortable*."

I could tell he nearly asked me if I was being serious about allowing him another question, as his mouth opened, but he stopped himself before any sound came out and pursed his lips together. He did not fall into my trap, but I'd not truly expected him to.

"You said you don't enjoy being looked at by me, but you enjoy being looked at by them." He paused. "Which do you prefer?"

"They both look at me in different ways," I said. "It's the same initial answer I gave you about loving them."

"Oh, I know they look at you differently." He grinned. "I'm asking which you prefer."

"If you're aware of that, then I'm sure you're aware of what my answer would be," I said nonchalantly. "I'll not answer a question you already know the answer to."

"Aren't you going to ask me why I seem so preoccupied with your love life when I don't even find you beautiful?" He took the liberty to ask another because I would not give him an answer for his last.

"I don't need to." I knew he was asking because he considered me to be a silly little girl who let love run her entire life. I was not. Or perhaps he kept asking because he was hoping to find a weakness in me. "And while you may not find me beautiful, you *are* attracted to me."

"I'm not," he said believably.

But when I looked over and smiled at him to ask, "No?" there was something about the set of his mouth and the look in his eyes . . .

I chuckled, and I did not have to tell him to put his eyes forward that day.

"Are you afraid of me?" was his question the following day.

"No," I answered.

"Do you know how quickly I could kill you?"

"And do *you* know how many times I've been asked that exact question?" I laughed. "Clearly, I'm still alive. I'm quite sure you're too intelligent to try, given you'd likely be killed before you could manage it. Even if you *could* manage it, you would be killed after. And even if you did it in some discreet way, everyone would know you'd done it and you'd still be killed." I offered him a small smile. "There's no need to threaten me simply because I embarrassed you."

He shook his head. "I don't know how they stand you."

"And yet *you're* the one who insists on riding beside me day in and day out." I sighed. "Who looks more ridiculous in this situation?"

"So you'll keep talking to me as long as I don't ask you questions." He nodded his head several times as though he finally understood the way this worked. "And I can see you're trying to insult me so I'll leave you alone."

"Is *that* what I'm doing?" I asked innocently. "Perhaps that *is* why. It would seem feasible, wouldn't it? But you *do* realize I could make you leave me alone at any time, don't you? Perhaps I allow you near me because I find it so *unbelievably* amusing."

"If that's true then you're not as intelligent as they all believe you to be."

I grinned. "And that would make me *precisely* as unintelligent as *you* believed me to be."

He said, "I *don't* think you're unintelligent."

"*Believed*," I clarified.

He grinned and, again, I did not have to tell him to look forward.

STELIN DID NOT STARE AT ME constantly the following day, only stealing glances here and there when I would move even slightly. I did not know if he was doing it in an attempt to get in my good graces or because he finally believed himself to have a somewhat proper understanding of me.

"How is it . . ." he began halfway between eating lunch and when we would stop for the evening. Then he paused in his speaking as if he'd not been planning this conversation for an entire day.

I knew he had.

"How is it that a beautiful girl who's never been allowed to be in love doesn't care for it once she's found it? So much of it, at that."

I asked, "Are you speaking of me?"

He smiled in response.

"I never said I don't care for love."

"Maybe not." His voice took on a thoughtful tone. "But you don't care about it as much as . . ."

"*Expected?*" I offered when he said nothing.

He nodded.

I glanced up at the sun for just an instant and sighed; it was real that time. I fought against heat rising in my cheeks when I informed him, "There's not one simple answer for that particular question."

"That's why I asked."

I looked at my horse's ears to say, "It's possible I don't care for it simply because I wasn't permitted feelings for such a long time. It's possible I don't care for it because I have such little understanding of it. It's possible I don't care for it because of my past. It's possible I don't care for it because I see such little place for it in the future. And it's also possible that it's simply . . . who I am." I glanced at him to shrug tightly. "I don't know."

He analyzed my face with this impish sort of grin on his for quite a while before saying, "That's progress."

A grin spread on my own which made his falter a bit.

I chuckled. "If you say so."

He narrowed his eyes and tilted his head. I could see it clearly on his face that he did not know if I was behaving this way defensively because I'd told him the truth or genuinely because I had not. Though it was the former, I wanted for him to believe it was the latter.

I kept a grin on my face periodically throughout the remainder of the day, only to keep up appearances.

STELIN TESTED ME AGAIN THAT NIGHT. It was more discreet than staring at me for hours on end and yet more invasive at once. When I was finished eating and on my way to my bedding area, I saw something resting on top of my blanket.

A flower. Just a harmless little thing that grew everywhere in the fields here.

My first instinct was to look at Chase when I found it, but I did not. It was ridiculous, of course. My second instinct was to rip it into shreds, but I did not do that either.

I took a deep breath, picked up the flower, and then tossed it gently somewhere away from me. It was far better than stomping on it, I thought. If I was a girl that did not care about love, it would make sense to throw it away from me. But I knew why Stelin had done it, and it had absolutely nothing to do of love.

I did not look to find him and see if he was watching me. I knew he was. I simply placed myself under my blanket and laid there stiffly, waiting for Jastin.

He and Chase no longer pulled the same shift in the night. While Jastin was asleep with me, Chandler was at my front with his back facing me. Then, halfway through the night, Chase would take up Jastin's position and Stanley would take up Chandler's. That had been put into place the next night after Stelin's arrival.

After nearly a fortnight of the two of them holding onto me while I slept, I knew which of them was there without having to be fully awake. My head still did not like it at all and my heart only liked it half the time. My heart always told me which of the two it was, though my head would say it was the feel of their arms or the way they smelled.

I pursed my lips together when Jastin came up behind me and put his mouth next to my ear several minutes later to whisper. "Would you have been so angry if I'd been the one to put that flower there?"

"You know better," I whispered back.

Then, the same thing happened that happened every night when he whispered things to me before bed. I heard him smile an instant before he nibbled on my ear. I giggled because I could not help myself until Chandler spoke.

Some nights he told me to be quiet, others he told the two of us to stop doing whatever it was we were doing behind his back. Either way, we always stopped.

I couldn't help giggling over it; it felt funny.

I did not peek over my shoulder at Jastin because I'd learned that doing so—and seeing the way he smiled at me when I did—caused nights with very little sleep. I did not want to lay awake thinking.

So as soon as my giggling had died down, I felt an all-too-familiar frown taking over my face as he settled in properly behind me. And I cried silently as Jastin rubbed my arms. I told myself I was preventing him from resting, as he would not fall asleep until I had, but I couldn't help myself.

The things I'd told Stelin about my feelings on love were all true in their own ways, but they were not the real reason I didn't care for it. I did not care for love because I *hated* the way it felt.

I hated that every day I fell more in love with the person I shouldn't and farther out of it with the one I should. I hated that I couldn't stop it. I hated that I couldn't make myself love one person and not love another. I hated the way my heart responded to everything and how it struggled and fought against my better judgment. I hated that the world was not better. I hated that I could not give Jastin the child his system had taken from him. I hated that nothing would never, *ever* be enough. I hated that I could not ever be what any of them deserved.

I hated absolutely everything about it, but my heart would not listen to reason.

Most of all, I hated that Jastin never had to ask me why I was upset. I hated it because it was so . . . *nice*, so perfect. So relieving, as if having a burden removed from you. It was like dangling food in front of a starving person and then laughing at them because they could never have it.

Why did seeing something and knowing it was beyond your reach make it all so much worse?

I stared through the darkness at the back in front of me as I took Jastin's hand in mine and forced myself not to think of flowers and love. He kissed me softly on the back of my head, and then I closed my eyes.

CHAPTER FORTY-FIVE

DEALS

FTER LUNCH THE NEXT DAY, Stelin said, "Two days."

I looked over at him.

"We'll reach Jarsil in two days."

"What of it?" I felt as though I did not have the energy to play games with him today, but I knew I needed to. I couldn't force my voice to sound a certain way, but I could still think of the appropriate things to respond to him with. Truly, that was what mattered most, or at least I told myself it was.

"My question for you today is what you want my role to be with you when we arrive there."

"Where's the play?" I asked curiously after watching his face for several seconds, expecting to find some hidden thing there.

"No play," he said believably. "And I won't ask you another question just because I worded the last as a statement."

"I want to know why you're asking me that," I told him.

"Because if I asked Jas, he would tell me it's your decision, wouldn't he?"

"That's not why," I stated. Though I didn't know Stelin, I understood some things about him. I figured out a little more about him with every passing day. And I could read him sometimes.

He grinned a bit. "Believe it or not, I like you. Maybe it's because you're not typical of the people I come into contact with. Maybe because you're not typical at all. Maybe it's just because you know how to interact with people to make them like you. I don't know, but I do either way." He paused. "I'm not asking to win points. I'm asking because I want to spend a few days mentally preparing myself for whatever you'll be having me do when we get there."

I knew Stelin could deceive me easily, but there was something on his face that made me believe he was telling me the truth about this.

I asked, "What would you prefer to do?"

He blinked hard for a moment, as if he'd never contemplated what he wanted to do in all his life. "They said you want to train. I know you have a little already. How much time?"

"A month."

"Two kills with a month of training. . . ." It seemed as though he were saying it to himself, like he was trying to process it.

To help him along, I said, "One of them was free." Both of them might've been, if one were being technical about it.

His forehead scrunched in confusion. "*Free*?"

"He more or less asked me to." I spoke to my horse's ears.

"Was it more, or less?"

"Is there an answer to that question?" I fought against the urge my body had to fidget.

He said, "I suppose not."

It was strange having a conversation with him where neither of us were being snarky with the other, to have a genuine moment. And it did feel that way. It almost made me even more uncomfortable with him.

He seemed to be thinking on it for quite a while before he appeared to come to some sort of decision. "I'd assume your lacking the most with your combative training. I'd like to assist you with that."

"Would you really?" I asked.

"Yes, I would."

"Could I trust you to be objective with me?" I noticed that my voice finally held some of its usual harshness while speaking to him. "I'm not so sure I could. I'd have to worry you'd intentionally teach me nothing."

Chandler would know of course, but I didn't need setbacks of any sort.

"I'd teach you," he said firmly. "If you keep going around running your mouth like you do without having more knowledge, you're going to get yourself killed. I can promise you that."

I blinked hard at him in disbelief. "It almost sounded like you cared."

He chewed on his bottom lip for a moment. "You remind me a little of my best friend. She, um . . ." He paused to shake his head and then he smiled a little. "She had this mad view on the world. She wasn't quite as hopeless as you, though."

"Had."

"Yeah." His voice turned quiet. "She got this idea in her head that we should take on the world together. I don't know . . . like the two of us could do anything. It was ridiculous, but I couldn't help listening to every word she said and believing it." He clenched his jaw for an instant. "My father killed her when he found out we were planning on running away."

A part of me felt like it broke a little at his words, while another part was screaming, *Liar!* I sat there blinking as I attempted to figure out which of the two was right.

"You don't believe me," he said with a sad smile. "You can ask your father. One of his men saw the entire thing and took me to him."

"And how could I know whether the entire thing was staged to get you into his city?" I asked blankly.

"I was fifteen. Your father hadn't even taken control of Jarsil when he took me in. I don't know many adult Reapers who could fake what you're accusing me of faking, not convincingly. If you think *you* could, then you're more heartless than I am." He nodded toward the front of our jagged line of people and horses. "Go ask your father and see how surprised he is that I told you. I've never told anyone the truth about it, apart from him and who saw it happen."

I said nothing.

"You may not like your father; you may even hate him," he said in a firm tone, "but my father is pure evil. Yours put me with you to help keep you safe from that. I'd much rather do my job than continue playing games with you."

That part, at least, I believed.

"You and Chandler may be in charge of that aspect together," I told him. "But I will put a stop to it immediately if I feel as though you're not truly helping. And I have conditions."

"Which are?"

"That you keep things to yourself," I insisted. "And that you never, *ever*, put a flower anywhere near me again."

He grinned. "Can I call you Flower?"

"No."

He sounded quite curious when he asked, "Can you tell me why I did that?"

"To throw me off for your question today."

He chuckled a little beneath his breath. "I did it to see which of the two you'd get angry at."

"That's exactly what I just said."

He smiled at me for some time before saying, "We have a deal. Discretion, hard work, and no more flowers of any sort." Then, he extended his hand toward me.

I frowned at it before taking it in mine and finally allowing him to shake it like he'd tried to do upon first meeting.

He grabbed hold of mine hard and stared at me intently. "Speaking of keeping things to oneself." His voice was both significant and quiet. "It would be a good idea for you to ensure no one finds out that I like you at all. There's a remarkable trail of dead bodies when I allow myself to go against my better judgment."

I said nothing to that, but I didn't have a chance to even if I would have.

"There *is* a spy for my father in your father's city," he went on. "I can tell you that much and I can also tell you it's not me. I don't know if your father assigned me to you because he thinks it *is* me or if he's trying to draw out my father by giving me a job that will be public knowledge. If I've gathered anything appropriately about you over these weeks it's that your guess would likely be as good as mine. Maybe we'll figure it all out together."

Then he released my hand.

After a moment of silence spent thinking over his words, I asked, "Do you know why our fathers despise one another so badly?" They despised one another badly enough for his to send Reapers to abduct me for leverage against mine.

It was the only sort of leverage I could be used for.

"Differing opinions on the way the world should be." He shrugged. "That's what they'd tell everyone, anyway. But given that Bethel was the city your father and mother were operating out of when they became pregnant with you . . . Well, I'd say there's something personal about it, wouldn't you agree?"

What could be—

"You think your father killed my mother," I said on a breath.

"Your guess is as good as mine." He shrugged again. "But yes, that's what I think. And if I'm right . . ." He shook his head. "I'm sorry."

"I believe that," I said in . . . disbelief.

"That's because it's true," he said. "I'm one of very few Reapers who have ever known their mother, even for a short time. After losing mine . . . Well, I think everyone should have a mother."

We were silent for quite some time until I had to give voice to a nagging thought in my head. "Why did you tell me about your friend? Was it to make me feel as though I could trust you?"

"I told you because I finally figured out I had nothing to worry about with you."

Careful, I said, "I don't understand."

"You know what it's like, don't you? Wanting a person to be objective with you?" He chuckled a little before continuing. "June . . . she used to talk a lot, and it always drove me mad. But after she was gone, I missed it. When I realized that, I went out trying to find girls that reminded me of her in some way." He stared off in silence for a moment. "They weren't her. I didn't want to fall in love. I just wanted another friend. I don't have to worry about you falling in love with me."

"How do you know that?" I taunted.

"Because you *can't*. Can you?"

I did nothing more than clench my jaw in response.

He said, "You don't have to keep playing games with me. Neither of us need to waste the energy on it when there are so many other things. And you don't have to answer that because I already know."

"I believe the only way you could come to that conclusion is if you broke your end of our bargain."

"You know I have." He chuckled. "And if you'd had a problem with it, you would've said as much."

363

"How am I supposed to know you won't break our current bargain, then?"

"You can't," he said nonchalantly. "But I have no reason to."

"Then how do I know *you* won't fall in love with *me*?"

He smiled a little to himself before saying, "Some people in the world . . . they can love unconditionally without thought or limits. I almost think someone did something to Reapers at some point in time to make them incapable of it. Like we only have so much blood we'll give to our hearts before they die. It's why your brother is so heartless—because the girl he loved was killed. He just . . . can't love anymore. Not completely. He tries to hide that. I don't. It's easier to fake things convincingly when you understand them, but I'd rather not waste the time and effort unless it's necessary."

I felt I had nothing I could say to that, but it made so much sense.

"You'd better hope you can keep Jas alive," he said. "Because if you can't . . . you're going to end up just like me. Unless he breaks what you have himself, of course. The love of friendship can sometimes be a much larger thing than any other sort."

"I'm not a Reaper," I said quietly.

"You don't have the training," he said. "But you can't deny your blood. These past few weeks have told me a great deal about what we are. So I'm going to work my ass off to help you."

"Why?" How was that even related?

"Because after you've been trained?" He chuckled. "I'd be scared of how good you could be, *especially* if no one is in the light about your training. It's going to take a lot of time and effort, but I'm sure it will be worth it. I just want you to make another deal with me right now."

"What is it?" Wariness built up in my chest at the prospect of more deals, and also because I couldn't think of anything I might be able to do for him. I couldn't come up with anything in general, but certainly nothing he would find a worthy exchange.

"I help you get to the point where there's nothing else I can do with you, and I keep your secrets from your father and everyone else. . . . As long as you promise me that when we find ourselves at that point, you help me ensure my father ends up dead."

I studied him. I watched his pulse pounding in his neck. I looked at his eyes and his flared nostrils. Slowly, I extended my hand toward him once more.

He took my hand, and he shook it. "Don't tell anyone."
I nodded my head.

EPILOGUE

JARSIL

TWO DAYS LATER, as Stelin had said, the city of Jarsil came into view. I heard myself laughing under my breath when I realized . . . it was the exact same city my father had shown me as a child. It was the exact same city he'd told me I would never see again as he'd concealed me inside his jacket and the stubble on his chin had pulled at my hair. The mountains surrounding it on two sides were . . . *unmistakable*. I'd had the image of it burned inside my head for most my life.

It put New Bethel to shame.

It was easily six times the size at a glance and, the closer we got, the more I realized it was not dilapidated and broken. It was beautiful—stone rising against stone in an attempt to reach the sky. It was better maintained but seemed much older.

Jastin rode close on one side of me, Stelin on the other, Chandler in front, and Chase behind.

The massive gate lowered, and then . . . there were so many people.

They were not screaming as they had when we'd left New Bethel. They were smiling as they stared at my father and the rest of us, but most gazes were locked on him. Some of them seemed to be crying while they smiled.

366

Joy.

I'd once tried to figure out why a person would cry when they were not sad. I could see now that these people were overcome with *joy* at my father's return. It did not seem real.

But I knew it was real because it was all so very wrong. *Wrong* was the only thing that made sense to me in the world.

What was this madness?

They tossed flowers.

I fought against the urge to scream profanities at all the ignorant people. Jastin patted me on the leg near the knee several times. It was likely the only reason I was able to hold my tongue, and my sanity, which seemed so ready to disappear.

I was so angry, I almost didn't notice Jastin's gaze roving over the crowd of people. I would not have noticed the searching at all if it had not stopped.

There was a beautiful girl with dark hair in the crowd, and she looked only at him. She smiled hugely when he found her.

I wouldn't have cared. It wouldn't have bothered me at all. Not if she didn't appear as though her stomach were on the verge of exploding all over the cobblestoned streets.

Jastin looked at me when we'd passed by her, but he said nothing. After that, I forced myself to stare at my horse's ears until it stopped moving.

"It feels so good to be home," I heard my father say happily with his carrying voice as I got off my horse. "I'll be so glad to finally sleep on a bed again."

I only realized I was staring at the back of my father's head and feeling as though I could murder him right here in front of his Reapers—directly underneath the noses of all his adoring followers—when Anders said, "I should show you to where you'll be staying. You look exhausted."

When I brought my eyes to his, I knew he was aware that I looked as if I were anything *but* exhausted. Still, I nodded my head and followed him. I distantly knew there were quite a few people around me as I plucked a stray flower off my shirt and crushed it in my hand.

The main House in Jarsil was not like the one in New Bethel. It was large and it was grand, but infinitely more so of both. And as I had assumed, much older. I walked through the halls without really noticing a single thing past the smoothness of the stone floor from traffic and age. And then we stepped back outside on the opposite end.

I stared around myself as I realized I was in a garden. It was not surrounded by an outside wall that had nothing on the other side; it was surrounded entirely by the walls of the House. Then, beyond that, the defensive walls of the House, beyond that the city, and beyond that the defensive walls of the city and the mountains.

In one corner of the garden was a decently large structure, but it was tiny in comparison to everything. I followed Anders as he walked toward it.

My hands were shaking when he held a key out to me.

I took it and said, "Stone walls," under my breath.

He smiled sadly at me and stepped out of my way.

I unlocked the door to my new prison, and then I stepped inside it.

It was intended to be beautiful, I knew. But I did not care for beautiful things. I felt as if everything inside the space was mocking absolutely every part of me as I stood there and took it all in.

I barely heard Jastin say, "You need to leave," from behind me.

I could not leave.

I could never leave.

I felt the key digging into my flesh where it was clenched in my hand. I felt when it cut through my palm, but only just. When I heard the door close, I lost control of myself.

I broke the vases that held the flowers, fresh like they'd just been cut and placed there. I pulled the paintings of flowers off the walls. And when I stepped inside my intended bedroom and saw the flowers embroidered on the blankets, I removed my knife from its strap on my arm and cut them into ribbons. I pulled the curtains with the same embroidery on them from the windows and cut them too. I did not care that someone had spent so much time making those beautiful things.

I did not care.

I'd not noticed Jastin following like a ghost behind me as I did those things, not until I was almost to the main door with my knife still in my hand. In one fell swoop, he'd grabbed hold of my torso from behind and done something to my arm that made my knife fall to the floor. He did not ask me what I'd been intending to do when I rounded on him; he simply stood there staring at me.

He'd just stopped me from going to kill my father. In that moment . . . I could've done it.

"I don't want to be here," I told him desperately instead, my voice shaking.

"Neither do I," he said as he pulled me into a hug. "But we *are* here."

He allowed me to cry into his shirt for quite some time before he took a step back and grabbed my hand.

He said, "Come on."

"What are we doing?"

He led me back into the bedroom and motioned for me to sit down on the bed. "I want you to sit there and think about how to make the most of this situation."

When he began gathering up the fabric that I'd destroyed, I asked, "What are you doing?"

"Taking care of you," he said without looking at me. "Sit there and think."

I did what he wanted for a time, though only in a sense. I sat and thought about the girl I'd seen because it was so much better than the alternative. Not *better*.

Easier.

If that was Cherise, then she was pregnant again. Would she be smiling at him like she had if it wasn't his? But he'd said he wouldn't have another child with her.

Had he been lying? Had he been lying about everything?

When having to choose between which of the two was worse—that girl or where I currently was . . .?

I could not decide. It was all so inescapable, and my heart and my head had differing opinions on the matter. So I sat there and cried until my thoughts went from somewhat rational into a jumbled mess of incomprehensible nothingness. And then I fell asleep.

I knew I'd done so when Jastin came back into my room. I knew because I smelled the familiar smell of my blanket from traveling as it was being placed on top of me. I knew it was him because I felt the familiar feeling of him settling in behind me and pulling me close. I felt the familiar sensation of breath near my ear before he whispered, "I love you."

He'd only said it because he thought I was asleep, I knew, and I mostly was.

I was only awake enough to know it had happened.

I was only awake enough to know that, even if he'd lied about everything, he was telling the truth about that one thing.

I lied to myself and said it was sufficient.

I was awake enough to have said it back, but my head kept my mouth closed. I felt silent tears falling from my eyes when he kissed me on the back of my neck.

I hated it. I hated everything. Part of me was starting to hate him for not being willing to give me as much as he could. And a part of me hated myself because the other part would be willing to give him everything.

I cannot allow that to happen, my head said in desperation.

My heart laughed and said . . . *You're too late.*

DEAR READER,

As we all (surely) know, things don't always quite work out the way we hope or plan in life. We make choices. We do the best we can, even when that 'best' doesn't look too good from the outside in. Even when our choices and the way we handle or deal with life makes people wish they could either shout at us or give us a hug that would actually make a difference.

Writing books in some ways is the ultimate form of teaching oneself patience with others, along with empathy. You walk the character's paths (lives) with them, feel their pains, rejoice in their joys. You come to understand and accept why they do the things they do, why they react and deal differently than anything you would ever. You at times look at situations and see no end, no hope. If there's one thing I've learned in writing books (more than even living my own life)?

There's always hope. It's just at times (and often) *very* difficult to find.

As much as I wish we all had nothing but sunshine and daisies, sometimes it's only when watching the darkness stretch beyond our view that we find ourselves able to appreciate the sun warming our skin after the clouds recede.

<3 C

If you enjoyed this book, I hope you'll consider leaving a review or telling a friend or family member.

Stories are much better when shared, even and sometimes especially through the difficult parts.

<3

WHERE YOU CAN FIND ME

WWW.CMILLERAUTHOR.COM

Email: contactcmillerauthor@gmail.com

Amazon: www.amazon.com/author/millerc

GoodReads: www.goodreads.com/CMillerAuthor

Facebook: www.facebook.com/CMillerAuthor

WordPress: www.cnmill.wordpress.com

Instagram: @dolly_llama

Twitter: @cn_mill

My website is where any and all information is and will be available. Any news, any updates, information about books and where to find them. If you're looking for any of that, it'll be there!

If you want to stay up to date on new releases, please consider subscribing to my newsletter. It's strictly for relevant information (NEW BOOKS!) and perhaps an occasional letter.

I am quite 'shy' and tend to shy away from social media as a whole. I do have accounts and would be happy to connect with you there, but if you're looking to get in contact with me, messaging me through my site or email would be the best way.

Questions, comments, or just wanting to say hi? I'd love to hear from you!

CONTINUE ASTER'S JOURNEY IN ...

ASCEND

SOMETIMES THE MOST BEAUTIFUL DREAMS CAN CAUSE THE MOST TORMENT.

Jarsil is a magnificent city, filled with happy, smiling people. To most, it would seem like a dream. The stone walls offer safety and comfort to citizen and Reaper alike.

For Aster, it's a nightmare she cannot wake from. After settling in to what life is and must be, something happens that changes everything. When truth reveals itself, some doors close while others open.

Though facing reality can be one of the most difficult things to do, it can—at times—offer more comfort than we believe ourselves able to find.

Made in United States
Troutdale, OR
03/02/2025

29425315R00222